STRANGERS *in the* NIGHT

STRANGERS *in the* NIGHT

SUSAN JOHNSON
KATHERINE O'NEAL
PAM ROSENTHAL

KENSINGTON PUBLISHING CORP.
http://www.kensingtonboks.com

BRAVA BOOKS are published by

Kensington Publishing Corp.
850 Third Avenue
New York, NY 10022

All Kensington titles, imprints and distributed lines are available at special quantity discounts for bulk purchases for sales promotion, premiums, fund-raising, educational or institutional use.

Special book excerpts or customized printings can also be created to fit specific needs. For details, write or phone the office of the Kensington Special Sales Manager: Kensington Publishing Corp., 850 Third Avenue, New York, NY 10022. Attn. Special Sales Department. Phone: 1-800-221-2647.

ISBN 0-7582-0529-5

First Kensington Trade Paperback Printing: December 2004
10 9 8 7 6 5 4 3 2 1

Printed in the United States of America

Contents

NATURAL ATTRACTION

Susan Johnson

Chapter One

Edinburgh, October 1785

Viscount Priestley, widely known in the fashionable world as "The Pope" for his utter lack of morals, observed the 80,000 spectators gathered round Heriot's Hospital Green with a mild frown. "I don't know why I let you talk me into coming to this crush, Harry. We could have just as well stayed in bed with the dolly mops we met us last night and read about this in the papers. In fact"—he surveyed the crowd from their vantage point atop a low wall, searching for a point of egress—"maybe the ladies are still at the hotel."

Baron Mayfield grabbed the viscount's arm. "Lunardi is about to take off. Wait," he said, his gaze on the large balloon being inflated in the center of the green.

"I'd prefer a warm bed and a bottle of claret." The viscount gently pried his friend's fingers from his arm. "Both of which will be adequately supplied me at James Dun's Hotel."

"I'll bet you a monkey Lunardi lifts off in the next minute." Harry knew the viscount rarely passed up a wager. The betting books at Brookes were testament to his passion.

"Double that says he doesn't." After having stood on the

windswept green for the better part of an hour, during which time Lunardi and his numerous assistants had dashed about to seemingly no good purpose, Jasper Amery considered the percentages on his side.

Despite his friend's reputation as an accomplished gambler to whom Dame Fortune had taken a special liking, Harry Mayfield knew aerial balloons a good sight better than either the viscount *or* Dame Fortune.

"This could be history in the making." Harry's excitement was plain. "If Lunardi's improvements work, it won't be long before we'll all be flying!"

"Pray, acquit me of your fantasies," the viscount demurred.

"You don't understand. Lunardi is using inflammable gas instead of fire to inflate his balloon. It's the damn fire that's always the problem—it was for Montgolfier and Charles—de Moret, too." The baron turned and winked. "If this works, think how it will shorten the journey to Paris."

"Perhaps there *is* reason to fly," Jasper said with a smile. "You could see Angelique more often."

"Or any of the other temptresses in the corps de ballet." The viscount had a decided preference for the dancers at the Comédie Française.

"The inflation tubes are being taken away," Harry murmured, once more engrossed by the scene before him. "Look, look!" Harry cried as the balloon began to rise. "By God, Lunardi's really done it!"

A murmur of astonishment rose from the crowd, augmented a moment later by a clamor of delight and wonder as the brilliantly painted silk balloon to which the basket containing Vincenzo Lunardi was attached climbed, caught a freshening wind, and soared upward. Awestruck, the spectators stared at the curiosity, all gazes on the marvel of man in flight. The bonds of earth were truly broken, the large balloon—thirty-three feet in height, one hundred two feet in circumference—mounting higher and higher into the clear blue sky with a kind of surety that seemed to prognosticate a successful mission.

"This is unbelievable," Harry murmured, his face wreathed in smiles as Lunardi was carried aloft, the balloon diminishing in size by slow degrees until it was the merest speck in the sky. "Man has transcended the earthly realm, and this is just the beginning, Jasper. Mark my words—we'll live to see our grandchildren flying like birds."

"Speak for yourself," the viscount said drily. "I don't intend to marry." Nor had he need, since his brother's wife had insured the Amery line with four sons. Not that the eager young misses and their mamas who descended on London each season didn't bestir themselves to prove the viscount wrong.

"Someday you'll meet a lady who touches your heart and you'll be swept away," Harry asserted.

The viscount looked pained. "Spare me your romantical fancies. In any event, I don't *have* a heart."

"So cynical, Jasper. Haven't you read Henry Mackenzie, one of the eminences of this town? Sentiment, not reason, is the social invention of our time."

"I find myself less prone to palpitations of the heart than Mackenzie. A defect, I'm sure," the viscount drawled.

"Perhaps meeting 'The Man of Feeling' will convert you to a more fashionable state of consciousness. I'll introduce you."

The viscount sighed. "I'm sure you will."

But Harry was no longer listening. He and a parson, from the look of the man dressed in somber black, were carrying on a lively discussion about inflammable versus elastic air as balloon propellants.

Jasper smiled, indulgent of his friend's passion for science. He'd watched Harry blow up many a laboratory over the years. Then again, it was as good a way as any to pass the time. Women, hunting, and cards could wear thin on occasion, although he wasn't sure he'd yet reached the point of ennui that would cause him to take a serious interest in Harry's scientific whimsies.

It was enough to tag along with Harry on his excursions, read an occasional feted book by one scientist or another, and watch the rapidly changing world through a dilettante's eye. Cynical he might be, but all in all, he was still sufficiently amused by his pleasures.

And truth be told, the viscount wasn't completely heartless. He took it upon himself to accommodate a great number of ladies who sent him *billets doux,* obliging them with the largesse of his sexual skills. In fact, many in the *beau monde* called him "The Pope" not only because of his title and propensity for vice, but for his stamina in bed—a blessing, as it were, that he bestowed on all the eager ladies.

Vincenzo Lunardi's balloon ascended three miles over Edinburgh before being affected by ice crystals, descending safely not far from his point of takeoff, and that inaugural moment for natural science as spectacle in Scotland caused a tumult of excitement that literally exploded in an uproar of screaming frenzy. The young Italian was carried through the streets in triumph, the riotous enthusiasm eventually spilling over into the ancient taverns of High Street, as well as into the elegant drawing rooms of New Town.

In the capital city of Scotland, where the natural sciences and a trail-blazing passion for innovation and ideas had been making advances for more than three decades, it was a glorious night for celebration.

Chapter Two

At an hour of the morning when most rational men were abed, Harry entered Jasper's darkened bedroom without knocking, strode to the windows, threw open the drapes, and, walking over to the bed, cheerfully announced, "The sun has risen!"

"I can see that," Jasper grumbled, squinting against the piercing light. "What the hell time is it?"

"Seven."

"Go away," Jasper growled, and checking to see that the rosy-cheeked blonde beside him slept on, he shut his eyes again.

"We promised to see Lunardi for breakfast. Don't you remember?"

Rather than Lunardi's conversation last night, Jasper had been focused instead on his companion's lush bosom as she leaned over the tavern table opposite him, her low decolletage a decided lure to the eye. "Go without me." His lashes lifted marginally. "I didn't get any sleep last night."

"What if I promise we'll leave on our hunting trip right after breakfast? Would that be suitable incentive?"

"Deal," the viscount murmured, having been cooling his heels in Edinburgh for over a week while Harry indulged his scientific curiosity. Carefully easing away from his companion, Jasper slid from the bed, preferring not to have to explain his hasty departure to the lady. If Harry was finally ready to leave, Jasper was more than willing to quit the city.

Moving toward the dressing room, he waited for Harry to follow him in before quietly shutting the door. Then, leaning back against the polished mahogany, the viscount briefly shut his eyes—long hours in the taverns, followed by a night of rather strenuous activity, had taken its toll. "Give me a minute," he murmured, taking a deep breath. "It's damned early to be up."

"Did she wear you out?" Harry teased.

A flash of amusement gleamed in Jasper's eyes. "Let's just say I worked up a sweat."

"You'll get your strength back after you eat."

The thought of food jarred the viscount's stomach. "Are you sure Lunardi's up at this ungodly hour?"

"His laboratory opens at sunrise." Harry poured steaming water from a covered copper pail into a basin.

"It might not today." Ignoring the towel Harry held out to him, Jasper sat down on a convenient chair instead. "Your hero was being carried from tavern to tavern most of the night."

"He wasn't drinking." Tossing aside the towel, Harry lifted the stopper on a small decanter.

"Then Lunardi must have been the only abstemious man in town. Or woman, for that matter." The Scots ladies were known to enjoy a wee dram.

"I didn't drink, either. Here." Harry held out a glass of brandy. "Hair of the dog. Take it."

The viscount took the glass. Tossing down the liquor, he felt the brandy warm his throat, its soothing narcotic flood his edgy nerves; before long, it was possible to contemplate moving. A second drink, together with his strong constitution, served to further dissipate the aftereffects of his profligate night, and by the time he'd managed to wash and dress, his appetite had begun to recover. After a brief detour to the hotel breakfast room for several cups of coffee, heavily laced with sugar, and a quick perusal of the morning papers that waxed triumphant over the events that had transpired yesterday on Heriot's Hospital Green, the men exited the hotel to walk the few blocks to Lunardi's laboratory.

The morning was sunny and warm, the streets quiet so early in the morning, only tradesmen and servants about on their errands.

"Now, just to be clear. We're leaving directly after this breakfast with Lunardi? No more laboratories to survey or lectures to attend?"

Harry nodded. "Immediately after. So you might want to think of some polite explanation should that pretty blonde still be warming your bed on our return."

"Rest assured, that won't be a problem," the viscount drawled.

Harry grinned. "So what's your excuse—a funeral, a wedding, an elderly relative with a lingering illness?"

"An expensive parting gift usually eliminates the need for explanations. But I'll tell her the truth if necessary—we're going hunting in the Highlands."

"And she won't cling?"

Jasper gave him a sardonic look. "I very much doubt it."

Harry laughed. "So we have no impediments to our journey north."

"None. And I warn you, if you linger too long over breakfast, I might consider saying something rude."

"No need, Jasper. You've been more than patient this week. An hour, no more, and we'll be riding north."

On arriving at the given address, they found what appeared to be a vacant store.

"I don't see Lunardi." Gazing through the paned windows at the empty interior, an unspoken I-told-you-so underlay Jasper's words.

"He's here," Harry said with assurance, as though his

acquaintance of last night was a friend of long standing. Pushing open the door, he strode into a room lined with shelves, most of which were empty save for various kegs and an array of mechanical devices strewn about willy-nilly. "Or if he isn't, he soon will be."

A muffled explosion suddenly rent the stillness, followed by the sound of shattering glass and a highly audible litany of curses. Quickly moving to the rear of the shop, the men walked down a dark hallway and found themselves on the threshold of a makeshift laboratory.

Sunlight poured through large windows, illuminating a long, narrow room, cut by aisles running left to right that separated two counters. The countertops were piled high with ropes and pulleys, crammed with large glass bottles holding various colored liquids and awash with yards of flowing, colorful waxed silk.

Taking note of a figure in the far corner, Jasper nudged his friend with his elbow and tipped his head toward the observed form. A boy, partially obscured by a drape of silk, was on his hands and knees trying to sponge up a yellow liquid.

"May we be of help?"

The lad jumped at Harry's inquiry, knocked his head on the edge of the counter, and swearing in some unintelligible language, backed out. Coming to his feet, still muttering under his breath, he swung around.

Both men registered surprise.

The viscount quickly reverted to type, however, his sudden smile one of appreciation. A beautiful woman outfitted in buff breeches and a boy's white shirt, her dark hair pulled back in a queue, gazed at them guardedly. "Our apologies for intruding." Bowing gracefully, his gaze on the magnificent breasts and taut nipples beneath the fine linen, Jasper unconsciously flexed his fingers. "Could we be of assistance?" He gestured in the direction of the spill. "Do you have a broom for the glass?"

Harry suppressed a gasp, not only astonished that Jasper was familiar with a broom, but even more shocked at his offer to use it.

"Thank you, but I'll take care of this myself," the woman replied coolly. She should have worn a jacket, Nicky thought, or more to the point, the tall, dark-haired Englishman should have had better manners. She remembered both men from last night, although she'd not spoken to them. The Baron Something-or-other had appeared pleasant enough. He and Lunardi had talked at length. As for the other man—too handsome for his own good—he'd been busy seducing Meg Hamilton. Not a difficult feat, even for an Englishman.

"We were to meet Vincenzo for breakfast," Harry explained. "Perhaps he forgot. May I present myself. Baron Mayfield," Harry offered with a bow. "And this is my friend, Viscount Priestley."

Nicky nodded, but didn't introduce herself, hoping they'd leave. She had little liking for Englishmen. "Vincenzo was here earlier. I'm not sure where he is."

"I am here, *cara mia,*" a melodious voice intoned, the Neapolitan ambassador's nephew appearing in the doorway with a wide smile and an expansive, arms-open welcome. "I remembered our breakfast, then I forgot, then I remembered again. Have you met my beautiful assistant, the Honorable Miss Nicky Wemyss?"

"Informally," Jasper pleasantly returned.

"Come, then, let's go to breakfast. Join us, Nicky. I insist," Lunardi said as she shook her head. "She knows more than I do," he declared, smiling at the men. "Nicky worked with both the Montgolfier brothers and Charles in Paris last year. Which is where we met, is it not, *cara mia*?" The Neapolitan blew her a kiss.

The viscount felt an instant irritation, as if a woman he'd just seen for the first time last night shouldn't be allowed a relationship with Lunardi. He must still be hung over. That was it—his nerves were raw. Christ, it didn't matter to him if Lunardi was fucking her. More power to him.

But during the course of breakfast, Jasper found himself increasingly fascinated by the beautiful, curvaceous Miss Nicky. She conversed like a man—straightforward and direct; understood scientific theory like a man—actually, better than most; and even ate like a man—her appetite was prodigious. Which caused him to speculate whether her sexual appetites were as unrestrained.

His ensuing thoughts brought his erection up, and shifting in his chair, he silently cursed his morning-after cravings. Although perhaps anyone in close proximity to the lush Miss Nicky experienced similar desires. She was unabashedly female beneath her mannish garb.

In fact, she was one of the most blatantly voluptuous women he'd ever had the good fortune to meet, the fine fabric of her shirt straining against her plump breasts, her breeches prominently displaying the curve of her hips as she lounged back in her chair, her long, shapely legs stretched out before her. She had the look of a wild gypsy, the front of her hair a riot of dark curls, her skin, in contrast to fashion, sun-washed, her violet eyes, full red lips, and flashing smile evocative of Romany blood. Although no Gypsy could afford the diamond buckles on her shoes. Such evidence of wealth, no doubt, allowed her her eccentricities.

Fascinated beyond his usual casual interest, he watched the animated discourse, particularly between Lunardi and Miss Nicky, as though his close scrutiny would disclose the exactitude of their rapport. Their manner was at times playful, other times serious, their conversation almost entirely related to aerial flight. Her Italian was as good as her English, her French flawless, her Scots accent equally fine. She was a veritable chameleon—impossible to type.

Although surely, a woman dressed like a man who immersed herself in science was well beyond the norm. No fashionable belle here, predictable and modish. A damnably refreshing change from the usual females who amused him.

Nicky took measure of the viscount as well during breakfast, but reluctantly. She disliked men of Priestley's ilk. Arrogant beneath their politesse. Aware of their exalted position and good looks. Too familiar with fawning women.

But she disliked even more the way she found herself regarding him with an unwanted degree of interest.

She must have been too long without a man, she told herself.

Or, more to the point, a man like him.

All male. Sensual. Handsome as a god. And ruthless, beneath his urbanity, with hooded eyes like that.

A brazen rake, unless she missed her guess. So he could go to hell with her blessings, she decided pragmatically.

With that pithy injunction, she dismissed his potent allure and her misplaced fascination and refocused on the conversation. Vincenzo was explaining the modifications he proposed on his next ascent, and she spoke with authority on the subject, losing herself in the normalcy of the topic.

Sometime later, when Lunardi said with regret, "We must return to our workshop. I've promised the university staff an impromptu tour this morning," Nicky rose and made her adieus with unruffled calm. The Englishmen were off to the Highlands to shoot several hundred animals, as Englishmen were wont to do, while she and Vincenzo would once again immerse themselves in the planning of their next flight. Her momentary attraction to the viscount was forgotten.

"Thank you for taking time from your busy schedule to visit with us," Harry offered politely.

"Our pleasure." Lunardi smiled. "Enjoy your expedition to the Highlands."

"We will. As a matter of fact, our carriage is waiting at the hotel."

"Really, Harry, there's no need to rush off. He has a tendency to be impatient," Jasper noted, offering Lunardi and Nicky a smile. "Actually, our plans are highly flexible." Jasper shifted his gaze to Harry. "Perhaps Mr. Lunardi and Miss Wemyss could be persuaded to have dinner with us tonight?"

Harry shot Jasper a surprised look.

"Is the hotel dining room not adequate?" the viscount inquired blandly.

"Of course," the baron hastily improvised. "We'd be honored."

"I'm afraid I'm busy," Nicky retorted, aware of the baron's startled look, more aware of the sudden leaping of her senses.

"Tomorrow, then," Jasper said.

"I couldn't." Fascination aside, she preferred not being added to the viscount's long list of conquests, her feelings apropos Priestley curiously volatile.

"Invite whomever you wish." The viscount smiled suavely. "We'll make it a local party."

"Really, that's not necessary."

"Surely you know persons of interest in the city. Harry tells me the great Henry Mackenzie is here. Could he be tempted to come?"

"I doubt it," she said with a smile as urbane as his.

"I'm a great fan of his work," Jasper observed mendaciously.

"I doubt that as well," she said, her smile in place.

"As a matter of fact, I know his publisher," the viscount lied, his expression amiable, as though he rubbed shoulders with writers and publishers on a regular basis. "Why don't I invite Mackenzie myself? Would you like that?"

It was obvious to even the most obtuse observer that the question of what Nicky would like had nothing to do with Henry Mackenzie—*or* dinner.

Harry and Lunardi exchanged glances.

The viscount took note, and, with a glance, dared either man to interfere.

It was male challenge, fierce and direct.

A riveting frisson raced up Nicky's spine.

How did Priestley do it?

Take possession like that—without a word?

Would she allow it?

Of course not.

"Pray, relent," Jasper murmured, moving a step closer so the fragrance of his cologne wafted into her nostrils. "Have dinner with me . . . us . . . whomever you wish to serve as duenna. I promise to behave."

She should say no. Was that musk and a hint of sandalwood? No, ambergris. She should have known a man like Priestley would prefer an aphrodisiac scent.

Walk away from his dark, bewitching gaze, she told herself, and from his promise to behave that meant nothing of the kind.

Ignore the invitation in his smile.

Stay as far away as possible from the handsome rogue.

"I could get a note from my curate," Jasper said, amusement in his voice. "Citing my very proper intentions."

"That won't be necessary."

His brows flickered. "Which?"

"The note. Your intentions are obvious."

"And?" It saved recriminations afterward, he'd found, to let a lady decide for herself.

"Perhaps," she murmured, when she should be saying no.

"When?"

"I didn't say I would."

"You didn't say you wouldn't," he countered softly.

It was only dinner, she told herself. There was no point in taking undue issue with a dinner invitation. Whatever decisions she had to make about his proper or improper intentions didn't have to be made now. "Very well," she said. "I'll come to dinner."

His sudden smile dazzled, and she almost reneged—such flagrant certainty was offensive.

But he touched her fingers in a light, brushing gesture and gently said, "Tell me when."

"Tomorrow."

"Send me your guest list. Do you like white roses?" His smile was boyish and warm. "My mother had your coloring, and she adored white roses."

He was unutterably disarming, or maybe simply deft. But any residual resentment dissipated before the sweetness of his smile and talk of his mother. "White roses have always been my favorite," she said. "Even in the heat of India."

Did that explain her exotic looks and the diamond buckles? "You lived there long?"

"Most of my life. I was born there."

"You must tell me all about it," he said, husky and low.

"Is dinner settled, then?" Lunardi interposed, pointing at his waistcoat watch, the pressure of his busy schedule eclipsing even possible repercussions from the viscount.

Jasper tipped his head toward Nicky and raised one brow.

"Yes."

"The professors will be waiting," Lunardi prompted.

Jasper bowed, his dark gaze holding Nicky's for a heated moment. "It was a pleasure to meet you, Miss Wemyss. Until tomorrow . . ."

As Harry and the viscount stood on the sidewalk outside the tavern watching Lunardi and Nicky walk away, Harry gave his friend a contemplative glance. "You might be poaching. Have you considered that?"

Jasper was concentrating on the lady's gently swaying

derriere. "She's old enough to make up her own mind, and independent enough . . . those breeches a case in point. I doubt she has to ask Lunardi's permission."

"How long are we staying in Edinburgh?"

"Does it matter?"

"If Lunardi doesn't mind me underfoot, stay forever as far as I'm concerned. But knowing you, I doubt we'll be here long."

"Long enough, I hope."

Harry grinned. "Do I detect a rare uncertainty?"

"Miss Wemyss is out of the ordinary." Jasper's brows lifted faintly. "But I have a feeling she's interested, whether she wishes it or not."

"A reluctant female. There's a change. You might have to be on your best behavior."

"I intend to. It isn't often you meet a woman like Miss Wemyss. If you weren't so enamored of Julia, you'd feel the same."

Harry had been in love with his cousin for as long as he could remember, the passion mutual. Just as soon as Julia was presented to the Ton, their betrothal would be announced. "I admit Miss Wemyss is admirable. Did you hear her suggestions for higher-altitude flying? They were ingenious."

"I'm sure," Jasper noted drily. "Do you think I should move to a larger suite?"

Harry smiled. "You may not need to."

Jasper looked smug. "I have a good feeling . . ."

"He's a rake and a rogue," Lunardi warned, giving Nicky a stern look as they walked down High Street. "In case you didn't notice."

"How could one *not* notice." Nicky smiled. "I may change my mind, in any event."

"His name is synonymous with scandal. Just a word to the wise."

"As if I worry about scandal, darling. We're not all innocents like your little Lucia waiting for you in Naples." Lunardi's fiancee was convent-bred.

"You're my dearest compatriot. I just wouldn't want you hurt."

"By sex?"

"By the disreputable viscount. His liaisons are numerous *and* fleeting."

"Maybe that's exactly what I want," Nicky replied lightly. "Transient, mindless pleasure."

Vincenzo snorted. "And maybe you want to fall in love someday as well."

"But not at the moment, darling. My life is far, far too busy to think of serious matters like love when I have more pleasant endeavors to consider, like making sure you break yesterday's altitude record. Now, enough of the wicked Priestley, if you please," she declared with a dismissive wave. "What are we going to do about keeping those ice crystals from forming the next time you go up?"

Chapter Three

Over breakfast in his suite the next morning, Jasper handed Harry a small note. "The guest list has arrived. I hope you recognize some names. With the exception of Lunardi, I'm at a loss."

Unfolding the single sheet, Harry whistled softly as he perused the names. "Feel honored to be in the presence of such genius," he murmured. "Every eminent man of science will be dining with us tomorrow. Not to mention two celebrated judges and, of course, Henry Mackenzie. They've all accepted."

"Wouldn't you, if you could spend an evening with Miss Wemyss?"

"Every man's not, shall we say, as single-minded as you. I'm sure everyone's looking forward to an evening of brilliant conversation."

"No doubt," Jasper drawled. "And having been witness to the Scots style of conversation on more than one occasion, we'd better order several cases of wine." Leaning back in his chair, Jasper gave Harry a narrowed look. "She's surrounded herself with a veritable phalanx of chaperons."

"You may find yourself relegated to mere host."

A low growl registered the viscount's displeasure.

Harry grinned. "Miss Nicky may not be as interested in sex as she is in aerial balloons."

Sliding up in his chair, Jasper grinned. "Are you suggesting I'm losing my touch?"

"No, I'm simply saying Miss Wemyss is not the style of woman you generally favor—frivolous, dare I say shallow, interested in pretty gowns and jewels and allaying their boredom with amorous pleasures. She would be out of place in your circle of friends. In fact, she may be indifferent to seduction."

"But then, I'm not interested in introducing her into society"—Jasper smiled—"other than my own. As for seduction, she seemed aware of the concept."

"Regardless, from the length of her guest list, I'd say she's planning on keeping her distance."

"Care to make a wager?"

"Seriously?"

"Five hundred says I'm serious."

"This could be the easiest wager I've ever won. On the other hand," Harry murmured, scrutinizing his friend over the rim of his coffee cup. Jasper didn't like to lose.

"Let's make it a thousand. If I lose, you can buy Cardiff's racer."

Such confidence gave Harry pause. "I don't know." He set down his coffee cup. "It doesn't seem right."

"Why? I'm not going to force her."

The baron debated, his friend's half-smile not reassuring. On the other hand, he'd fancied Cardiff's racer for a long time. "Very well," he said finally. "If you promise you won't force her."

"Jesus, Harry. Since when have I ever done that?"

"She seems . . . different, that's all. Natural. I wouldn't go so far as to say unsophisticated, but somehow pure. And because of that, maybe not capable of withstanding your seductive skills." Jasper had earned his nickname, "The

Pope," even before he'd reached his majority, and the intervening years had only added to the legend.

"I understand the meaning of no. You needn't worry."

In all honesty, Harry understood, women were more apt to chase Jasper than the other way around. "I suppose she's safe enough," he murmured. "A thousand it is. Although, she might be the first to turn you down. Have you thought of that?"

Jasper's mouth quirked in a faint smile. "I never think about losing."

Chapter Four

By the following evening, the hotel's private dining room had been bedecked with white roses in dramatic profusion. Three enormous epergnes spilling over with pale blooms marched down the long, damask-covered table. Several vases full of fragrant blooms adorned the sideboards, two towering arrangements sat atop gilt pedestals on either side of the door. The glittering crystal chandeliers and wall sconces were wreathed in garlands of roses, their wafting scent heightened by the heat from the candles.

Jasper had instructed the hotel manager to buy up every white rose in town and to good purpose, he decided, surveying the opulent display with satisfaction.

Even the scent was heady, not that he needed any further stimulation.

In fact, he could use a dose of saltpeter, the mood he was in.

He'd dressed early and come downstairs, too impatient to remain in his suite. A brandy in hand, he'd restlessly moved about the room—paced, in fact, if he allowed himself an honest assessment—critiquing every detail of the elegantly set table and decor as though he was the head butler instead of the host. When he found himself straightening a knife, gauging the exact distance to the adjacent plate, he jumped back, downed his drink, poured himself another, and drank that down as well. He needed to calm himself, or more aptly, what he really needed to do was fuck the voluptuous Miss Wemyss and be done with it, he thought.

There was something about her that was making him feverish—he didn't exactly know what, but he was anticipating her arrival with almost an adolescent excitement. Pouring himself another drink, he wondered if it was her feigned indifference that incited such rare feelings. Had not his French governess pretended that same unconcern until he'd worked up his youthful courage and kissed her that day so long ago? He half smiled at the fond memories, their attachment one of long standing until she'd left him for a wealthy countryman of hers.

Or maybe his desires had nothing to do with adolescent longing, but rather were provoked by the rare sight of a lady in breeches. Such reckless disregard for convention suggested an unrestrained nature that would be fascinating to explore.

Nor could anyone deny that Miss Wemyss was beyond the ordinary in beauty and intellect, qualities that were bound to entice.

But her long sojourn in India perhaps intrigued him most, her exotic beauty reminding him of numerous voluptuous eastern goddesses he'd seen in various illustrations of Indian temples and manuscripts. Indian art displayed copulation and the intensity of sexual passion with startling openness and tantalizing variety. Was Miss Wemyss capable of twining her lush limbs in the same provocatively supple ways?

His pulse quickened at the thought.

He glanced at his watch.

Nicky persuaded herself as she left her town house that there was a perfectly good reason for her arriving unfashionably early for dinner. She ignored the fact that the sun had just recently set, although the dinner hour was earlier in Scotland than in England. But the thought that she might interrupt the staff setting the table was a genuine concern.

Not that she could have waited any longer, regardless the reason.

She'd already tried.

She'd even had her ayah make her a nice cup of tea to help her relax. But after one sip, she'd set the cup aside, stood up, and even while she'd called herself every kind of fool, she'd ordered her wrap.

"Take care of yourself," her old nurse had warned as she'd helped place Nicky's mantelet on her shoulders. "The English are scoundrels, every last one of them."

"I know, Madhu. I'm on guard," Nicky lied, when she'd not been able to dislodge the viscount from her thoughts. She'd assessed the beauty of his glorious face and form in endless variation, reviewed and dissected the words he'd spoken, found herself haunted by his smile. And whether she could resist his allure was moot at the moment. Or, more to the point, what was moot was whether she wished to resist. "Jai need not accompany me," she added, adjusting the flounces on her short, silk cape, dismissing her Indian manservant who normally accompanied her at night.

Madhu nodded, and with a glance, warned off Jai, who stood at attention in the shadow of the stairs.

"I may be late."

"You're always late."

"I just mean, you needn't wait up for me."

"Yes, Missy." As if she wouldn't wait up, Madhu thought, when she'd been watching over her little girl since the day she was born.

The moment the door shut on their mistress, the servants exchanged knowing looks.

"I will watch the hotel," Jai murmured. "She won't see me."

"Our little Missy was dressed three hours ago," Madhu

said with a sniff of disdain. "And in her best gown, may the gods consign every pestilence to the Englishman's black soul. We must be ready to pluck her from the abyss."

Jai stood well over six feet, his body muscled and hard despite his years, his loyalty uncompromising. "I will keep her safe."

"See that you do. Go now—the English devils are not to be trusted."

Chapter Five

At the sound of the door opening, Jasper turned, then immediately set down his glass. "I've been waiting for you," he said, smiling at Nicky as she walked into the room. "For hours . . ."

"How nice, and this as well." Nicky lifted her hand to indicate the floral splendor, although the opulent, scented display was eclipsed by the more impressive sight of Viscount Priestley in full evening rig. Unspeakably handsome, dark as the devil, the stark contrast of predacious male against billowing white roses was striking.

He seemed to dominate the room—his height, the width of his shoulders, his power and strength barely masked by his perfectly tailored clothes.

He was beside her a moment later, deftly untying the bow on her cape. "I was hoping you'd arrive first," he said, lifting her mantelet from her shoulders, tossing it over a nearby chair back.

"I thought I should," she said, as temperately as he. "To introduce you to the others." A small lie or partial truth or perhaps only empty words to serve politesse.

"Perfect."

Her gaze rose to meet his, the soft utterance replete with nuance.

"You must know you intrigue me." Whispered words, husky and low.

"Yes," she said. "As you do me, with some—perhaps more than some—reservations."

"Tell me what they are and I'll—"

She smiled faintly. "Change my mind?"

"I was going to say, I'll do my best to make whatever adjustments are necessary."

"Such obliging sentiments from a rogue."

He laughed. "Consider it a testament to your charms."

He didn't deny her designation of *rogue;* he was honest, at least. As she was in her reply. "I'll have to think about your offer. I'll let you know."

His surprise at her frankness showed for a transient moment, and then he smoothly replied, "Take your time. Would you like a brandy before our guests arrive?"

Nicky smiled, not only at his fleeting discomposure, but at the way he'd said *our guests* as though they were intimates already. "I gather plain-speaking women are an oddity for you. And yes, please, a brandy would be welcome."

"One brandy coming up. And I'm more than happy to accommodate your plain-speaking. Tell me what you want, or think or dream about." He winked. "I'm adaptable."

She smiled. "I'll keep that in mind."

My god, she was delightful. Absolutely straightforward, without subterfuge or flirtatious guile. "Since the Scots never leave before the last bottle is drunk, I'm tempted to throw out a case or two of wine before they arrive."

"There's no rush."

He glanced over his shoulder as he stood at the drink table. "Speak for yourself. I'm ready to make a complete and utter fool of myself."

She'd followed him over and stood close by. "I doubt you'll play the fool. You've been doing this too long."

"I'd say you've done this once or twice yourself."

"Is that a problem?"

Turning, he handed her a glass and lifted his in salute. "On the contrary. I look forward to your expertise. To a pleasant association, Miss Wemyss."

"Call me Nicky. Everyone does."

"Everyone does what?"

"My lord, Priestley," she said with a smile. "Surely that's not a note of censure I hear."

"This is novel for me, these feelings of reckless abandon," this man of facile charm and seductive artifice declared. "Allow me a blunder or two."

"Have you read the Kama Sutra?"

"Only portions in translation," he said as calmly as possible, her abrupt question extraordinary, although definitely in the way of miracles. And at that moment, if it were possible to lock the dining room door and send their guests away without damaging her reputation, he would have given away a good portion of his fortune to do that.

"Ah, here's your friend, Baron Mayfield," Nicky said, her voice perfectly calm, her smile bland. "Do come in, Mayfield. We were discussing the culture of India."

"I see," Harry said, smiling as he approached. "And what the hell do you know about Indian culture, Jasper?"

"I'm hoping to learn," Jasper replied silkily. "Miss Wemyss has promised to tutor me."

"I haven't exactly promised," she said. "But Priestley is aspiring to put himself in my good graces, are you not, my lord?"

"With the most burning fervor, my lady."

"My compliments on your self-command, Miss Wemyss. Jasper is rarely put in his place."

"That particular state may be only temporary. I haven't entirely decided if I'm up to keeping him in his place. Do you have a lady in your life, Baron Mayfield?" Nicky asked, preferring to change the subject, the concept of keeping Viscount Priestley in his place open to highly provocative interpretation.

"He's in love," Jasper offered with a teasing smile.

"How wonderful," Nicky said. "Tell me what it's like to be in love?"

"You've never been in love?" Jasper's brows lifted, a skeptical note in his voice. "In my experience, ladies are always in love."

"Really. How interesting. I've never been so inclined. Have you?"

"Of course not."

"My feelings exactly. Tell me about your lady love, Mayfield."

And as Harry explained how he and Julia had been neighbors and played together since childhood—or more exactly, he'd played with her older brothers and fallen in love with her when she was fourteen—Jasper watched Nicky from beneath his lashes. He couldn't believe his good fortune. Not only was she amenable to amorous pleasures, she knew of the explicitly carnal Kama Sutra and didn't believe in love. Was it actually possible she would dispense with all the usual specious games ladies played once you took them to bed? And if so, how soon might he explore that possibility?

He glanced at the clock on the mantel. Bloody hell—how was he going to last through dinner?

Any further speculation on the duration of dinner in relation to his self-control gave way to a flurry of introductions as Joseph Black, who had discovered carbon dioxide, and Adam Smith, the author of *The Wealth of Nations,* suddenly arrived, followed by James MacPherson, who had resurrected the oral poetry of the Highlands in his influential book, *Fingal, An Ancient Epic Poem.* Soon after, Hugh Buchan, the City Chamberlain who held the Council's purse strings, entered with Henry Raeburn, an artist recently returned from Rome. And moments later, James Hutton, who had been devising a theory of the Earth's development based on geology, walked in with the "Man of Feeling," Henry Mackenzie. When Lunardi rushed in some minutes after, apologizing for being late, their guest list was complete.

Jasper had been counting heads even before Nicky said, "There, now everyone's here." As he escorted Nicky to her seat at the end of the table opposite his, he said quietly, "I'm tempted to feign an apoplexy and send everyone home but you."

She smiled up at him. "What makes you think I'd stay?"

"Such indifference," he said, grinning. "I'm demoralized."

"You don't look demoralized."

He made a grotesque face.

She laughed and patted his arm with her fan. "Be polite, my lord, and you may still win the day after all. These men are my friends and they're looking forward to a convivial evening."

"With you."

"Perhaps." Her shoulder lifted in a faint shrug. "But then again, if and when I leave Edinburgh, they'll still be friends. Much as you're still "The Pope," even outside London."

So she knew. "It doesn't mean anything, that name," he remarked urbanely, pulling her chair out for her. "Pray disregard it."

"On the contrary, I find it intriguing. Does that encourage you, at least a little?" She glanced at him over her shoulder as she sat, a faint smile on her lips. "Now, go amuse our guests, and we shall see what we shall see."

She'd winked at the last, or had she? The fluttering movement was so fleeting, he couldn't be sure. But she hadn't said no, nor was her presence here tonight indication of disinterest, he thought.

Bowing gracefully, he moved to his chair at the head of the table.

As host and hostess, in a manner of speaking, they oversaw an evening of brilliant conversation, excellent food, and extraordinary wines. With Scotland a favored trade partner of France for centuries, the Scots had developed a distinguished palate for French wines, and the hotel cellar was superb. Although Jasper drank sparingly, preferring to remain sober tonight. He did, however, do his utmost to play the gracious host in an effort to gain favor with the equivocal Miss Wemyss.

Not that he intended to allow her to continue in her equivocation once the party was over. Good manners were all well and good—to a point—at which time he intended to do what he did best. And having spent years perfecting the art of seduction, he knew that any lady who asked point-blank whether he'd read the Kama Sutra was unlikely to require much persuasion to join him in bed.

From time to time, when it was unavoidable, Jasper would engage in the various discussions, his education diverse enough to allow him to speak with some authority on any number of subjects. But he much preferred watching Miss Nicky. And to that end, he spoke as little as possible, kept his comments as brief as good manners allowed, and considered instead the pleasant possibilities of the night ahead once their guests were gone.

Nicky sat directly opposite him, masses of white roses at her back. The glow from the chandeliers was reflected in the glittering diamonds at her throat and ears, the warm golden light illuminating the dark, silken sheen of her hair, the rosy flush of her cheeks, the satiny curve of her throat and modicum of bare shoulder visible beneath her filmy fichu. Her white silk muslin gown was all the rage since Marie Antoinette had taken to playing milkmaid at Versailles, the simplicity of the design heightening the exotic nature of her Gypsy-like charms. The decolletage was modest, bordered with ruffles and lace, the elbow-length sleeves edged with more flowing lace, the full, gathered skirt a delicious soft pouf. The only color in the pale confection was a wide, emerald-green silk grosgrain ribbon circling her waist and tied in a bow at her back. She sat up straight, he noticed, so as not to crush her bow, perhaps. Or maybe she'd been taught proper comportment in faraway India and always sat thusly. He half smiled at the contrast of her restrained pose with his erotic thoughts apropos Bengali maidens in all manner of supple sexual contortions. Although, at the moment, Miss Wemyss didn't look as though she was capable of accommodating his fantasies.

Her gaze suddenly came up and held his as though in response to his smile, and he realized she'd been watching him as well.

He lifted his wineglass in salute.

But she'd already turned to speak to James Hutton, leaning slightly to her right, the swell of her bosom marginally visible in the deep vee of her fichu. Sit up, sit up straighter, he ordered silently, as some jealous lover might, only to chastise himself a second later for such adolescent behavior.

For the next few moments he concentrated on the conversation between Harry and Lunardi sitting to his left and right. They were speaking about valves or the lack of valves or the merits of valves; he was having trouble focusing.

Because Nicky had just picked up a spear of asparagus with her fingers and was bringing it to her mouth.

With the spiky green tip approaching her half-opened mouth, all he could think of was experiencing the exquisite sensation of her luscious lips closing around his cock. Taking a deep breath, he forcibly looked away. Running through a number of platitudes having to do with patience and virtue, he turned to Harry and gave every appearance of listening to him for . . . maybe a count of ten . . . before returning to the ravishing sight of Miss Nicky biting into the tender asparagus spear.

Lust spiked through his body, his breath caught in his throat, and he seriously debated striding down the length of the table, scooping her up into his arms, bidding their guests good night, and carrying her away.

Quickly regaining his reason, he took solace in the fact that no one seemed aware of the shocking violence of his feelings.

Conversation was going on apace, the steady buzz of voices testament to the fact that Miss Nicky consuming her asparagus had apparently gone unnoticed, save for himself.

But then, he was obsessed with fucking her.

He shifted in his chair to ease the tightness of his trousers and checked the time once again.

"She does as she pleases," Lunardi said, amusement in his gaze.

Jasper frowned slightly. "I beg your pardon?"

"It's obvious, Priestley. You're salivating. But she'll decide, not you."

Jasper's frown deepened. "And how do you know that?"

"We've been friends a long time."

"Friends or more than friends?" The viscount's tone could as well been suggesting pistols at dawn.

"I'm engaged to a Neapolitan lady," Lunardi retorted, a spark of temper in his gaze.

"So?"

"For God's sake, Jasper," Harry reproved, his voice hushed. "May I remind you we have esteemed guests?"

"Who aren't above noticing Miss Nicky's decolletage," Jasper drawled.

Harry glowered at Jasper. "Mind your manners."

"I'd suggest you do," Lunardi noted. "She might shoot you, if you offend her." At Jasper's look of surprise, he added, "She did once in Paris. The Duc de Louvain limps to this day. And there was talk of some Rajput prince who changed his mind about adding her to his harem after viewing the business end of her pistol."

"Perhaps the gentlemen were ungallant," Jasper murmured sardonically.

Lunardi's brows lifted. "Apparently so."

"I appreciate the advice." Jasper's tone made it clear,

however, that he wasn't in the market for advice. "Do you plan to marry soon?"

Lunardi understood challenge when he heard it, but knew as well that Nicky was capable of choosing her suitors herself. "As soon as my aerial flights are complete," he answered.

"And when will that be?"

Lunardi made one of those ambiguous hands-up gestures. "Soon, I hope."

"Once your flights are successfully finished, you return to Naples?" This might be a good time to make a donation to Lunardi's efforts, Jasper decided. He was always short of funds, Harry had said.

"Yes." Lunardi smiled. "Not that my absence or presence here will affect Nicky's decision."

"Nor would I expect it to," Jasper said blandly, but he preferred Vincenzo in Naples rather than in close proximity to Miss Nicky. Not that he would have been able to say why, should he have been asked.

"Could we get off this subject?" Harry inquired brusquely. Before he had to stand second in a duel, he thought.

"By all means," Jasper returned smoothly. "More wine, Lunardi?" And raising his hand, he signaled a footman.

Chapter Six

Dessert had been served, the table cleared for the port decanters, glasses filled for the first round of toasts.

Gazing down the polished mahogany table, Jasper said in a carrying tone, "Miss Wemyss, I was wondering if I might avail myself of your expertise for a few moments. Mr. Creech delivered a collection of rare books on India. I was hoping you could authenticate them."

Conversation came to a standstill and heads swivelled to take note of the lady's response to so blatant an overture.

"Bide a wee bit, my boy," Joseph Black suggested in an effort to ease the air of shock. "This is a bra' fine port. The books will wait."

"For God's sake, wait," Harry muttered.

"Don't want to waste a splendid port like this, Priestley." MacPherson held his glass up to the light. "I'll help you later. Know a thing or two about India myself." MacPherson had earned his fortune as the London agent for the Nawab of Arcot.

"Thank you, but this won't take long." Jasper's expression was bland, his voice blander. "The collection is from Delhi." MacPherson's nawab had been from Calcutta, as he'd mentioned more than once tonight, which accounted for Jasper's chosen provenance. He dipped his head in Nicky's direction. "Delhi was your home, as I recall. If you would be so kind, my lady."

She waited a moment before she answered, because Priestley's audacity required at least the appearance of reluctance on her part. Actually, she should refuse him on principle. He was much too familiar with female assent. But she said instead, "I'll take a brief look, my lord," because she'd decided long before dessert that the viscount would serve as her dessert tonight. "I doubt I can be of much help, however," she added mendaciously. "I spent more time in the hill stations than in Delhi." Rising, she smiled at all their guests, who had come to their feet. "Enjoy your port, gentlemen. I won't be long."

Jasper led her from the room a moment later, immune to the stares that followed them, the fact that he'd taken her hand in his further raising eyebrows.

As the dining room door shut on them, Nicky looked at him, a teasing light in her eyes. "Have you no patience?"

"I've been patient for thirty-four hours, twenty-two minutes—give or take a few seconds—not to mention," he added with a flicker of his brows, "I've listened politely to philosophical and scientific discussions while more or less sober. An act of considerable patience, I'll have you know."

She smiled. "Courtship is not your strong suit, I gather."

He came to such an abrupt stop, she half stumbled.

"Courtship?" he said, very low and very heated and so inhospitably she found herself reminded of her father's blanket condemnation of Englishmen.

"You're hurting me." She tried to pull her hand away.

He instantly let go but didn't apologize.

A heated silence fell.

"If you'll excuse me." Affront overwhelmed her clipped reply.

"No," he said as she turned away, and grabbing her around the waist, he swung her back. "You're not excused."

She met his gaze with one as glowering. "You can't do this."

He glanced up and down the empty corridor. "We're quite alone." A curt pronouncement, his meaning clear.

"How dare you play barbarian with me!" She lifted her chin. "I'll scream."

"And then what? Lunardi will call me out? Or old Adam Smith or Dr. Black?"

"Don't think to intimidate me. I'll scream if I wish."

"Suit yourself."

His calmness was provoking, along with several dozen other factors, some unfortunately of the kind that made her acutely aware of his hands on her waist. "I suppose women don't scream with you," she said snappishly, trying to disregard the treacherous direction of her thoughts.

He tried not to smile but didn't quite succeed. "It depends."

Damn his arrogance. "For your information, Priestley, I'm Scots or at least half Scots, and not some stupid, missah Englishwoman. Your exalted position might make such women swoon, but it won't—"

He moved to silence her with a finger to her mouth, but jerked back when she tried to bite him.

"Press me at your own risk," she said, with a challenging lift of her brows.

Since that was exactly what he wished to do—press her, or, more precisely, press into her luscious cunt—some appeasement was in order. Holding his hands out at his sides, he offered her his most charming smile, one that had been honed to perfection in many a boudoir. "A truce, please? I meant no harm. Truly. Could we start over?"

She hesitated.

"I spoke out of turn. It won't happen again."

His smile was artless. And whether it was sincere or not, it was bewitching to behold. "Perhaps," she said, as easily charmed by that smile as all the others, "if you apologize."

"Yes, of course, I apologize for—" He raised his brows in query.

"I believe it was the word *courtship* that caused you such consternation that you wrenched me to a stop and practically broke my hand."

"Ah . . . as to that . . ."

She resisted the urge to smile at his tactful hesitation. "So they all want to marry you. Is that it?"

He didn't answer.

"You won't offend me, Priestley, or rather, you already have. Speak up."

"Yes, they do."

"Then, let me put your mind at rest. I do not wish to marry you or anyone. If I wished to marry, I could have done so any number of times these past ten years. Is that more reassuring?"

"Very much. And I do apologize for thinking—" He paused, searching for a more appropriate phrase than "the worst." "You were like the others," he said, deciding that would offend least.

"I'm very much *not* like the others. A shame you won't have the opportunity to discover that," she added pithily, taking issue with his assumption that all women were available to him.

She stood ramrod straight, her splendid, upthrust breasts brought into even more prominence with her posture, their soft plumpness beneath the filmy muslin of her gown close enough to touch. As if he needed any further incitement after waiting for thirty-some hours. "Couldn't we reconcile this in some way? Deal with this like adults? Come to some agreement?"

"Negotiate, you mean? Like in a brothel?"

"Look," he said very, very softly. "You choose the words—I'll agree to anything you wish." A faint edge had reentered his voice. He wasn't in the habit of begging for sex.

"There's nothing to agree to. I dislike your utter selfishness."

"If this is still about sex"—he wasn't entirely clear at this point—"surely your interest is no less selfish than mine. You want something, or you wouldn't be here—and you needn't look affronted. I understand the feeling, because I want something, too. Additionally, neither of us wishes to marry. We're much alike in our enjoyment of, shall we say, the pleasures of life."

"You don't know what I enjoy."

"Then show me, or I'll show you—or we could show each other. In fact, I have a masterful translation of the Kama Sutra if you'd like to see it." He made a dismissive gesture with his hand. "Not one of those missionary translations."

"So, you've seen those?"

"Yes—prurient hypocrisy at its best. If the subject matter is so offensive to a cleric, why bother to translate it?"

"Exactly."

He smiled. "So we agree on something."

"The missionaries in India are, by and large, an unsympathetic lot," Nicky said with a grimace. "That fact, however, doesn't mean you're exonerated."

"Tell me how I may make amends, and I will."

She sighed softly. He was still—despite his knee-jerk reaction to women trying to gain his title—gloriously handsome, powerfully male, and, truth be told, one of the most desirable men she'd ever seen. Or maybe it was the ambergris scent in his cologne that made her liquid with longing. "Very well," she said, reminding herself she *had* come here tonight for this—for him. Her body understood that better than she. "We have to set some ground rules."

He restrained his gloating impulses. "Name them. I'm amenable."

She half smiled. "You *are* obliging."

He couldn't repress his grin. "Give me a moment of your time, and I'll show exactly how obliging I can be."

"Do you actually have books upstairs?"

"Four cartons full. They were delivered this afternoon."

"So you'd have an excuse to lure me upstairs?"

"I thought they might amuse you."

"Because you could lure me upstairs on your own?"

"Something like that."

"Arrogant rogue."

"You're not exactly submissive yourself."

"Do you like submissive women?"

His mouth quirked into a faint smile. "At times."

"I like submissive men at times as well."

His gaze went shuttered.

"Are you thinking of changing your mind?"

A flash of amusement suddenly warmed his eyes. "Not since I first saw you in Lunardi's laboratory."

"You'rc sure, now."

"Oh, yes, definitely."

"So—what next?"

"It's up to you. I have no reputation to uphold."

"Or maybe you do."

He laughed. "I don't keep score."

"Some men do."

"Good for them."

"As I live and breathe!" a raucous cry rang out. "If it isn't "The Pope"—the greatest cunt-hound in England!"

Recognizing the inebriated voice, Jasper swore softly. "Ignore him," he said in an undertone, turning to meet the drunken man staggering down the hallway toward them. He moved forward to ward him off.

"You've had too much to drink, Dudley," Jasper muttered, meeting the disheveled man still dressed in hunting garb, holding him steady with a harsh grip on his shoulders. "Why don't I see you in the morning when you're sober."

"I'm sober enough to see that little filly you're trying to

hide," Lord Dudley bellowed. "Somebody's wife? Eh, Priestley? Won't say a word. Your secret's safe with me," he hissed in an attempt at reticence that was so loud, Jasper glanced down the corridor to see if anyone was within hearing distance. "You always did like'm with a bit of danger and risk on the side." Dudley leered. "Better sex, eh what?"

"No, Eddy. Now turn around and go away," Jasper growled, manhandling the young lord and marching him toward the hotel lobby.

"Don't want to go! Want to see the little tart! Christ, Priestley, since when haven't you shared?"

After that disastrous utterance, even if he hadn't heard the dining room door shut with a sharp bang, Jasper wouldn't have expected to find Nicky still in the corridor when he returned from handing Eddy over to the hotel staff. And for a transient moment, as he stood outside the private dining room, he debated going back to his suite, opening a bottle, and drinking himself into oblivion in lieu of spending the remainder of the evening with Harry's "esteemed" scholars and Nicky's wrathful resentment.

But he wasn't a coward, nor was he in the mood for his own company.

And despite Eddy's inopportune appearance, he was still hopeful he might change Nicky's mind.

Call it arrogance.

Or years of practice.

Or maybe just blind hope.

In any event, at least he'd be in erudite company as he drank himself into oblivion.

Chapter Seven

But it was one of those nights when, regardless of how much liquor Jasper poured down his throat, he remained sober. Maybe Nicky's fiery gaze burned away the alcohol from his brain, maybe his adrenaline was racing so fast it absorbed the liquor, maybe he was so focused on his ultimate goal that he was immune to the effects of strong spirits.

Or maybe he was more drunk than he thought, for when the painter Raeburn suggested that Nicky come to his studio as the party was breaking up, Jasper invited himself along.

"No," Nicky said, her voice mild but her gaze forbidding. "Thank you for dinner, but Henry doesn't like interruptions."

If only she had used some other phrase.

"I'm sure Henry wouldn't mind," Jasper retorted, his voice cold as the grave.

"He may not, but I do," she said, rebuffing Jasper in an equally chill voice. "You're not welcome, Priestley. I'm ready to go, Henry." And twirling away, she walked from the room in a rustle of silk.

"Some other time, Jasper," Harry cajoled, pulling on Jasper's arm. "It's late. It was a pleasure to meet you,

Raeburn. Vincenzo, a hand here if you please," he muttered, clutching harder on Jasper's arm.

Having followed the interchange between the viscount and Nicky with interest, if not understanding, Henry Raeburn opted for neutrality in what appeared to be a lover's tiff. Offering his thanks for dinner, he bowed to the three men and followed Nicky from the room.

"You've done your duty," Jasper snarled, shaking the men's hands away. "Now go away."

"You make sure you leave her alone," Harry ordered. "You've had too much to drink."

"What about you?" Jasper inquired churlishly, arching a brow at Lunardi. "No words of warning?"

"Would you listen?"

Jasper snorted. "A man of acuity at least."

"Come to bed now," Harry commanded.

"With you? I'm not *that* drunk."

"You know very well what I meant."

Jasper surveyed the table. "The Scots have left a bottle or two. Surely that must be a first. Was it something I said?"

Harry hadn't seen Jasper in such a vicious mood in years. "If you won't come upstairs, then I'll keep you company."

"I don't need a chaperon."

"I beg to differ with you."

"At least allow Lunardi to find his bed. Good night, Vincenzo. Harry will keep me from harm."

"It's not you I'm worried about," Harry muttered.

"Thank you for the fine dinner, Priestley," Lunardi said, bowing gracefully. "I wish you the best of luck."

Jasper glowered at the young Neapolitan. "With the formidable Miss Nicky, you mean."

"But of course, my lord." Lunardi smiled. "I doubt you need luck in any other arena."

Up to this point, Jasper had viewed making love to the ravishing Miss Nicky as no more than a familiar game. But something in Lunardi's tone, or maybe the substantial amount of liquor he'd consumed, suddenly parlayed the scaling of Miss Nicky's amorous citadel into a conspicuous challenge. If he read Lunardi correctly, at issue was his success or failure.

And he didn't like to lose.

"Thank you for your good wishes," Jasper replied smoothly. "I'll let you know how events transpire."

Vincenzo made an elegant bow as only a Neapolitan could. "I look forward to hearing from you."

Harry was waving Lunardi out from behind Jasper's back. Another few exchanges between the two men, and Vincenzo would be involved in a duel that would certainly put an end to his promising career. Jasper fought as well drunk or sober, with pistols or swords, his reputation so formidable he was given wide berth in all the London clubs. "We'll see you in the morning," Harry cheerfully proclaimed, morphing his go-away wave into a good-bye wave as Jasper turned around. "Bright and early, as usual. Bright and early. Do you want brandy or claret, Jasper? I'm in the mood for claret."

Moments later, the dining room was silent, Jasper slumped low in a chair, a glass of brandy balanced on his chest, his eyes half shut. Harry sat at the table with his chin propped in his hands, his elbows on the table, his gaze on the clock, wondering how long Jasper would last—or worse, remain biddable.

When he rarely was.

Furthermore, Harry understood better than anyone that Jasper's not following Miss Nicky had little to do with his admonitions. "Have you calmed down?" he gently inquired.

Jasper's lashes levered up slightly, and a faint smile curved his mouth. "Do you know how many years you've been asking me that?"

Harry nodded. The two boys had met at Eton as ten-year-olds thrown to the upperclassmen wolves, as were all the young nobles sent from home. They'd stood together against the bullies and survived. "Maybe she's not your type."

"I've been thinking about that."

"She's not pliant."

Jasper snorted. "The understatement of the century."

"You might not like to fight in bed."

Jasper suddenly grinned. "I've been thinking about that, too."

"I'm not sure that tone of voice calms my fears."

"You needn't have fears. When next I see her I'll be the consummate gentleman."

"With anyone else, I might believe you. But she triggers some response in you I haven't seen before. Male possession, perhaps. You've always been the byword for indifference when it comes to women. You know that."

Jasper grimaced. "Do we have to analyze this?"

"No. If you went up to bed, I wouldn't say another word."

"And if I don't?"

"One of us will drink the other under the table."

Actually, it didn't take as long as Jasper had thought. Harry must have been tired. When Harry's eyes closed for the last time and remained closed for ten minutes, Jasper found a servant, had a blanket brought for Harry, and left him with his head on the dining table.

He could have had Harry carried upstairs, but didn't want to take the chance of waking him.

Not when he had plans.

Chapter Eight

Henry Raeburn's portrait studio was well known.

Shortly after receiving directions from the concierge, Jasper was standing outside an elegant town house ablaze with lights.

Hopefully, they weren't in bed yet, he thought, surveying the three floors of windows glowing in the night. And a potentially embarrassing scene could be avoided.

Not that the painter had had the look of a lover, his mild manners tonight unlike a man with an intense interest in a woman. But then, artists were by nature less predacious, he supposed. Or perhaps they were besieged by society women in their capacity as portraitists to the aristocracy. Perhaps they were blasé about females in pursuit.

As he had been.

The operative verb in the past tense.

Which altered circumstances now brought him here in the middle of the night to this strange street and house where he was faced with deciding how to enter the house, and once inside, find the woman who had occasioned his radical departure from long-standing custom.

And perhaps, more difficult, persuade her to come with him.

Or in the absence of that, carry her away.

It was not only astonishing but unprecedented that he should be contemplating such a shocking act. If he weren't feeling almost completely sober, despite the prodigious amount of liquor he'd consumed, he would charge the bewildering improbability to alcohol.

He was very far from intoxicated, however.

In fact, he was sober as a judge, not a particularly apt expression here in Scotland where the judges were known to drink their supper at the bench. But in his current case, true.

So his choices were plain: do something or go home. And he'd not come this far, figuratively speaking, to turn away from a challenge.

He actually craved this woman, a concept that would have been foreign to him two days ago. Although, her refusal may have contributed to the curious intensity of his feelings. On the other hand, even on first sight, she'd provoked a primal lust quite distinct from his usual casual desire.

So, Henry Raeburn and good manners be damned.

Swiftly crossing the street, he took the shallow flight of stairs fronting the entrance in a leap, and banged on the door.

A serving lad answered, his eyes drowsy from sleep.

Stepping over the threshold like a man on a mission, Jasper said, "Mr. Raeburn's expecting me."

"He's in his studio, sar, and don't like to be disturbed."

The young boy jumped into Jasper's path as he moved toward the stairs. Scowling, Jasper came to a stop. "Kindly tell your master I'm here."

"He won't see no one when he's workin', sar."

"Tell him Viscount Priestley is here," Jasper enunciated in clipped, cool syllables, his impatience clear. "I'm sure he'll see me."

Shortly after the servant reached the main floor and entered a room at the top of the landing, Jasper heard Nicky's voice clear as a bell, her indignation echoing down the stairs. The word *no* in various guises was the pithy gist of her message. Not that he'd expected less.

Taking a deep breath, he ran his fingers through his unruly hair, his mood uncertain. Would this enterprise prove too embarrassing? Did he care?

How much did he care?

When the servant returned to the entrance hall, the viscount was gone.

A fact he reported to his master.

"Good. He's a rogue and a rake and of no interest to me," Nicky said crisply as the young boy exited the studio and closed the door. Taking care not to move in her pose despite her perturbation, she said with a sniff, "Priestley's audacity is outrageous."

Raeburn half smiled. "Certainly not an unusual characteristic in a London rake. Why let him bother you?"

"He doesn't bother me. Don't look at me like that, Henry. He simply displeases me in numerous ways. I'm annoyed with his bold-faced impertinence, that's all."

"Your color's high, my dear. Just an observation as an artist," he added with a grin. "Is something afoot I should know about?"

"No, nor will there be. Priestley's an attractive rogue, I don't deny. That doesn't mean I intend to succumb to his insolent charm."

The artist's brows rose. "You surprise me. I wouldn't have thought you likely to succumb to anything you didn't wish to."

"Nor will I," she retorted firmly. "Now, if you please, the subject is closed. Entertain me with more of your marvelous descriptions of Rome. You so bring the city to life, I may be inclined to go with you when next you travel there."

"I'd be delighted. Did I tell you about Raphael's tomb? Lift your chin just a little . . . there . . . like that. Perfect. It's truly moving to feel Raphael's spirit in the Pantheon. I'm painting your left ear now, so not a twitch."

Raeburn was painting Nicky's portrait against a bucolic landscape with an aerial balloon rising from the distant horizon. She wore a wide-brimmed, flower-bedecked hat tied with a bouffant bow under her chin, the stylish hat a modish adjunct to all the fashionable, gauzy gowns.

But her smile was strained, and a certain tension was visible in her shoulders since the viscount's intrusion, Raeburn noted. And after wiping away the flesh-colored tones of what should have been the left ear in the portrait for the second time because his model was restless, he politely inquired, "Would you like to take a short rest? We could have some of that malmsey you like."

Nicky's smile was rueful. "If you don't mind, I find myself out of sorts tonight." Stretching her arms over her head, she arched her back. "Perhaps we could do this some other time."

"Whenever you wish. Go home, get some rest. I have plenty of work to do on the landscape."

"Lunardi's always at the laboratory by dawn. I expect I should sleep for a few hours at least."

"You're excused, darling." Raeburn smiled.

"You're always so understanding." Untying the bow under her chin, she rose from her chair, lifted the confection of a hat from her head, and carefully placed it on one of the numerous Roman busts scattered about Raeburn's studio.

"One of my servants will see you home." Raeburn was already working again, brushing on paint with intense concentration. "You don't mind, do you?" he said without looking up.

Nicky shook her head, understanding an answer would likely go unheard. Bent low over the painting, Henry's brush hand flicked over the canvas, leaving behind a wispy cloud exquisitely true to nature.

Picking up her cape, Nicky tossed it over her shoulders

and left the studio. She enjoyed Henry's company; she liked more that he'd traveled enough to understand that a world existed beyond Scotland.

Descending the stairs, she chose not to wake the young servant asleep in the porter's chair. Quietly opening the door, she walked out onto the porch, tripped, and fell.

Jasper barely moved from his lounging pose, his back to the wrought iron railing, his outstretched legs the obstacle causing Nicky to conveniently tumble into his waiting arms.

Her shocked cry instantly changed to a suffocated gasp as she lay sprawled atop the man she least wished to see. Struggling to free herself, concerned with not making a public spectacle, she hissed rather than screamed, "You, you reprehensible! wicked! shameless . . . disgraceful . . ." But her voice trailed off and her struggles lessened as her senses responded in a completely indefensible way.

Dear God, or Shiva, or Buddha, or whoever would steady the chaotic dither in her brain. Was it good or wildly bad that Priestley had waited for her, barricading her exit, that his hard-muscled body felt much harder and more muscled than she would have liked to admit. That she was feeling decidedly tremulous and susceptible to his legendary charms.

The lady's skirts were topsy-turvy, her bodice in disarray, the silken friction of her limbs violently distracting. Reining in his base instincts, Jasper reminded himself that honeyed phrases accomplished infinitely more than brute force. "I would like to apologize for all I've done to offend you." Releasing her from his light embrace, he held out his arms as though in supplication. "I throw myself on your mercy. I'm quite willing to wear sack cloth and ashes, if necessary."

She looked momentarily incredulous before mistrust altered her gaze. "Is that so?"

He nodded.

"Really—sackcloth?" She suddenly smiled as she pushed

herself upright and sat astride his legs. "I'm sorry"—her mouth twitched into saner alignment. "You don't really expect me to believe that."

"I'm serious," he said.

She looked amused. "No, you're not."

"I could be."

Her gaze was direct. "What if I were to take you up on your offer to wear sack cloth and ashes?"

"You don't think I can be humble?"

"I don't think you know what the word means."

"Perhaps we could go somewhere less public," he murmured, "and I could show you."

"Your humility?"

He suddenly grinned. "Among other things."

"That's what I thought."

Hearing her tone of voice, he was about to begin apologizing afresh when she made a small moue, shrugged one shoulder, and said, "I shouldn't, of coursc."

It wasn't necessary to have her spell out what she shouldn't do. He knew better than to ask what she meant in that regard. "Why not?" he asked.

"Because you do this all the time."

"How would that affect your pleasure or mine?" He sensed she might prefer the truth to suave fabrication.

"So I should be grateful for your expertise?"

"Whatever form your gratitude took, *I* would be extremely grateful, believe me."

"That's the problem."

His brows rose.

"Your interest is too casual. It's the chase, isn't it, Priestley? Never the getting."

"Perhaps," he replied truthfully, "but in your case, there's nothing casual about my interest. You're one of the most beautiful, intelligent, captivating women I've ever met."

She half smiled. "Did you say, *one* of the most—"

His brows rose in piquant raillery. "Conceited chit. Very well, the most superior woman in every way, who has enticed me beyond comprehension. Now may we get up off this landing and go elsewhere?"

"Where, exactly, would that be?"

"A warm bed, preferably. Yours or mine." He smiled the most natural, open smile. "Mine, of course, is available."

"Just like that?" she said, thinking a smile like that was too good to be true; he was a very good actor. "You say 'my bed' and I'm supposed to fall into it?"

"I think you forget the rather elaborate foreplay in the form of dinner tonight where I performed my duties as host for you—and *only* you. Whether I ever see Adam Smith fall asleep over his port again or hear another word about the lamentable loss of Highland traditions interests me not. Consider the magnitude of my effort to please you as the most prolonged foreplay since Abelard met Heloise."

"Does that mean tonight will be devoid of foreplay?" Her voice had taken on a teasing note; you couldn't fault him for the grandness of his gesture.

"Tonight will be devoid of nothing your heart desires—word of honor—if you give me leave to get up off this cold limestone and escort you to my bed."

"I don't know whether I'm fatigued or whether you've overcome my last scruple with that generous word of honor promise, but you have and I am and," she leaned forward and kissed him lightly on the mouth, "your bed sounds truly divine."

Taking her hands in his, he immediately came to his feet with effortless grace, pulling her up as he rose. "You're very light," he murmured, steadying her for a moment. "You should eat more."

"If I had been inclined to further equivocate, such blatant charm has surely sealed our bargain."

"Bargain?" The faintest frown marred his brow.

"I'm sorry." She looked entertained. "Would you prefer a more romantic term?"

The word *romance* effectively quelled his moment of unease. "No, of course not," he replied smoothly. Her blunt speech was very different from that of the ladies in his past who never said what they thought or meant what they said. But he was more than willing to adjust his perceptions of females as a class. With a bow, he offered her his arm. "May I interest you in—"

"Sex with you? Yes, Priestley," she softly returned. "You finally may."

Chapter Nine

As they were approaching Dun's Hotel, Nicky said, "Wait," and turned around. "You may go home now, Jai. I'm perfectly safe. Tell him, Priestley."

A tall Indian dressed in a hybrid combination of eastern and western garb walked out of the shadows and came to a halt a short distance away.

Meeting the man's bold gaze, Jasper said, "Your mistress is safe with me, I assure you."

"And tell Madhu to go to sleep," Nicky ordered. "I'll be home in the morning."

"As you wish." Jai's deep voice was bland.

"I mean it," Nicky insisted. "I don't want you sleeping outside my door."

Jai bowed again, his expression impassive.

"Come," Nicky murmured, taking Jasper's hand.

With a last glance at Jai, Jasper fell into step beside her. "He doesn't sound as though he follows orders well."

She snorted. "Or at all."

"So will he be sleeping outside my door?" A small dubiousness shaded his query.

"More than likely."

He cast another glance over his shoulder.

"Jai never interferes."

Her declaration wasn't particularly comforting. In fact, it was slightly unnerving. The man, while not young, was fit and clearly protective of his mistress. Jasper wasn't sure whether Jai's presence outside his bedchamber might not present some problems in terms of, say, spontaneity.

On the other hand, having performed in rather more public venues on occasion when some wager was at stake—Madame Adelaide's brothel last month coming to mind—perhaps performance wouldn't be an issue.

Since a footman was about to open the door to the hotel for them and the lady who had been on his mind almost constantly since yesterday was finally willing, he dismissed any further speculation. Only a fool would quibble over some manservant's presence at a time like this. "Did I tell you I've decided to invest in Lunardi's venture?" he asked as they entered the hotel.

"No." Nicky smiled. "How very nice. Vincenzo will be pleased."

"Once his mission is complete, he tells me he intends to return to Naples."

She glanced up at him with a twinkle in her eye. "I haven't slept with him, if that's what you're thinking."

"He said as much."

"But you were just checking?"

His brows flickered in sportive response as they walked through the lobby. "For unknown reasons."

"Similar incomprehensible motives have brought me here tonight," she replied with a quirked grin.

He winked. "It must be kismet."

"I dearly hope so. I wouldn't want to think it was a signal weakness in me."

He half turned to her as they mounted the stairs. "Because you like sex?"

"No, because I succumbed to your many charms."

"Or me to yours," he countered. "And add ten thousand."

Her gaze was playfully arch. "I like that much better."

"While I like everything about you," he pleasantly said. "Now if I might offer you the hospitality of my suite." Having reached the first apartment at the top of the stairs, he opened a pair of ornately carved doors and waved her in. "I look forward to becoming better acquainted."

Moving past him, she swung around in the center of the sitting room, her full-skirted gown belling out around her. "*Much* better acquainted," she purred, twirling away, her arms flung wide.

He stood against the closed doors, watching her pirouette in the candlelight, her lighthearted merriment beguiling, as was everything about her. She was a complex, captivating woman who engaged his interest beyond his usual lascivious designs. Not something he cared to contemplate now—or ever.

She came to rest at that moment, conveniently checking whatever pernicious sentiment had insinuated itself into his brain. "I just adore sex," she playfully proclaimed, bowing low, her arms open wide in imitation of ballerinas on stage, sweeping upright a second later with a candy-sweet smile. "Don't you?"

"Very much," he said softly. Turning the key in the lock, he slipped it in his pocket. "Insurance," he said to her raised eyebrows. "I don't care to take on Jai when I have better things to do."

"He won't intrude unless I ask him."

"Or I let him in."

She didn't answer for a moment. "Yes, of course."

Her pause was mildly disquieting. "Would he break in?"

"If he had to." She smiled and kicked off her slippers. "I don't anticipate such a need, however."

"How reassuring," he replied sardonically.

"Really, Priestley, don't be concerned." Reaching behind her back, she untied the bow at her waist and stripped the bright green ribbon free. "I don't expect your notions of sex are so bizarre as to require my rescue." Dropping the silk ribbon to the carpet, she smiled at him. "Help me with these hooks, will you?" Turning her back to him, she lifted her dark curls from her nape.

In his current covetous mood, no actual thought was required to accommodate her, and moments later, he was lifting her gown over her head.

She swung around. "Would you like me to undress you?"

It took him a moment for her words to register, her voluptuous form clearly visible through her sheer chemise, the shadowed juncture of her thighs the particular focus of his gaze. "No, no need," he answered, stripping off his dress coat, reaching to untie his neckcloth. "Would you like some wine?" he inquired, remembering his manners.

"I've had enough. Dinner was long."

"Too long." He unwrapped his neckcloth and tossed it away. "I was tempted to carry you away a dozen times."

She looked up from untying her garter. "And me you."

"Ah." He paused, his shirt half over his head.

"Don't look at me like that. Surely you've had women want to have sex with you before." She slid off her silk stocking.

"Not one for whom I've waited so long," he murmured, jerking his shirt over his head, his erection surging at the sight of her shapely leg.

Her brows rose. "A day?"

"It seemed forever." Stepping out of his shoes, he pushed them aside.

"You have no patience." Her second stocking joined the first on the carpet and she lifted her chemise over her head.

He drew in his breath, her sumptuous breasts quivering slightly as their heavy weight fell back into place, her slender waist and rounded hips female perfection, her plump mons, the springy dark curls between her legs inciting every carnal nerve in his body. "No," he said softly, consummation a raging impulse, "I'm not a patient man."

Tossing away her chemise, she surveyed his powerful, muscled torso with appreciation. "I could seduce you if you like. I've read the chapters on courtesans in the Kama Sutra." She smiled. "You certainly are one of the men-about-town they describe."

"Seduction won't be necessary." Glancing up from unbuttoning his breeches, he grinned. "I'm well past any need for that. In fact," he said, stripping off his breeches and stockings, "I'm hard-pressed not to—" Arrested by her gasp, he looked up again.

She was staring, her cheeks flushed, her lips slightly parted.

The Kama Sutra categorized penises by size as a hare, a bull, or a stallion, and there was no doubt Priestley qualified as a stallion, Nicky reflected, the twelve fingers in length that designated the status of stallion conspicuously manifest in his enormous, upthrust erection. A little frisson of anticipation rippled through her vagina, a melting warmth suffusing her tissue. "That is very, very alluring," she murmured.

"I could say the same, Miss Wemyss," he said, velvety and low, the nude beauty before him with tousled curls and diamonds at her throat and ears inflaming his senses. She excited rapacious cravings quite different from the usual sportive play he engaged in. She made him feel as though he might be entering a combat zone instead of the graceful ritual world of the Kama Sutra.

She put out her hand. "Show me your bed."

"Are you sure?" He felt as though he should warn her.

Pointing, she made a small circle with her index finger and softly said, "I'm very sure. You haven't changed your mind, I hope."

He moved his head in the faintest negation and, moving forward, took her hand and led her through the sitting room into the bedchamber where a fire had been set in the hearth and candles lit by the well-trained hotel staff. They'd also accommodated his wish for a luxurious display of white roses.

"How pleasing you can be, Priestley," she murmured, taking in the enchanting excess of roses. "You've made all the flower stalls much richer today." Dropping his hand, she strolled from one arrangement to another, inhaling the scents, admiring the blossoms, turning at the bed to smile at him. "If I weren't so selfish, I might almost be content already. You've been most charming—dinner and all this," she said with an encompassing wave.

"I think it's too late to be content with only this," he said, advancing toward her.

"I couldn't stop you at this point, you mean?"

His lashes lowered infinitesimally as he reached her. "It would be difficult."

"But not impossible."

"Impossible, actually," he said, sliding his hands around her waist. "I was being polite." Lifting her, he seated her on the edge of the bed, forced her thighs open with a brushing motion of his palms, and moved between them. "It's too late to go back," he whispered. Taking her face between his hands, he bent down, his mouth brushed hers, and he said against her lips, "I hope you don't mind."

She should say she minded—out of principle, because Priestley never experienced dissent from a woman. But were she to take serious issue and force him to let her go—Jai's presence outside her guarantee—she would lose as well as he.

It was a shame he was so gloriously endowed, his kisses so enticing. With anyone else, she might consider her principles. With anyone else so audacious as to ask her if she minded, when he obviously didn't care, she would have bitten him hard, as she could right now if she wished, and called for Jai.

"If I minded, I wouldn't be here," she murmured instead, her breath warm on his mouth.

"I know." Kissing her gently, he slipped two fingers into her vagina and stroked her sleek, turgid flesh, her engorged clitoris, sliding his fingers up and down and around, expertly, adroitly, knowing exactly where to touch and how, making her vagina softer and wetter, making her forget about arrogant men who had always had their way.

Making her want what she'd come here to have.

Pushing his mouth away, pouty and sultry and perhaps as audacious as he when it came to her sexual pleasures, she said, "That's enough. I want more. At your earliest convenience, of course," she added impudently.

For a fraction of a second, he considered refusing; he didn't give command performances.

"Don't tell me you *want* to wait," she said in a husky contralto, taking note of the spark of anger in his gaze.

"You like to give orders, don't you?"

"Not unless I have to." Lying back on the bed, she spread her legs, opened herself with both hands, and gazed at him from under the fringe of her lashes, a faint smile lifting the corners of her mouth. "Perhaps you could think of it as a request."

That carnal offering was impossible to resist, and she knew it.

Holding his gaze, she ran her tongue over her plump, red bottom lip. "I'd really adore if you'd put that lovely lingam—"

"In your hot little cunt?" he returned gruffly, roughly pushing her hands aside, guiding his erection to her dewy cleft, and doing what he'd been wanting to do from the first moment he saw her. Plunging into her soft flesh, he drove in with a barely controlled wildness, forcing her to yield, pressing deeper and deeper still, his hands on her thighs spreading them wide, the sensation of her tight cunt closing around him only whetting his appetite for more.

Constrained by his fierce grip, she whimpered and squirmed, made little panting noises, helpless captive to his fevered penetration.

He didn't hear her or didn't care enough to listen or couldn't have stopped after thirty-six hours and counting if he'd had a gun to his head. She was slippery wet, and any cunt that drenched was definitely in the welcoming category regardless that it was a damned tight fit. Needing better ingress, he lifted her legs and twined them around his waist. She was panting and sobbing, clinging to his shoulders, leaving marks with her nails, and he knew what that meant.

She wanted more.

He was so huge, so deliciously huge, she could feel him in every taut nerve and pulsing cell, his downward pressure wildly intoxicating, riveting. No wonder he was so vain. Women must beat a path to his door. Damn him. Although she wasn't going to take issue with his vanity right now. Not when she had, oh lord, a jolt of pure, unalloyed pleasure streaking through her body as he achieved maximum depth. Her toes curled, her hair tingled, her sobs rose upward in frenzied little exhalations, and she began to come as if he had only to fill her completely and she instantly climaxed. There was no stopping it, the intensity overwhelming, the ecstasy bombarding her senses, the orgasmic tidal wave of sensation so intense she screamed when she shouldn't have, when Jai—

Jasper arrested her cry mid-pitch, covering her mouth with his as her explosive orgasm rolled through her body like a ferocious storm.

Taut with restraint, he waited until she was conscious of reality once more before easing his mouth away. "Keep it up, and we're going to have company."

"I'm sorry," she breathed, willing to acquiesce readily if she could feel the way she'd just felt again, every necessitous throbbing bit of vaginal tissue acutely aware of being crammed delectably full. "It won't happen again."

"Thank you."

The brusqueness of his tone obliterated her rare compliance. "You might consider being more polite." Moving her hips in a graceful undulation, she contracted around him with a serene smile. "I don't believe you've come yet."

"That's not a problem," he said with effort. The grip of her vulva was sensational.

"What if I were to leave?"

"Then you'd miss a dozen orgasms."

"You're very annoying."

Holding her waist, he moved inside her, left and right, in and out, smoothly, with a finesse born of considerable practice. "How annoying?" he whispered.

It took her a moment to answer, the strumming pleasure like a hard, pounding drumbeat through her vagina and body and brain. "Fine, I won't leave. Satisfied?"

"Not yet," he said with a wicked grin. "Let me know what you think of this." Leaning forward, he eased her legs over his shoulders and caressed her breasts and nipples in several of the thirty-two variations detailed in the Kama Sutra, his lower body moving all the while—in and out, in and out, slowly, deliberately, in a silken flux and flow, until she was whimpering softly and so liquid with desire, he found himself anticipating the night ahead with unbridled delight.

She was easily aroused, quick to climax, obviously highly sexed, and so ripe and succulent she could last for hours. The possibility of such lascivious sport brought his erection surging higher.

She moaned softly, his added dimension stretching her more taut, bringing another climax shuddering on the brink.

Recognizing her sudden stillness, no longer capable of waiting himself, he whispered, "Now, now, now, *now,*" and drove in up to the hilt.

She uttered a suffocated little cry as the first wild tremors began.

"Good girl," he whispered, half in praise, half in warning, should she be inclined to scream, more intent, however, on gauging the exact moment her orgasm exploded, like . . . right . . . now. Pouring into her, he met her frantic, frenzied release, pumping into her, flooding her with a river of white, hot semen, every nerve in his body alive to the soul-stirring ecstasy.

Immediately afterward, he jerked away, silently cursing his stupidity. Grabbing two towels from those piled at the end of the bed per his orders, he tossed one on her stomach, swiped himself clean, and dropped the towel as he strode away.

Motionless, she watched him walk to the bureau, pick up a bottle of brandy, and pour himself a drink.

Draining the glass, he told himself he should have had more sense than to come in her, told himself as well that it was too late to worry about something unalterable. Muttering a curse, he poured himself another drink, tossed it down, and set the glass on the bureau.

Still unmoving, her diamonds twinkling, she surveyed his scowling return.

"I shouldn't have come in you," he said gruffly. "I don't normally make such mistakes."

"All is not lost, Priestley," she said tranquilly. "My ayah will make me some tea and elixir when I return home, and your worries will be over." She smiled. "Mine as well. Is that better? Will you stop looking at me with such brooding ill humor?"

"I wasn't aware there were options for unprotected sex without consequences."

"While I thought noble lords ignored such problems," she noted with a touch of sarcasm.

"You thought wrong," he said, sitting down beside her with an enormous sense of relief. Picking up the towel from her stomach, he wiped her dry with an unaffected naturalness. "I make it a habit to avoid by-blows, the last few moments notwithstanding."

"I didn't realize you had a conscience."

"Nothing so fine," he replied. "I dislike responsibility." He touched her cheek with the gentlest pressure and smiled. "And apparently, I have none to contend with tonight."

"Certainly not on my account."

He ran his finger down her arm as she lay beside him. "How charming you are."

She shook her head. "Just self-indulgent. I dislike responsibility, too."

He laughed. "How nice we found each other."

"I agree," she murmured. "Especially after those last two orgasms. Would you be available for more?"

"You may have as many as you want." A woman's desire is eight times that of a man, the Kama Sutra said. Tonight he was looking forward to putting that maxim to the test.

"When?" she asked, very, very softly.

He laughed.

"Greedy minx."

"I've been working so hard, I've forgotten to—"

He stopped her statement with a kiss, not inclined to hear about her desires unless he was involved. Had he taken note of that moment of possessiveness, he might have been alarmed. He was pushing her up on the pillows, though, and more aware of the heated kisses being offered by the delectable lady in his arms. Introspection wasn't his strong suit, anyway. Sexual intercourse was.

The newly met, but mutually compatible, couple explored a good many of the sixty-four positions detailed in Vatsyayana's manual of love that night, keeping in mind the author's declaration that "When the wheel of sexual ecstasy is in full motion, there is no textbook at all, and no order." Nicky knew the Kama Sutra well, Jasper less so, but then the art of love was a natural pleasure transcending cultures. And the viscount had been playing the game for a very long time.

Miss Wemyss was remarkably supple, and had not her expertise been so satisfying, Jasper might have questioned the amount of schooling necessary to be so proficient.

For her part, Nicky was only grateful for the viscount's noteworthy stamina.

They talked superficially of their lives in the quiet intervals between their love play. He wasn't exclusively a rake, his activities more numerous than she would have thought. Her stories of India were intriguing, her travel there extensive, her descriptions of business dealings with native merchants fascinating. He'd never met a woman so exempt from feminine frivolity and giddiness.

She was truly exquisite in numerous ways.

While "The Pope" performed with appropriate benevolence.

Nicky would very gratefully attest to that.

Chapter Ten

"Where are you going?" Against the first light of dawn, Jasper took in the delicious sight of Nicky struggling to pull her chemise down over her plump breasts.

"To work. It's early. Go back to sleep."

"I'll come with you," he said, throwing aside the covers.

"That's not necessary. How do I say this politely? Last night was lovely—more than lovely, stupendous and blissful—but I really have to go to work. So thank you for everything, and pleasant dreams."

He'd never been dismissed by a woman after a night of sex or given his conge by a woman for *any* reason. It gave him pause—for the briefest of seconds—before his well-honed self-interest came to the fore. Rising from the bed, he closed the small distance between them, tugged her chemise down for her, and straightened the batiste folds with a flick of his fingers. "I don't know how to say this," he murmured in gentle parody, brushing her cheek lightly. "But last night was beyond stupendous for me, and with that memory still newly fresh, I have no intention of letting you go. I hope you understand."

"Don't be ridiculous." She gazed at him from under her lashes. "You are, you know."

He blew out a breath. "Probably. But I'm coming with you."

"And do what?"

"Whatever you do. Give me orders." He smiled. "You're good at that, as I recall."

"This isn't a seduction, Priestley. I'm tired as hell and not in the mood to put up with this foolishness. Weren't you going hunting?"

"I was until I met you."

"You don't understand. I have no time to be polite."

"You can't work every minute."

"Very nearly. I don't indulge in a life of leisure like you."

"Let me put it this way. Tell me you really don't want to come ten or twenty times tonight, and I'll go hunting for whatever Harry feels is in need of being hunted."

The fact that Jasper was standing very close, his erection at full mast as usual, made it almost impossible to avert her eyes from its splendor. Be sensible, she told herself; don't surrender to Priestley as diversion. There were hours and days, perhaps weeks of work ahead before the balloon was restructured for higher altitudes. "I'd prefer a polite good-bye. I'm sure there are legions of women who would be delighted with your offer."

"Why are you being difficult?"

"Because I'm really busy."

"Then why don't we just say I'll be available whenever you're *not* busy." He ran his fingers up the length of his upthrust penis. "Like now, for instance, if you could spare a few minutes."

"I can't," she said hoarsely, clearing her throat to quickly add, "Really, Jasper, I have to go." Not that her body was in agreement; the hard, steady pulsing between her legs accelerated, her sexual appetite permanently ravenous in close proximity to the viscount's glorious cock.

"Why don't I see if I can change your mind," he murmured.

"No!" She backed away.

"Give me five minutes of your time, and I'll buy Lunardi another balloon. Ten minutes, and I'll buy him two."

She hesitated.

His cock took notice, swelling higher.

"Damn you," she croaked, sorely tempted.

"Think of it as advancing science. I'm sure Lunardi will be grateful."

She'd contributed a good deal of her fortune to Vincenzo's project; another affluent patron—in this case, an influential English one—would be helpful to Lunardi's cause. Damn Priestley for his casual wealth—and impertinence.

Although, if she were honest with herself, refusing Jasper's offer of sex was difficult even without his generous incentive. Nearly impossible, she thought, gazing at the huge, engorged object of her lust.

She shifted in her stance as though so slight a movement would negate the fevered demands of her throbbing flesh and the small voice inside her head whispering, 'Think of the gluttonous, sensual pleasure.'

She resisted a second more before deciding, the word *capitulation* faithlessly leaping into her mind a second after that.

As sop to her independence, she decided a quid pro quo would be necessary. She was not so lost to all reason that she would join the ranks of Priestley's paramours without due compensation. "I will agree to your offer, but you'll have to wait until evening. Vincenzo's expecting me to arrive on time."

Out of jealousy, Jasper almost said, no, you must do it now. But in that portion of his brain still functioning outside the tidal wave of unquenchable lust, he understood how much her work meant to her. He understood even better how pleasing her would ultimately be his gain. And perhaps, at base, he refused to acknowledge the concept of jealousy. "You have yourself a deal," he agreed pleasantly.

"I won't interfere in your work. I'll stay out of the way. Harry will be there, no doubt. He can allay my boredom."

"As I said from the beginning," she declared crisply, "you should remain here."

"Let me rephrase that. I don't wish to be a hindrance. But if I can help in any way, please, by all means, tell me."

"If that's double entendre, I don't appreciate—"

"You misunderstand. I meant it sincerely."

"Hmmm."

"You needn't be so suspicious. I'm capable of controlling myself."

She smiled for the first time that morning, recalling the astonishing extent of his control. "I stand corrected, Priestley. You definitely have control."

"I suggest we keep our conversation devoid of sexual allusions in an effort to, in my case, tame the wild beast."

Easier said than done, she thought, taking in the splendid sight before her eyes. But she understood duty and responsibility. "I agree," she said, with the same attempt at composure as he. "I'll have Jai bring me workclothes. You may use the dressing room first. How would that be?"

She wouldn't care to hear the truth. "Whatever you say."

Halfway to the door, she turned and looked at him, her expression testy. "I hope you won't pout all day."

He was at a loss as to why he put up with her damnable temper. Then again, a roisterous night of the hottest sex he'd ever experienced might be a good enough reason. "I won't pout if you don't," he said pointedly.

She opened her mouth, then shut it again.

"Exactly," he murmured. "And there's more of that tonight if you wish."

"I should send you packing," she snapped, turning around and flouncing to the door.

"If it wasn't my suite, you could," he drawled.

Swivelling back, she leaned against the polished oak and met his amused gaze. "You're too good to give up, Priestley.

Not that you don't know it. But, just for the record, I never take orders."

There was no point in arguing; he could dominate her a hundred ways to Sunday if he wished. "Fair enough," he said politely. "Should I ring for breakfast?"

She smiled. "No argument?"

He shrugged. "What's the point?"

What was the point indeed, when you could order the world to your liking, she thought. But contrary to Jasper's opinion, she could be as agreeable as he, especially when he would make it worth her while tonight. She smiled. "Well said. I'll have coffee and scones. Two eggs and bacon." Turning, she opened the door and gave her instructions to a waiting Jai.

Careful to keep their distance, for reasons of insatiable lust, they took turns washing up in the dressing room and by the time Jai returned with Nicky's clothes, Jasper was dressed, breakfast had arrived, and they were about to sit down.

After a quiet conversation at the door, Nicky sent Jai away.

Looking up from the paper, Jasper lifted his brows. "Will he actually leave?"

"He feels I'm safe when I'm at work." Taking her parcel, she disappeared into the dressing room and emerged short minutes later, attired in breeches and shirt, her hair pulled back in a queue.

It was going to be a very long day, Jasper thought, quickly averting his gaze from Nicky's curvaceous form boldly displayed in the tight breeches and shirt that clung to her breasts rather more than he would have liked. He would definitely have to see that Harry found him something to keep him busy at the laboratory. If he were forced to simply watch Nicky all day, his manners would be sorely taxed.

There were limits even to his self-control.

Chapter Eleven

In the course of the next fortnight, if it were possible to put a value on perfect sexual rapport and contentment, the two occupants of Viscount Priestley's suite at James Dun's Hotel would have been the gold standard for that reckoning.

They worked together each day, the viscount rolling up his sleeves and getting his hands dirty along with everyone else, as intent as the principles at making the balloon flight a success.

And at night, he and Nicky explored the breadth and depth of bliss, of wild sensation, of a quiet intimacy neither had ever known.

They found themselves finishing each other's sentences.

They found themselves looking forward to waking in each other's arms.

They reveled in a kind of boundless enchantment that enveloped them and made their world complete, a very circumscribed world, as it were, of New Town and Lunardi's laboratory.

But it was enough—more than enough; it was their own special paradise.

And the specter of the future never intruded.

Nicky understood what Priestley was and didn't care. Her own life was as self-centered and worldly as his.

Jasper chose not to think beyond the moment. It had long been his pattern, anyway.

At long last the next balloon flight was scheduled, the day dawned clear and bright, and Lunardi successfully reached a cruising altitude of such height, the celebration on his descent continued uninterrupted for days.

All the papers praised Lunardi's success, his newest innovations testament to his brilliance. His career was on the ascent. Even the king sent congratulations.

When the festivities finally came to an end, the laboratory crew met at the tavern in High Street to make plans for the next mission.

"We're off to Paris—immediately," Vincenzo announced. "Last year, the Montgolfier brothers offered me carte blanche in the use of their facilities. I'm finally ready to take advantage of their superior laboratory." His eyes shone with delight. "Now, *we* have the expertise they lack. I assume you're going, Nicky. As for you, Harry and Jasper, consider this your invitation as well. Paris is splendid any time of year."

"If I didn't have a country house party I promised to attend, I'd go in a minute," Harry said. "Perhaps I'll come over later."

"What about you, Priestley?" Lunardi had reconciled himself to the liaison, despite his reservations. If Nicky was happy, that was enough.

Jasper turned to Nicky beside him. "Are you going?"

She smiled. "Of course. I wouldn't miss it for the world."

The viscount's gaze went shuttered, although none but Harry took note, for excitement gripped the table, the conversation running apace, a flurry of questions going round having to do with the particulars of the Montgolfier brothers' facilities. How far was it from Paris? What accommodations were available for families? Would they be working in conjunction with the Frenchmen or on their own? How soon would they be able to launch another balloon? Everyone was laughing and smiling and talking as fast as they could. Sweet anticipation perfumed the air.

Nicky squeezed Jasper's hand from time to time, but she was fully engaged in the conversation, making plans for their departure, flushed and animated, clearly thrilled with the prospect of working with the Montgolfiers.

"You'll come, won't you?" she murmured, turning to Jasper and smiling.

"I can't."

"Of course you can." Distracted by a question about a specific mixture of gases, she turned back to answer the query, and Jasper stood to leave. Smiling, she blew him a kiss and returned to the lively discussion. As often happens when like minds and interests meet, the debate and analyses were vigorous and lengthy, after which all the participants proceeded to the laboratory to begin packing their equipment for transit to Paris.

It was hours before Nicky returned to the hotel.

Raising his glass as she entered the sitting room, Jasper drawled, "Bon voyage, darling. Lunardi is on his way to fame and fortune on the Continent."

"In good time and with a certain amount of luck," she murmured, sinking into a chair opposite him and reaching for the brandy bottle on what normally served as a tea table. "Why did you leave?"

"Harry insisted."

"Ah . . . and he's where?"

"Off writing letters or some such thing for Julia's country house party."

Taking a sip of brandy, she relaxed against the chair back. "Everything is in piles at the laboratory, waiting for crates. To the next phase of aerial flight," she said, lifting her glass to him. "You *are* coming with us, aren't you?"

"I wish I could."

"Why can't you?"

"Why can't you stay?"

"Certainly, that's not a serious question. It's the Montgolfiers, it's Paris, it's the very epicenter of research on flight. Come with us, Jasper. You'll love it."

"You want me to follow you wherever you go?"

"What's come over you? Why wouldn't you wish to go to Paris?"

If he could answer that question, he wouldn't have had to empty two bottles already, nor would a gnawing resentment be overwhelming his normal live-and-let-live disposition. "I'm not sure."

"Then come. You can equivocate over there."

"What if I said I didn't want you to go?"

A small silence fell, and then she said, "I'd ask what gave you the right to make such a demand."

"I like your company."

"Then join me in Paris."

"Perhaps I might," he said in lieu of continuing a highly unsatisfying conversation.

"That's more like it. Now what do you want to do on our last night in Edinburgh?"

He smiled. At least they were in agreement on one thing.

"Dinner first or after?" she inquired. Her spirits were high; she felt sure she could convince Jasper to come along.

"After."

She smiled. "Any requests?"

He laughed. "You don't have the time."

She'd made him laugh, which was her intent. "I have a request of you."

"The answer is yes."

"You don't know what it is?"

"Of course I do."

"I could have been asking for—"

"I know what you're asking for. The same thing you always ask for. More and more and then some more."

"I hope you're not complaining."

"I hope you don't think I'm that stupid."

She pouted prettily. "You're not very tactful."

"I didn't know you were looking for tactful. I thought you were looking for this." He swept his hand downward as he lounged in his chair.

His tight chamois breeches left little to the imagination, and she wondered how many times he'd been casually available to please a lady. "The habitual satyr, are you not, Priestley?"

"Only for you, darling."

"Hmpf," she sniffed, suddenly aware that she didn't wish to leave him behind—for some other woman (realistically, women plural) to enjoy.

It was a novel sensation, but powerful, and like Jasper, she was inclined to be willful. She might have to consider employing some of the courtesan arts enumerated in the Kama Sutra in order to entice him to Paris.

Subterfuge was no basis for friendship, sexual or otherwise, her voice of reason pointed out. Her selfish disposition, however, opted for whatever means would serve her ends. With the bulge in Jasper's breeches not only visible but highly motivational, her debate was brief. "Be a dear and pour me another drink while I get my robe. My workclothes are filthy."

Returning from the dressing room a moment later, she carried a porcelain wash basin half full of water, a towel, washcloth, and her robe.

Jasper observed her with a narrow-eyed gaze. "What have we here?"

Was she that transparent? Was she so inept after all? Had she been pursued by men so often that she'd never acquired the subtleties necessary to seduce? "I haven't seen you all day. I thought you could keep me company while I change."

His brows flickered as though in query. But his voice when he spoke was mild. "Be my guest."

Taking the brandy bottle from the table, she handed it to Jasper, set down the basin and towel, dropped the washcloth into the water, and stepped out of her buckled shoes. Rolling off her silk stockings, she discarded them and took a sip from her glass of brandy before giving it to Jasper. "So I don't spill water in it."

Making room on a nearby candlestick table, he placed her glass beside his and the bottle and settled back in his chair, a faint alertness in his heavy-lidded gaze.

Untying her shirt collar, she said with a smile, "I missed you today."

"I missed you two bottles' worth. I'm glad you came home." The word *home* slipped out unintentionally, but to correct it would only call attention to his blunder. "I'm glad so much packing was accomplished," he added smoothly.

His use of the word *home* warmed her heart; perhaps very little subterfuge would be required, after all. But at base, she was willing to do whatever was necessary to have him in Paris. He'd become the great joy of her life. "The worst of the moving is over." Pulling her shirt from the breeches' waistband, she began unbuttoning the cuffs. "The crates come tomorrow. Workmen will load them and cart them to the docks."

The ruffled cuffs fell over her hands with the buttons free, the long shirttails draping nearly to her thighs; her dark curls had come loose from their queue, and unruly tendrils framed her face, the whole a picture of artless, youthful innocence.

Until she slipped the shirt over her head a second later and dropped it at her feet. And a sensual, voluptuous temple sculpture came to life.

Her full breasts were improbably rounded, the plump, fleshy mounds pressed together so tightly—in the words of the Kama Sutra—as not to admit even a blade of grass between them. Her breeches rested on her ripe hips, her slim waist rising above the snug kerseymere, her thighs softly inviting.

And Jasper suddenly became fully conscious of what was taking place.

Not that he was averse to being seduced.

"Come here," he murmured, sliding up in his chair. "I'll help you with those breeches."

As she approached, he opened his legs, and she came to rest between them. "Look," he said, his mouth only inches from her breasts.

She already knew before she looked, the sweet ache pulsing between her legs, and as she lowered her gaze, he touched one nipple with the tip of his finger.

"Closer."

It was an order, no matter how hushed and low, and she could no more have denied him than she could have stopped breathing.

"Up a little—here, put it in my mouth."

She immediately obeyed, no longer sure who was doing what to whom, or whether her courtesan ploy was for him or her. Taking her breast in her hands, she lifted it slightly so the taut crest grazed his mouth.

His lips opened, slid over her nipple, then his teeth, lightly, gently, and when his mouth closed over the tingling tip and he gently sucked, she arched her back, compressed her thighs, and quivered with an all-consuming need for sex. He had only to touch her, and she wanted him; she had only to glimpse the glorious dimensions of his erection, and she was lost.

Having unbuttoned her breeches as he tenderly suckled her, Jasper slid the soft jersey down her hips, and raised his mouth enough to say, "Lift your feet."

Even while damning his coolness when she was dying for him, lusted and fevered for him, she stepped out of her breeches, the small movement elongating her nipple caught in his mouth once again, the resultant tremor racing downward like wildfire, exploding in a sudden brief, wholly inadequate orgasm.

Crying out in frustration, she pummeled him.

"Relax," he said, grabbing her hands and holding them firmly. "We have all night." Shifting his mouth to her other nipple, he checked her movement and bit and nibbled and sucked with an intensity that speedily aroused and inflamed and soon had her moaning and writhing, not in frustration and anger but in desire. Blazing-hot sensation streaked, pounded, raced downward to her throbbing vagina in another apparent breakneck sprint to climax. Softly pleading, she tried to free herself from his grip, from his mouth, desperately wanting him inside her. "Jasper, please . . . I beg of you," she cried.

Abruptly setting her at arm's length, as though she only had to ask and he would comply, he calmly said, "I thought you were going to wash first."

"No." She shook her head, tried to break his grip on her waist, her gaze focused on the stretched leather at his crotch. "I'll wash after."

"After what? Look at me. After what?"

Shuddering faintly, her gaze swung up and met his. "After we make love."

"After we have sex, you mean."

"Yes, yes, after sex. Don't be cruel, Jasper." She tried to shake him off. "I haven't felt you inside me since morning."

"You could have come back with me." He restrained her effortlessly, her struggles futile against his strength.

"I know. I'm sorry, truly I am."

"You'll say anything now so I'll fuck you."

"No, that's not true. I should have come back with you. I wish I had."

"I should make you wait."

"Please, no, don't make me wait." He was right. She'd

say anything to have him inside her. "Would you like me to do The Spinning Top?" she whispered, so wet and needy she would promise him anything. "You like that."

"You like that, you mean."

"Let me, please . . ."

His orgasm was staggering when she rode him like that. Refusal was out of the question. Releasing her, he brusquely said, "Undo my breeches. And wash yourself first," he added gruffly. "You're dripping wet."

She instantly complied, dropping to her knees between his legs, and hastily began unbuttoning his breeches, so frantic for surcease her hands were trembling. He could have helped, but he didn't, letting her fumble with the silver buttons, driven by an inexplicable need for retribution. When, at last, the front placket fell open and his erection sprang free, she reached for it as though it was a sacred lingam to be worshiped, and she was its adoring supplicant.

Catching her hands just short of their mark, he stopped her. "You must wash first."

"I don't want to," she repudiated, sullen and petulant. "I want that."

"You can't have it until you wash." Perhaps there was more than sexual dominance at play, perhaps umbrage over personal freedoms, desires, and the shifting rules of amour were distractions as well. "You decide." Like you did this afternoon—or perhaps that thought was buried so deeply beneath the nonchalance of a lifetime that he didn't actually think it at all.

"I should say no," she grumbled, coming to her feet.

Leaning back in his chair, he let her go. "Or you could wash quickly and have what you want." Measuring the length of his engorged erection with a languid sweep of his finger, he smiled up at her.

She glared at him. "Insolent brute."

"So what will it be?" he said with unruffled calm.

"Damn you!" she spat, flouncing away. "That, of course—you . . . or you and that or—"

"You and me and that," he drawled roguishly.

"If I had any other choice," she muttered, wringing out the washcloth.

"I beg your pardon?"

His voice was so chill she felt a moment of unease, followed quickly by remorse at her tantrumish declaration. "I apologize. I didn't mean it."

"Are you sure? We could *find* someone for you," he said, smooth as glass.

"I don't want anyone else. I want *you,* as you must have surmised by now. I haven't been in the least subtle about it. Rest assured, Priestley, you're unequaled in bed—as if you didn't know."

She was as well, but he wasn't as open about his feelings. "Bring that washcloth here, and I'll help you," he said gently. "I apologize as well."

"We both want what we want," she said with a sigh, walking toward him.

He smiled. "With you that goes without saying."

She hit him with the washcloth and the tussle that ensued ended in sweet kisses and sweeter words.

He washed her, then washed himself before lifting her onto his lap. "I don't need any grand gestures," he said softly. "No spinning tops . . ."

When all else in their volatile relationship was precarious, of one thing she was sure. "You like everything, darling." She touched his bottom lip and smiled. "And it's not a grand gesture—it's for me."

He chuckled. "I don't know what came over me—suspecting altruistic motives from you."

"I haven't heard any complaints," she replied playfully.

"Nor will you, as long as I have breath in my body."

She smiled. "How reassuring . . ." And turning toward

him, she opened her thighs and adopted the lotus position—right foot on her left thigh joint and left foot on her right thigh joint. Placing her hands on his shoulders, she raised herself with Jasper's help and settled down on his erection with a gratified sigh. This position allowed the deepest penetration, and a moment later, when both their pulse rates had subsided from a tremulous shuddering splendor, she whispered, her eyes half closed, "Slowly, now . . ."

He was well aware how difficult the position, how much experience and caution were required. Clasping her arms, he turned her slowly until her back was to his chest and, holding her breasts lightly, waited for her to find the physical equivalent of bliss. The exact placement, site, and point of maximum contact.

She drew in a breath when the entire length of his erection was embedded precisely where she most wanted it. "Don't move," she gasped, rocking ever so slightly, stirring in a slow, languorous rhythm, grinding downward after a timely pause as her tissue stretched and yielded.

Adept at recognizing sexual cues, he flexed his hips upward to meet her downward pressure, and was gratified to hear her rapturous gasp, his own explosive sensations the equivalent of fireworks on his birthday. Although he was forced to pause for a breath-held moment while his beleaguered nerves regrouped.

"Don't stop," she whispered.

"Never," he breathed, unquenchable lust overriding imperiled nerve endings.

Very shortly, they climaxed, and then came again and again and again, scarcely moving, joined in fathomless, wondrous desire, awash in sexual obsession, shifting only enough to reach the momentous, miraculous, ultimate crescendo.

When Nicky finally fainted away, Jasper carried her to bed and held her close while she slept, the certainties he'd always accepted suddenly suspect, his entire way of life hanging in the balance. Nothing was clear and absolute any longer. All order was chaos.

Unaware of Jasper's turbulent thoughts, Nicky slept on.

But sleep eluded him; he knew it would.

And long before morning, he kissed her gently one last time.

Chapter Twelve

When Nicky came awake the next morning, Jasper wasn't beside her. She didn't have to look in the dressing room to know he was gone. The bedroom had an air of emptiness quite separate from its baronial furniture and colorful decor—his jacket no longer on the chair, nor his books on the table. The bed was cold where he should have been, only a faint indentation evidence of his presence. Rolling over, she pressed her nose into Jasper's pillow, inhaling the fragrance of his cologne, the light scent still lingering on the linen.

And for a wistful moment, she wished she could have kept him.

Although, in her heart, perhaps she'd always known he wouldn't stay—not a man like Jasper.

His liaisons were, by choice, temporary.

She would miss him dreadfully, though . . . despite any logical understanding to the contrary. And had she not the prospect of the Montgolfiers' laboratory in Paris to look forward to, she would have been hard-pressed to hold back her tears.

But she understood his desire for independence, enjoying a degree of freedom herself that was rare for females. Her empowerment had been born of necessity, and she'd no more relinquish it now than give up her dream of flight.

When her mother died, she'd run away in order not to be sent to school in England. She and her ayah had been tracked down, of course, but even at ten she'd had the courage to challenge her father's edict. Hard-bitten East India company man that Andrew Wemyss was, he'd recognized his daughter's need for autonomy as only a Scotsman in the employ of the English could, and had given in to her.

So, with or without Priestley, she would live her life, the habits of a lifetime not likely to be altered by a fortnight of sex, no matter how glorious.

And once she was in Paris, she would be far too busy to pine over what might have been.

"You didn't have to travel south with me," Harry said, lounging across from Jasper in the viscount's well-appointed carriage, watching his friend empty a bottle in record time. "It isn't *your* country house party."

"I had to return to London anyway, for something worse," Jasper grumbled, not mentioning another more significant reason why he'd quit Edinburgh. "My sister-in-law has dragooned me into serving as host to some affair for Prinny. She doesn't understand that he hates boring dinners as much as I. But Charlotte will insist. Apparently, she's breeding again, her nerves are on edge, and my brother has asked me to oblige her."

"I don't suppose the *père* will attend?"

"I expect he's too busy with his other family," Jasper said coolly. Since his father had taken a permanent mistress long before Jasper's beloved mother's death, the two men rarely spoke.

"Has he asked you for money since—"

"I threatened his life? No. I doubt he'll be so foolish again." Jasper had inherited his fortune from his mother,

her marriage settlement ironclad when she'd wed the scapegrace Earl of Umfreville.

"You won't be seeing him at Charlotte's party, then."

Jasper's brows lifted faintly. "I expect not."

"What of the delightful Miss Wemyss? Will you be sharing her company any time soon?"

"Not unless she comes to London," he said, his voice clipped.

Something had happened in Edinburgh to transform the man who was a byword for transient sex—or, more aptly, someone by the name of Miss Nicky had happened to him. His entire persona had altered, although exactly how was not entirely clear yet. "I might go to Paris once my obligations to Julia are concluded," Harry remarked. "Perhaps next month, if the seas aren't running too high. Why don't you join me?"

Jasper shook his head. "My interest in balloons was never scientific."

"That's no surprise. But Miss Nicky will be there."

"I don't care."

"Allow me to disagree. You're bloody blue-deviled this morning, or rankled, or both."

"I'm neither. It's damned early, that's all. I'm tired."

"Fatigued from a gratifying night of hot sex?"

The last thing Jasper needed was to be reminded of last night; he was in serious withdrawal already, and he'd only left Nicky a few hours ago. "Keep it up," Jasper growled, "and I'll have the carriage stopped and have you put out."

"Would you like me to tell you about Julia's country house party?" Harry offered cheerfully, in lieu of walking to London. "She sent me the guest list."

Jasper groaned. "I have a feeling it's going to be a long sixty hours."

Denials aside, Nicky Wemyss had touched some hitherto hidden emotions in Jasper whether he wished to admit or not, Harry decided. But they'd been friends for a long time, and the baron was more than willing to oblige his friend. If Jasper had something to divulge, he would find out soon enough. Harry spoke no more of Edinburgh, conversing instead on the usual topics: horses, gaming, mutual friends, and adventures. As they journeyed south, the men stopped only long enough to change horses and pick up fresh supplies of liquor, their arrival in London the afternoon of the third day hours ahead of the long-standing record. Instead of sixty hours, they'd completed the trip from Edinburgh to London in less than fifty-seven.

After dropping Harry off at home, Jasper arrived at his bachelor apartments with a distinct feeling of satisfaction. The familiar, commonplace sights did much to mitigate his unwanted memories of a woman who only pleased herself.

Taking his coat, his valet greeted the viscount like a long-lost friend—Jasper had never gone so long without his ministrations. Jasper's secretary welcomed him home with the agreeable news that one of his most demanding lovers had left the city for an extended stay in Wiltshire.

For a brief moment of panic, Jasper wondered whether Eliza might be pregnant and had gone to the country to escape scandal. Her husband was old and beyond joining her in bed, while she was young and extremely fond of sex.

Aware of the viscount's sudden alarm, young Drayton quickly explained, "The Countess of Bramley's father has had an apoplexy. She was required at his bedside."

Jasper blew out a breath, promised himself to be more circumspect in the future with the French *lettres* he used, and said, "Thank you, Drayton. I appreciate the information." He glanced at his hovering valet. "I could use a brandy, Sam. Make it a double." After that scare, perhaps the entire bottle, he thought. Stripping off his gloves, he tossed them on a table, strode into the comfortable environs of his study, and dropped into a chair by the fire.

"It's a pleasure to have you home, my lord," Drayton

said, following his master into the study. "The house seemed dull in your absence."

"Well, I'm back now, and here I intend to stay."

There was something gruff and final in the way Lord Priestley had uttered that phrase, the secretary explained to the steward over dinner in the small dining room they shared.

"You don't suppose he's ill?" the steward remarked. "He seemed less attentive than usual when we went over some business matters."

"He's just tired, I suspect. Although, he dressed and left for Brooke's as usual tonight." Drayton pursed his mouth. "Now that I think of it, he wasn't in his normal high spirits. He nearly emptied a second bottle before he left."

"Sam thinks it's woman trouble," the steward said, one brow raised in dubious query.

Drayton snorted in disbelief. "Not likely that when the man can pick and choose from any woman in England."

"That may be all well and good, but Sam knows him better than anyone. He also talked to Mayfield's batman. Seems there was some woman up north who dressed like a man and was with the viscount day and night." The steward shrugged. "Such devotion's not Priestley's usual style."

"Then why did he return?"

"Dunno. Why do these swells do anything?"

"There *was* that time he was pursuing Bathurst's wife," Drayton murmured. "It was nearly a month before he grew bored."

"I remember. Well, bored with the Edinburgh chit or just bored, we'll find out soon enough."

The steward was right about that. Nothing was private from those below stairs.

Chapter Thirteen

While Jasper returned to his familiar haunts, Nicky was immersed in a more hectic schedule than usual because of the coming winter. Vincenzo was hoping to put one more balloon aloft before the weather turned cold. They worked practically around the clock to accomplish the task. And when it was over, when Vicenzo had triumphed once again, when French accolades had been added to those of the Scots and English, Lunardi took a hiatus to return to Naples and receive another delightful prize.

His Lucia had come of age.

Nicky stayed in Paris for a time. The season had begun, and she amused herself in society—or at least tried. But flirtation was a bore, the salons were a bore, even old friends were no longer entertaining. She debated traveling to Rome; Henry Raeburn often spent some of the winter months there, and he was always good company. She thought of returning to India for an extended stay. Edinburgh, however, was not on her itinerary—and not because of unwelcome memories, she told herself. She was simply tired of the city.

Out of ennui and indecision, she did nothing and went out less. She only read and read and read some more. There were times she didn't get out of bed for days. Her excuse was that it was too drizzly and cold. By the end of the month, her ayah was beginning to worry.

"Don't look at me like that. I'm fine," Nicky firmly declared when she could no longer abide her old nursemaid's dolorous gaze. "Very well. I'll get dressed. Find me something colorful to wear. I'll go shopping."

But her shopping almost always involved another bookstore that involved another extended stay in bed reading, until one night she lay abed in what had become her normal insomniac state rereading the same lines in the book that lay open on her lap. "The important thing is not to think much but to love much; do, then, whatever most arouses you to love." St. Teresa of Avila had written those lines in 1577. The candle flame suddenly flickered, as though in emphasis. Choosing to ignore the fact that winter drafts infiltrated the room through the floor-to-ceiling windows, she preferred instead to consider it a sign.

She looked around, a new clarity to her thoughts. What day was it? What month? How long had she been in decline, like some fainthearted female without a brain or spine or purpose? Throwing the covers aside, she decided it didn't matter the time or date. If she wanted Priestley, or even *thought* she wanted him, or wished to discover *if* she wanted him, there was no point in staying in Paris. He wasn't here. He was in London. Or presumably so. Which was another quandary altogether that she wasn't in the mood to consider.

The crossing was treacherous in mid-January, the Channel storm-tossed. Having reached Dover only slightly worse for wear after a ten-hour crossing that took twenty, the road to London turned out to be a quagmire. Two broken axles later, the third coach brought her into the city just as winter twilight fell. Intent on her mission, she hired a hackney at the coaching inn, and in short order she was deposited at Viscount Priestley's home in St. James's Square.

She stood before the dwelling, her bags in hand. If she'd been sensible, she thought, she would have found an inn for the night and faced Jasper in the morning. On the other hand, she'd rarely been sensible.

Perhaps never.

Picking up her bags, she mounted the stairs and knocked on the door.

When the imposing portal opened, she requested the footman to inform Jasper of her arrival.

The young man's eyes flared wide at a female being so bold as to beard the viscount in his own home. "Jes' a moment, miss," he said, and scurried away.

Setting her bags down, she surveyed Jasper's residence—a bachelor one, without a doubt. While elegant, it was neither large nor ostentatious. The small foyer displayed no Roman busts or family portraits, the furniture had the look of casual use rather than show, the fabrics sturdy leathers and wools.

Her musings were cut short by the arrival of an imposing butler in full livery who surveyed her travel-stained appearance with haughty disdain and informed her that Viscount Priestley was not at home. Nor was he expected any time soon. What was left unsaid, although crystal clear, was that he would never be home to a woman who arrived uninvited.

When it came to disdain, Nicky had spent her entire childhood watching the British govern what they considered the inferior races in India. "My name is Miss Nicky Wemyss," she coolly declared, meeting the butler's gaze with equal hauteur. "The viscount will see me, I assure you. If you would bring me a hot cup of tea while I wait. Sugar, no milk." And she walked by him without a glance, moving toward what appeared to be a small drawing room.

After days of chill travel, a glowing fire beckoned her like a beacon of hope, and soon she was warming her chilled fingers and toes before the blissful warmth.

In the meantime, the staff was gathered in the kitchen, all in a dither, her name having sparked a violent debate.

"It's her. The one from Edinburgh. He *has* to be found," Sam exclaimed.

"As if anyone knows where he is," a footman muttered. "He's gone for days at a time—and only God knows where."

"It's her, all right—that's the name. He'll want to know." The steward had gleaned the entire story from Mayfield's valet, and in the ensuing weeks, the viscount's descent into dissipation had been laid solidly at her door. "Someone stand guard near the drawing room and see that she doesn't leave."

"She gave me orders for tea as though she were a queen." Still not certain whether he was offended or impressed, the butler frowned.

"Of course she must be treated like a queen, by all means." The chef was French and already warming to the occasion, a delicious amour just what the viscount needed. "The master has been sunk in gloom of late. The lady will bring him the sunshine, eh?"

"He's been drunk of late, you mean," Drayton murmured. "And I don't know about sunshine, but Mayfield's valet says the viscount didn't leave her side when he was in Edinburgh," he added with significant emphasis. "So send out every footman—scour the city and find Priestley. I'll see that the lady stays."

Percy Drayton accompanied the maid with the tea tray and introduced himself to Nicky. "Please make yourself comfortable, Miss Wemyss. The viscount is out this evening, but we've sent for him."

"Thank you." Nicky smiled. "I apologize for arriving so late."

"Nonsense. No apology is necessary. May I offer you a withdrawing room later to freshen up?" To her slight frown, he said, "The viscount's schedule is erratic. He may not be located immediately."

Her first thought was that she shouldn't have come, followed by her second, which dismissed propriety and decorum. When on a Messianic quest as she was, such issues were insignificant. Or maybe she simply wanted what she wanted, conventions be damned. "An opportunity to freshen up later would be most satisfying," she said, as though she were an invited guest and Jasper would come walking in the door any minute and welcome her with open arms. "Would you care to join me for tea?"

He would indeed, his curiosity towering. Over several cups of tea and numerous servings of cake and sweets, Drayton asked what questions he dared, as politely as possible. And much later, when he returned to the kitchen as Nicky went to freshen up, the entire staff descended on him and clamored to hear all that had transpired.

"She's beautiful, charming, and intelligent." Percy went on to inform them of the entire conversation and finished by saying, "There's no doubt why the viscount is enamored."

"*If* he's enamored," one of the footmen said, the viscount's countless assignations over the years having inspired a good deal of doubt.

"He's bound to be drunk, *that's* for certain. Someone should be in attendance when he meets her. Just in case," Sam said ominously.

"I agree," the steward declared. He'd seen Jasper's temper too often to discount the possibility of disaster.

The butler scowled. "If he's even found tonight."

Word of his coming arrived before Jasper did, a footman running through the back lanes to reach the house ahead of the viscount's carriage.

"He were . . . in a gambling den, drunk and hot-tempered and . . . none too happy to hear . . . the lady was here," the footman panted. "He swore . . . a blue streak at . . . the news."

"He *is* coming home, is he not?" Sam uttered the question, but everyone waited for the reply, no one certain the viscount would comply.

"Yes, yes, he be on his way. He'll be here right quick."

"I'll make some coffee," the chef muttered.

"He ain't gonna drink it." The footman had seen Jasper's face.

"The lady fell asleep," a maidservant pointed out. "Poor dear, must have been exhausted. He's going to frighten her something fierce."

"We'd better all be in the entrance hall when he arrives. Show our presence en masse," Drayton suggested. "We may be able to deter his most violent urges."

"No *may* about it. We'll just *have* to," the steward asserted, and everyone nodded, the secretary's glowing description of Nicky and their conversation having prompted a collective impulse to protect her from the viscount's wrath.

Chapter Fourteen

Jasper stood arrested on his threshold, surveying his staff. "What the hell are you all doing standing there like some goddamned militia?"

"We wish to welcome you home, sir," Drayton replied courageously.

"Bloody hell you do. I'm not going to harm the chit, so you may disband. Now, where is she?" Throwing off his coat, Jasper tossed it on a chair.

"We'll show you, sir." Drayton stepped forward, the rest of the staff following his lead.

"Jesus," Jasper muttered, scanning the stiffly arrayed ranks. "You have my word. The lady is safe. Now go."

No one moved.

"I'll sack you all on the spot if you don't leave," Jasper growled.

Mute disobedience.

"God Almighty," he said. "Am I really that terrifying?"

"No, sir," they answered in unison, but no one stirred.

He sighed. "Very well, you've made your point. Get me some coffee, Andre, with brandy. Drayton, you may act as chaperon. Everyone else, stand back. At your convenience, Drayton," he drawled.

Straightening his shoulders, young Percy faced the viscount with calm; his father would have been proud. "Follow me, sir."

The staff parted and Drayton and Jasper passed through, moving down the hall to a room reserved for ladies to powder their noses on those rare occasions when Jasper hosted a dinner party.

"Miss Wemyss's fallen asleep, sir," Drayton explained quietly before he opened the door. "She said the crossing was rough, and the road from Dover almost impassable."

"She came from Paris?"

"Yes, sir. On the spur of the minute, I understand."

"I see." Jasper almost smiled, reminded of Nicky's delightful spontaneity on numerous occasions in the past. "Open the door, Drayton, and then you're dismissed." He met the young man's gaze. "I'll speak to the lady alone. I want no argument. You may bring in the coffee when it arrives."

Something in the viscount's voice soothed the secretary's apprehension, or maybe it was the way Jasper ran his fingers through his hair, straightened his cuffs, and softly exhaled.

When Percy opened the door, Jasper stepped inside and quietly closed the door behind him.

The room was lit with wall sconces and a single branch of candles, flickering firelight further illuminating the scene. Shadow and light played across the sleeping form lying on the chaise, a golden sheen glossing her soft flesh.

She looked more French than he remembered. Was it her fashionable traveling gown? Were her Parisian mother's features enhanced by candlelight? Had he seen too many Boucher paintings of blushing vixens made for love reclining like that on pillowed chaises? And then he realized it was her hair, all tousled curls and modish disarray, pulled back with jeweled trinkets like the queen wore at her Trianon hamlet when she was playing milkmaid.

Pretty as a maid she might appear, but juxtaposed was a defiantly sumptuous female. The simple innocence of her rosy cheeks in contrast to her expensive, glittering jewels; her opulent breasts nearly bursting the seams of her bodice against a small stockinged foot peeking out from under her skirt; the way she lay half on her side, the pose both child-like and profoundly erotic.

However mismatched the images, his misery of the weeks past instantly disappeared and a rare and novel tenderness warmed his heart.

A light rap on the door shattered his reverie, and Drayton entered, bringing his coffee.

Nicky came awake at the sound, blinking against the light.

"Thank you, Drayton," Jasper murmured as his secretary set the tray on a table. "That will be all."

The phrase, though softly spoken, was dismissive. After a glance at Miss Wemyss to ascertain whether she contemplated the viscount with fear, Drayton perceived that she did not, and, with a bow, left the room. Not so lulled into compliance that he would abandon the lady completely, however, he remained outside the door should his assistance be required.

"They found you." Nicky's voice was still drowsy with sleep.

"Yes."

At his clipped, curt tone, she pushed up into a seated position. "Are you angry?"

"No." He stood motionless at the door, as though he wasn't certain whether he'd stay or not.

"You *sound* angry."

"I'm not. Why did you come?" A blunt, uncivil question.

Anyone else might have taken pause. But she was here after an arduous journey, for a reason. "I missed you."

Absolute silence engulfed the room, only the sound of their breathing and the crackle of the fire breaking the hush.

Jasper shifted slightly in his stance, the creak of his heeled shoes the faintest of sounds. "Are you in London long?"

"It depends on you." Without the truth, her journey was pointless.

"What does that mean?" He, too, needed definitive answers after weeks of drinking and discontent.

"It depends on whether you want me to stay or not."

"Have you run out of Frenchmen to seduce?" Jealous and resentful, he knew how passionate and insatiable she was.

"Have you run out of Englishwomen to seduce?" He was notable in many ways, but most famously for the women he entertained. She, too, could feel the sourness of distrust.

"I asked you first."

"None appealed," she said. Because she was inconsolable, not virtuous.

"I see."

"How about you?"

"The same." There were times when he'd questioned his sanity when the temptations of the flesh held no appeal.

"Liar."

"Not at all." He smiled, her admission having mitigated his resentments. "I blame it on the winter megrims."

"You haven't been sitting home, though. There was some question whether your staff could find you or not." The drollery of winter megrims aside, she still had her doubts.

"I've been drinking and gambling here and there. What have you been doing? I hear Vincenzo amazed the royal family as well as countless others."

"The flight was truly marvelous," she said with a sudden smile, recalling the events of that day. "The balloon rose with absolutely flawless precision, for which Vincenzo received a medal and, more importantly, an annual stipend from the king's brother. He's in Naples, getting married as we speak. As for myself, I've been reading."

"Alone?" Perhaps his suspicions were not so easily appeased.

"It's the best way, I've found. I expect you've been drinking alone as well," she said, a modicum of sarcasm in her words.

"I might as well have been," he replied gruffly.

"I found I missed you dreadfully. To the point of paralysis at times. Does that frighten you? You may send me away if you wish. I would understand. Obsessed women are unnerving."

"Normally, yes. However, with you, I find the prospect gratifying."

"Tell me you missed me, then," she said.

"I did. Very much. Too much."

She swung her legs over the side of the chaise, having heard the answer she'd come for. "I'd like to stay for a time, as an experiment," she said with a smile. "To find out if what I'm feeling is life-altering or not, although certainly those weeks in Paris were a change for the worse. You may send me packing whenever you tire of me."

He scowled faintly. "I'm not in the mood for sport."

"Nor I."

"You understand, this is different."

"I know. Are you as terrified as I?"

"I am gripped by immeasurable terror."

She grinned. "That much? Mine is occasionally manageable."

"Perhaps you haven't been amusing yourself as long as I—don't answer that. I don't want to know."

She came to her feet. "Could we continue this discussion in your bedroom?"

With effort, he restrained himself from taking a step back. "If we go to my bedroom," he said softly, "we won't be doing any talking."

"I was hoping you'd say that."

"I may not let you leave."

"Ever?"

He nodded, shocked at his response, but meaning it.

Overwhelmed by eagerness and hope, he fancied this was love he was feeling, although he had no standard with which to compare.

He moved toward her; she put out her hands, and when he reached her, he gently took her hands in his.

"What if we fight?" she said abruptly.

He'd been expecting something more endearing, although her candor was what he most loved about her. There it was—the word *love* slipped in, smooth as silk. "I don't care if we fight. You still can't leave." He smiled faintly. "And there's worse—you have to meet my family."

"Are there many?"

"A father I avoid, a brother, his wife, and four and a half children. His wife will be disconsolate when we marry. She's expecting the title for her eldest."

Nicky's brows lifted. "You never mentioned marriage."

"Is that a problem?"

"I'm not sure," she said in a musing tone. "I've never considered marrying anyone."

"I'm not anyone."

Her smile was bright. "You certainly aren't."

"If you agree to marry me," he offered with a wicked grin, "I'll take you upstairs right now."

"I'd love to marry you."

"Shameless coquette."

"If that's the only way I can get into your bed," she purred. "A lady must do what a lady must do."

He laughed, the joyful sound echoing through the room, bringing smiles to the servants waiting outside the door. "In that case," he said, picking her up in his arms, "there's no reason for further delay. Although once I have you in my bed, I may be tempted to keep you there indefinitely."

"I shan't raise any argument," she whispered.

"I'm glad you came to London." He spoke with his heart.

"I thought I'd better. You need me."

He smiled. "More than you know. Have you any qualms about an expeditious wedding?"

"Is there a rush?"

"There is for me."

"Not tonight. I have other plans."

"Agreed. Tomorrow. I'll get a special license." He tipped his head toward the door. "They're all waiting outside. Are you ready?"

She nodded, well aware of how Madhu and Jai watched over her.

Jasper swung the door open and cheerfully announced, "You may congratulate us. We marry in the morning."

A cheer rose, followed by a hip, hip hooray, as Jasper and his bride-to-be moved through the gauntlet of exuberant servants and ascended the stairs.

Entering his bedroom, he locked the door before carrying Nicky to his bed.

"One last thing," she said, as he settled between her legs.

"Anything," he murmured, brushing her lips with his.

"Never mind, then."

He looked up and met her amused gaze. "There's nothing I can't give you."

"What a pleasant thought. Does that mean the Queen of Heaven will be in your repertoire tonight?"

It was—along with Frolicking Like a Sparrow and The Deer and, of course, The Spinning Top.

Love and lust were united in full and luxurious measure.

There were no more lovers' quarrels.

When the clergyman arrived the following afternoon, having been preceded by several barristers and one expensive jeweler, the happy couple greeted him from bed. Since the curate's generous living was supplied by the viscount's largesse, he greeted them with courtesy and particular care not to comment on the venue.

The scandalous news of the viscount's marriage spread

like wildfire through the Ton, although the sequestered bride and groom were immune to gossip.

And by the time the viscount and his lady finally exited their home a month later, more scandalous news was on the wind. The viscountess was with child.

Already.

Tongues wagged and eyebrows were raised and everyone anticipated counting the months until her delivery.

In fact, so delicious was the news, that Lord and Lady Priestley's first meeting with the viscount's brother and his wife was interrupted by a tidal wave of callers who stopped by on the flimsiest of pretexts.

As they drove away from the family visit in the comfort of the viscount's luxurious carriage, Jasper said, "You need never return there if you don't wish."

"Your brother is pleasant enough, and Charlotte did her best. But I was thinking we might better spend our time launching balloons, say, in the country somewhere."

"We could invite Lunardi and his wife over."

She smiled. "You must have read my mind."

Propping his feet up on the opposite seat, he lounged back against the squabs. "I already wrote them, and they've accepted. You may expect Lunardi and a boatload of equipment a fortnight hence."

Throwing herself at him, Nicky wrapped her arms around his neck and grinned from ear to ear. "Have I told you lately how adorable you are?"

He looked amused. "I don't believe I've ever been told I'm adorable."

"You are, nonetheless, and I'm so so lucky to have you," she whispered.

No one knew better than Jasper what the odds were that they would meet in Edinburgh, of all places, and more improbable still, that he would fall in love. "I'm luckier," he murmured, this man who had always scoffed at the notion of love. "I'm the luckiest man in the world."

Fool Me Once

Katherine O'Neal

Chapter One

Ixtapan de la Sal
October 1933

Kate Frost was in bondage.

Not the bondage of chains or the captivity of a dungeon, but bondage nonetheless. The prison of a Svengali's strong mind. Psychic bondage. The most consuming—the most dangerous—of all.

She had to break free.

But as she stepped from the long Bugatti limousine, she felt her shackles tighten. She took a composing breath and looked out over the crowd waiting in the gathering twilight to meet her. Stifling the impulse to run, she braved a glance at Rhys.

Rhys . . . her captor. The man who wielded her emotional leash.

His cold blue eyes ordered her forward.

At that moment, a thin, nervous man in a crisp black suit stepped before her and bowed. "Welcome, *princesa,* to the Hotel Ixtapan de la Sal. I am Senor Vega, the manager. I have the privilege to offer you every amenity and to assure you that all reporters have been barred, so there will be no repeat of the . . . unfortunate circus atmosphere in Mexico City."

With the grace that had been drilled into her, she offered a hand. His was clammy as he gripped hers with the fawning fascination she was coming to know well. "Then I put myself under your protection, Senor."

He blushed with pleasure. "If you will permit me, I will show you to your bungalow. But first, may I introduce to you some of your illustrious fellow guests?"

It was these illustrious guests who caused her stab of panic. The popular press of Mexico City had been one thing—second-rate newshounds eager to embrace a new sensation and easily duped. But the crowd that had motored here in a caravan from the capital was a different challenge altogether. This was the elite of Mexico: the wealthy, the famous, the sophisticated—public figures in their own right who were accustomed to celebrity and not as likely to be taken in by the tale she'd come to tell. An incongruous, uneasy mix of poets and playboys, matadors and movie stars, revolutionaries and industrialists. Denizens of pure-blood Spanish aristocracy standing shoulder to shoulder with grizzled veterans of the armies of Zapata and Pancho Villa. Each looking at her through the veil of diverse beliefs and expectations.

They'll never believe this preposterous story!

They moved further into the crowd—a cocktail party, it seemed, arranged in the forecourt of the hotel to greet her. Every head was turned her way. Momentarily, the manager stopped before an enormous man, exuding a glow of confidence, standing beside a short woman wearing a colorful Zapotec dress. "May I present Senor Diego Rivera, Mexico's most treasured muralist . . . and his wife, Frida Kahlo."

Before she could respond, Rivera's ham of a hand grasped hers and brought it with devout appreciation to his lips. *"Dios!"* he exclaimed. "What beauty! What bone structure! The soul of Mexico is in your face. I would have picked it out of a crowd of a thousand women. It is so obviously the mirror of our lost Aztec glory. I *must* paint it! You will be the centerpiece of my new mural."

His unconditional acceptance startled her. She possessed, as far as she knew, not so much as a drop of Aztec or Mexican or even Spanish blood. She'd been positive, in fact, that the people of Mexico would never accept her as the long-lost Aztec princess she was pretending to be. But Rhys had insisted that with her newly dyed blue-black hair and faintly exotic features—and with the right prompting—she would fool them all. He'd even rejected her idea of wearing tribal-inspired clothing along the lines of Rivera's nationalistic wife. *That's what they'll expect,* he'd told her dismissively. *We're going to give them something they* don't *expect.* So he'd dressed her simply and with understated elegance in a black satin gown that hugged her curves with just the ideal amount of Carole Lombard glamour. Her long hair was knotted low on her neck in a stark chignon. She wore no jewelry, because Rhys had said, *Let the attention be on your face. Let them see in it what they want to see.*

Now, Diego Rivera himself—legendary collector of Aztec artifacts and painter of the Mexican Everyman—was looking at that face and claiming that he could pick the English-born Kate Frost out of a crowd and just *know* she was of native Mexican descent. So once again, Rhys had been right. Even the practiced eye of a great artist could be tricked into seeing what the experienced confidence man wanted him to see.

But as Rivera continued in this extravagant vein, Kate noticed that his wife was peering at her with narrowed, suspicious eyes.

She's on to me! Get away from her!

Even as she thought this, she felt the warning grip of her captor's hand on her arm. She steeled herself to ignore the woman and concentrate once again on what Rivera was saying.

"Look over there, *princesa.*" He gestured toward the pool cabana where a crowd of the hotel's maids, spa attendants, waiters, and lawn boys were assembled in hopes of catching a glimpse of her. "Look at them. Your people. See how you symbolize for them a dignity and pride in their heritage they never had before. You are their link—*our* link—to a more noble past. Yes! That will be the essence of my mural! Your presence giving hope and inspiration to the downtrodden masses of our beloved *Mexica.*"

She couldn't look into their hungry eyes. If she did, she'd feel ashamed. She couldn't afford to ask herself what would happen to their hope once she disappeared. Because she *had* to disappear. She had to get out of this, one way or another.

But once again, as if sensing the impulse to bolt, Rhys's hand on her arm tightened. The hand that was the true shackle of her bondage. Because even as it gripped her, imprisoning her, controlling her, the touch of it also thrilled her. Because her body—her heart—loved what her mind despised.

Because even the slightest touch of that hand could make her want him in her bed. And that was the *real* control he exerted.

She heard the voice of the hotel manager saying, "And over here I would like to present some guests who are most eager to meet you, and I'm sure you will want to meet in return."

She *didn't* want to meet them. But she had no choice. She was here for a reason.

The gauntlet that had been waiting with martinis in hand suddenly swooped in on them, eager to be presented. The faces began to blur as the names were rattled off. But even before the introductions were completed, the crowd was calling out questions in a jumbled rush.

With a charming smile, Rhys held up his hands. "*Señores*

y señoras, por favor. We'll be happy to answer all your questions, but please, one at a time."

Gilbert Roland—suave, virile star of the silver screen—stepped forth, putting hands on hips and peering at Rhys with flamboyant disdain. "And who, sir, might *you* be? The gringo Prince Charming to the Mexican *princesa*?"

It was a blatant challenge from someone accustomed to being the center of attention and not accepting things at face value. The two men squared off: the movie star and the intruder on his home turf. It seemed a wildly uneven confrontation. But as the room quieted and the tension crackled through the air, Rhys gave a slow, bemused smile. And suddenly, all the energy in the room shifted his way.

Because for all of Roland's macho authority, he seemed to shrink in this man's presence. For the moment, even Kate was forgotten. It was as if only Rhys existed. A tall and powerfully masculine man, wickedly handsome in his Panama suit, the jacket skimming his cat-burglar torso with an unstudied Chesterfieldian polish that hinted—enticingly so—of the musculature of the naked body underneath. The hair he'd plastered down had been tousled in the breeze, so the riot of black curls sought escape in a way that framed his strong face magnificently. Even the fiercely penetrating gaze beneath the masking smile turned his eyes into torrid blue flames that made a woman want to sizzle in their heat. Because this aura he could turn on like a spotlight wasn't the typical appeal of a stylish and well-built gentleman. It was blatantly sexual.

Every woman there felt it in her bones.

And Kate—*damn him!*—was no exception.

Finally he spoke, in that soft tone that underscored his power more than antagonism could. "Prince Charming? Hardly, sir. In fact, in the scheme of things, I'm nobody at all."

In the wake of the personal magnetism he'd just exhibited, this seemed an extraordinary statement. "But, Senor," gasped someone close, "are you not Burton Brandt, the American producer who has come to our country to make a motion picture?"

Rhys bowed his head, acknowledging the false identity with a show of silent modesty.

"And are you not," asked another, "the same man who discovered the existence of the *princesa*?"

"By chance, Senor. Merely by chance."

A woman sidled forward, all bleached, marcelled hair and draped champagne silk. "Surely not by chance alone," she breathed, giving him a glimpse of her strategically bared shoulder. "You strike me as a man who always gets what he's after."

Rhys favored her with an intimate glance. "Would you like to hear the story?"

"I'd love to," she purred, all but falling over him.

A disgruntled man, obviously her husband, stepped between them, giving her a seething glare. "We all know that story. It's been in all the papers."

"*I* don't read the papers," hissed his wife.

In the midst of this nuptial crisis, other voices raised themselves to be heard.

"Who believes the papers, anyhow?"

"Rumors and hearsay."

"Tell us the story yourself."

"Yes," sneered Gilbert Roland, reissuing his challenge. "Let us hear it from the horse's mouth."

"If you insist," Rhys acquiesced, although this was what he'd intended all along. "Very well. What you've all heard is true. We have, indeed, come to your splendid country to make a motion picture called *The Conquistador and the Princess*. It will be an epic historical romance about a lusty Spaniard who, in the process of conquering—" he gave them a meaningful look—"some might say *defiling* Mexico, falls in love with a ravishing Aztec princess. And from this union is born a child who is the genesis of today's Mexico—a fiery fusion of the best of two rich and ancient cultures that come together to create a proud and vital nation."

With one masterful stroke, he succeeded in allying every person there. For, as contradictory as their outlooks might be, they shared a love of country that, in that moment, united them through his words.

All but the frowning Gilbert Roland, who seemed to view Rhys's triumph as a personal affront.

"It's also true," Rhys continued, "that our movie princess will be played by none other than—" he extended his palm toward Kate like a ringmaster presenting his much-anticipated headliner—"Maria Consuela Isabela Dominica Reyada, the last survivor of the Aztec royal line."

Once again, attention focused on Kate. But only because he'd allowed it.

Someone piped up, "But you were going to tell the story of how you found her."

He drew a slow breath, looking around the room so it seemed he met the gaze of every person gathered, heightening their anticipation. Then, with the flourish of a true showman, he launched into his story. The story of how, in researching his movie, he'd acquired a collection of Colonial-era documents at a Seville auction two years ago. Of how he discovered in those papers the journal of a priest who'd accompanied Cortez to the New World and taken part in the *Conquista.* Of how this document chronicled the amazing saga of Cuatemoc, the last Aztec emperor, and of his family who, with the priest's help, had escaped the Spanish destruction of the city of Tenochtitlan—today's Mexico City—and had fled to the south. Of how this surviving family—which the priest renamed Reyada, using "Rey," the Castilian name for king—continued to move ever southward over five hundred years and many generations until it settled at Tierra del Fuego, the very bottom of the world. Of how he, "Burton Brandt," had doggedly tracked the odyssey of the Reyadas until he finally found the last of their lineage—a daughter, educated and now living in London. Of how he decided this young woman, a bonafide princess, was so beautiful, so photogenic, and so completely the embodiment of Aztec glory that he *had* to star her in his picture.

Kate had heard this story—this fraud—countless times, and each time she heard it or saw it on a newsreel or read it in *Time* magazine, or *The Saturday Evening Post,* or *The New York Journal,* she marveled at how convincing it was and how captivatingly Rhys told it. He had all the necessary details and forged papers to give it absolute credibility. It explained everything, including her tenuous grasp of the Spanish language, and why she spoke with an English accent. It was so good she almost believed it herself. But, from long experience, she also knew that no scam was perfect, and even now, as Rhys spoke, she could see the resistance building in the shrewd eyes of Gilbert Roland.

"And why is it, Mr. Brandt," the movie star drawled, "that we in Hollywood have not heard of you before this time?"

Rhys faced him once again. "Because, Senor Roland, even though my picture is being made in partnership with MGM, the most powerful of all Hollywood studios, it's my first movie project. We all have to start somewhere, don't we? We can't all be as illustrious and accomplished as you. In fact, I'm an admirer of your work, and would be grateful for any advice or assistance you'd care to give. I would have asked sooner, but naturally I hesitated to bother you when you no doubt came to Ixtapan to rest."

Oh, he was good!

The charismatic actor's chest expanded noticeably. "But . . ." He glanced about the room as if struggling with the sudden shift in gears. "But my dear sir, it's no bother whatsoever. Perhaps we could dine tomorrow? I already have a number of ideas. This story you've come to film is, after all, dear to all our hearts." Then, suddenly, "You don't perchance need an actor to play the *conquistadore*?"

"We'll talk," Rhys promised.

Kate had had enough. "I see our friends the de Guzmáns over there," she reminded Rhys in a deceptively sweet tone. "We should pay our respects."

Rhys's eagle eyes pierced the crowd and picked out the object of their mission: the real reason for their journey to this plush resort in the mountains of Central Mexico.

"Yes," he agreed. "Let's."

The manager pushed an entry into the crowd and they followed him toward Ramirez de Guzmán, the wealthiest man in Mexico, and his twenty-three-year-old son, Monolito. Both men were similarly dressed in white dinner jackets, but there the resemblance ended. The father was a stout, balding man in his sixties with predatory eyes above a charming smile that couldn't quite disguise the cruel twist of his mouth. His son stood beside him uneasily, a sensitive young man with blunt bangs crowning an angelic face that reflected his late mother's bashfulness and none of his father's ruthless ambition.

The elder de Guzmán greeted Rhys with a warm handshake before turning to Kate. "You are more lovely every time we see you, *querida*. I do not think it would be telling tales to confess that you have made quite an impression on Monolito. Since that party at Chapulchapec Palace, he has spoken of nothing else."

The son reddened and thrust his hand behind his back, as if to conceal what he was holding. But Kate had seen the small, neatly wrapped package and asked the embarrassed young man, "Is that for me?"

"I hadn't planned to give it now . . . so publicly . . ." he mumbled miserably.

His father nudged him. "Go on, boy. Where are your manners?"

"It's nothing, really," Monolito demurred. But he handed forth the package as instructed.

Feigning a smile, Kate unwrapped her gift. But instead of the expected jeweled bauble, she found nestled in the box a single blue ribbon.

At the sight of it, the world rushed in on her. She remembered their last meeting. She and the boy had spoken of many things that night. In a moment when her guard was down, she'd confessed a small truth from her real past: that she'd been desperately poor as a child and had dreamed of having a blue ribbon to tie in her hair like other girls. It had represented all the things she'd never had, all the love she'd never been given. Monolito had obviously taken her confession to heart. She was so touched by his consideration that for a moment, she lost her voice completely.

Misreading her reaction, Ramirez de Guzmán wheeled on his son. "And what kind of present is that for such a woman as this?" He looked angry enough to strike.

But Kate forestalled him by gently touching the boy's arm. With tears prickling her eyes, she told him brokenly, "It's the most wonderful present I've ever received."

Seeing that the tears were genuine, Rhys intervened. "The princess is exhausted from the trip. I should see that she rests."

"Of course," Ramirez agreed. "We will meet in the morning, *si*? Perhaps you and I may talk business. I can see to it that you have access to the choice locations at bargain basement prices—anywhere you want to film. There is much we can discuss. And that will give the young people some . . . time to themselves."

"Tomorrow, then." Kate was still staring dazedly at the ribbon in her hands. Taking her arm once again, Rhys said with a command beneath the silky tone, "Come, Princess."

The manager led them back through the crowd and out into the warm night. Up a lighted walkway they passed a series of charming mission-style bungalows before he came to a halt in front of one, and unlocked the door. As he flicked on the lights and was about to give a tour of the accommodations, Kate suddenly became aware of Rhys's edginess. Dropping his solicitous air, he snapped out, "That's enough."

The manager disguised his surprise. "Very well, Senor. Your bungalow is across the way. If you will follow me—"

"Just give me the key and I'll find it myself."

The manager handed over the key and left them. Rhys hardly noticed. He gripped Kate's arm, pushed her inside, and all but slammed the door behind them.

She had only time to catch a quick glimpse of the comfortable sitting room before he turned on her, assessing her with those hooded, impenetrable eyes—eyes that seemed to smolder with a fire all their own. His energy, in the more confined quarters, was volatile, misleadingly leashed, like a simmering volcano on the verge of eruption. He began to close the distance between them, slowly, crossing the room like a jungle cat stalking his quarry. His eyes locked with hers, his look stealing her breath. Slowly . . . slowly . . . one measured step at a time . . . closing in on her . . . making her feel trapped.

And then he was before her, looking ruggedly irresistible. Looking so delicious that she felt the treacherous tingling of her loins. His gaze roaming up and down her satin-clad body as if feasting his eyes on his possession. As if making ready, with the heat of that gaze, the feminine curves and soft flesh his hands would soon claim.

Go away . . .

He didn't, of course. He took her chin in hand and tipped it up to look into her eyes. But she couldn't look at him now. If she did, she might succumb to him once more. So she closed her eyes and prayed.

Please, God . . . give me the strength to fight him.

Chapter Two

How did she get into this? She, Kate Frost, who'd never been out of England in her life . . . here, in a country as foreign to her as Timbuktu . . . in a role she had no desire to play . . . with a man who was so mysterious, so threatening, so determined, so . . .

Perilously seductive.

It all began seven months ago in London when she'd so foolishly thought he was the mark and she the masquerader. But he'd turned the tables on her. He'd shown her how naïve and ignorant even she—someone who considered herself an expert in the art of flimflam—could be.

But in a way, her entire life had been a journey to this entrapment. From the moment she'd been left in a basket on the doorstep of Saint Andrew's Orphanage in the East End of London with nothing to identify her. A pretty child with golden blond hair and gold-flecked emerald eyes, the only clue to her heritage being a faintly exotic appearance that, despite her light skin, hinted of some foreign blood. They called her Kate.

Life at the orphanage wasn't so oppressively strict as it was disorganized and undisciplined. The children grew up wild, the most ambitious of them learning early to become pickpockets and petty swindlers who worked the Limehouse streets and alleys. Kate herself was among the cleverest, and by the time she was eight, she'd perfected her own version of what was known as the "tourist con." Wearing a tidy dress she'd pilfered off a line in Islington, she would haunt Victoria Station looking for likely prey. When she spotted feasible candidates, she'd appeal to them with teary eyes and quivering lip, pretending to be a tourist who'd lost her family in the crowd and begging a bit of change for food to tide her over until her family came to find her. She was careful only to approach obvious visitors, as they'd be less likely to spot the scam and notify the police. Travelers, after all, were always in a hurry and eager to be on their way. From careful observation, she was able to pick up their accents and pose successfully as an Australian, a New Zealander, or an American, depending on the nationality of her intended victim.

One day she was pocketing a particularly hard-won shilling when an older man approached her with an amused twinkle in his eye. "You're good, m'girl," he told her candidly. "But you could be better."

She gave him a dainty sniff, pretending not to understand, but he chuckled, undeterred. "Your accent's serviceable enough, but you give yourself away with your choice of words. Colonials don't call a man 'guvna' and they don't ask for a 'quid.' You go on like you are, and you'll be pinched sure. But you have potential. You're a fetching little thing, and you've got pluck, I'll grant you that. Might be I'd give you a pointer or two."

Even at that tender age, Kate knew better than to trust seemingly well-meaning strangers, and she lost no time in giving him the air. But she incorporated his suggestion, and a week later noticed him once again observing her act. This time he complimented her. "Well done, m'girl. You're a quick study. I could do with someone like you."

Once again she brushed him off. But in the following weeks she spotted him again and again watching her with a reflective gaze. Each time he'd offer some small correction to improve her technique and increase her take. Soon she began to look for him.

His name was Tolly Frost. She didn't know it then, but he was a legend among the touts, pickpockets, and confidence artists of the London slums. He was also the gentlest, kindest, and most protective human being she'd ever encountered. In the weeks and months that followed, he continued to tutor and encourage her until it seemed the most natural thing in the world that they should work together, posing as father and daughter. His schemes were cunning in their seeming simplicity, but he left nothing to chance, and he never involved her in any endeavor that might jeopardize her safety. Without effort, without pushing her, he accomplished what no one else ever had. He made her trust him.

That Christmas, he gave her the present she wanted most and had never thought to have: he legally adopted her. Finally, she had a father to call her own.

As the years passed, Tolly continued to train her. He taught her to speak well, with an aristocratic accent. "People mark you by how you talk," he stressed. He gave her books to read. He taught her to dress, to walk, to conduct herself like a lady. By the time she was sixteen, she had the equivalent of a finishing school education and could easily pose as a Mayfair debutante. By the time she was twenty, she was a confident young woman who could be taken for the cynosure of any Belgravia drawing room.

But Tolly schooled her in more than manners and comportment. Slowly, through the years, he acquainted her with all the scams that had made him the most accomplished con artist of his generation. He shared the secrets of identifying the most lucrative suckers, the many ways to charm them and gain their trust. She thrived under his tutelage, loving the thrill of losing herself in a false identity, delighting in the danger, pushing him to try ever more inventive and daring methods. The proud heir of his artistic legacy. And yet it was her own talent that made her shine. As Tolly said time and again, "M'girl, you're a natural."

Her life couldn't have been happier. Until one day, it ended—and it was all her doing.

Against his better judgment, she talked Tolly into swindling a Member of Parliament into buying a nonexistent South African diamond mine. "Think of the audacity of it. An MP! Why, it shall be the highlight of our careers."

But what she didn't understand was that behind Tolly's reluctance was a realization that he was growing old. His wits had been dulled by time, repetition, and the painstaking process of passing his knowledge and experience to her. In the climactic moment of the con, when the MP was handing over a bank draft for a hundred thousand pounds in the lobby of the Dorchester Hotel, a team of Scotland Yard's finest descended on him and took him away in shackles.

Three days later, he was dead. He'd died in his cell in Wormwood Scrubs Prison. Official word was that he'd succumbed to bronchitis, but Kate didn't believe it. She knew they'd beaten him, trying to sweat out details of his career in crime and likely the name of his young female accomplice.

Kate was destroyed.

Immobilized by grief, ravaged by guilt for what had happened to this man who'd given her so much, she lost all trace of her confidence and steely nerve. For months, she wanted to die. And when that passed, she developed a paralyzing fear of going to prison because some part of her believed if she did, she would, like Tolly, never walk out again. She was rudderless, self-destructive, afraid to face the future without the man who'd guided her every move.

But soon her money ran out, and her old will to survive began to reassert itself. Knowing no other way to earn a living, she knew she had to get back into the game. It was what Tolly would want her to do.

But it was 1930, the year the wave of unemployment and

bankruptcies, instigated by America's stock market crash, hit London full force. Wealthy visitors were few and pickings were slim. It took some time and a lot of effort, but eventually there was a success. Then another. And another. It took her three years, but she finally regained her confidence and found new ways to survive in these harder times. Although she realized she was only half of what she'd been with Tolly, the rest of the London underworld considered her, at age twenty-three, to be the most creative woman flamster in all of the British Empire.

Then she met Rhys.

He was a wealthy American on holiday, one of those charmed few whose fortune hadn't been in stocks and who'd been relatively unaffected by the Depression. He seemed like a godsend. But from the first, there was something different about him. It wasn't just that he was so arrestingly tall, dark, and handsome. She'd fleeced handsome men before. His appeal was more than just physical. Everything about him seemed larger than life. The assurance and grace with which he moved his athletic body called to her mind visions of a cat burglar traversing rooftops on moonless nights. He didn't smile but grinned broadly, showing strong white teeth in a wickedly sensual mouth. Every gesture of his big hands seemed like poetry in motion. And when he spoke he enunciated every word, drawing it out, as if savoring the sound of it on his tongue.

Still, all that paled beneath the force of his presence. He was so bold, so innately sensual, that every time she saw him, she felt as if the breath had been knocked from her lungs. He made her feel, for the first time in her life, completely submissive to a power more potent than her own. He made her feel trembly and whispery and . . . womanly.

It wasn't that she was a stranger to sex. It was just that passion had been one of the tools she carted out, when necessary, from her bag of tricks. Used as a last resort, when only seduction would secure her success. She'd never minded using her sex appeal—she viewed it with the same dispassion as she viewed her looks, or her affinity for accents, or what Tolly had called her "pluck." The fact that she never felt anything for her victims was, in truth, a relief. It made her feel safe.

But she never felt safe with Rhys. The first time she'd seen him, with his shirtsleeves rolled to the elbows, her eyes had lingered hungrily on his strong wrists and darkly haired forearms and her knees had gone weak. She'd known then that he was a danger to her.

She'd never imagined how truly dangerous he'd become.

It had begun well enough. She was determined to view him as a challenge. If she could best him—this remarkable man—it would be a pivotal triumph, her crowning glory. And because he could be bested, she'd lose all respect for him—and with it, this precarious attraction that was such an inexplicable threat.

What she hadn't counted on was the emotional effect he had on her. Suddenly, because of him, she saw her life with newly opened eyes. She recalled her years in the orphanage when she'd cried herself to sleep at night, feeling hollow because she knew she wasn't loved. She realized now that the love Tolly had bestowed had merely scabbed over the wound. Now that wound was exposed once again. Being with Rhys made her more aware than ever of the emptiness inside.

And so she shut herself down and proceeded with fierce determination, resolving to beat her own weakness as surely as she planned to beat him. She played him along—avoiding his bed at all costs—and smiled shrewdly to herself as he handed over the exorbitant sum she'd extracted for a paste emerald necklace she'd tricked him into believing had once belonged to Catherine de Medici. Knowing she'd won.

Until the door to his suite at the Savoy had opened and

two men swarmed in, grabbing her and cuffing her hands behind her back.

"You've been outconned," Rhys announced with that damned wolfish grin.

As she spat invectives at him, he raised a silencing palm. Even then his power was too much for her.

"There is, however, one way out of this—and *only* one way."

He proceeded to tell her in that same infuriatingly calm tone that he'd been looking for a woman like her, someone he could use to perpetrate a deception of mammoth proportions.

"If you choose to go in with me, you'll turn yourself over to me completely. I won't mislead you. It won't be easy. You're good, but not good enough." Just what Tolly had said to her all those years ago. "This will be special training for a particular job. By the time I get through with you, you'll fool the entire world. I intend to make you into a goddess. I'll teach you and reshape you. You'll do what I say when I say it, and you'll do it the way I say to do it. If you don't, you'll do it again and again until you get it right. This is no job for amateurs."

"Amateur!" she shrieked, indignant.

He merely raised a brow. "If you weren't an amateur, would you be in this situation now?" That silenced her once again. "What you need to know will be told to you when you need to know it. From what I can see, your training will take months. That's immaterial. I'm willing to invest as much time as is necessary. But once you agree to put yourself in my hands, I never want to hear the word 'no' from your lips. The only decision you'll be allowed to make is the one you make today. So if you're going to say no, do so now."

"And if I do?" she demanded, shaking with fury at his unspeakable arrogance.

He merely shrugged. "Then I'll see to it that you get a nice, long vacation in Wormwood Scrubs."

The Scrubs.

She wanted more than anything to spit in his face. But his threat shriveled her resistance. She recalled so vividly her nightmares following Tolly's death that she broke out in a cold sweat.

Prison.

She could almost hear the cell door slam.

It seemed that they stood there forever, each sizing up the other. Was he bluffing? No. She was adept enough at reading people—even though she'd failed so miserably to read him—to know this wasn't a trick. Whatever he was after, he wanted it badly. Enough to have gone to all this trouble, allowing her to see her charade to the end, biding his time. Instinct told her he would stop at nothing.

Finally she caved in. Not just because the promise of prison was so abominable. Because when he glared at her that way, she felt the impulse to surrender take hold. She knew then that she'd met her match.

Reflexively, she raised her chin to a haughty angle. "Very well. I shall do as you demand. But I shall hate you at every moment."

His next words startled her more than anything that had happened so far.

He just crooked a grin and told her, "No, you won't."

Then he strode deliberately to the door, opened it, and dismissed his private detectives. She heard the door close softly. A moment later, he was standing before her once again.

Slowly, he took her shoulders in his hands. She felt the shock of the contact in her loins.

"No," she croaked.

"I told you," he said between his teeth. "I don't want to hear the word 'no' from your lips again." He used his thumb to trace the swell of her mouth. Her heart was thundering in her breast. Everything within her screamed for escape. But there was nowhere to run.

He wouldn't let her if she tried.

"You won't always know what I'm training you for," he said softly. Still trailing her lips with his thumb. "But you *will* obey me."

Then he dipped his head and kissed her. And she knew she was lost.

He kissed her possessively, with a conqueror's authority. Not sweetly or tentatively or hoping to please. He kissed her as if saying, *You now belong to me*. As if, with the domination of that beastly, sensual mouth, he was searing her with his brand. As if his tongue, taking possession of hers, was drawing from her all life and energy and spirit, empowering himself as he turned her to putty in his hands.

She melted with that kiss. She'd have done anything he wanted in that moment. Because his mouth seemed made for hers. Because as he clutched her in his arms, it seemed that she'd finally found the nook where she belonged. Because her mind had ceased to function.

Until he lifted his head and looked down at her. Until she pried her eyes open—painfully—and saw him standing before her, assessing her as if gauging the extent of his supremacy. Until she saw in the inferno of his blazing blue eyes a ruthless control that brought a flush of embarrassment to her cheeks.

Gasping for breath, she told him, "I shall never give myself to you completely."

His gaze flicked over her, down and up the length of her vulnerable form, still fettered at his command. And he told her, enunciating every word, as was his way, "Yes . . . you . . . will."

Something stirred in her. Some last vestige of pride, of independence, of free will. She fought him this time as he came for her with all the strength she had.

He let her. Almost patiently, he fended off the slam of her

shoulder into his chest, the kick of her shoe against his shin. Stoically. Impassively. With vastly superior strength, as if allowing her this final rebellion before taking what was his by right of claim.

And then . . .

When she'd exhausted all her surpluses and was limp . . .

Only then did he reach forth with one hand and snap free the buttons of her blouse. One at a time, effortlessly, unhurriedly, as if showing his contempt for her pathetic display of temper. Opening it with measured leisure, pausing to look at his prize. Gazing at the extravagant curve of her naked breasts as if sizing up their usefulness to him. Not with passion or desire. Just judging the goods.

She was so frustrated by his exhaustive scrutiny that she wanted to cry. Damn him! How could he incite such a reaction from her—the first such response of her life!—and feel . . . *nothing?*

But then she remembered. He was only doing what she'd done countless times.

Only she'd had the good sense to pretend.

She quivered in anticipation. Not certain what he'd do. *Could anyone ever be certain of him?* Despising him yet wanting him, all at the same time. Feeling that she'd scream if he didn't do something soon.

At last he stepped toward her. Took her shoulders and hauled her close with a jolt that made her gasp. Ran his hands down her arms, as if to emphasize that they were bound behind her for his pleasure. She waited with held breath for him to remove the cuffs from her wrists. But he didn't. He just stood there looking down into her eyes as his mouth twisted into a smirk. As if he knew already what she hadn't—that being tied and helpless to him was oddly . . .

Irrationally . . .

Thrilling!

And then he kissed her. Kissed her as if he knew she'd do anything he demanded. Kissed her until she lost all track of where she was and why. Kissed her until she was mewling softly in her throat. Unbidden permission to take what he would.

She didn't know how she ended up draped across his bed. She only knew that his hands—so expressive—touched her flesh with a scorching heat. Making her body rejoice with his forceful caress. Making her feel ripe and juicy and wanting.

Wanting *him*.

And when he entered her—filling her so completely that she wanted nothing else—she shivered in ecstasy. Giving herself to him completely, despite her rash proclamation. Rising beneath him like an instrument played with devastating skill by a virtuoso of the art.

He never bothered to uncuff her hands. He just took her. But he took her so exquisitely—his mouth on her flesh making her swoon—that she gloried in his possession.

And when it was over—when she'd shamed herself by loving *every moment*—he stood and gazed down upon her, rumpled and disheveled in the ruins of his bed. Only then did he remove the handcuffs that had bound her. Without a word. Taking them with him. Leaving her there and closing the door.

She curled herself up into a ball, rubbing her chafed wrists. The worst of it was, now that she was free, she missed their confinement. She already missed the feel of his massive body pounding into hers. The feel of his feasting mouth on her nipple.

She'd never felt so humiliated in all her life. To make her pleasure so obvious to him seemed a betrayal of self. She hadn't even had the presence of mind to pretend to loathe his touch. In that explosive union, she'd forgotten all her training.

She'd forgotten everything but him.

Trembling now with a tumble of emotions, she pulled together the tattered shreds of her resolve. Somehow . . .

someday . . . she would have her revenge. For what he'd done to her—what he'd turned her into—she'd make him pay!

They stayed six months in his Savoy suite overlooking the Thames, working seven days a week, ten hours a day. He never told her exactly what his con would be. From the specifics of the training, she gradually gathered that their mission would take place in Mexico, which was, in this Depression year of 1933, exploding with a fervor of revolutionary sentiment; and that she was to impersonate a woman who was the sole heir to the Aztec royal line and thus the glory of a lost tradition. But how it would all come together, she had no idea. He clearly had no intention of telling her until she needed to know.

During those months, he worked on her tirelessly to mold her into the quintessence of grace, breeding, and effortless royal demeanor. He taught her enough Spanish that it could pass as her nearly forgotten childhood language, along with some words of Nahuatl, the ancient Aztec tongue. Dyed her honey hair a rich, smoky black. Taught her to use makeup to accentuate the exotic shape of her eyes. Coached her on how to speak in public and win a crowd, how to shine for a pack of photographers. How to move, how to react, how to look at people in a way that was so regally appealing, so enchanting, that it would cause a demoralized nation to say: yes, this is our Louis XVII . . . our Anastasia . . . our very own lost princess.

There were times when she lost herself in the intensity of the training. In those moments, she recalled those wonderful days when Tolly had imparted the wealth of his knowledge to her. There were even moments when Tolly and Rhys seemed to blend together in her weary mind, and she'd have to snap herself out of the spell, reminding herself that this wasn't Tolly. This was her captor.

Her enemy.

And yet, Rhys's manner wasn't sadistic or cruel. Indeed, he was unfailingly tolerant. He never raised his voice to her. If she did something wrong, he just made her do it again . . . and again . . . and again. When she did it right, no matter how long it had taken to manage it, he merely looked at her and nodded his satisfaction.

The hours were long, the work grueling, and she often felt she'd collapse from fatigue.

But the nights . . .

Oh, the nights! Just when she was sick to death of him and his demands, just when she thought she couldn't hate anyone more, he'd reach for her again and she'd forget everything in his arms. It was then that she found herself wanting to please him, longing for some sign, some kind word, some gesture of approval. It was then that he exerted his greatest power over her. Because she loved his body. She loved what it made her do and feel. Every touch, every kiss, each masterful thrust made her blossom more. If she was sometimes sullen and rebellious during the day, she was more than willing through the long, idyllic nights. She knew he was using her weakness for him to control her. *She knew it!* But she didn't care.

And then one day, he told her she was ready. Just that. No praise, no congratulations.

She was crestfallen. More than anything, she wanted some validation for all she'd endured.

Remembering his words on that first day, she jutted her chin and asked, in a tone seething with sarcasm, "Am I now the goddess you wanted me to be?"

He turned and looked at her the way he always had, without a trace of emotion that might give her a clue to the workings of his mind. But then, incredibly, his eyes softened with the first look of tenderness he'd ever exhibited, and she saw the trace of pride lurking behind his gaze.

"Every inch," he said simply.

It was then that she knew she loved him.

It appalled her. She couldn't afford to love him. *Not him!* She was nothing to him. Just a pawn he was using for his own hellish designs. She didn't even know anything about him, who he really was, or even what he was after. She could *never* trust him . . .

No, loving him was an abomination. It was humiliating. She couldn't let it happen.

She wouldn't.

Not if it killed her.

Only then did she comprehend the true extent of her peril. And she knew in that moment that her only hope of deliverance was to escape his grasp. She had to get as far away from him as she could.

No matter the cost.

Chapter Three

And now she stood before him, her chin in the grip of his fingers, praying for the fortitude to find a way out.

She waited with a pounding heart, steeling herself to withstand the kiss she was sure would come. That blinding kiss that always made her feel as if she were melting into a puddle at his feet. But it didn't come. The moment stretched between them as she felt her nerves tauten. As he didn't move.

Eventually, she opened her eyes, driven by curiosity. He stood towering over her, assessing her with a cold, hard glare.

He removed his hand from her chin and took the ribbon she still held, dangling it from his fingers, allowing it to unfurl. Staring at it as if it were a snake he'd just found in his bed. "What's the meaning of this?" he demanded.

She could see that he was steaming. It surprised her, since she'd never seen him angry before. She raised her chin a mutinous notch, determined to stare him down, then affected an insouciant shrug. "I should think you'd be elated. You wanted the boy to become enamored with me, and so he has."

On the ship from Southampton to Vera Cruz, Rhys began to tell her about Ramirez de Guzmán, a landowner and industrialist who was reputed to be the wealthiest man in Mexico. He was currently mounting a campaign for the presidency, but had a rough road ahead since he was reviled by the socialist-minded common folk as the country's most vicious capitalist. But after arriving in Mexico City amidst a cyclone of publicity, after making sure the elder de Guzmán would be the first man she'd meet, and after coming to Ixtapan because it was the favorite retreat of the man, Rhys had offhandedly informed her that her object wasn't the magnate's pocketbook, but a marriage proposal from his more weak-willed and passive son Monolito.

"The son!" she'd exclaimed in surprise. "You want me to marry the son?"

"You won't be marrying him," he'd assured her. "Once the engagement is announced in Mexico City—once Ramirez takes each of your hands in his, raises them high, and proclaims the forthcoming union—your job is done."

How, she wondered, was anyone to profit from a marriage that wouldn't take place? Obviously there was more to know—much more. But he wouldn't tell her.

Now, even though she was rapidly advancing along this path, Rhys was reacting strangely to the matter of the ribbon.

"Why did he give you this?" he asked, still suspending it from his fingers.

She surveyed the sitting room airily, determined not to nibble at his bait. "I suppose it's because he finds me more charming than you do."

"You know what I mean. Why this? A ribbon he could pick up in any market for a peso."

"Perhaps he ascribes to the theory that it's the thought that counts."

She was about to turn her back on him when he took hold of her arm and swiveled her to face him. "What did you tell him?"

She could see he wasn't going to let it go. "Oh, very well. The moonlight was dreamy, the jasmine succulently scented, and the boy loquacious. He told me the horror it was to be the son of his beastly father, and I told him when I was a young girl I'd always wanted a blue ribbon."

"What else?"

"He brought me one. He's not quite the dreadful bore you led me to believe. There's something rather agreeable about him."

"And where, exactly, were you supposed to have been when you were a little girl pining for this blue ribbon?"

"I didn't say."

"Well, that, at least, is a relief. I was beginning to think you'd regaled him with stories of your dreary days at Saint Andrew's."

It had never been necessary for her to tell Rhys anything about her past. His private detectives had compiled a complete dossier on her, detailing her childhood, her career with Tolly, everything.

"You must take me for a complete imbecile."

"Not a *complete* imbecile. But let me ask you this—who were you supposed to be when you were praying to heaven for a blue ribbon to call your own?" When she gave him a blank look, he persisted. "The cockney orphan? Or the lost Aztec princess?" She suddenly saw what he meant. "Was it in Tiera del Fuego where Maria was being gently reared by the loving last remnants of the great Reyada family?"

He might have spent the last half-year tearing her down and reconstructing her, but she could still think on her feet. "You needn't worry. I've never blown a cover in my life."

"Haven't you? Then why are you here?"

It infuriated her that he should throw her bondage to him in her face. "Thankfully, Monolito isn't the snake in the grass that you are. Do give me *some* credit. I've fooled my share of gullibles, after all. I know a bit more about the handling of men than you seem to think."

"Then he's asked you to marry him?"

Damn him! Must he always be so quick, so sharp? Sometimes she wished he was as doltish as the boy Monolito.

Then she wouldn't love him so desperately.

Don't think of that. Keep your wits about you, m'girl. You'll need them.

"No, he hasn't asked me. But he will."

"This pathetic romantic gesture—" He flung the ribbon aside and stood rigid, breathing hard.

She studied him thoughtfully for a moment. His irritation was so at odds with the withdrawn patience he'd shown her for the last six months that she might almost think he was jealous.

Jealous . . .

Was it possible?

Her heart leapt with hope. But then he fixed his explosive gaze on her and said, "At this rate, it could take him a year to propose."

She slumped. And because she was furious with herself for her fleetingly futile optimism, she snapped out, "What do you want me to do, sleep with him so he'll *have* to ask me?"

She saw something flicker in his eyes. For some time he was silent. Then he said quietly, "You've changed."

She met his gaze and began to lose herself in the deep cobalt magnet of his eyes. *It's because I love you. Because I can't be in the same room with you without wanting to crawl out of my skin. Because every time you're near me I can't eat, can't sleep, can't think of anything but you.*

And because I hate myself for it.

But all she said was, "Have I?"

"For some time now. I don't know when it started, exactly . . . but certainly since we arrived in Mexico. It couldn't have anything to do with that little balloon ride in Mexico City, could it?"

This surprised her. She studied him more closely and detected, behind that steely gaze, a ghost of . . . insecurity?

The day before, at a gala reception at the Chapulchapec museum, de Guzmán had arranged in their honor a hot air balloon ride over the city—the princess surveying her domain, as it were. The prospect thrilled her, but as they'd climbed aboard, she'd noticed Rhys turn white. As the ropes were untied, his hands began to tremble and he'd swayed on his feet. Then, just as the last tie to the ground was about to be freed, he'd leapt off. It caused a bit of a scene, which he'd explained with a cryptic, "I don't like heights." Now, like any man, he assumed it made him look smaller and less masculine in her eyes. But the truth was, it made him more attractive. There was nothing more appealing than a single vulnerability in a man normally so strong and self-assured. It had made him seem touchingly human. It had made her love him all the more.

"Perhaps," she said carefully, letting him squirm.

Absently, he reached up to loosen his evening tie, letting it fall open on either side of his collar, then unfastened the top two buttons of his Saville Row shirt. An endearingly nervous gesture. She caught a glimpse of the dark hair furring his chest and swallowed hard.

"Or perhaps I like the boy," she continued. "Maybe I'm feeling pangs at duping him. Or perhaps I resent being called on the carpet like some tot in knickers who hasn't a brain in her head. I wasn't, after all, hatched the day you met me. I do have talents and potential of my own. Would it kill you to show some occasional faith in me?"

She stood before him with her chest heaving. She'd meant to throw him off the scent, yet had ended up by spilling some small part of her carefully guarded truth. The room was so quiet that she could hear the whisper of his trousers as he stepped toward her. Taking her arms in both hands, he told her in an oddly throbbing tone, "I have so much faith in you that I've put my entire future in your hands."

She felt herself begin to thaw.

Don't say such things. I can handle it when you're arrogant and even dictatorial. But when you're kind . . . when you pat me on the head like a puppy, and my heart constricts in hope . . . when you show me up for the wretched fool I am . . .

That I can't abide.

He turned his right hand and with the back of his finger traced the line of her arm. She felt the ache of longing shudder up her spine. She turned from him and went to open her trunk, which had been delivered to her room. Rifling through it for the peignoir he'd bought her in London, she said, "It's late. And I'm tired."

He came up behind her with disquieting abruptness. Grabbed her hips and pulled her into him. She felt the length of him against her back, felt his hand on her buttocks, smoothing the slim-fitting satin of her gown. Then, with a savage lunge, he reached up under her, between her thighs, his hand searching with relentless confidence until he found her throbbing clit. Roughly, with ungovernable strength, he held her pinned to him as he stroked her through the barrier of her dress until she could feel herself wet beneath his hand. Her breath was coming in startled gasps that sounded too much like purrs of pleasure. With his hand he played her, expertly building the escalation of her lust as he jerked her back so she could feel his erection against the crack of her ass. Ravaging her self-control with a wave of yearning, forcing to the surface all she'd stamped down with her pride. She could feel herself lean back into him, her head falling to his shoulder, her lips slackly parted. Feel the expansion of her slumbering passion, too long denied. All the careful nights since leaving London, sleeping in her lonely bed for the sake of the con, wanting him without *wanting* to want him.

And then his mouth was at her ear, nibbling, tasting, sending alarming pulses of pleasure through her like flashes of fever. The warmth of his embrace, the power of his seduction making her drunk. Her head spinning as her body arched into his hand, seeking the delectable release only he had ever given her. Wanting to ruck up her skirts and feel his unsheathed fingers on her moist and shimmering flesh. Wanting them inside her, moving with the feathery flicks that had brought her to unwilling climax time after time.

And then he spoke. Softly, huskily, in that graveled voice that drove her wild in the dark of night. "You've been quite the little rebel lately."

His words penetrated the numbing mist of her mind. And then she knew what he was doing. Asserting his authority over her, controlling her in the way he knew she could be most controlled. Using the cravings of her body to abate her insurrection.

She pushed herself away. Away from the oh-so-easy surfeit of thought. Away from the one thing that would temper her. Away from him.

"No."

The word sprang from the depths of her soul. She wheeled on him and saw the surprise in his eyes. Taking satisfaction, she drew a breath and said, more succinctly, "You'll never touch me again."

She stood with clenched fists at her sides, awaiting his reaction. Waiting for the fury she thought would surely come.

But he didn't rail or threaten as she expected. He just lowered his gaze, masking whatever emotions her mutiny had driven from his hardened shell. He turned and took a slow circuit of the room, looking it over as if noticing the details for the first time. The multicolored native weaving on the wall depicting the feathered serpent Quetzalcoatl. A Taxco silver bowl filled with mangoes and papayas atop the Zenith console radio. The sand-and-lapis-colored Mexican tiles beneath the vibrant throw rug. She watched him, waiting, the silence unbearable.

Finally, he looked at her. But his gaze was mild, lacking the anticipated anger or blame. "I owe you an apology," he said.

She scoffed. "What sort of trick is *this?*"

"No trick. You've made me see myself with different eyes. You've been so . . . wonderful . . . and I've been . . . unappreciative at best. My only excuse is that I've been so wrapped up in my own objectives that I've failed to . . . express my admiration. I'd planned to, but I can see now it's too late."

If he'd said it glibly, she'd have deepened her suspicion. But he was uncharacteristically hesitant, as if the saying of the words was costing him some measure of his own pride. She didn't want to—couldn't afford to—but she almost believed him.

Was it possible that she hadn't been crazy, after all, in thinking him jealous?

As if he'd just had an idea, he asked suddenly, "Will you wait for a minute? I have something for you. Please."

He'd never said "please" to her before.

He took the key from his pocket, glanced at the number, then hurried to his own bungalow. A few moments later he returned with a flat blue velvet box in his hands. It was slightly worn, as if it had passed through countless generations.

"I'd planned to give this to you when we announced the engagement. But perhaps you'd accept it now."

She was staring at him, speechless. When he handed forth the box, she couldn't bring herself to move, so he flicked the lid open. Inside was a magnificent necklace fashioned entirely from blue diamonds. Her practiced eye told her they were real. And they were worth a fortune.

"May I?"

He waited for her to nod mutely, then took the necklace and, reaching around her, fastened it behind her neck. As he did, she could feel the intimacy of his breath on her cheek. He said, "I spent two years looking for the right woman. But I never imagined I'd find someone like you. You've surpassed all my expectations. Time and again I've marveled at you. I couldn't have done this without you." He paused, as if the saying of it was difficult, then added simply, "Thank you."

She could feel the necklace over the lump in her throat. She managed to ask, "Where did you—?"

"Get it?" Her question seemed to throw him. She could see on his face the signs of some internal struggle. Finally he admitted, "It was my mother's."

His mother's . . .

He narrowed his eyes and peered at her, then said, "You're stunning."

She didn't know what to do. No words would come. She felt more shocked than she ever had before.

His mother's!

He stepped closer, and slowly, so as not to raise her hackles, touched the choker at her neck. As he did, his fingers brushed her throat.

"It won't be easy to keep my distance," he was saying. "You've done something to me—touched something in me. I've missed the nights when you were curled up in my arms. I've missed the way you feel, the way you smell. That delicate scent that's all your own. The way you murmur in your sleep. Tonight, when everyone was looking at you, all I could think was, how can I go one more night without her? I hadn't counted on missing you, and yet . . ." He trailed off.

His fingers were so warm against her throat.

"But you've played square with me. If that's what you want—" He shrugged. "I owe you that, at least. Forgive me if I've overstepped my bounds. It's just that I—" He paused, then said with a catch in his throat, "How can a man look at you and not want you for his own? I've come to think of you as mine. That you . . . belong to me. It's foolish, I suppose, but I can't seem to help wanting you. For that, you have only yourself to blame."

Her head was reeling.

"Would you at least give me one thing? One last kiss. I

hadn't planned for this to be the end. You've caught me, I'm afraid, unprepared."

He leaned over and gave her lips a gentle kiss. Just a soft, sweet pressure of his mouth. But he kept it there, the moment drawn out, tasting of her breath. Then kissed again. Tenderly, lingeringly, as if he couldn't bear to tear himself away. She was still so dazed that she stood suspended in time, a sense of unreality making her sluggish and slow. Unable to move away.

"I have only one regret," he said against her lips.

"What?" she rasped.

"That I wasn't the one to give you a blue ribbon."

Her heart broke.

He lifted his head and his gaze flicked to the necklace, then back to her teary eyes. "Will a ribbon of blue diamonds suffice?"

She didn't know how it happened. One moment she was choking back the tears, and the next she was in his arms, kissing him madly. Pouring all her grief and love and need into that one adoring kiss as her arms found his neck and clung. And then his arms were crushing her to him, and she was being lifted in his strong embrace. And the sitting room was whirling by and she felt the feathery folds of the bed at her back. And the weight of him was upon her as he shoved aside the dress he'd chosen for her to wear.

He was kissing her divinely. Somehow in the process she found herself unclothed, naked to his touch. His hands exploring her like something prized as his mouth plundered hers. Stoking the dormant flames of her starvation, but elegantly now, as if relishing every touch. Making her body pulsate with a spirit all its own, making her feel beautiful—clad only in blue diamonds—as his mouth explored her shapely curves. Loving her—*loving her*—with passionate devotion.

Waiting until she whimpered with need. Then bringing his mouth to her responsive inner thigh. Licking her with long, slow swipes of his moistly devouring tongue. Sparking new and dizzying elevations of lust as her thighs parted, begging silently for more. Finding her core, teasing her with the tip of his tongue, sucking on her clit, until she was so hot, she nearly burst into the succor of his mouth. And then . . . only then, when she was desperate to feel him plunging inside, filling the emptiness without him to make her whole, did he take his stiff cock in hand and ram it home. Making her arch up with a cry of joyous welcome, receiving him with tight, juicy spasms that rocked and thrilled her with delicious shivers that carried her away to a world of dreamy bliss.

And when she'd ceased her shudders, he continued moving within her with long, hard thrusts that forced the breath from her lungs in loving sighs. Carrying her once again to that sense of harmony where nothing was wanting save that she could make this moment last for all time. Kissing her mouth, nipping at the lobe of her ear, as the collar of blue diamonds pressed into her throat, sealing her as his.

When they'd climaxed together—he with mighty groans, she with uncontrollable, soft cries—he lay atop her, searing and substantial, and stroked her face as if, even now, he couldn't get enough.

And then, unhurriedly, he eased himself up and looked down into her eyes. "Remember this."

"Always," she sighed.

"And remember one more thing."

"Anything." Awash in love and exquisite fulfillment.

He leaned into her and kissed her mouth. Then put his lips to her ear and whispered, "I can take you whenever I want."

It was a moment before the true meaning of his words penetrated. And when they did, she pushed him away and stared at him in horror. Struggling to disbelieve even as her scalded heart sank within her breast.

"And that," he told her, rising from the bed with an air

of finality, "is precisely why you need me. Because you're too easy to con."

He was straightening his clothes as if he had all the time in the world. As if he hadn't just driven a knife into her heart. Gradually her sense of mortification seeped from her to be replaced by a simmering rage. She bolted up in bed and, reaching behind to struggle with the clasp, wrenched the necklace from her throat and hurled it at him.

It fell to the floor. He didn't bother to pick it up. He just looked at it, then back to her with a raised brow. "I'd be careful with that, if I were you. It's borrowed."

She felt as if the wind had been knocked from her. Eyes glinting, she ground out between clenched teeth, "You son of a bitch."

Something unfathomable flickered in his eyes. But he gave her a steady glare that seemed full of contempt. Then, with a derisive smirk, he told her, "For once you're right."

With that he left her.

She was so outraged, she couldn't bring herself to move. But then her gaze fell on the necklace, gleaming with blue lights from the carpet by the bed. She rose with a lunge and swept it up, bent on destruction. It would serve him right if she ripped it to pieces.

But the gems seemed to warm to the touch of her hand. As if wishing they belonged to her. A ribbon of blue diamonds, he'd called it. The lonely child she'd been had only thought she'd wanted a blue ribbon to call her own. But it was this she'd wanted all along. This, and all that went with it.

It was my mother's . . .

So she'd been a complete imbecile, after all.

She put it back in its box with shaking hands. No wonder he'd seemed so touchingly hesitant as he'd confessed his longing for her. He'd been choking on the words.

Back in the East End, they think I'm the queen of the con artists, the best in the British Empire.

But I can't hold a candle to you.

Chapter Four

Rhys couldn't sleep.

He paced his room like a caged beast. Trying not to think. Cursing himself for being such a sucker. Using all his willpower to make his mind a blank.

To keep him from thinking about Kate.

What was going on? Why was she having this effect on him?

It wasn't as if he failed to realize that this beautiful, gifted woman represented a certain threat to his mission. He'd deliberately kept a psychological distance, telling her nothing of his past, sharing nothing that would allow her to know who he really was. Resolving to use her, because he must, but taking no emotional risk.

In the beginning, he hadn't even planned to sleep with her. It was only after he saw the effect his physicality had on her that he'd consciously decided to use it to control her. But now he realized that was only a lie he told himself. The truth was, there was something about her that he'd found impossible to resist. Even that first day at the Savoy when he'd unveiled his surprise, when he'd treated her with such contempt, flinging her failure in her face. Using the fear he'd instinctively discerned—the threat of prison—to make her comply with his plans. Even then, when he'd bested her so thoroughly, there had been a look of pride gleaming from her eyes. She was a woman who'd learned to take care of herself. She held herself aloof, as if surrounded by some impenetrable shield. A mystery to be unraveled.

But he'd expected some of that. What he hadn't foreseen was the faintest glimmer of vulnerability lurking behind the gold-laced emerald of those eyes. The hint of fragility that made him realize she could be hurt.

It was that defenselessness that fascinated and perplexed him most. If she'd been tough, he would have used her skills and gone about his business without a second thought, comforting himself with the notion that she deserved everything she got. But when she'd looked at him that way, he'd felt himself grow hard. More than her beauty, more than the body that seemed perfectly formed for the shape of a man's hands, that look had made him want her. It had given her a power over him that alarmed and unsettled him. It wasn't part of his plan.

And because it wasn't, it angered him. Challenged him to prove to himself that it, like all the rest of her, was a façade. And so he'd taken her. Thinking to extinguish his lust for her by fucking her blind. Making her loathe him so she'd never look at him that way again.

But she'd loved it. Handcuffed like some goddamned pasha's sex slave, she'd given him the most magnificent union of his thirty-two years. She'd made him feel, for that brief time, as if the possibility of being healed and whole existed—the past forgiven, his blackened heart restored. It was, for him, the most deceptive and dangerous trick of all.

He'd tried to fight her effect on him. Tried to ask himself what kind of woman would love the bondage he imposed, and open herself to him so completely that he felt he'd glimpsed her soul. Telling himself the punishment he imposed was for all such women who lived to mislead.

But she hadn't taken it as punishment. And because she hadn't, he lost track of his intent and found instead sublime satisfaction in the compliant flesh his own body loved and craved like a second, finer skin. Sheathed inside her, he felt as strong, as content, as a sun-drenched lion watching over his domain.

He found he didn't want to hurt her at all.

But the success of his mission *would* inevitably hurt her. There was no escaping that fact. He'd known this from the beginning. That was why he kept her at arm's length, letting nothing slip, training her like a taskmaster, focusing with an iron will on the epic revenge he was here to extract, the quest that gave his life meaning. Telling himself he'd use her to help him accomplish his purpose, then wash his hands of her.

Except that he couldn't stay away. Each night at the Savoy he told himself he'd take another suite and purge her from his mind. But then she'd turn and give him that cursed look and his resolutions turned to dust. And so he went to her again, coiled like a serpent ready to strike. This time, he vowed, it would be different. This time he'd block out that fatalistic sense of rightness in her embrace. This time he'd be in control.

But he never was. She was like a fever in his blood. She had to know she was driving him to his knees. *She had to!* This, after all, was what she did for a living. She was a con artist! That look that pulled the rug out from underneath all his determination had to be the shrewd device of a skilled charlatan.

Or was it?

The uncertainty nearly drove him mad. Made him go out of his way to hurt her.

Once they'd left London—once he'd dyed her hair and she'd assumed the new persona—it had been easier. She looked so different that he could tell himself she was another person. And so he used the occasion to distance himself—to take the separate rooms the con required and root himself to his own bed. It had actually been a relief.

But tonight it had all fallen apart. He'd seen her face when the boy had given her that shabby ribbon. So luminous, so touched. Startled out of her role.

He'd wanted to see her look that way at him.

He'd actually been jealous! But that was absurd. Jealous of what? That pitiable roughshod-ridden squirt and his miserable little gift? Because the boy had genuinely, with his simplicity, touched Kate's hidden heart? The way Rhys never had?

Ridiculous. He was only jealous because . . . what? Because the boy had, without trying, exerted more control over Kate in that moment than Rhys ever had?

So he'd given her the necklace. He'd just wanted to bring her to heel, to belay the rebellion he saw brewing in her. Too, he'd wanted to see if he could elicit such a response. But he'd done something he hadn't done in years—he'd told her the truth. He'd actually told her the diamonds had been his mother's. And he'd found himself saying things to her that didn't seem like the ruse he'd intended them to be. He'd found himself meaning them.

He'd fallen for his own con.

What was wrong with him?

What was this power she had over him that made him act like . . .

Like some lovesick pup.

He must be losing his mind. He'd spent three years of his life planning this operation. A great deal was riding on its success. But to make that happen, he'd have to keep a clear head. He couldn't afford to let her distract him.

He stepped over to the bar and poured himself a healthy shot from the bottle of tequila. Drank it down in one gulp, letting it burn his throat and momentarily drive these menacing thoughts from his mind. Poured another and drank it down, then began to undress. He had to get some sleep. Tomorrow the real game would begin.

* * *

The next morning he felt ravaged and hung over. But as he sat down to breakfast with Ramirez de Guzmán on the outside terrace overlooking the pool, the customary wave of loathing for the man gave him a jolt of adrenaline. It was all he could do to keep from reaching for his leathery throat as he leaned conspiratorially close and slyly explained how Monolito and "Maria" would make such a suitable match. "Maria is good for Monolito. Such a charming girl. My son, despite my urging, is such a . . . how shall we say it? . . . such an awkward young man. She gives him the grace he needs. And do not forget, my friend, he has the best prospects."

The hypocrisy of this was so cloying that Rhys had to strain to keep a straight face. There was something harrowingly obscene about this man and his ambitions of being president of this country. Didn't he realize he was the most despised villain in all of Mexico? Even now the waiters glared at him with proletarian hatred.

"Of course they are only children," Ramirez was saying. "And it may be that we grown-ups will have to help Cupid along, no?"

These unctuous words gave Rhys a stab of alarm. Yet it was exactly what he'd counted on when he'd devised this plan. It should have buoyed him considerably. Instead it filled him with inexplicable rage.

He kept glancing toward the glass doors, waiting for Kate to make her appearance. Wondering if last night's scrap had affected her as bleakly as it had him. But when she showed up, she looked as freshly radiant as if she'd just awakened from a long and restful slumber. She wore a sleeveless white silk blouse and palazzo pants that flawlessly offset the faint tan he'd had her acquire to lend credence to her claim of *indio* blood. Her lustrously dyed black hair was knotted in an elegant chignon at the nape of her neck, lending her an otherworldly, imperceptible aura of what could well be mistaken for Latin allure. She wore no jewelry, as they'd planned, but she carried herself with such an innate sense of grace and style that she made the bejeweled society matrons look tawdry and overdressed. She was as polished, as sleek, as the native jaguar the Aztecs had worshipped.

But there was nothing cold or aloof about her now. She floated from one wrought iron table to the next, outrageously beautiful beneath the tropical palms and splashy bougainvillea, greeting each and every guest with warmth and interest, as if each one were a potential friend. She paused at his table and addressed him courteously before taking Ramirez's hand and favoring him with an especially delighted smile. Looking at her, no one would guess that she was anything but what she claimed to be.

Or that she'd spent a good part of the night with Rhys's cock between her thighs.

Good God, he thought, *she's magnificent!* And then corrected himself: *I trained her well.*

She didn't flinch when Frida Kahlo asked her to join her party. Greeting her by saying, "*Mixpantzínco,*" the traditional greeting in the ancient Aztec language of Nahuatl, which meant, literally, "In your august presence." She merely dipped her head a fraction and answered, as he'd taught her, "*Ximopanólti.*" *At your convenience.* But she said it with such dignity that it made Frida's attempt to undermine her seem petty.

Frida, with her braids wrapped tightly about her head, mustache proudly visible, dressed in her conspicuously colorful garb. Peering at the "*princesa*" with a mingling of suspicion—because she, alone, doubted the veracity of their story—and jealousy because her husband had, no doubt, spoken—as Rhys had known the lecherous artist would—of nothing but the princess since meeting her the night before. He made a mental note to watch her. An envious woman could be the broken spoke in his carefully fashioned wheel.

Kate didn't even blink when Frida suggested an outing she'd planned. "Not far from here is a complex of ruins called Teotenango, where the Aztecs once worshipped. I feel certain you will want to walk in the footsteps of your—" an indiscernible pause—"ancestors."

Kate had to know this was a test. But she merely beamed at the scheming woman. "I'd hoped for just such a jaunt. How kind of you to suggest it. But I warn you, I shall be an awful pest. I'm hoping that you'll tell me all you know. The details of our heritage that were passed down through the family are few and vague, I'm afraid. Some words of Nahuatl, some distorted facts and memories . . . I'm embarrassed to admit that you know more about my people than I. But we'll change that, won't we? With your help, if I might count on it." And, turning to Rhys, she said offhandedly, "Aren't we fortunate, Burton, to have the services of one who's so well versed in the history we've come to learn?"

He repressed a smile at that. He'd seen Frida blanch at the word "services," as if she were part of the hotel staff. *Bravo,* he thought, relaxing just a bit. So far, Kate was having no trouble putting this meddlesome woman in her place.

Just after lunch, Frida, the two of them, Gilbert Roland, and a half-dozen of the other hotel guests piled into a small bus and drove out into the hilly countryside. Kate was the picture of the interested tourist as they passed a succession of burros, white-clothed peons working their cornfields, nearly naked children chasing each other in an arroyo. After a half-hour or so, the bus stopped at a tiny village nestled against the base of a steep hill. Kate actually seemed to enjoy the grueling hike up the hillside that had the others wheezing—particularly Frida, who had chronic back problems from an accident suffered as a girl.

When they came to the crest of the hill, they were met by a flight of red stone stairs that would take them up the outer wall of the ancient complex—thirty-one narrow steps up an incline that was nearly ninety degrees. Rhys stared at them in frustration. There was no way he was going to attempt that dizzying climb. And yet, it made him nervous to have Kate and Frida out of his sight. Damn this irritating affliction! Every time he turned around, it slapped him in the face.

Kate glanced from the steps to him, noting his hesitation. "You go ahead," he told her. "I'll stay here."

As the others ascended the stairs, he stayed behind. But momentarily, Gilbert Roland returned to keep him company. "There is not much to see up there," he said. "You were wise to remain here. By the way, I was thinking about the film you are making . . . "

For the next half-hour, as Frida took the others on a tour of the panoramic complex of pyramids and open courtyards above, the actor regaled him with his ideas for the movie that would never be made. Occasionally, Rhys could hear Frida's voice pointing out where the bloody human sacrifices were held, explaining the pantheon of gods the Aztecs worshipped, and dramatically assembling her audience on the very spot where, twenty years after Cortez, the conquistadors had crushed a last stand of Aztec warriors. As she rattled off the litany of historical events, he began to think he'd misjudged the woman's intentions.

Then, later in the afternoon, on the way back to the resort, Frida struck. She told the driver to pull over on the dirt road dissecting the ragtag collection of shacks below the hill that served as a town. "I've saved our special treat for last," she told them in a tone that stiffened Rhys's spine. "The old woman who lives here is the latest in a long line of revered shamans. They say she has remarkable psychic powers. She can read the mind of even the most stubbornly resistant stranger. She can tell you things about yourself that even you don't know. Even in this backwater, she has heard of the discovery of the last Aztec princess. I promised to bring you to her, so that she might—" a momentary pause "welcome you in person."

It was the trap Rhys had been dreading. Instantly alert, he gave a cool but firm smile. "The princess is tired, as we all are. Perhaps another time."

Frida peered at Kate the way one woman looks when sizing up another. "*Are* you too tired, *princesa*?"

Rhys held his breath. It was touchy, but there was no way in hell he was going to allow her to walk through that door. He bored his gaze into Kate's back, willing her to refuse.

But she didn't even glance his way. "I wouldn't miss it for the world," she said as if delighted by the prospect.

Rhys stepped forward and put his hand on her arm with a warning touch. But she just turned and, when no one else could see, gave him a seething glare. After her show of acquiescence all day, it shocked him. He recognized the haughty tilt of her chin. And suddenly he knew what she was doing.

She was going to show him what she was made of.

Panic seized him. With this ridiculous show of pride, this attempt to prove herself to him, she was endangering years of meticulous planning. She could even, given what he knew of Ramirez, be endangering their lives. All this psychic shaman had to do was declare Kate to be an impostor, and, at the very least, it could plant a cancerous seed of doubt in de Guzmán's mind. Rhys knew people with psychic ability existed—his mother had believed in them and taught him to respect the possibility—but for all he knew, this woman could be as much of a phony as he and Kate. Frida may well have arranged with her beforehand to discredit the alleged *princesa*.

All this because Rhys had felt threatened the night before and had made Kate feel inadequate.

He cursed himself and tried to think of a way out. If he raised another objection, it might set off an alarm. He had no choice. He had to risk it. Frantically, he tried to think up some story to undermine whatever this so-called shaman might say. Anything to divert the impending disaster.

The hut was small and dusty. The woman—who must have been a hundred if she was a day—sat before an altar of flowers and Catholic icons, in a veil of incense. Her eyes found Kate at once amidst the small group. Showing her toothless gums, she held her hands outstretched and said, "Come, my child. Let us see if you are really our long-lost daughter, after all."

He had to admire Kate's cool as she stepped forward and took the woman's gnarled hands in her own, bowing respectfully as she said, "It's an honor to meet you, Mother."

The woman's rheumy eyes peered deeply into Kate's for what seemed an eternity as Rhys clenched his teeth, his mind racing. And then he saw the comprehension in the old woman's gaze.

She knows.

The silence was oppressive. Minutes seemed to tick by as Rhys felt his nerves tighten. *Say something,* he willed her. *Give me something to work with.*

She closed her eyes. It seemed to Rhys that there was a perceptible shift in the energy in the room. As if the shaman were listening to something only she could hear. It mesmerized her audience, which stood in rapt attention, awaiting the verdict they sensed was imminent.

Finally she opened her eyes. It seemed in that moment that some unspoken understanding passed between her and Kate. And then—remarkably, unbelievably—she took Kate into her arms. "Welcome home, my daughter."

Rhys watched, stunned. Frida, just as staggered as he, approached slowly, staring at Kate now with shining eyes. "Forgive me," she begged of her. "I doubted you. I am much ashamed."

With an air of authority, the shaman said, "I will speak

with my spiritual daughter in private." As Rhys hesitated, she told him, "You may stay."

They were left alone with the icons and incense. Again, the silence was palpable.

When Kate spoke, her voice was tremulous. She was clearly as shaken as Rhys. "Do you truly have the second sight?"

"I do, my child. A gift, and often, to my dismay, an annoyance."

"Then you know me to be . . ."

"An impostor? Yes."

"Why didn't you expose me?"

The old woman took Kate's hand and squeezed. "Because the guides have told me that, although you are not who you pretend to be, you have been brought here to be of use to Mexico. This is your destiny. And this I respect."

Then she lifted her gaze to meet Rhys's with a look that told him she did, indeed, perceive secrets about him that even he didn't know.

There was no opportunity to talk to Kate after that. When they reached the resort it was time to dress for dinner. They ate by the pool in the warmth of the night, beneath the shimmering stars. Ramirez cornered Rhys, animated because the shaman had given the "princess" her blessing, and word had spread through the premises like wildfire. By morning the whole village of Ixtapan would know, and from there, all of Mexico. He was rubbing his hands together in anticipation of how this would reflect on him.

Rhys tried to listen to his prattle, but he couldn't seem to take his eyes off Kate, dancing with Monolito to the strains of the mariachi band. Wearing the boy's blue ribbon about her throat.

In place of the blue diamonds.

It made him furious. Again he cursed himself. Why should he care? It was what he wanted. Everything hinged on the boy's asking for her hand. She was right to wear his offering. It was good business.

But when the couple wandered off from the crowd and disappeared, he found he could no longer concentrate on the flow of chatter around him. Time dragged, and still they didn't return. The band packed up and left. Guests lingered over nightcaps. And still no sign.

When the last of them had gone to bed, he suddenly remembered her taunting words. *Do you want me to sleep with him?*

Sleep with him . . .

He'd seen the anger in her eyes this afternoon. But how angry *was* she? Enough to carry out her threat?

What difference did it make? Let her. As long as it brought the results he wanted, she could do as she damn well pleased.

So why did the thought of Monolito's hot little hands on her body make him want to smash his fist into the nearest wall?

He went in search of her. To her bungalow, which was dark. To pound on the door, only to be received in silence. Was she in there—with him?

Was she whispering "yes" in his ear with that way she had of making a man feel like a king? Was she kissing him as if she never wanted it to end, moaning helplessly into his mouth? Were her hands on his ass, urging him to fuck her harder until he couldn't bear it any longer and had to explode inside her?

He had to find her.

He searched the grounds. The lobby, which was still and empty, its floors gleaming. The pool which lapped softly as bits of leaves fluttered down from the trees on the breeze. The landscaped pathways beside the man-made stream.

Nothing. No sign of them.

It was almost three o'clock in the morning.

He was fighting back the urge to storm to Monolito's bungalow when he whirled and nearly collided with her. She was a vision in the moonlight that, for some odd reason, seemed to rest on the blue ribbon at her throat. Lifting his gaze, he caught the glisten of some unfathomable triumph in her eyes.

She took his breath away.

"You may congratulate me," she announced.

"Congratulate you?" he asked, hoping she didn't mean what he thought she did.

"On my engagement. Monolito has proposed."

"Oh. That."

"That, indeed. I told him I'd give him my answer in the morning. But I'm going to say yes."

With effort, he recovered his wits. "Naturally. That was the plan."

"The plan? Oh, I see you don't understand."

He frowned at her, feeling thrown off-center by the infuriating breeziness with which she spoke. "*What* don't I understand?" he asked carefully, all his instincts warning him that some unpleasantness was to come.

"I'm going to do it." She walked a few steps past him, then turned and grinned like a child bent on mischief. "I'm actually going to marry him."

Chapter Five

"Marry him!" Rhys exploded. "Like *hell* you will!"

It did Kate's battered heart good to see the fury on his face. She'd known last night that she couldn't go on like this—loving and hating him all at once. Allowing him to toy with her emotions like some bloody puppeteer pulling her strings. She had to end it. And the only way to do so was to get away from him.

But get away to what? What would her life be like once the job was completed and he went on his way? She hadn't wanted to love him—God knows!—but love him she did. She knew she'd never love another man. What was left for her? To return to her old life? To marry some sod who'd be safe as a church but never thrill her the way Rhys did? What kind of escape *was* there for her?

She'd stewed over it all day. It was agony being near Rhys, having to play her role, having to pretend last night's debacle hadn't happened. Throughout the outing, when she'd known she was under Frida's scrutiny, all she could think was *I have to break away from him.* She'd always loved the danger of her life, but being with Rhys was the sort of danger she could no longer afford. He was a jeopardy to her heart, her soul. For the first time in her life, she longed for security. A haven from emotional peril.

But how?

And then, in the midst of near calamity, the shaman had given her an idea. A way of fulfilling the destiny the old woman said was hers, and of finding the refuge she so needed.

She'd simply go ahead and marry the boy.

It didn't hurt that she'd be throwing a wrench into Rhys's plans. So he thought he'd bested her, did he? Not by a long shot!

Looking at him now, she felt a surge of satisfaction. He hadn't even seen this coming!

Who's been conned now?

Silkily, she told him, "Oh, I most certainly *am* going to marry him. You heard that woman today. She said I'm fated to help Mexico. Well, this is how I shall do it."

He was glaring at her incredulously. "By marrying the son of its most detested exploiter?"

"By marrying the son of its wealthiest *caudillo*."

"Don't you understand? Ramirez wants to use you."

"Oh, that's a novelty."

"Are you blind? This man means to be president of Mexico. And the reason he wants his son to marry you is because it will give him the credibility he needs with all those *mestizo* voters who currently hate his guts."

He'd never spelled it out this way before. Naturally, she'd known she was the bait to hook the man's presidential ambitions, but she'd never understood how. This made perfect sense, although it still didn't explain how the plan would work or what Rhys would get out of it. But she didn't care anymore. She was finished.

"Well, then, if he's such a monster, maybe I'll just use my status as his daughter-in-law to influence him when he comes to power."

"A *woman* influence an old-school Latin man? You must be out of your mind."

"Ah, but I'm not just *any* woman, am I? Thanks to you,

I'm an Aztec princess. The progeny of Mexico's cultural heritage—isn't that what you said? I speak for the people, and Ramirez will listen, or I shall use my influence to turn the people against him. You've seen how they look at me, as if I'm some sort of savior. I can't even tell you how it's torn my heart out, knowing I was deceiving them, knowing I'd disappear one day and with me, their one small vestige of hope that someone will care about *them*. It's a despicable scam. But if I marry Monolito—*when* I marry him—I can use my influence to help them. And justify that hope."

"*Now* who's falling for her own con?"

She narrowed her gaze. "I'm not falling for anything. I'm repaying you for every abomination you've inflicted on me. If you're furious, I say, 'Cheers!' I *want* you to squirm. I want you to feel some of what I've felt all these months. I've outsmarted you, Rhys. I've beaten you at your own game. And there's not a ruddy thing you can do about it."

"I've told you," he corrected her automatically. "When you say 'ruddy' it makes you sound like the backstreet urchin you really are."

"And I believe I've just told *you* to go to hell."

His lip curled. "You have a fanciful imagination, but a short memory."

"What is it I'm forgetting? Oh. You must mean that little matter of the detectives you have all ready to cart me off in chains. I think it's you whose memory is failing. We're in Mexico, my fine friend. Now, I may well be just a street urchin, as you so sneeringly infer, but even *I* know what Mexico means. Asylum for fugitives, that sort of thing. Mexico is where people run to escape big, brutish bullies like you. You should have thought of that when you chose this particular location and this particular con. Those English detectives you're so fond of conjuring can't touch me here. And let me assure you of one thing, should you have any doubts—I'm not getting on a plane, a train, a ship, or so much as the back of a *donkey* with you unless you carry me kicking and screaming. And I should imagine my future father-in-law has enough restless thugs lurking in the wings to belay *that* little scenario. So face it, darling. You've lost."

If looks could kill, she'd be dead at his feet. But he was trumped and he knew it. He scraped a hand across his jaw and began to pace up the moonlit path and back again. Suddenly he stopped. "I'll expose you," he said. "I'll tell the boy the truth."

She shrugged. She'd been expecting that. "I'm going to tell him myself. He will, after all, be my husband, and I owe him honesty at least. I shall lay you a wager that he's besotted enough with me to forgive such a minor infraction. He doesn't care a fig if I'm a princess or not."

"And if I tell his father?"

"You can't do that without exposing yourself, which—for some odd reason—I can't think you want to do."

He stared at her, rubbing again at the stubble on his jaw. For a moment, it seemed he couldn't think of a retort. Then, closing his eyes wearily, he said in a more thoughtful, reasonable tone, "Maybe this is my fault. I should have explained this to you earlier." He opened his eyes and looked at her with renewed strength. "Ramirez de Guzmán is one of the vilest human beings who's ever walked this earth. His newspapers tell us he made his fortune in mining and railroads, which is partly true. But the real basis of his wealth is the string of brothels he's maintained along the U.S.-Mexican border for the past twenty years."

"Oh, come now. You can do better than that!"

"And do you know why his whorehouses are so popular? How he's managed to drive out his competition? By staffing them with the youngest, most comely girls in Mexico. And do you know where he gets those girls? Some of them as young as ten or eleven? By kidnapping them or buying them from poor villages all over the country. The man is a flesh-peddler on a scale that has no equal anywhere on this planet."

She felt queasy but managed a withering glance. "You'll have to do better than that. I grew up in Whitechapel, don't forget. I'd scarcely be shocked by the thought of a doxy house."

"Think about it, Kate. As it now stands, this man—who is despised by his countrymen simply because they know him to be a greedy capitalist—doesn't have a chance in hell of being elected president next year. But if his son were to wed the Aztec princess, those millions of downtrodden peons would have to see him in a new light. By marrying his son you'd be giving Satan the pitchfork he needs to bury this country."

She was feeling sicker by the moment. "Oh, you bastard. You *are* good. But you're wasting your breath. Whether Ramirez is or isn't what you say, I don't care. I'm not marrying him. I'm marrying his son."

He nodded. "What if I were to tell you that this Prince Charming of yours isn't quite what you think he is? That you, in fact, are not the love of his life. That part of the reason you were such a great candidate for this job was because of your resemblance to his *real* love?"

"And who might that be?" she taunted, confident enough in her power over Monolito to pity Rhys this paltry attempt.

"Her name was Lupe."

"Oh, you're a marvel, *you* are," she hissed. "You have a name for her and everything."

"She worked in one of your future father-in-law's establishments in Ciudad Juarez. A lovely young thing Ramirez bought from her family. She was eighteen when she met the boy."

"You must really think me an amateur to fall for this cock-and-bull."

"Your precious Monolito was a frequent patron of his

father's fun houses. Discreetly, of course. Until the unfortunate day when he committed the one unpardonable sin for a Latin gentleman of means—he fell in love with a whore."

Despite her best efforts, Kate swayed just a bit on her feet. "I don't believe you."

"He wanted to marry her, you see. You can imagine his father's reaction when he found out. And the speed with which he split up the two lovers. So you're not exactly the love of the boy's life. You're just an acceptable substitute for a whore."

The night was quiet in the aftermath of this declaration. The breeze stirred, rustling the overhead leaves. From the village, the church bell clanged, tolling the hour.

And Kate fought with everything in her to keep from wringing Rhys's sorry neck.

She couldn't let him see her humiliation. *Not again!* So she wracked her brain to think of something—anything—to hurt him.

"Fine," she said at last. "If Monolito spent his youth frequenting brothels, that relieves the one fear I had."

"And what's that?" he growled.

She looked him squarely in the eyes. "At least he'll be good in bed."

Chapter Six

The next morning, she went to the outdoor terrace to meet Monolito for breakfast as planned. Every movement seemed forced and heavy—hardly the spirit of a woman about to tell her suitor she was accepting his hand in marriage. In fact, she'd never felt more depressed in her life.

She realized now that this whole crazy scheme had been an unconscious attempt to force Rhys's hand. How was it possible that she could love him so *desperately* without him harboring some secret feelings for her? She'd thought—complete imbecile that she was—that if she told him she was marrying Monolito, Rhys would realize he really loved her and be forced to declare himself. But he hadn't.

He'd given her nothing.

He hadn't even tried to seduce her out of it.

She felt somewhat soothed when she saw Monolito sitting alone, waiting for her. He looked so innocent and shy and nonthreatening with his Blue Boy bangs falling over his forehead—not at all the man Rhys had described. She tried to picture this boy frequenting his father's whorehouses, and couldn't. Rhys must have lied. He'd fooled her before, and would no doubt make up the worst story he could to try and change her mind. Yes, she decided, she'd give Monolito the benefit of the doubt. She didn't love him, but if she had to go through with this, as her self-respect dictated, at least he wasn't an ogre—or a liar. He was gentle and kind and, perhaps, after all, would make a good friend.

But when she told him she was accepting his proposal, his reaction was pleased but not that of a man passionately in love. He kissed her cheek with brotherly affection and said, "Let us go tell Father. He will be so happy."

As if that was all that mattered.

Ramirez de Guzmán was playing tennis. With his shirt off—his skin richly tanned, his large but muscular body covered with curly white hair—he appeared much more powerful and virile than he had the other times she'd seen him. Noticing them, he volleyed the ball back over the net with a mighty swing and raised his racket to end the play. An attendant handed him a towel which he used to dab the sweat off his bald head as he approached them, saying, "Well, what is it to be, my children?"

"She has accepted me, Father."

"Santa Maria!" Ramirez grabbed her and planted a delighted kiss on her forehead. "This is the day of days! You will be married by Cardinal Villegas himself. Now let me see . . . Friday is *Día de la Raza*. What more auspicious time to announce the engagement than on the day when we celebrate our national heritage? Wednesday morning we will leave for Mexico City. We will stay at my hotel while the arrangements are finalized. And Friday night we will make the announcement before a public gathering in the Zócalo. You have made me a happy man, my children. Tonight, we fiesta!"

Word of the engagement spread throughout the resort. The de Guzmáns and the hotel staff spent the rest of the day arranging the celebration. Kate kept expecting Rhys to make some play—try to seduce her, threaten her . . . something. But she saw no trace of him.

That afternoon while she was sunning herself, waiting for him, Frida Kahlo came up to her with fire in her eyes. "I believed in you. I gave my *heart* to you. And now I learn this vile news. By marrying his son, you are surrendering your legacy to a capitalist bloodsucker who will keep Mexico's proletariat in chains. You have disgraced your ancestors and betrayed us all." With that she spat on the ground and stormed off.

Kate wouldn't have thought it possible, but her spirits sank even lower.

That night, the pool area was decked out with colored lights and *piñatas*. A long table overflowed with regional delicacies and an abundance of champagne. The hotel guests—except for the Diego Rivera party, which had abruptly checked out that afternoon—had been joined by the landed gentry of the surrounding Morales state, who enthusiastically congratulated the couple and kissed the hand of the proud father of the groom.

Rhys was nowhere to be found.

Kate's heart ached. As dusk settled over the party, his absence was soon noted. At one point, Ramirez said to her, "Where is your . . . producer?"

"I'm not sure," she admitted.

"He does not seem to have taken well to your news. Could it be that he is jealous?"

Swallowing a wistful sigh, she said, "I hardly think so."

"Well, *hija,* I still want to see you in a movie that will show you off to your people. But with my resources, we do not really need an inexperienced gringo to make problems for us, do we, now?"

Grimly, she responded, "I suppose not."

But she was only half listening. Where was Rhys? His absence—and his silence—was ominous. She knew he'd do something. He wasn't going to let his cherished plan—whatever it was—go down the drain without some fight. And with the de Guzmán clan leaving the day after tomorrow for Mexico City, he'd have to do it soon.

But what would he do?

After an extravagant toast to the "happy couple," Ramirez took up a mallet and walked over to a *piñata* suspended over a nearby patio. There a crowd of the hotel workers and local villagers waited. Addressing them, he raised his voice and called out, "Here, my *companeros*, witness the generosity of Ramirez de Guzmán."

With that he smashed the papier maché bull, and an avalanche of ten-peso coins clanged on the bricks below. The sight of these poor people fighting each other for such a paltry treasure as the wealthy jeered them on seemed to sicken Monolito as much as it did Kate. He took her by the hand and led her off into the darkness.

They could still hear the merriment, but the voices were muted and distant, and they could feel some of the peace of the surrounding garden. They wandered along the man-made stream beneath the palms until they came to a canopied courting swing. Monolito dropped down onto the seat with an air of embarrassed defeat. Kate waited for the swing to still, then settled herself beside him.

"He is quite something, my father," he mumbled.

She didn't know what to say. In the face of Monolito's misery, Rhys's accusations hovered in her mind. She felt the need to ask about them, but wasn't sure how to begin. "He seems . . . larger than life."

He shrugged but said nothing.

"I've heard . . . stories about him."

"And they are probably true."

"They can't be."

He gave her a bleak look. "Do not be naïve, Maria. This is Mexico, not an English boarding school."

"I'm not naïve, Monolito. I know impressions can be deceiving. But he does seem to care about you."

"He cares about what I can do for him. Or how I might hurt his image. Do not delude yourself, Maria. He is a most ruthless man. There are many bodies strewn on his climb to success."

His tone chilled her. She realized now that there was no way to avoid this. She had to know. "I've heard he owns brothels all along the border. And—"

"He has kidnapped children from poor villages all over Mexico to staff them? It shames me to admit it, but yes, it is true."

So Rhys hadn't lied. "How could you possibly put up with that? Be part of it?"

He sighed. "I am not strong like he is, Maria. I tried to buck him once. But he broke me."

"Was that when you fell in love with Lupe?"

She felt him jerk in surprise. "How did you know about Lupe? *No one* knows about Lupe!"

"Does it matter how I found out?"

He squirmed uncomfortably beside her. "I do not wish to speak of that. It is over and done, and nothing for you to think about."

She put a hand on his sleeve. "Monolito, I know you loved her. I know you wanted to marry her. And I know I'm just a substitute you're marrying because your father wants you to."

"No, Maria, I—"

"I know, Monolito. You like me. You're relieved that the woman your father chose is someone you find pleasing to be with. But I want you to know that if I'm not the love of your life, I can at least be your friend. I'd like to think that you might talk to me about things you can't say to others."

He slumped as if his spine had suddenly collapsed and he had no more will to fight. Fixing his gaze on the ground before him, he admitted with flaming cheeks, "You are right, of course. I did love her. She was a . . . she worked for my father, but she was a saint. You might wonder why I went to such a place. But I was—awkward with women and the girls there required little of me. I did not have to be strong or charming or ambitious . . . all the things my father wanted me to be. But then I met Lupe. And when I was with her, I found that I *was* all those things. I didn't have to try. With her, I was the man I was meant to be. She saw my heart. Her parents had sold her as they would sell a goat, so she understood the hatred I feel for my own father. How we would talk . . . how we would plan! I was going to marry her, to take her away from that foul life. But my father found out. He beat me so hard I thought I would never get up again. He had Lupe sent to an even more brutal brothel that serviced the mines in Zacatecas—"

His voice broke.

"But why didn't you—"

He turned to her. "Because I can't fight him, Maria! I am fortunate that he did not have her killed. And he probably would if I ever tried to see her again. Fighting him is like trying to fight what Mexico is."

"It's not too late, if you really love her."

He put his face in his hands and shook his head. "All my life, my father has told me I should be strong—be a man. But don't you see? In order to do that, I would have to rise up against him. Lupe made me believe that I could do it. But he crushed me completely. And he . . . he hurt my poor Lupe. He claims he wants me to be strong, but he does not. He wants me to be like *him*."

"Maybe you were fighting him in the wrong way—"

But he shot up and cut her off. "Maria, if you want to be my friend, you will never, ever speak of this again. Now, come. We will return to the fiesta, before they send a rescue party to find us."

She followed him, feeling dejected. Everything Rhys had said was true. What was she going to do?

She wished she could ask someone for advice, but the only person she could speak honestly to was Rhys. And he was the last person who could help her.

He didn't make an appearance at the party. When she went to bed around midnight, his window was dark.

Though she scarcely slept, she never heard the sounds of anyone walking down the gravel pathway or entering the bungalow. Had he left? She felt profoundly depressed.

But the next morning, just as the first rays of the sun slanted through her shutters, she heard a soft knock at the door. Without putting on a robe, she went and cracked it open.

It was Rhys.

Unbidden, her heart began to race.

"I'd like you to go somewhere, Kate."

It was so good to see him that she cursed herself. But as she took a moment to control her natural impulses, she began to notice his appearance. He was slightly disheveled and hadn't shaved. There was a gleam in his eyes that she couldn't read, a look she'd never seen before. But when he spoke there was no trace of liquor on his breath.

She had to be careful. He looked so unlike himself and, by now, had to be desperate. "Go where?"

"Away from here. Where we can be alone and talk."

When he said it, he seemed so different that she felt disconcerted. There was nothing arrogant or dictatorial in his attitude now. Only a quiet composure, as if he'd been through some crisis of the soul and had come out the other side.

"All right," she said guardedly. "Give me a few moments to dress."

He was waiting for her in the hotel driveway, where he'd arranged to rent an immaculate maroon '31 Cord. She settled herself in the car and he drove off through the streets of town and out into the countryside. The sun cast a vibrant orange glow over the hills, giving the day a promise of freshness that contrasted sharply with his mood. He drove silently, with no pretense of small talk, navigating the winding road with that same concentrated calm. So calm that she felt a stab of alarm.

Maybe his mood didn't reflect a crisis of the soul at all.

Perhaps he'd simply reached a decision he was determined to carry through. Her mind began to cast about as the questions she should have asked earlier surfaced in the eerie stillness. Where was he taking her? What did he intend to do? What were the possibilities? He could kidnap her, to keep her from going through with the marriage—which wouldn't be so bad. Or . . . he could be planning to do away with her. She didn't, after all, know him very well. She didn't know what he was really capable of doing to preserve his scheme. He could kill her and have it blamed on Ramirez.

Or . . . he could do what he'd always done to bend her to his will—seduce her. Or, in these circumstances, force himself on her.

Was it a mistake to come with him?

Finally, in a bowl surrounded by mountains, he pulled over to the side of the road, switched off the engine, set the handbrake, and turned to her. "We're here."

"Where?"

"The Cacahuamilpa cave. It's a cavern that runs two miles beneath the mountains. Diego Rivera told me about it. It was supposed to be sacred to the Aztecs."

A two-mile-long cave. The perfect place to hide a body. "Why do you want to go in here?"

"It's the most private place I could think of."

She swallowed hard.

It was hot now, and still bright despite the gathering clouds, but when they climbed down the long series of crude stone steps into the cave, they were suddenly submerged in cool darkness. A darkness rife with danger, and yet . . . undeniably exciting, exhilarating, deeply sensual at the same time.

Rhys turned on a flashlight he'd brought along, and all at once a scene of absolute splendor was revealed. She'd never been in a cave before, and had no idea what to expect. But this cavern was so expansive, so massive, so majestic, that being there was like entering Saint Paul's Cathedral in the hush of dawn.

As if drawn by its beauty, they began to walk, their breathing audible in the silence. They came to a huge formation, and as Rhys scanned the light over its towering height, she found it supremely phallic, rising like a mighty erection. She waited for him to comment on the obvious analogy, but he said nothing. Just lowered the light and moved on.

They passed a succession of natural formations that looked as if some pre-Columbian sculptor had carved them from the native rock. Sauntering deeper into the widely winding tunnel, so deep they could no longer see the light of the entrance. Kate listened with taut nerves to the sound of his footsteps as she waited for Rhys to make his move.

Finally he stopped. He shone the light on a flat, elevated area and said, "Let's sit here."

Once she had, he turned off the flashlight and they were consumed by utter blackness, as if they'd been swallowed by a whale. A blackness that wasn't possible in London. A blackness that suddenly frightened her, so she reached over and instinctively touched his arm, wanting some human contact.

"I realize it's crazy to come here," he said, his voice rich and resonant in the darkness, but strangely monotonic, "but it's not going to be easy for me to say this, and I don't want to see your face when I tell you."

"Tell me what?"

He hesitated a moment, then asked, "Does the name Mace Archer mean anything to you?"

She blinked. "No. Why?"

"If you'd lived in America, it might. Mace Archer was the owner-publisher of the *New York Globe*. His wife was his equal partner in running the paper. They were one of the glamour couples of Manhattan society. Mad about each other. Their newspaper made its name championing the cause of the underdog, the people instead of the robber barons."

Forcing herself to concentrate, wondering where this was heading, she mumbled, "And . . . ?"

"They were my parents."

She glanced toward him in the darkness, truly startled. He'd never before told her anything about his past. "Then your last name is really Archer?"

"Or so I thought."

"You—thought?"

He ignored the question. "I grew up privileged—social standing, the best education at the best schools. I worshipped my father and wanted nothing more than to follow in his footsteps as a crusading newspaperman."

She couldn't believe what she was hearing. She'd expected something dire, and instead he was opening himself up with a totality she wouldn't have thought possible from him. It was baffling. What journey had taken him from that golden background to this pitch-dark cave in the middle of Mexico? And why was he telling her this? Why now? "Go on," she prompted cautiously.

"Let me ask you something else. Have you ever heard of the names Blackwood and Sherwin?"

Blackwood and Sherwin! They were only the two most famous names in the annals of English con-artistry. Tolly had put her to bed with stories of the exploits of the two notorious clans. "Of course I've heard of them. But what do they have to do with—"

"Those were my parents' real names. My father was Mace Blackwood, and my mother was Saranda Sherwin."

"You're jesting, surely!"

"I'm perfectly serious."

She reached for the flashlight, too startled to tolerate the dark any longer. But his hand stopped hers. "Please don't," he requested softly.

She barely noticed. "Rhys, do you realize what you're saying?" she cried excitedly. "Mace Blackwood and Saranda Sherwin were the last of two dynasties of the most celebrated English pickpockets, thieves, and masters of the con who ever lived! Two families that had been in competition—not to mention that they hated one another—for three hundred years. But you say they were your parents?"

"Yes. They went to America, where they butted heads, took turns besting each other, and finally fell in love."

"Blimey! It's like Romeo and Juliet. And they went *straight*?"

"More or less. They assumed new names, faked entree into the upper crust, finagled their way into owning the newspaper, and used their unique skills for the cause of good. So you could say they reformed. But of course they never told anyone."

"Did you know?"

"Not until the end."

"The end? What do you mean?"

He took a breath. "Three years ago, they threw the entire weight of their newspaper behind a crusade to bring down the most evil man in this hemisphere—Ramirez de Guzmán. But in their zeal to nail him, they did something they'd never done before—they underestimated their enemy. You see, de Guzmán had connections of his own, and he used them to ferret out the secret of my parents' background. This he promptly supplied to their competitors on Park Row, which created a huge and embarrassing scandal. 'Archers Revealed as Scions of Criminal Cockney Dynasties.' That sort of thing."

"And that's when you found out about them?"

"Yes. To a spoiled boy who'd grown up thinking of himself as a member of the New York Four Hundred, it was quite a blow. Not just because of who they really were, but because they'd lied to me all my life. I didn't know who I was anymore. It was as if someone had ripped the rug out from under me. Nothing was as I believed it to be. Our lives—my life—was a fraud. The only thing I knew for sure was that my parents were criminals. I felt utterly humiliated. I went to my mother for some kind of explanation that would make some sense. But she wasn't a bit contrite. She was *proud* of their background. Said they were just doing what they'd always done—only in a different guise and for a higher purpose. 'Life is a con, Rhys,' she told me in an East End accent I'd never heard before."

"She was right to be proud," Kate told him. "The Blackwoods and Sherwins were the best of the best. They were what all the rest of us dreamt of being."

"I didn't see it that way at the time. In fact, I didn't take the news at all well. I whaled into her unmercifully. For some reason I didn't hold my father half as responsible. But the idea of my precious mother being the daughter of a line of Cheapside pickpockets was unbearable. I'm ashamed to tell it now, but I was . . . extremely cruel to her. It was the last conversation we ever had. That same night, they decided to fly to our summer home in the Adirondacks to collect themselves and figure out a strategy to deal with the scandal. My father was piloting the plane. Just minutes after takeoff, it went down over the Hudson River. They were both killed instantly."

She found his hand. "I'm so sorry. To lose them that way, without ever having the chance to reconcile . . ."

He withdrew his hand and continued speaking in the same unemotional tone. "In my grief, the only thing I could think of was that the man responsible for their deaths was Ramirez de Guzmán. Scandal or no, I had inherited a perfectly good newspaper. My first impulse was to keep up the journalistic campaign against him. Then, gradually, another idea began to take shape. What if I brought this man down in the manner and tradition which he'd exposed? What if I destroyed him by conning him like the Sherwin-Blackwood descendant I was? Wouldn't *that* be poetic justice?"

"So instead of rejecting your roots, you decided to embrace them."

"Yes. I went to London. Went to their old haunts, talked to their old colleagues in crime. Read books and magazine articles. Became engrossed by their exploits. By the imagination and creativity of their operations. And gradually I got my idea for the con of cons. I would dangle before this man's greedy eyes a means of neutralizing the hatred his countrymen feel for him—a public relations coup that would give him the presidency of Mexico. And for this, I needed a very special woman."

"Me."

"You. I used you. I molded you to my purposes. I seduced you to try and control you. But what I didn't realize was that I was falling in love with you."

She froze. It seemed to her in that moment that all of the hushed cavern—the tunnel, the stalactites, the monolithic structures—resounded with the echo of his words. *He loved her.*

Before she could react, he continued speaking in that soft, steady, oddly lifeless voice. "And I couldn't face that, you see, because despite my resolution to come to terms with my family's past, the truth was, I couldn't accept what my mother really was. I was just too much the pampered New York aristocrat for that. I was too . . . small."

"And I reminded you of your mother," she said, beginning to understand things for the first time. "In a way, we were like the same person." She thought back over the last few days, this new realization making sense of his actions. "And the blue diamonds . . . they really *were* your mother's?"

"Yes. I see now that's why I was so cruel to you. I was still rejecting my mother, and trying to reject you, too. But I also see just how demented this whole enterprise happens to be. I can blame Ramirez for being a procurer of children, but I can't blame him for my parents' deaths. I'm as responsible as he is. And the truth is, no one is really to blame. It was an act of God. So I'm giving it up. And I want you to know that I'll back you in what you're doing. The fact is, someday Monolito will inherit everything his father owns. And who better than you to be in a position to influence what happens to that empire?"

Through the darkness, she stared his way in horror and disbelief. What was he saying? He loved her—that was shock enough. But that he loved her and was *giving her up?* Giving her his blessing to go ahead and marry the boy?

It wasn't supposed to be like this! He should be taking her in his arms, kissing her madly, making wild, possessive love to her, and telling her over and over: *I love you. I love you.* Lovingly. Joyfully. In celebration.

When he turned on the flashlight, she looked at him. The dear, beloved face, his vulnerability palpable but cloaked in a quiet dignity. "Rhys, what if I told you . . ." she began.

But he cut her off with a raised hand that was more entreaty than command. "Please," he said wearily. "Don't say anything. I didn't make this decision lightly, but I've made it and it's given me peace. I know now that everything I've done since learning the truth about my parents has been the act of a selfish child. I just wanted my revenge, and I didn't care who I hurt in the process. But that's over now. I've turned the corner. And I won't go back."

Kate was so horrified, she couldn't speak. She could see that he meant every word he'd said. He'd found his peace in the noble, unselfish act of sacrificing himself for her.

But what he was really doing was throwing her to the dogs.

Chapter Seven

Kate was numb with shock on the drive back to Ixtapan, Several times she tried to say something, but couldn't find the words to express her jumbled feelings. In her wildest imagination, she couldn't have dreamt what would transpire in that massive cave. It changed everything, yet it changed nothing.

Through her lashes, she watched Rhys at the wheel. He drove fast, but not hurriedly, maneuvering the hairpin curves with a quiet assurance and determination that reflected his new inner peace. He'd made his decision and had moved on. He was already gone.

In what seemed but an instant, they pulled into the long drive of the resort. After the strained silence, it was a relief. All she wanted was to retreat to her bungalow and be alone. To think. To sort things out. To decide what to do. But when she stepped from the car, she was immediately surrounded by people: the hotel manager, some of the staff, and various lackeys of the de Guzmán family. Where had she been? There were a million things for her to do. A designer had come from Mexico City to measure her for a wedding gown. Arrangements for Friday's announcement had to be finalized. A delegation of politicians and industrialists was coming in for a special cocktail party that evening, for which they wanted her to look particularly stunning. The rising Mexican photographer Gabriel Figueroa had been commissioned to shoot the engagement photograph and was waiting with his equipment by the pool, feeling anxious because grey clouds were rapidly moving in, and there was a threat of rain in the air.

Somehow, in the midst of all this bedlam, Rhys disappeared.

For the next several hours, Kate was led from one thing to another, barely conscious of what was going on around her because her mind was in a daze. Frantic plans for a wedding that now wouldn't—*couldn't*—take place. All she could think of was: *I've got to go to Rhys. I can't let it end like this. I've got to get him back.*

But how?

Tell him she loved him? Determined as he was, would he believe her? Would he even listen? The peace she'd sensed in him was so profound that she was going to have to fight him in order to rip him out of it. To make him understand—no, feel—that their physical and emotional union was more important, more powerful, more essential than any other consideration . . .

But there was no time. They'd be leaving for Mexico City—to announce this nightmarish engagement—early in the morning. If she was going to extricate herself from this mess she'd created, it would have to be today. The time was passing too quickly. She could almost feel the ticking of the clock inside her head.

Suddenly she felt a hand on her shoulder and started. It was only Monolito. He'd been watching her keenly. Now, his eyes softened and she saw in them a compassion, a comprehension, that gave her the eerie feeling he was reading her mind.

"Go, Maria," he told her softly. "Do what you must. I will try to buy you a couple of hours."

She stared at him, wondering how much he knew—or

had guessed. But the look he gave her was so supportive, so uncannily understanding, that she could have cried. He deserved more than a wife who didn't love him. And it seemed, as he gazed at her, that he was giving her permission to do what she *had* to do.

With a trembling hand she touched his cheek. "Thank you, sweet brother Mono."

Two hours to determine the course of her life. Two hours to change the mind of a strong man set on being a martyr. Two hours to salvage three lives.

She hurried to the lobby and wrote a hasty note, which she gave to a bellboy with instructions to deliver it to Rhys's hand. "Check his room," she told him. "If he's not there, find him."

Then she set out along the deserted back road and began to climb the dirt path into the hills. She still wasn't accustomed to Ixtapan's altitude, so it wasn't long before she was puffing, her lungs burning from the effort of the steep climb. But she persevered, telling herself it was worth it. Telling herself it was her only chance. Her only hope.

The trail took her through the woods, higher, higher. The clouds that had been gathering all afternoon were black now, shot through with grey, and the hills throbbed with the threat of rain. The air was warm but heavy, oppressive, so thick it seemed she was breathing moisture into her lungs. As she trudged on, still climbing, still panting, a raindrop splashed on her cheek. But still she walked, willing herself not to think. Not to put words to the fear gathering inside.

If it rained, he wouldn't come.

The path wound higher still until at last she came out onto the precipice. It was a flat mesa, stretching out toward the horizon. Close to the crest was a large, rocky pool of the hot mineral waters that had made the region a resort destination from the time of the Aztecs.

Standing at the edge of the jutting crag, high above the world, she could almost feel like the native princess she'd been pretending to be. The valley fell before her, wooded and hilly, cloaking its secret caves and streams. Across the vast distance, the mountains loomed, mantled now by the ominous, dark clouds. No town was visible, no trace that humans inhabited this vast and empty land. As she looked out at the savage beauty of it, a crack of thunder echoed through the basin like the roar of drums, entreating ancient gods. And then a fork of lightning split the sky, followed by another and another, crackling and sparking through the dense cloud cover as if Tlaloc himself, Aztec god of rain, was hurling from the hereafter proof of his displeasure. The sky seemed to open, and the rain fell.

It drenched her in seconds, cooling her sweat-sheened body, washing her clean. But as she felt her clothes cling to her skin, her heart grew heavy. He'd have to be crazy to come out in this.

As crazy as she.

But then, the rain was just a handy excuse. Would he have come without it? Or had he closed himself off from her so completely that he wouldn't even allow her one last try?

She closed her eyes and offered up a prayer. Appealing to the spirit of the land to help her. To Tlaloc. Or better yet, to Xochiquétzal, goddess of love and flowers, who'd brought ardent suitors to eager Aztec maidens.

Bring him to me. Please give me this chance.

As if in answer, a boom of thunder shook the earth. A moment later, lightning streaked and flared, traversing the great length of the sky, coming so close that she could feel the electric charge in her veins. She was frightened suddenly, all alone—so alone—in this alien realm where nature's fury pummeled her like angry fists, the height of the overhang towering above the verdant valley where safety and comfort seemed too distant to reach. Alone and desperate, and suddenly not knowing where to turn.

A monumental fool.

The storm raged around her, through her, as she stood paralyzed atop a world gone mad, her clothes heavy and cloying, her sodden hair torn free from its pins in the rising wind, lashing her face like whips. She tried to gear herself to return the way she'd come. To trek back down the track—muddy now—and slink into her bungalow in defeat. But she couldn't bring herself to move. Her mind took on the rhythm of the thunder, persistent, booming through her, asking over and over: what then?

What then?

She had to go. The gale was howling now, threatening to sweep her off the ledge. Perhaps it would be best. To float to the ground far below on the hot exhalation of the wind. No more hopelessness. Sweet surrender. The ultimate escape.

Once more, she closed her eyes. She felt the drowsiness come over her. Felt herself sway seductively in the storm. Blotting out the chaos all around her. Retreating into her own cocoon.

And then, so suddenly that it startled her, she felt someone grab her from behind. Felt strong hands press into her arms as she was yanked around. Felt those same hands shake her as the voice roared over the thunder, "What the hell are you doing?"

Her eyes flew open and she saw him standing there, shaking her as if to shake some sense into her. Looming above her so that she no longer felt precipitously high. Bringing back a sense of proportion. Bringing her back to earth.

She looked at him the way she would gaze at something she'd already lost and never again hoped to see. Soaked to the skin, his black hair plastered around his fine head. The white shirt molded to his chest so it took on its rugged form. The alarm in his cobalt eyes. But even as his distress registered, she noticed, too, that the lashes of those compelling eyes were damp with tiny droplets of rain, as if sprinkled with the dust of diamonds.

"What do you think you're doing?" he asked again, his words finally penetrating the numbness of her mind.

"I don't know," she called over the wind. "Maybe I don't want to live without you."

She saw the change in his eyes. The quest to understand her meaning. Then the sharp suspicion. Thinking she'd called him here—in all of this—to toy with him once again. One last scam, perhaps.

Having no idea how fervently she'd meant it.

His hands dropped from her. "Do you know what it took for me to tell you what I did today?"

"Yes," she breathed.

"And you can still do this? Don't you know what you're doing to me? Don't you care?"

Again the thunder roared and with it came the lightning, casting a brief glow upon his ravaged face. But suddenly, the elements that had frightened and lulled her seemed to fuel her, energize her, to spark a rage she wouldn't have thought possible a moment before. The wind whipped her hair across her face, but it was the wind that powered her now. The lightning that made her eyes gleam. The thunder that flowed through her and came out as her voice.

With her hands to his chest, she shoved him back. "What I'm doing to *you*? What about what you've done to *me*? What about the pain I've felt every minute of every bloody day that I've been with you? Loving you with all my heart and soul, while you let me think you didn't love me! Telling myself what an imbecile I was to love a man who thought of me as nothing more than a pawn. Wanting you desperately, but not *wanting* to want you. And all that time . . . all those months while I was torturing myself . . . you loved me, too."

He stood stock still, staring at her, letting the driving rain drench him. She'd never seen a more shocked expression on a man's face.

She pressed on, too angry now to stop. All of her repressed fury and frustration tumbling like the rain. "And now, after finally making your precious confession, you want to give me up like some magnanimous sacrifice on the altar of your nobility. You think you've grown because you've reached this grand and righteous decision that allows you to cast me aside for the sake of all you've learned. But let me tell you something about your self-imposed martyrdom. If you'd really grown, you'd know that we were brought together for a reason. That the love we've found is more important than anything. That nothing on this earth matters if you push me away. And if you don't know that, you're as stunted as you ever were."

His mouth moved several times before any words would come. But finally, he croaked, "I thought you wanted—"

"To marry Monolito? You blithering idiot! I *never* wanted to marry him. I just wanted you to tell me I couldn't. I wanted you to move heaven and earth before you'd allow me to belong to another man." She gasped for breath, then told him, "Well, I *won't* marry him. Even if you leave me, even if I never see you again, I won't do it. My only pain was in thinking you didn't love me. And now that I know you do, I could strangle you for what you want to—"

He didn't let her finish. He closed the distance between them with a lunge and crushed her to his chest. Molding her body to him as if he'd never let her go. Clutching her in powerful arms as his lips sought hers and he kissed her as if seizing from her mouth the very breath of life.

And then he was grasping her head with desperate hands, murmuring in her ear the words she'd so longed to hear. "I *won't* let you go. I can't. No matter what I have to do . . . You belong to me. Do you hear me?"

"And sacrifice be damned?"

"And sacrifice be damned."

All the anger drained from Kate. With a heartfelt cry, she leapt into his arms. They kissed again in a fever of passion, all the bottled-up emotions tumbling free. Wanting life and love with an intensity that made them soar. Ripping at their clothes as they kissed, lips locked, as one by one their garments were tossed aside in a soggy heap. And when they were naked at last, he pulled her to him so he could feel her tender flesh pressed against every rigid part of him and stroked her with the hands of a man so long starved that no amount of touching her could fill his void.

As he did, she felt the world around her shift. No longer was she lost and alone. She felt safe in his virile embrace, cherished and adored. Comforted as no substitute haven could, yet greedily aroused. Shimmering in the warmth of his love, in the anticipation of adoring him openly, freely, without restraint or pretense. Caressing him now with the knowledge that he was hers to touch and hold.

Hers.

She'd lost all track of her surroundings. Of the tempest raging around them, of the wind and rain. But just as she was pressing herself closer, longing to have him buried deep inside, longing to be truly one with him, the lightning blazed again and he lifted his head and watched it streak across the sky.

She read his thoughts as clearly as if he'd spoken them aloud. And as the thunder shook the ground beneath them, she wailed, "We can't stop now!"

He peered at her keenly, dripping in the shower of rain, her breasts, her hips softly curved yet gleaming like glass. And all at once he grinned. A titanic, wolfish, devilishly handsome grin that split his face as he glanced again at the thunderous firmament and roared to it, "You're right, by God. The storm be damned, too."

She realized with a shock that he was happy. That it was she who'd made him so. And on the heels of that monumental revelation, she felt her own happiness fill her heart and overflow. And then they were laughing into the wind, laughing as only those reborn to the glory of life could. Laughing because the storms that had sought to divide them had dwindled, and they were left standing. Together.

In a burst of playfulness, Rhys scooped her up and held her in his arms. And then he turned with her in a great, wide circle, round and round like a spinning top, shouting laughter to the skies as she kicked her feet and squealed in delight.

They turned and turned, the two of them above the world and all its petty trials, in the midst of the receding wind and rain and the lightning that now seemed like fireworks of celebration, just for them. But soon he slowed until at last he stood still, gazing down into her eyes with such tenderness and appreciation that the laughter left her. Softly, he said, "The whole world be damned. You're all I need."

Her heart skipped erratically. She noticed then how warm the rain was. It seemed now not a driving force of destruction, but a welcoming, cleansing, baptizing cascade. Washing away the painful past. Making way for a fresh new world, full of infinite possibilities. Full of love and hope.

He carried her across the expanse of ground and walked with her into the pool. Held in his arms, she felt the warm, silky water envelop them. And as the lightning crackled above them, he kissed her. Deeply, passionately, with all of his soul, giving himself to her absolutely. Beyond superstitious warnings. Tempting the fates, afraid of nothing now. If the lightning would strike, let it do its worst.

Nothing mattered but this.

She slid down his body so she was standing before him in the waist-high pond. But as she reached to wrap her arms about his neck, he caught her wrists in his hands and stood looking at her as if seeing her for the first time. As if his eyes couldn't drink in enough of the sight of her. Pinning her eyes with his, he ground out, "I must have been insane to think I could ever live without you."

Slowly, he turned her so her back came up against the edge of the pool. Equally slowly, his gaze still locked with hers, he bent her backward so she was draped across the bank. Moving with masterful deliberation, holding her gaze as if commanding her to feel the power of the moment. Transferring both wrists to one hand and pressing them back over her head to anchor them to the ground so she was laid out helplessly before him, hands fastened, breasts prominently displayed. He never took his gaze from hers as he leaned into her. As his free hand caressed her in a sensuous trail along her cheek, her throat, her breasts. Pinching the nipples just enough to arouse the need for more. Moving lower with delicious skill, over her ribcage, the gentle mound of her belly, the swell of her hips. Touching tender places that were so unexpectedly erotic, it made her gasp: the junction of her buttocks and thighs, the inner crack of her ass. Ambling his fingers in a circle around her cunt, close enough to elicit shivers, to heighten her anticipation, to deepen her breathing in her out-thrust breast. Watching her eyes mist over as her breath grew wispy and her mouth fell unashamedly open, loose and quivering. Watching her need escalate in the fierce penetration of those eyes. Driving her mad as she tried to will his fingers closer . . . closer . . .

"You're mine, Kate," he told her. "I'll never let you go again."

And then he leaned into her and kissed her. But even as he did, he kept his eyes open. Watching. *Watching* . . . And because she felt his power now—as powerful as any god of lightning—she, too, kept her gaze on his. Clinging to him with her eyes because the rest of her was pinned and couldn't move into him as she wished. Noting the pleasure in his eyes as his fingers finally found her clit and she gasped into his mouth. His hand tightening on her wrists as she sought to move them, imprisoning them as his fingers began to fuck her. Slipping inside her, moving, thrusting, as his thumb worked her clit. Angling them with astonishing confidence as he found all the hidden spots that opened her to lust and made her arch up into his hand. Driving her to climax now at his own pace, controlling it, watching his effect on her as if savoring every liquid movement of her body, every mewling sound escaping her throat.

And even as instinct compelled her eyes to close, she found she couldn't do it. She wasn't capable of wrenching her gaze from his. But soon, as her body ached and soared and screamed for release, she began to lose herself in his eyes. She began to see not just him, but *into* him. The Rhys no one else had ever seen. She felt herself meld into him in a way she never had before. As if their physical cloaks were stripped away and they glimpsed the beauty of each other's soul.

She came just so, her wrists pinned back by his gripping hand, her lips on his as his fingers in her drove her like a stampede. Her eyes never flinching from his gaze. Their bodies, their minds, their spirits joined completely.

It was the most intimate experience she'd ever known.

And when it was over, he let her go and they clung to one another for one long pause in time. She kissing his shoulder, he stroking her hair. Basking in the lovely warmth of having braved their own vulnerable fears and giving themselves to one another as fully as it was possible to give.

Then, wanting more, he lifted her hips in his hands so she floated down onto his rigid standing cock. Her moist chasm closing on him in blissful spasms, she rode him weightlessly in the water as he thrust mightily into her, holding him close, feeling her emotion peak until it was spilling from her as she gasped with each thrust, "I love you, Rhys . . . I love you . . . I love you . . ."

Until even the thunder seemed to echo it through the canopy of heaven.

Chapter Eight

She wanted to stay in his arms forever, floating in the steaming pool, feeling the warm shower bond and seclude them. But as the rain began to lighten, she remembered the world they'd left behind, and the things still left to do.

She took his fine head between her hands and smoothed back the riot of dripping black curls. He was still gazing at her wondrously, as if even now he couldn't believe the way his life had altered in such a short span of time. She hated to spoil the mood, but time was running out and she knew she must.

"Listen to me, dearest," she told him earnestly. "I'm going to go back and take up where we left off. We're going through with this. I won't marry Monolito, of course, but you're going to have your revenge. We shall make Ramirez pay for what he did to your parents. And to you."

But he was already shaking his head. "We can't."

"Whyever not?"

"Don't you see? The final step in my plan was to expose you to the world. I have a letter ready to go to Luis Valderez of the *Mexico City Gazette*, telling him you're an impostor—with a long history as a shamster. The morning after Ramirez announced the engagement, Valderez was to break the story, making it appear that de Guzmán was the one trying to pass you off as the Aztec princess. Effectively ruining his chances forever. It seemed like the perfect plan at the time. I told myself you were nothing more than a con woman who deserved to be exposed. But I hadn't counted on loving you. I can't do it now."

She chuckled affectionately and caressed his face. "Darling, I don't give a hang if you expose me. It was a brilliant plan, and it will still work. Once Ramirez is finished, we can find a way to explain why I went through with it. We shall say I was doing it to bring him down. I shall be quite the heroine. I'd fancy that."

"No. You might go to prison. Ramirez might kill you, for all I know. I can't take the risk. I won't. Nothing matters to me now but you. I won't consider endangering you for any reason."

"It's no more of a risk now than it ever was. Your parents began to right a monumental wrong, and you need to finish it."

He took her hands from his face and held them tightly to emphasize his words. "No, Kate, I don't. That's the past. I meant it when I said I've let it go. All I want now is to start over. With you."

She kissed his hand. "You may feel that way now. But what about a year from now? Five years from now? Ten? It will eat you up inside. What if Ramirez *does* become president? You'll read about his atrocities and know you could have stopped him and didn't. And every time you look at me, you'll remember that I was the one who kept you from it. You'll hate me for it."

"You're wrong. I've learned that all I really need is you. Don't you understand, Kate? Ever since I found out my life had been a grand lie, I was drifting . . . searching for the place where I belonged in this world. I thought ruining Ramirez would give me those answers. But it won't. It's an empty ambition. This plan did have a purpose, though. You said it yourself. It led me to you. My place is with *you*. Not in vanquishing political dictators. Once you start doing that, there's no end. I have to stop it now. I have to get you safely out of this mess and out of this country."

His face was set in resolution. Softly she asked, "What about that little boy who wanted to follow in his father's footsteps? The one who wanted to use the newspaper to expose the evils in this world?"

"My father was a fraud."

"Maybe. But he still used his newspaper to do good. What difference did it make if his name was Archer or Blackwood? Think of it, Rhys. You come from grifter royalty, and I've been trained by you, the Blackwood crown prince. Together we can find a way to beat Ramirez *and* get out of here in one piece. I know we can!"

His eyes flashed as he stared at her. "Now, you listen to me, Kate. I won't do it. You don't know de Guzmán the way I do. You don't know what he's capable of if things go wrong. I won't let you do it, and that's final."

She sighed, churning now with frustration. She was touched by his concern for her, but she couldn't help feeling there had to be a way. "What do you want to do, then?"

"Leave. Sneak out of here as soon as we can safely get away. Tonight. I'll make all the arrangements. You go through with the party as planned. Behave naturally, as if you're delighted by the upcoming trip to Mexico City. Be charming. Stay until the end. Don't let them suspect that you're eager to get away. When it's over, go to your bungalow and change clothes. Don't pack. We'll leave everything here. I'll have a car waiting for us. Can you do that?"

"Yes, of course. But there's one thing. I have to tell Monolito something. I have to tell him I'm leaving and why."

"Oh, no, you don't."

"Rhys, I can't just leave him like this without a word. He's a good man. We can trust him with our secret."

He bolted up. "That's crazy. You don't know that you

can trust him. He's a Latin man, and his ego is going to be shattered because you don't want to marry him. We're going to have a hell of a time getting out of here safely as it is—"

She interrupted, "Mono has been a friend to me, and I trust him. You just gave me an ultimatum about leaving, and I accepted it. Now you have to accept my judgment about this."

He studied her determined face for several moments. Finally, he acquiesced. "All right. I'll trust your judgment." But he couldn't help adding under his breath, "I just hope you're right."

Knowing the chance she was taking, Kate thought, *So do I.*

The evening seemed endless to Rhys. After a brief appearance at the cocktail party, he returned to his bungalow, using the time alone to concoct an escape plan. Kate, the center of attention, would remain at the party, looking for an opportunity to have her private conversation with Monolito.

Monolito!

He couldn't believe he'd gone along with this. It seemed utter insanity. It went against all his survival instincts. But he was stuck. He had to do what he'd promised. He had to trust her judgment. She knew Monolito better than Rhys did, and her ability to read people was astute. She was the best there was at this sort of thing. That was integral to the art of the con.

Still . . . to go out of your way to divulge your plans to the son of your enemy . . . What could be more natural than for the son to tell his father that they'd both been had? Even though they didn't get along, family was everything in this country.

He tried to push it from his mind. Even without the specter of such a betrayal, their escape was bound to be a dicey affair. Ramirez had announced a six o'clock departure the next morning for the caravan of cars leaving for the city, which didn't leave them much time. It was bound to be after midnight before he and Kate could get away. He'd arranged to have a rented car waiting for them just outside the gate, but which way to go? It wouldn't take much more than two hours to get to the Mexico City railway station, but there was no telling how long they'd have to wait for a train heading north. Once they were on board, it would be relatively easy for the powerful de Guzmán to intercept them at any stop along the seven-hour journey to the U.S. border. The other obvious alternative was to make for the port of Vera Cruz and hop onto a passenger ship. But Vera Cruz was over two hundred meandering miles away along potholed roads, and Ramirez, learning of their escape at dawn, would no doubt think to call ahead and have them detained by the port authorities.

No, their only chance would be to make for the tiny Cuernavaca air field with hopes of hiring—or stealing—a light plane. His father had made him learn to fly, hoping to offset his fear of heights. He'd learned, but every moment in the air was agony, and it had done nothing to alleviate his vertigo. Still, in this case, he'd have to do it. With a fuel stop at San Luis Potosi, and another at Monterrey or Saltillo, they could make Texas before Ramirez could fully comprehend what had happened. It gave him a chill, thinking of being in a plane again, but it was the only way. De Guzmán knew of Rhys's hatred of heights and would never expect such a move.

The hours dragged on until it was well past midnight. Sitting alone in his room was driving him crazy. Where was Kate? What was taking so long?

Could something have gone wrong with Monolito? Christ, don't think about that!

Suddenly he heard the sound of footsteps coming his way along the path outside. Then a soft rap at the door. He opened it, and she ran into his arms.

"I'm sorry to be so late. They were determined to drink a hundred toasts in our honor."

He held her tight, inhaling the scent of her freshly washed hair. "You told the boy?"

"I told him."

"And . . . ?"

"It's going to be fine. He'll help us."

Rhys wasn't convinced, but he said nothing. "All right, then. We'll wait a while, then go."

He turned out the light, and they sat on the bed, holding each other, not speaking, for a half-hour as the compound grew still. Finally, Rhys said, "Okay, let's go."

As he was about to open the door, Kate put a detaining hand on his arm. When he looked at her questioningly, she smiled. "Whatever happens, dearest, I want you to know that I love you."

He bent and gave her a quick kiss. "Tell me again in Texas."

He closed the door quietly behind them, and they walked stealthily down the path, pausing momentarily behind a hedge by the pool while one of the yard boys finished his smoke and returned leisurely to the main building. From there they sneaked past the lobby, up the main drive, and out the gate. There, waiting for them, was the car . . . and, just maybe, freedom.

But as he reached for the door handle, they were suddenly caught in a crossfire blaze of car headlights. Blinded, Rhys spun around to make out the silhouetted forms of a half-dozen men moving in on them. Several rifles pointed at them. Then the detested voice of Ramirez de Guzmán taunted from the shadows.

"So, my friends . . . taking a little midnight drive, are we?"

Raising his hand to block the glare of the headlights, Rhys could see Monolito standing beside his father. Kate cried, "Mono, you didn't!"

"I am sorry, Maria. But blood is blood."

"What an extraordinary development," Ramirez cooed in a satisfied voice. "This man I knew as Burton Brandt, this man I thought had come to my country to make a motion picture, turns out to be none other than the son of my old nemesis, Mace Blackwood. Come to seek revenge for his father's ignominious defeat. When I first learned of your true identity, I confess that I was seized by a fierce anger. Would this plague of Blackwoods never cease? But then I calmed myself. Success is a mighty pacifier, is it not? And after all, I succeeded in outwitting the father. I turned his ambitions of slandering me to dust. I outflanked him so spectacularly that all he could do was run away. How difficult, then, could it be to best the pretender son?"

Biting back his anger, Rhys ground out, "Okay, you've got us. But as you can see, we've decided not to go through with our plan after all. So if you'll just put down those guns, we'll be on our way and out of your lives forever."

Ramirez gave a sarcastic grin. "Oh, but I do not want you out of my life. You are the best thing ever to happen to me. You are going to give me the presidency. A great irony, wouldn't you agree? Even you can see the beauty of it. Your father must be reeling in his grave."

"But you know now that this was all a fraud. There is no Aztec princess."

"The four of us know that, but no one else. These *pistoleros* don't speak English, and I will eventually have the clods exterminated anyway, so they cannot tell even *this* part of the story. No, Senor Blackwood, you have done such an exemplary job of creating a believable fantasy that I see no difficulty in making it a reality."

"But surely your son won't—"

"Ah, but Monolito is smitten with the girl. Besides, he will do as he is told. No, my friend, we will proceed as planned. We *will* return to the capital. We *will* announce the engagement. The girl *will* marry my son. And it *will* buy me the love of the people of Mexico."

The sight of this man was an obscenity. A hateful montage of images tumbled through Rhys's mind. Child brothels . . . his parents' deaths . . . the prospect of the villain's inauguration as President of Mexico . . . and Kate . . . most of all, Kate . . .

All his resolutions to leave his vendetta behind and start over suddenly seemed a vain delusion. This man was his enemy! Like it or not, he'd inherited the obligation to bring him down. How could he possibly have thought to ignore this sacred duty?

Without warning or hesitation, he flew at Ramirez and grabbed for his throat, choking him with all his might before rough hands pulled him away.

Clutching at his bruised neck in a fury, Ramirez croaked, "*Bastardo*! You have just signed your death warrant."

Rhys spat in his face. "You'd *better* kill me."

With eyes blazing, Ramirez barked at one of his men, "*Cuchillo*!" A knife.

In desperation, Kate lunged forth, putting herself between the two men. "No!" she screamed. "You touch him and I swear to God I'll kill myself."

Ramirez had his hand out, waiting for the weapon, when all at once he froze and glared at Kate. "Foolish girl. Do you suppose I would allow such a thing to happen?"

"I'll wait," she vowed. "I'll find a way. I'll break a glass and slit my wrists. I'll use my bedsheets to hang myself. Sooner or later, you'll overlook something, and I'll do it."

Monolito stepped into the fray. "Father, it might indeed appear suspicious if the man suddenly disappears."

In the silence that followed, Kate continued. "I shall make a bargain with you. I shall go with you willingly and promise not to do myself harm. But in return, you must promise me Rhys's life. I want him with us Friday when we make the announcement. And once that's done, I want to see him put safely on a ship for America. You do this, and I shall comply with anything you like."

Rhys was struggling against the guards who held him. "Kate, no—"

But she turned on him and put her fingers to his mouth, cutting off his words. "You have to trust me," she urged.

He jerked his head. "I trusted you, and look what's happened. If you think I'm going to leave you to this, you're crazy."

Her gaze softened on him. "Rhys," she said tenderly, "I know you want to protect me, but you can't. You have to let me do this. You have to love me enough to let me go."

Chapter Nine

The beefiest of the *pistoleros* tied Rhys's hands and shoved him into the back seat of one of the waiting automobiles. Joining him there, he signaled to the driver, and the car pulled away, its wheels spinning gravel behind it. Rhys looked back and saw Kate being similarly placed in another automobile, which would caravan with de Guzmán's Rolls Royce for the 75-mile drive to Mexico City.

Rhys spent the trip smoldering with a combination of feelings: frustration with himself for allowing Kate to so gullibly tip their hand to a spoiled playboy; anger at his own naïveté in thinking he could turn his back on his obligation to destroy this monster; fear of what was going to happen to them once they'd served the villain's purpose. Somehow, there had to be a way out. But how? It seemed hopeless.

Dawn was breaking when they reached the outskirts of Mexico City. They descended into the immense, sprawling metropolis, and turned onto Paseo de la Reforma. This grand boulevard, built by Emperor Maximilian to resemble the Champs Élysée, showcased the ostentatious remnants of colonial splendor, disguising the fact that not far away, impossibly narrow side streets teemed with abject poverty. But Rhys barely saw the trees, the imposing buildings, the passing statues, as he gazed out the window distractedly, straining his brain to devise a plan. He had to try something. *Something.*

After a stop-and-go drive through the already congested streets, the cortege pulled into the forecourt of the Gran Hotel de la Ciudad on the west side of the Zócalo, which de Guzmán had bought two years before from its bankrupt British owner. Here, Friday evening, he would make his "joyous announcement" that would "have a huge impact on the future of the nation."

Rhys's guard untied his hands but kept a firm grip on his arm as he led him into the dazzling art deco lobby, filled with a contingent of Ramirez's burly henchmen. As they entered the open-grill elevator, Rhys could see Kate coming in the front doors with her own guards. Their eyes met. Hers seemed curiously confident, as if she knew that somehow he'd find a way. That after finally coming together, their love could conquer even this most hopeless of situations. In a way this look of faith buoyed him. But ultimately it put more pressure on him to succeed.

The elevator opened on the tenth floor, where there were more armed guards filling up the hallway. His escort pushed him toward a room at the end of the long corridor. As he stepped inside, he could see Kate leaving the elevator and being taken to a room at the opposite end.

The guard closed the door behind them and Rhys surveyed the room where they would spend this day and the next before the staged announcement. He crossed to the window that looked down over the largest public plaza in the Americas. The Zócalo had once been the heart of the Aztec world, where the Great Pyramid had dominated a city the conquistadors had called the Venice of New Spain. Even though it was October, it was still hot in the city, and the window was open.

He spent the afternoon watching the guard play solitaire,

and staring out the window trying to figure out when and how to make his move. If somehow they could escape the hotel, his original plan of making for the Cuernavaca airport still seemed workable. De Guzmán would head straight for the train station, or the road to Vera Cruz. But how to get away? He could likely overpower this one sentry, but what would it buy him? There were half a dozen guards in the hallway, and a dozen more in the lobby.

After a late dinner, the room suddenly seemed sweltering. He went over to sit on the windowsill to catch the whiff of a breeze that was stirring the curtain. Biting into an apple, he absently glanced out the window. He felt a little queasy at the feel of being perched so high above the ground. But as he stamped it down, he noticed three things. First, there was a narrow ledge—not even a full foot in width—that ran the length of the building just a few feet below his window. Second, like all the buildings facing onto the Zócalo, the façade of the hotel was lit at night, but the bright lights cast a shadow over the upper floor where the prisoners were ensconced. And third, there was a long drainpipe running down the far side of the building just beyond what must be Kate's room. But Christ! It would take a human fly to step out on that ledge and . . .

He brooded on this as his escort played game after game of solitaire with his tattered deck of cards. It was insanity. Even if he could conquer his fear of heights enough to step out onto that precarious ledge, he was sure to lose his nerve and freeze along the way. No. Never in a million years. Never in *ten* million years. Don't even think about it. Don't even—

With a savage spring, he reached out, grabbed his guard by the hair, slammed his face into the table, and watched him fall unconscious to the floor as the cards rained around him.

Then, without giving himself time to change his mind, he

rushed to the window, stepped out onto the minuscule ledge, and began to edge his way in the darkness toward Kate's room.

He heard the sounds of honking horns below, of people laughing companionably in the square. Making him realize how high up he was. *Sweet Jesus, what am I doing? No, don't think. Whatever you do, don't look down. And don't stop. Not even for a second.* A wave of dizziness swept over him. His fingers gripped the flat, rough stone surface so hard he could feel them begin to bleed. His legs threatened to buckle beneath him. What if the plaster of the ledge gave way? *Think of Kate! Think of Kate in the rain. Think of the feel of her body, warm and nude . . . the taste of her nipple . . . her fingers on your dick. See her now and keep moving. Kate . . .*

He didn't know if he was on that ledge for twenty minutes or two hours. It seemed like twenty hours. But somehow he made it. Defying gravity and all good sense. Made it to the last window and thanked God it was open to the night. Peering inside, he could see Kate sitting at the vanity, brushing her hair while her guard was flopped on the sofa reading a cheesy Mexican movie magazine with Gilbert Roland on the cover. As every strained muscle in his body ached from the ordeal, he noiselessly crawled into the window.

Seeing his reflection in the mirror, Kate shot around. As Rhys stumbled onto the floor, the guard looked up. His jaw dropped and he stared at the phantom before him, trying to figure out who he was and what was going on. Within another moment, he had. He reached for his shoulder holster and flung the magazine aside.

Rhys sprang from the floor like a panther, grabbed him by the throat with one hand, and slammed his other fist into the man's face with a mighty crash of bone and cartilage. With one shocked look, the guard slumped back into the sofa, unconscious. Rhys caught the pistol before it could fall and tucked it into his belt. Then he grabbed Kate's arm and propelled her toward the window, whispering, "Come on, we're getting out of here."

She stopped in her tracks. "Getting out? But how?"

"The drainpipe. We can do it."

He tried to pull her forward, but still she held back, staring at him. "How did you get here?"

Hurriedly, he told her, "I scaled the ledge."

She rushed to the window and looked down at the narrow ridge running the length of the building. "You did that—" she turned and looked at him "for me?"

She looked so touched, so shocked. But there was something else lurking in the back of her eyes, something he didn't comprehend. Ignoring it, he said in a low, urgent tone, "Let's go, before they hear us."

Again, she pulled back. "Rhys, it's wonderful what you did, but I have to tell you—"

He cut her off. "There's no time now. We can talk later. I'll go first and help you out."

But as he was stretching his leg over the windowsill, he was jarred back into the room by the crash of breaking glass. A tray that had held a decanter and drinking glasses lay shattered between them. It took him a moment to realize it hadn't been an accident. When his back was turned, Kate had gone to the vanity and hurled the tray to the floor.

As the door burst open and the guards came flooding in, he stared at her in disbelief. She stood before him, returning his look, defiant but sad.

The guards surrounded them, grabbing each and holding them fast. But still Rhys glared at her.

"You did that on purpose," he accused, hardly feeling the rough fingers bite into his arms.

"I had to," she told him. "I can't let you risk your life."

Swearing at him in Spanish, the guards wrestled him to

the floor and began to kick him viciously. Struggling against her own captors, Kate cried, "Don't hurt him! The deal is that he's not to be hurt!"

At that moment, Ramirez came charging into the room. Taking in the scene before him, he demanded, "What goes on here?"

The man Rhys had knocked unconscious had come to by now, mopping at his bleeding nose with a dirty kerchief. He growled something to de Guzmán, who turned back to Rhys as the guards pulled him to his feet. "The ledge . . . ? That tiny sliver of cornice out there?" He raised a cynical brow. "But this is amazing! A man who's afraid of heights? This surely must be true love."

He cackled. But before the sound had barely left his lips, he backhanded a blow to Rhys's face.

Kate cried out, "If you touch him again, the deal is off. So help me God, I shall jump out that window the first chance I have."

Ramirez gave an expansive shrug. "But I have no intention of hurting him. In point of fact, Mr. Blackwood and I are going to be the best of friends. He is going to go back to his country and return to the helm of the *Globe-Journal*. But from this day forward, this newspaper that has been such a thorn in my side is going to be an enthusiastic supporter of Ramirez de Guzmán. Everything we do here will be praised. He will, in fact, portray me as a cross between Simon Bolivar and Saint Francis of Assisi. Yes . . ." he added, savoring the thought. "The savior of Mexico!"

Rhys struggled against the hold of the guards, grinding out, "I should have slit your throat while I had the chance."

Ramirez just smiled, taunting him. "That would, indeed, have been the clever move. Before I knew who you really are. It would have been so easy in Ixtapan. You could have slipped into my room at night and cut my throat and blamed it on socialist *banditos*. Now, granted, I run a risk at letting you go. You could well decide to—how do you say it?—blow the whistle on me. But if you do, let me tell you what will happen to . . . Maria." He glanced at Kate. "I won't just kill her. I will send her for a long vacation in a little place I own in Mexicali called La Casa de Tormenta. A most unusual establishment. Frequented by only the wealthiest, most perverted individuals in all the world. Do you realize, amigos, that there are actually people who will pay fantastic sums to see a beautiful young woman raped again and again by all sorts of men and beasts? Who will sit there for hour . . . after hour in intense excitement, beholding the spectacle of a poor, pathetic victim being slowly tortured. It makes my skin crawl to even think of it! But there are such people in this world. And they would pay a king's ransom to see a woman as captivating as our Maria getting the full treatment before she is finally put out of her misery forever."

Rhys snarled, "You sick son of a bitch!"

Before Ramirez could answer, Kate intervened. In a firm voice, she announced, "I won't be going to the House of Pain. Not now, not ever. I alerted the guards bccause I have every intention of going through with this plan. I shall go through with the announcement tomorrow, and so will Rhys. He'll sit beside us and applaud the upcoming marriage and won't so much as give an indication that he disapproves. You have my word."

Rhys watched her as she spoke so decisively, and with so much grace. "Why?" he asked her, his sense of betrayal gnawing at him. "We might have made it. But you brought this on us. Why?"

When she raised her gaze to his, he saw a look of such tenderness that it confounded him all the more. "Because I love you, Rhys Blackwood," she told him. "Because I'll do anything I have to . . . for you. You think I'm going to a prison that will be intolerable. But I'm telling you, it won't. My prison was in thinking you didn't love me. As long as I know you do, I can withstand anything. You were willing to conquer your demon for me, and that touches me more than I can ever say. But you're wrong to think we could run away. Ramirez would hunt us down and have his revenge. I won't let you go through life looking over your shoulder, waiting for him to come. So you have to let me do this. You don't have to understand it, or agree with it, but you have to promise to help me keep my word."

He still didn't understand. *All for nothing* . . . Everything in him still wanted to fight.

But he was licked and he knew it.

"If you love me," she insisted, "do this one thing for me. Help me have the courage I shall need. Promise me."

He'd never loved her more than in that moment, when she was being so brave. But he couldn't bear to look her in the eyes. Knowing how colossally he'd failed her.

He dipped his head and gave a single nod.

And felt himself die inside.

Chapter Ten

The crowd began to build in the Zócalo early the next morning. Word had been spread that on this most auspicious *Día de la Raza,* an announcement would be made that would have a momentous impact on the future of the nation—that indeed, a new Mexico would emerge from it—and it was hinted that it involved the famous and already much beloved Aztec *princesa.* Shortly before noon, workmen hammered together a grandstand in front of the hotel, directly facing, across the vast square, the National Palace—the residence of the president that Ramirez hoped to inhabit soon. In the early afternoon, loudspeakers were set up as well as the apparatus needed for a nationwide radio broadcast. Later in the day, delegations of foreign correspondents and a large contingent of socialist action groups joined the steady stream of peons from the countryside and poorer districts of the city who continued to pour into the square to make it one vast wall of humanity. By nightfall, when the lights flooded over the facades of the stately colonial buildings, the packed square was as charged, as dramatic as a scene from a Cecil B. DeMille spectacle.

Rhys watched the formation from his tenth-floor window, feeling bleaker by the moment. Late in the afternoon the luggage had arrived from Ixtapan, and an hour after that, there was a bang on the door and a voice told him it was time to change into his tuxedo. Until then, the day had been endless with nothing to do except wait. But now that the moment had arrived, it seemed too soon.

The guards came for him, marching him down to the lobby and out the front door. He knew the moment Kate had arrived—just ahead of him—from the deafening roar that rose from the crowd. In the wake of the commotion, he was shoved up the makeshift steps to the top of the grandstand. As he came out onto the stage, the floodlights blinded him, adding to his sense of disorientation as the million voices continued to chant. He brought a hand up to shield his eyes, sensing more than seeing the crowd stretching out before him, staring at the podium with breathless anticipation. As his eyes began to adjust, he could make out the ocean of faces, highlighted by the brilliant illumination of the square.

But then he felt the presence of something that, for him, was a stronger pull. He turned. And there, across the stage, stood Kate, looking for all the world like Cinderella at the ball. The white satin gown Ramirez had commissioned caught the light in such a way that it seemed to cast a halo all around her. The effect was dazzling. But as she turned and caught his eye, he saw something he hadn't when she was standing in profile. Something that seemed to glow with a special radiance meant just for him.

His mother's blue diamonds.

He lifted his gaze and saw the love shining in her eyes. She'd worn them for him, as a secret symbol. To let him know where her heart really belonged.

The stab of pain was nearly unendurable. He couldn't go through with this. He felt the panic sweep over him and settle in his throat like bile. But a quick glance about revealed de Guzmán's platoon of henchmen, scattered around the dais and inconspicuously armed. Many of them with their gaze fixed steadily on Rhys.

There was nothing he could do. But when he glanced back at Kate, he detected a gentleness in her look that baffled and frustrated him all the more. It was as if she were asking him—astonishingly—to have faith. Faith in what? The hope she'd helped ignite had been snuffed out. How could she go through with this so calmly, so . . . *willingly*?

Would he prefer that she go kicking and screaming? A part of him said yes. He'd rather she fight for him—for them—as he'd been willing to fight. This bland acceptance was more than he could stomach.

All for what? To save his life? He'd rather be dead than let her go through with this.

As if sensing the direction of his thoughts, her expression changed. Her eyes now pleaded with him to conquer any rash inclination that might endanger him. So forceful was her silent plea that he finally began to understand. Kate felt compelled to go through with this. But in order to do that, she needed his help. She needed his strength.

His guard prompted him to take a seat in the VIP section to the right, where he recognized many of the celebrities from Ixtapan. Just beyond Kate, he could see the smug, fat face of Ramirez de Guzmán, and beside him, the turncoat Monolito, who stared unemotionally into the crowd.

The host of the festivities, sweating in his white dinner jacket, raised a hand to silence the clamor. When the multitude had finally, gradually, quieted, he began to address them in Spanish. The loudspeaker beside him gave a grating squeal.

Momentarily, the man invited Ramirez de Guzmán to the podium. As he stepped before the row of microphones, his sprinkling of lackeys, carefully positioned in the crowd, began to cheer wildly. But they were soon drowned out by the boos and catcalls of a crowd that was yet to be won over. His voice over the immense loudspeakers began to override the angry tumult. And as he spoke, his voice—soothing, accommodating, full of fatherly joy—expressed his eagerness, his excitement, his pride at being able to bring them such magnificent news. Sparking their curiosity, building the suspense, until even his dissenters were hanging on his every word. Only then, after a pause for dramatic effect, did he turn and gesture to Monolito. "Earlier this week I was given the most joyous news a father can hear, that his son and heir has chosen for himself a wife. And what a wife! A woman whose story embodies the very soul of our country. Whose vibrant blood pulsates with the rhythm of our ancestors. A symbol of our past and a beacon for our future. I could sing her praises all night long, but I know the suspense must be killing you. So I will leave it to Monolito to present her for your approval."

With that, he stepped back and made way for his son to present his *novia*—fiancée. Monolito rose slowly and took his place at the microphones. He drew a long breath, then began to speak.

Mis paisonos . . .

"My countrymen, I want to present to you a special woman. A woman who is everything my father claimed, and more. A woman I love with all my heart and who I am honored to take for my wife." He turned to Kate with a small smile. But as everyone watched, he veered in the opposite direction and extended his arm. A young woman with jet-black hair—a woman who might have been mistaken for Kate, except that she was shorter and more fawnlike—climbed onto the grandstand and took his outstretched hand. Bringing her close, he said to the crowd, "This is Lupe Sanchez. And I would like to tell you her story."

Rhys bolted upright from his slumped position. Lupe . . . ! He looked at Ramirez, who started to rise, but checked himself, as if unsure of what was happening or what he could do about it. Just then, Rhys noticed that a phalanx of Mexican army regulars and municipal police had encircled the grandstand, neutralizing the hegemony of Ramirez's thugs.

Rhys wheeled around and looked at Kate. She was

watching him, as if to see the effect this would have. As if she'd been waiting . . .

All at once, he began to understand. *She'd planned this all along . . .*

Monolito continued. He spoke earnestly, passionately, charismatically, with an assurance and vigor no one had ever seen in him before. He told the story of Lupe Sanchez, who'd been purchased like some beast of burden from her family as a young girl, forced to work as a *puta* in the despicable brothels owned by a cruel conquistador of a businessman named Ramirez de Guzmán, brutalized beyond belief . . . yet who'd never lost her soul.

This was what Kate and Monolito had talked about before leaving Ixtapan. This was why she'd insisted on "telling him the truth." This was why the boy had turned them in!

Monolito, worked up now, began to shout out a litany of his father's crimes. "This man, my father, is more evil than even his worst enemies have charged. He is guilty of—"

In a rage, Ramirez leapt from his chair and charged at his son. But even as he wrestled with him, trying to pry him from the microphones, Monolito continued his invective. "Corruption . . . political manipulation . . . harrowing abuse of women and children . . . unprecedented violence against the social fabric of Mexico." Ramirez was pulled off him by two policemen who'd vaulted onto the grandstand. It didn't even break the rhythm of Monolito's indictment. "I renounce this vile man and ask all of you to reject his obscene bid for even more power! I have been weak in not standing up to this infamy. That is my shame. But today I make my amends. From this day forward, Ramirez de Guzmán is no longer my father!"

Ramirez dropped back into his seat. One by one, his henchmen—in the crowd and on the grandstand—began to sneak away, abandoning the corpse of their fallen leader and disappearing into the throng.

When Monolito had finished, his audience, with tears in their eyes, began to chant his name. *Monolito . . . Monolito . . .*

A new political champion had been born.

Finding himself suddenly and unexpectedly alone, Rhys rose and slowly crossed the stage to where Kate stood, waiting for him with a beguiling smile on her face.

He quickened his pace and crushed her in his arms. Holding her, kissing her, cherishing her. This astonishing woman.

His woman.

Epilogue

As Rhys reached for her, he felt something cold and metallic touch his wrist, and then the unmistakable click of a handcuff. "What's this?" he asked, surprised.

There was another click and he realized he'd just been manacled to the iron bedpost. "This is *my* revenge," Kate grinned.

"I've got an appointment this morning."

"*Oh, no,* you don't. We're not leaving this room. I don't intend to see anything but that ceiling for the next month!"

They were back in their old suite at the Savoy in London, with its sweeping view of the Thames. They'd stayed in Mexico long enough to see Ramirez indicted on an avalanche of charges and to stand up for Monolito and Lupe at their wedding following Mono's announcement that he would run for office. His impassioned chronicle of Lupe's life story had captured the hearts of his people.

Then they'd left for London, taking a series of privately chartered planes to Rio, then boarding the commercial Ford Tri-Motor to cross the Atlantic. To distract Rhys from his nervousness, Kate had impulsively suggested that they be married by the pilot of the plane. After the impromptu ceremony and a round of champagne toasts from their fellow passengers, they retreated to a private rear compartment to plan their future together. How they would, after a month-long honeymoon in London, return to New York where Rhys would take up the reins of his father's newspaper and use his inherited skills to continue his parents' mission. How Kate would be a partner in this enterprise. But instead of hiding behind the Archer name, they would now live openly as Blackwoods.

So here they were, Rhys and Kate Blackwood, in the same suite where, months before, Rhys's detectives had handcuffed Kate and he'd offered her his ultimatum. The same suite where she'd lived in agony with Rhys for six long months during her training. But this time they were here for their honeymoon. This time it felt like home.

And this time, she was turning the tables on him.

"Come on, Kate," he urged, tugging at the handcuffs that bound his arms above his head so that his biceps bulged magnificently. "I don't do this."

She tossed her head so the mane of newly dyed blond hair fell about her shoulders in a shower of golden light. "Oh, you always have to be in control, do you?" she grinned.

"That's right. Now give me the key, and be quick about it."

She dangled the tiny key before him playfully. "If you want it, come and get it."

He made a lunge for it, but she was just out of his reach. He fell back, rattling the cuffs in frustration.

"This doesn't work with me," he warned.

"Oh, doesn't it?"

She reached over and put her hand on his leg. He recoiled slightly, but she proceeded with a firmer hand, caressing the rigid curve of his calf, parting with her fingertips the dark, crisp hair of his deliciously muscled thighs.

Somewhat less vehemently, he suggested, "Why don't you unlock me, and we'll have some fun."

She gave him a mock scowl. "I shall say to you what you once said to me. You're my prisoner. Enjoy it."

With that, she grasped the prize. Despite himself, it stirred to life. She used her fingers to tease him, to alternately stroke and squeeze. Smiling triumphantly as he grew immense in her hand.

"Just what do you intend to do with me?" he asked, guarded now that his body was responding against his will.

With her other hand, she fondled the velvety soft head. "I intend," she cooed, "to do just what you did to me. I intend to tease you, to drive you mad with lust, and then, just as you are about to explode . . . just when you think if you don't, you'll die . . . then I shall pull away and deny you. Because you come when *I* want you to now. You're my plaything, and I intend to play with you to my heart's content."

She took the key to the handcuffs and used it to trace a mischievous pattern across the tightly stretched sinews of his chest. He bulged bigger in her hand. But when she came close enough, he made another dive for it with his teeth. She laughed and placed it on the bedside table.

Then she parted his legs and knelt between them. As her mouth closed over him, he gave a wretched groan. "I hate this," he croaked.

"Yes," she smiled. "It shows."

She began to suck up and down the mighty length of him, using one hand to follow the path of her mouth, the other to cup and gently embrace his balls. Her hands moving in a continuous flow with her mouth, her tongue, so that he lost track of where each sensation was coming from. Sucking as if she was ravenous for his cock.

Gradually his head rolled back against his arm and he closed his eyes, surrendering himself to the undeniable pleasure. Feeling himself move with her . . . arching gently into her . . . lifting and receding into the succulent warmth. Fucking her mouth.

Feeling his lust rush like a river toward the channel where release was but an instant away. Surging faster, charging like a runaway train, building . . . stampeding . . . heading toward . . .

Nothing!

The succor of that moist and talented mouth was gone.

His eyes flew open, and he saw her sitting before him, wiping her mouth the way a gunfighter would blow on a six-shooter. "We're going to do a *lot* of this," she purred.

He met her gaze. "And what about you?" he asked.

"I shall be in charge."

"Will you?"

"I should think that's obvious."

He continued to stare into her eyes. "You realize, of course, that by denying me, you'll be denying yourself. You've never struck me as being particularly patient where your pleasures are concerned."

"I can be as patient as you'll be forced to be."

"Are you sure that's what you want? It's quite a responsibility, isn't it, calling all the shots? You have to think instead of feel. And isn't that what you like about the little games we've played . . . how I make you feel?"

"Ah . . . so the mouse is trying to talk himself out from under the cat's paw!"

Rhys shrugged. "The mouse knows what the cat really wants."

"And what is it the cat wants?"

"She wants the mouse to be a lion."

Something stirred in Kate, which she did her best to tamp down. He had such a determined look in his eyes. What was he up to? "You may be a mouse or a lion, whichever you please. You're still in my power."

"Now, that's an interesting word . . . power. It's something I noticed about you right away."

"What's that?"

"That you're a woman who likes to have her power

taken from her . . . at least, in bed. You're so bright, so clever, so capable. You can turn a man to mush with just a look. But you were tired of that, weren't you? Tired of all the foolish men who so eagerly jumped through your hoops. You wanted something more."

"And what might that be?"

He pinned her with his fierce blue glare. "You wanted a man who would take the responsibility from you. A haven, if only for a while, where you didn't have to be clever or capable, where you didn't have to think. Where you could lose yourself to a man's touch and simply feel."

Her hand had gone limp at her side. She swallowed hard. "I know what you're doing. And if you think you'll succeed, you're wrong. You've fooled me once, and I'm not about to—"

"How *could* a man fool a woman like you? You know all the tricks of the trade. It wouldn't be possible unless . . . you wanted to be fooled. I saw what you wanted right away. That first day in this very room. You stood before me with your hands cuffed behind your back, doing your best to defy me and spit fire with your eyes. But I saw behind the defiance. I saw a woman who was secretly thrilled. A woman who wanted a man to do to her what no other man ever had. A woman who wanted to trust a man so much that she could turn herself over to him and say, 'Do with me what you will.' "

Her heart was beating fast. She remembered all of it as he spoke so vividly that it seemed to be happening all over again.

"And when I touched you . . . I could see that you loved the power I had over you. Why do you think I made love to you the way I did? Because you loved it. Because you needed it."

She felt herself begin to succumb to his words, to the soft, mellow persuasion of his voice. Begin to grow excited by the picture he was painting in her mind.

"The key, Kate," he urged. "All you have to do is reach over there and get the key and unlock my hands. Think of what these hands can do to you . . . *for* you. Think of how they feel on you. What a waste to keep them idle when they could be touching you in all the ways you like to be touched. You remember how it feels when I push your knees open and run my hands up your thighs? How my fingers feel inside you?"

She could almost feel them now. His voice was lulling her, hypnotizing her. *Arousing* her.

"The key, Kate. Get the key and unlock a lifetime of excitement. Let me give you what you *really* want."

She bit her lip, torn between the plan in her head and the aching need he'd incited in her body. "For someone who denied being a con man, you're making a fine show of it."

"But what *is* a con man, really? Just someone who can be all you want him to be. So let me be that for you, Kate. Unlock the cuffs and set your true fantasies free."

For a moment she didn't move a muscle.

Watching him as his eyes blazed into hers.

Feeling drowsily mesmerized and shockingly alert all at the same time.

Not certain what to do.

He gave her a slow, wicked grin.

Finally, she returned the smile. And with absolutely no hesitation, reached for the key.

A House East of Regent Street

Pam Rosenthal

Chapter One

Monday
London, 1816

"Pompeiian Red."

"Turner's Yellow."

"Zoffany Blue."

The rooms glowed. Rich afternoon September sunlight poured in through tall, graceful windows; the air shimmered as though suffused with the earths, stones, and metals that lent their hues to the walls.

"And the green?" Jack Merion waved his cane at the walls of the front parlor. The room was nearly empty; his voice echoed as he wandered among a few chairs and a settee, discreetly swathed in holland covers.

"What's the green called?" he asked the property agent.

"Sorry, Mr. Merion. I've forgotten what they call the green paint. But it's got verdigris crushed up in it. Lapis lazuli in the blue paint, verdigris in the green." Mr. Wilson's pale, plump face had caught a slanted ray of sunlight; his cheek was mottled with faint splotches of color from the walls. He shrugged, as though to slough off any personal identification with all that rowdy brilliance.

"One doesn't usually see such expensive paint, but the

tenant"—he allowed himself a bit of a snigger here—"evidently considered it worth the investment."

No need to be patronizing, Jack thought. Whatever the tenant's taste or motivation, the investment had paid off handsomely. Situated just off Soho Square, the house had been a popular and highly profitable brothel, maintaining its luster even as the neighborhood grew shabbier and less fashionable, and while more elaborate houses farther west attracted a richer custom. The lease having finally expired, however, the tenant had chosen not to renew.

One could easily imagine this parlor in its heyday: glowing green walls, delicate furniture, bronze brocade at the windows. You'd come here first, to choose a girl for the evening. It must have been . . . inspiring.

Solid woodwork; fine, ornate plaster ceiling. Still, Jack thought, the whoremaster tenant had been right to close down. The district wouldn't support a brothel of this elegance for much longer. Best to get out now; the property should be subdivided, rented out as separate units. Really the only thing to do with it, with Soho Square so clearly on the decline.

For a time, in the raucous, jostling way of a bourgeoning metropolis, the lines of social distinction between London's separate districts had remained companionably blurred. But the Prince Regent, like an eager puppy, had lately begun to mark his territory, his architects laying plans for parks and crescents, canals and arcades, and a boulevard to rival the great shopping thoroughfares of Paris. Some of these designs were still merely marks on paper and proposals before commissions, but ground had been broken, neighborhoods destroyed, and populations dislocated, in order to make way for the coming glories of Regent's Park, Regent's Crescent, Regent's Canal.

And, most notably, the new commercial thoroughfare. People were already calling it Regent Street; when completed, the fashionable corridor would constitute itself a sort of rampart, a bastion of social exclusivity, neatly dissociating the city's *ton* from the remainder of its populace. Let the lesser sorts go about their business eastward of Regent Street; the Polite World would concentrate its pursuit of pleasure to the west, in Mayfair and St. James. Even a striver, a "paper-money man" like Jack, would endeavor to locate himself in the West End, establishing a family (well, hoping to establish one, anyway) in some trim little stuccoed crescent going up in Marylebone. *This* property, splendid as it was, could only be an investment, one that he was considering quite seriously, for the rents it would bring in.

It was gratifying, he thought, that an ex-sailor could afford to buy such a building. For, contrary to the proverbial way of sailors, Jack had saved and invested what he'd gotten over the years, be it from wages, prize money, or some early smuggling ventures that were now safely buried in his past.

And equally gratifying to be treated as a man of means—though he might still encounter the occasional uncertain moment, usually with minor functionaries. It was usually the flunkies, he'd observed—like petty property agents or obsequious butlers—who were most eager to show their contempt for low origins and new money.

Wilson, however, had been most decent, murmuring the obligatory catchphrases like a benediction. *Viscount Crowden's letter of introduction . . . family well known to our firm . . . his father the earl in your deepest debt . . . A grateful nation recognizes its heroes.*

To which Jack had turned his best public smile: modest, dashing, and high-minded, all at once. Leaning on his cane in the entrance hall, he'd paused for a moment under the skylight: War Hero, Justly Rewarded, Entering his Sober Middle Years as a Man of Commerce. It helped, as he'd learned these past months, that he so perfectly *looked* the part. The grateful nation found it easier to recognize a handsome hero.

And so he and Wilson had managed a cordial acquaintance, the pale, plump, younger man expatiating upon the house's fine design and good construction, while the broad-shouldered, sun-darkened, older one contributed an ex-sailor's working knowledge of the inside of a brothel. By now, Jack had quite won the young property agent's affections.

"Someone else is interested in this property," Wilson confided. "Can't afford to buy it, though. He wants to lease it, to use for its original purposes. A Frenchman. I'd been expecting him this afternoon as well. But as he's quite late already, I doubt we need worry about him."

Jack shrugged, not worried at all.

"Well, then," the young man continued, "we've seen the kitchen downstairs and the dining room at the back of the house—nice, eh, to imagine the girls taking their meals there? So I think we'll want to go upstairs now." A broad wink. Silly youth, Jack thought.

Having mounted the stairs to the second story, they found a lovely little bedroom, painted in that rich Zoffany blue. Good, springy Elastic Bed, well covered against dust. Elaborate plasterwork on the ceiling—cherubs, it looked like.

Beautiful house. Had he ever been here? Possibly, quite some years back, during the smuggling days. Occasionally, after a venture had gone particularly well, he and a few of his mates had treated themselves to places like this, rather than their accustomed cheap haunts in Wapping. They'd clean and smarten themselves up, contain their rowdiness, give the girls a break (as they liked to joke) from the *softer* sort of gentlemen who made up the house's usual custom.

There were additional small bedrooms on this second story, and other, more interesting spaces as well, like a large room that held various bulky and oddly shaped items, ghostly in their cloth covers.

"They'd do their more public entertaining in a room like

this," Jack said. "Pageants and such. They'd be half dressed, singing and playing musical instruments—that's a harp, I suppose, and that thing looks like a barrel organ."

The room would have provided a graceful setting for it, though in fact he'd never had a lot of patience for such entertainments. To him, the point had always been the fucking.

Whereas for Wilson . . . the younger man gazed dreamily at the harp until Jack cleared his throat.

"And on the next story . . ." he suggested.

"Quite," murmured his guide, leading the way up the stairs.

Upon peering into the first room on the house's third story, however, Wilson's cheeks flushed a sudden dark red. Perhaps a reflection of the paint on the walls again, Jack thought, but not likely.

"Yes, well, and *here* we h-have a . . . a . . ."

". . . torture chamber." Abruptly, Jack finished the young man's sentence for him, in a sharp tone that disallowed of any discomfiture on his own part.

The walls were done in dark Mediterranean red. No windows: airshafts had been built at the edge of the room to allow light from skylights in the roof. Curious dark panels were mounted high on the walls; wooden gargoyles appeared to be perched atop iron contrivances bolted into the panels' carvings. And hanging down from the bolts? Chains, with wrist cuffs attached. Cranks and pulleys to adjust them, and some odd hinged mechanisms whose workings he didn't quite understand. The gargoyles grinned and grimaced in a mute frenzy of anticipation.

He pulled the holland cover from a large, square object. The tooled ebony cabinet hadn't been shut correctly. Its door swung open, revealing the whips and floggers, the switches, straps, and scourges neatly ranged in order of size and formidability.

Wilson let out a sort of squeak that might have been a

scandalized giggle, while Jack remained silent as the gargoyles, his face circumspect and just mildly ironic, trying to deal with whatever complex of emotion the room had churned up in him.

Not shock or surprise, exactly. And certainly not disgust—live and let live; if you paid your money you were entitled to whatever entertainment was available. No, what he was feeling was more complicated, a sort of unwilling envy of anyone so confident of his place in the world that he'd pay for a taste of helplessness and humiliation. Where Jack came from, you got your ration of helplessness and humiliation for free.

The gentlemen who'd used this room had probably pretended to be little boys at Eton again—Lord Crowden had once explained a little of what *that* had been like. Jack had noticed a bundle of slender willow canes in the ebony cabinet. There'd also been a cat-o'-nine-tails: no doubt the gentlemen had also played at being seamen, spread-eagled and stripped to the waist, waiting for the hideous bite of knotted rope at their naked backs. They probably fantasized a whole ship's crew assembled on deck to watch. And very arousing it might be, too, Jack supposed, as a fantasy.

Rather less so, as a memory.

"The room is sealed," Wilson announced solemnly. "When the door is closed, no sound can escape."

Jack nodded. Enough of the red room. The two men took a slow, meditative stroll through an elegant bedchamber, all done in bright yellow.

Well, he had to admit that the house had stirred his imagination. And more than that—no point trying to ignore the physical facts of the matter—it wasn't *only* envy and resentment that had taken hold of him. He took a deep breath and exhaled slowly, as he'd learned to do these past few years, in preparation for a battle at sea.

Mercifully, the stirring began to subside. *Some* advantage, anyway, to approaching one's fortieth birthday.

"Yes, well, I think I've seen what I needed to see, Mr. Wilson. I think we both have."

They could skip the servants' rooms at the very top. He'd quite gotten the idea of the place by now. Yes, Mr. Wilson, he concluded, yes, I'll be considering the investment.

Soothing to begin thinking in money terms again. And it was also time to begin discussing his other (actually more exigent) needs in the way of houses and property.

Mr. Wilson? he repeated softly, for the younger man was clearly having his own difficulties in the matter of self-management. Jack cleared his throat.

"Perhaps it's time, Mr. Wilson," he announced, "to move on now. I'd like to hear about some venues more appropriate to the setting up of a household. Houses the young lady I'm presently paying court to might find to her possible liking."

He laid mild, didactic stress on the word *lady*, his gentle, almost avuncular smile meant to turn the property agent from the dangerous currents of his imaginings and steer him toward the shores of decency, propriety, commerce. The young man gulped, his eyes slowly regaining their focus.

"Of . . . of course, quite so. I left the list of properties downstairs. And may I congratulate you, sir, in advance . . ."

"Hah! A bit early for that, Wilson, but you can wish me luck . . ."

The self-consciously jaunty exchange faded into the clatter of their boots on the stairway. The smooth, beautifully bleached pine boards were uncarpeted at the house's upper levels; bathed in warm rays of sun streaming from a skylight, the wood felt sturdy, springy, and slightly yielding. They descended another floor, walking on good, thick carpet now, and gaining the entry hall on the first level.

His knee ached a bit. Always did, walking down stairs.

A mirror hung in the hallway. He straightened his cravat and ran his fingers through his thick hair to order it a bit—

or to make it stand up as it was supposed to do. He missed the feel of a sailor's queue at his nape, but Lord Crowden had insisted he get it cut in one of those poetical new styles that suggested a soul buffeted by winds of passion.

His brow was a bit sweaty. The house was stuffy; all the windows were closed. Or perhaps he felt taxed by the pain at his knee.

"Enjoy the knee," Crowden had counseled him. "Exploit it. The ladies love a war wound." He'd been right, in the case of a wound as little disfiguring as this one, anyway—at least when hidden under well-tailored, narrow buff pantaloons. Draped in good clothing, his wound was, in truth, rather an adornment. Ladies liked to fuss over an attractive hero; Jack would never have stood a chance with his young lady, were it not for the fortuitous combination of his good looks and bad knee.

Her parents had wanted someone better born. But in the patriotic haze of these post-war days, they were willing to indulge her—even, finally, to welcome Jack's daily presence at their house on Cavendish Square.

With his sharp nose for turbulent weather, however, Jack was in a hurry to seal the bargain before Miss Oakshutt (Evelina, as she'd lately allowed him to call her,) conceived a fancy for some other suitor and whatever novelties he might offer.

A loud, clacking noise interrupted his thoughts: an unexpected rap at the front door's big brass knocker. Wilson shrugged and hurried to answer it, while Jack nodded absentmindedly—perhaps the phantom Frenchman had materialized after all.

Evelina was a good deal younger than he was—pretty enough, blond, and well-shaped. With her dowry and her merchant father's connections in the City, she was as satisfactory in her way as Andrewes, the tailor Crowden had recommended, was in his.

Not that Jack wouldn't keep his end of the bargain. He'd

provide well for her and the children they'd have; act the sober, faithful husband. And, of course, he'd do his duty in bed—after all, as Nelson had famously expressed it, *England expects that every man will do his duty*.

In any case, he'd had enough of whores and whore-houses. He'd steal a kiss from Miss . . . from *Evelina,* this very evening.

But what had Wilson been doing all this time?

There were voices at the front door. Jack turned from his reflection, to join Wilson and the new arrivals.

They were an interesting trio: the hugely tall, crag-faced servant wheeling an invalid chair; the distinguished, rather wizened gentleman seated in it—the Frenchman, evidently; and the simply dressed but extremely elegant woman.

Woman, rather than *lady*.

Unless, Jack supposed, one knew how to pronounce the word *lady* with a certain ambiguity—a tone of voice like a wink or smirk exchanged with the other men in the room, to show that one really meant quite the opposite. A courtesan. Or even better, the French phrase Lord Crowden had taught him—trust the French to come up with an expression like *grande horizontale* to describe a very expensive whore. He himself had never encountered such a woman at first hand, and so he'd never been quite sure of all the nuances of implication.

But *this* . . . ah, *lady* could quickly fill the gaps in his education. He need only contemplate her posture and manner of address; it would be like memorizing an entire lexicon of new uses for ordinary words that her extraordinary presence had suddenly rendered inadequate.

One couldn't, for example, exactly say she was *small,* not with her posture so regal that only the proximity of the lanky servant called attention to her lack of stature. *Slender*? He doubted that the possessor of such a voluptuous bosom could correctly be called slender. She was hardly *young* but it wouldn't do to call her *old,* either; the word *ageless* came to mind, but here his common sense rebelled. No woman was ageless—her youth, or lack of it, was always a critical index of her value.

Beautiful? He wasn't quite sure—he'd always thought that beauty brought with it a comforting, disinterested sort of serenity. Well, *striking*, then—she was certainly that. Sparkling eyes slanted catlike above well-drawn cheekbones; her mouth was expressive, the sinuous upper lip curving in a wary half-smile above the full, appetitive, lower one. The afternoon sunlight seemed to embrace her as its own, her bright eyes and creamy skin outshining the brilliance even of these surroundings.

And oddly *dignified*, Jack thought, dignified and defiant—though *world-weary* might have been a more accurate word for the bored, rather contemptuous look in her blue cat's eyes, the tilt of her head and ironic curl of her mouth as she waited for him to get hold of himself and cease this clumsy ogling.

While Wilson was fairly panting and wagging his tail, like a spaniel begging to be taken into her lap.

"Ah, Mr. Merion, may I present Monsieur Soulard, Prince d'Illiers." He'd put some energy into managing the French pronunciation. "And,"—his shining face leaving no doubt as to the source of his energy—"may I also present Miss Myles."

She directed a warm smile at Wilson and a minimal nod at Jack, while the gentleman in the invalid chair reached out a cordial hand. "Soulard is sufficient. The title is a bit worse for wear." He glanced down at his legs, covered in slightly threadbare paisley. "As I suppose I am as well. Do please accept my apologies for our lateness—my health is not what it might be."

The woman's expression softened; Jack felt himself staring at her again, even as the tall servant glared at him. The barometric pressure in the room had risen discernibly. An awkward silence clogged the air.

No doubt, Jack thought, Soulard understood exactly what was going on. One wouldn't have such a creature as Miss Myles under one's protection and *not* be familiar with the effects she'd inevitably produce in male company. But the invalid's manners were as perfect as his lightly accented English, and he cleared the freighted air with graceful chatter. "And anyway, a prince in France is not what a prince in England is. I was, and then wasn't, and now am again, a rather petty nobleman."

The woman smiled and touched his shoulder, and Soulard reached up a thin hand to grasp hers for a moment.

Jack felt a shudder of envy. Or was it confusion?

Or only a spasm of helpless, jealous lust?

"And is the house as you remember it, *ma chère*?" Soulard had turned slightly in his chair to address her.

"Yes, yes, quite so. Well, the little we've seen, anyway." She moved forward, to save him the effort of shifting in his seat. "Of course, we'll have to inspcct the rooms, see how much repair the paint and plaster will need. *And* check against the furniture inventory."

She frowned. "They've already sold off some of the most valuable items, you know, like the Elastic Beds: there are only two of those remaining, and a decent house needs considerably more of them, especially for an older custom. But we'll have to see. It might do very well. Mr. Wilson, will you be so kind as to lead us upstairs?"

How casually, Jack thought, she spoke of Elastic Beds. It was disorienting to hear her speaking so briskly, like a shopkeeper. One expected so elegant a woman to speak in a languid, aristocratic drawl—like Crowden's mother and sisters, when the viscount had brought Jack home to tea.

But that was nonsense. Miss Myles's profession didn't draw its adepts from the ranks of countesses. Though he was beginning to wonder if some countesses might not copy their style and bearing from members of Miss Myles's profession.

The servant was evidently going to carry Soulard, invalid chair and all, up the steps. Miss Myles leaned down to smooth the paisley over her companion's lean hips.

And Jack couldn't quite believe the words he heard issuing from his own lips.

"It *might* have done very well, Miss Myles, Monsieur Soulard. But you see, before your arrival, I was so taken myself with the house's, um, proportions, that I made Mr. Wilson a rather impetuous offer. . . ."

The 5500£ he mentioned was considerably higher than the amount he'd planned to offer. Wilson opened his mouth, widened his eyes, and then nodded eagerly, swallowing his surprise in a quick gulp and clearly wondering how much of the surprise fee might stray into his own hands.

Jack watched the trio's silent response; as he'd suspected, they'd clearly wanted this house quite a bit more than they'd been letting on. The tall servant bared his teeth in fury. Soulard maintained his elegant reserve, though he slumped a bit in his chair. And Miss Myles simply squared her slender shoulders and gazed thoughtfully at Jack as regrets and good-days were exchanged, turning to glance at him once more as she and her companions quitted the house and joined the busy crowds in the street outside.

As it turned out, Jack hadn't stolen (or even begged) a kiss from Miss Oakshutt that evening, after all. In fact, he'd sent her a message instead, begging her pardon and professing his disappointment, but he felt a bit peckish and had to forgo the delight of her company. A recurring touch of the malaria he'd once contracted in . . . he'd shrugged and written "Gibraltar." He dined heartily (especially, he thought, for a man suffering a touch of malaria), and took brandy and a cigar in his small, very orderly sitting room.

And waited.

Calmly, at first, trying to divert himself with a fat book he'd bought, in the vague apprehension that a man of substance should have some volumes on the shelves of his home. It was a collected Shakespeare—Jack had been reading *The Tragedy of Antony and Cleopatra*, a bawdy, colorful thing about silly, passionate people well past their primes. He rather liked it. But tonight it failed to hold his attention.

It was growing late.

Had he miscalculated? Underestimated her?

Impossible. There was only one way to interpret her final glance, out there on the front steps.

Finally, he heard a low rap at the front door of his sitting room.

"A Miss Myles to see you, sir."

"My word, and at this hour." He tried to affect a note of stuffy surprise: *whatever might the lady be doing, out alone so late*? "Well, show her in, Weston, show her in."

She seemed a bit wan in the lamplight, her eyes dark smudges against her pallor, her body indeterminate in a hooded blue velvet cloak. But still the dignified, upright posture, the dark, jewel-like glints in her eyes. Eyes that might have taken their tones from lapis lazuli and verdigris. Eyes like a northern sea with a squall on the way.

"Miss . . . Myles, is it?"

A brief nod, as though it were too wearying to evince the scorn his silly charade warranted.

"Good evening, Mr. Merion."

He rose to greet her. "Here, let me help you off with that cloak."

"Thanks, I think I'll keep it on. Unless," she spoke more softly, "you'd prefer I remove it."

"No, just as you choose. Well, then,"—he gestured vaguely—"do sit down, Miss Myles, and tell me what brings you out so late this evening."

She did, however, let the hood slip back off her hair, which was black, thick, and caught in a simple Grecian knot at the back of her head.

She took a small, hard chair straight across from his. Settling comfortably back in his own wide armchair, he crossed his legs and brought a polite, attentive look to his face.

"You know why I'm here," she told him. He was becoming familiar with that blunt, businesslike tone of voice. "You intended me to come tonight."

He widened his eyes in mock befuddlement, reached for his drink, and took a slow sip, waiting for her to continue.

She let a few beats of silence pass, as though to underscore his boorishness. "You wasted money on a house that you don't want," she said.

Which brought him up sharply enough. "Of course I want it. It's an excellent investment. Unless,"—but why was he telling her this?—"you don't think a former sailor is capable of managing his money. Unless you think it takes a cultivated sort, or a nobleman like your poor petty prince who sent you here to bargain with me."

She raised her chin. "He didn't *send* me. He and I agreed that I had to come—you gave us no other choice. But we'll leave Philippe Soulard out of this discussion, if you please, Mr. Merion."

"Have you been with him for a long time?" Jack asked—mostly, he supposed, to demonstrate that he'd discuss any confounded thing he pleased. Upon having asked the question, though, he found that he was actually quite interested in what she might say in reply.

She sighed, drew herself up to protest once again, and then stopped herself. And when she did speak, her manner was exaggeratedly patient and condescending. "I've been with him for twelve years. And before that, I spent ten years at the house in question."

Her mouth twisted. "You like numbers, do you? Well, here are a few more for you. He visited me there for six months, before taking me home to live with him. Redeeming me cost him 100 guineas. He's got a wife in Paris. They have serious differences of opinion—about France and its political destiny, among other things.

"I was twenty-six when I met him," she added, "a bit long in the tooth even then, for a gentleman to make a fool of himself over. Or so the madam thought."

She paused. "And *that* should give you all the numbers you'll need—to tell you what you want to know about me."

He almost had to laugh—at the catalog of information she'd presented (germane and extraneous both), and the unembarrassed candor with which she'd delivered it. Not to speak of the fact that she'd nonetheless made *him* do the calculations.

He wouldn't have guessed that she was almost as old as he was. But, yes, he could see it now that he knew it. Her lightly powdered cheeks were exquisitely smooth, but they lacked Miss Oakshutt's careless glow. And below the pure line of her jaw, the skin—well, it didn't sag, but you could see where it would, when it finally did. He blinked, suddenly wondering how long she'd been watching him assess her.

Age—hmmm—*age cannot . . .*

But what a botch he was making of this. And it didn't help that his thoughts had suddenly got tangled up with the play he'd been reading.

"All right, then." A hint of a smile played about the corner of her mouth. "Would you agree that we've established that I am no longer young, that you were a sailor and I was a whore, and that you are rich and I am not?"

He nodded dumbly.

"Good," she told him. "Well, anyway, you're right that I

came here to make a bargain. You've got something we want, but luckily . . . well, turnabout's fair play, you know. So perhaps *now* you'll tell me what I'll have to do, in return for your granting us a lease on the property you bought today."

But he'd had enough of playing the buffoon in this comedy. After all, *he* was the one with the money.

"Quite right, quite right, Miss Myles. But I'm sure you'll be more comfortable if you remove that cloak. It's very warm in here."

Pleasant, anyway, to watch the fledgling smile fade from her lips.

She rose, loosened the ties below her chin, and allowed the dark velvet to slide down to the floor around her. Her gown underneath was pale and gauzy—a very fine pearl gray muslin, piped in that same velvet, and cut very low in the front.

Oh yes.

She stood in front of him a little longer than she needed to, before sinking into a sort of mock curtsey at his feet, remaining there long enough to afford him a splendid view of her breasts—firm white flesh, delicate blue veins, even a peek at her darkly sculpted nipples.

(But of course it wasn't really a curtsey—he'd been mad to imagine a curtsey, even for a moment. She was merely picking up the cloak she'd dropped.)

And having picked it up, she rose quickly, draped the cloak over a slender forearm, and regained her chair, the velvet flowing over her legs, her back straighter even than before.

Carefully, he reached for his brandy. The glass was cold in his hands, the alcohol hot in his throat.

"Yes, well . . ." It was time to speak, but his tongue felt swollen. He took another sip, rolled it around his mouth, and cleared his throat.

"You'll meet me at the house at three in the afternoon

for the next five days. A different room each time, I'll specify which. You'll do everything I ask. Don't worry, I've no diseases, nothing of that sort. Though I've been told I can be rather . . . demanding. Still, nothing you haven't, ah, handled, I'm sure.

"And if you do your best to please me—but I'm sure you will, I'm sure you always *did*—at the end of the week I'll lease the property to Soulard and wish the two of you all due prosperity of it."

She nodded. If he'd insulted her, she was doing a masterful job of hiding it.

(And why, he wondered miserably, had he felt obliged to boast? *Demanding* indeed.)

Not only didn't she seem insulted, she seemed mightily uninterested—except in specifying the terms of their agreement.

"Because of course, Mr. Merion, the rents we could afford to pay you would never make you back the sum you offered Mr. Wilson. But you already know that."

She fumbled in her reticule, handed him a sheet of figures. He cast his eye over it; the calculations were reasonably accurate, even if lacking in a few fine points of accounting. Jack hadn't gotten rich by missing the fine points. Still, she—or Soulard, or both of them together—had grasped the general idea.

"Quite right. I'd be renting to you at a loss."

"A considerable one. And you're not the sort of man who does business at a loss. Let's be clear on this, Mr. Merion."

He narrowed his eyes. "The difference—the loss I'll absorb—is my fee to you for services rendered. I want to be assured that you will do *everything* I wish."

She gave a small, rather Gallic, and very cynical shrug.

"If you promise to sign over the lease to us at a rate we can afford," she told him, "you can have me any way you like. As many times as you may *demand*, and of course making use of any of the house's facilities, if you're pleased to do so."

A gargoyle smirked at him, from against a dark red wall, somewhere at the edge of his inner vision.

"Any way you like," she repeated. "Even in those ways that you can't seem to believe a woman could enjoy."

Difficult not to gape at her.

"Sorry if I've shattered a cherished illusion, Mr. Merion," she said. "And oh, one more very important consideration. I'll supply a good, slippery lubricating ointment. Promise me that you'll use it when the proper time arises. Otherwise we don't have a bargain."

"I'll use it," he muttered. There ought to be something he could add at this juncture, but he'd be damned if he knew what it might be.

"So we're agreed," he said. He reached into his pocket and handed her a key, which she put into her reticule. "Three o'clock tomorrow afternoon, in the front parlor, first story."

She nodded. "Where normally you'd begin your evening, where you'd go to choose a girl. Yes, of course, quite right. We shall begin in that front parlor.

"Don't worry," she added. "You'll get your money's worth."

Briskly rising to her feet, she told him that she'd be arriving a bit early each day. To—well, to set the scene before he arrived. If he had no objection, of course. And thank you, she added (though he hadn't asked), the afternoon schedule would be quite convenient. Monsieur Soulard hadn't been able to sustain a good night's sleep lately, and so he almost always took a long nap after luncheon.

And before he could offer his assistance, she'd once again wrapped herself in her blue cloak.

He reached for his cane, intending to rise and accompany her to the door. But of course his knee *would* choose that moment to refuse to cooperate.

He needn't bother, she assured him; his servant could see her out.

"Um, one more thing, Miss Myles. Your name—um, I should like to know your first name."

Oddly, given the forthrightness with which she'd conducted herself up until now, she hesitated for a moment. "Will a *nom de guerre* be all right? For some years now, I've been called Cléo."

Clay-OH.

He blinked. The bawdy old play. What *was* the line? *Age . . . age cannot wither her, nor . . . nor something . . .*

Cléo.

"It will do very well, Miss Myles—ah, Cléo. Well, tomorrow then.

"The front parlor. At three."

Chapter Two

Tuesday—The Front Parlor

He hadn't slept well.

She'd haunted his dreams, but not in the pleasant, teasing, voluptuous way he'd anticipated. The images flickering against his eyelids had been fragmentary, uneasy. *He was late getting to the house; somehow he'd lost his way. Confused by all the new constructions going up, he'd wandered for what had felt like hours through labyrinthine streets; his knee had slowed him down—perhaps he needed an invalid chair.*

Ah, but there she was, just around the corner—well, there was the hem of her velvet cloak, anyway. He tried to hurry his steps, keep pace with her. Not too far to go now—Soho Square was just a few yards away. The house's fine front of gray stone and red brick materialized like a ship in the mist.

His cane disappeared, and so did the ache in his knee. He bounded up to the front door, stopping to stroke the thick black curls of the little housemaid scrubbing the shallow marble steps. Somehow, he knew to be careful; someone had spilled some sort of slippery ointment.

A blue-eyed cat sat perched on an iron railing. It watched as he tossed the housemaid a coin, and then it leaped out of sight. The girl turned a hideous gargoyle face to him, stuck out her tongue, and hissed.

He woke with a pounding heart, a headache (he'd drained the brandy bottle after she'd gone), and a guilty, sweaty awareness of how shabbily he'd behaved the night before. Yes, she was beautiful, fascinating, the most desirable woman he was ever likely to have (in *this* world anyway, and he wasn't counting on the possibility of another). And yes, she could be bought, but not because she'd intended to peddle herself. She'd consented to the deal he'd proposed because she'd had no other choice. He'd exploited her and he'd cheated the Frenchman, who'd actually seemed quite a decent chap. He'd taken cruel, petty advantage of their evident financial embarrassment. Which is, of course, always the surest method of increasing one's own capital.

But he hadn't done it to make himself richer. He'd done it because he was in such blatant, humiliating need of her.

Which made it all the more unconscionable, an insult both to her and to himself.

Still, he told himself, it wasn't too late to make it right. He could still invalidate the bargain, free all parties from obligation. He could find a way to transfer the property to her companion, even at a considerable financial loss to himself.

But . . . *you're not the sort of man who does business at a loss*, she'd told him. You're utterly lacking in grace or style—she hadn't said *that*, but surely she'd meant it. You're *nothing*, compared to the refined gentleman I'm used to.

With his mind's eye, he saw Soulard grip her hand, watched her slender fingers straighten the paisley shawl about the invalid's lap. They'd been together for twelve years; casually, unconcernedly, they'd flaunted their intimacy, their mutual sympathy, like a king adjusting his fur-lined greatcoat in sight of a shivering beggar. It was a mortification, he thought, to have barged in upon them with his lonely, jealous lusts. The only thing to do was apologize and make it right; back off and leave them to their poorly conceived business venture.

But he'd never backed off from an opportunity. If he were that sort, he wouldn't have begged a job on a merchant ship when he was twelve. He'd have stayed in Lancashire; he'd probably have died in the colliery.

If he couldn't have the sort of touch he coveted, he'd have whatever sort of touch he *could* buy. And as for his lack of grace and style—she could bloody well think anything she liked of him. A woman who could speak so casually of beds and lubricating ointments oughtn't to be judging him. And in any case, he intended to get his money's worth.

For he'd also awoken this morning with a monstrous hardness between his legs. And—as he swung his body around to get out of bed, dragging the bad leg behind him—he knew that there was no possibility he'd apologize. And not a chance in hell that he'd break the compact he'd bound her to last night.

Three o'clock, was it? He'd probably specified three in order to see her again in the sweet light of afternoon. Or because three was supposed to be a magic number, or simply a nice, leisurely time of day to have at her. In any case, it had sounded right when he'd proposed it, but now it sounded a damnably long time away.

Well, how did one usually pass the time?

Breakfast—no, he was still too queasy for breakfast.

Wash, dress, have his man shave him.

Walk about Town. Aimlessly, and then sometimes with dogged, mechanical rapidity, even when his knee pained him. He barely took note of where he was: Holborn, Bloomsbury . . . the next time he looked about him he'd wandered deep into the East End, where the buildings crowded so closely upon each other that they blackened the morning sky. The streets were filthy, the buildings hideous rookeries; he kept a firm grip on his purse and held his cane like a weapon. Cold eyes appraised him from doorways. As a boy, he'd learned how to put up a wary, aggressive front; he supposed it was a good thing he hadn't lost those instincts. The men watching him could tell that he knew how to fight—one-on-one, anyway. He hurried away before a gang could gather. Or before his knee could buckle and give him away.

Circling back to the City, he lingered at his accustomed coffeehouse, reading the newspaper and trading bits of gossip about the price of securities and movement of commodities on the 'Change. None of his regular acquaintances were about, but then, it wasn't his regular time: midday usually found him at the Oakshutts'. He buried himself in the newspapers for an hour and a half more, making his way to Cavendish Square around two.

Where he learned (though it shouldn't have come as a surprise) that the young ladies and their mother were on a shopping expedition. The butler didn't try to mask his disapprobation: the oldest miss *had* thought you might be here an hour ago, Mr. Merion, but . . .

They'd be home about three. Jack murmured something about an engagement of his own at three and resumed his wanderings.

Astonishing, though, just how slowly the time passed when you deliberately set out to waste it. Unless, like Crowden and his intimates, you belonged to one of those West End gentlemen's clubs. Gambling and betting were prodigious time-eaters; according to the viscount, clubmen's conversation was more effective still. Analysis of the cut of a coat or the cuttingness of a remark could occupy the better part of a day. Before you knew it, it was time to hurry out to supper or the opera.

Of course, Jack could never aspire to membership in such a fraternity; the best he could hope for was that someday a son of his . . . Dutifully, he made his way back to the Oakshutts'. He left his card, along with a promise to call again in the evening, when he hoped the young lady would be free to receive him.

After which errand he discovered that he was late (*just as he'd been in his dream*) and obliged to hurry eastward, across the half-laid pavement of Regent Street, through the raw constructions of what would someday be a graceful boulevard. He ran the last few blocks, limped up the white marble front steps (*no gargoyle scrubbing them, anyway*), put his key to the lock, and made his wild-eyed, dusty, disheveled, apologetic entrance into the blue front parlor.

Where no apology was required. A customer, after all, could arrive any time he wished. He'd hired her to please him, and it was clear that she intended to do exactly that. Yesterday's negotiations were all in the past. Today, she would give him everything she'd promised.

Beginning, just as she'd said, with an appropriate setting. Remarkable what she'd done, just by moving things here and there, adjusting the light, and placing herself at the center of the scene. As though she were an actress in a play, delivering her lines in front of a couple of potted plants the audience would come to take for an entire forest. The house *was* a brothel again, Jack an eager customer, and she . . . but was it the kohl outlining her eyes, the inviting curve of her painted lips, or the languor of her slouch? Whatever it was, she looked entirely natural: mildly bored, reasonably good-humored, a bit relieved that he wasn't an entirely unsavory piece of work. Because what he wanted—what they'd do in the next hours—well, it *was* all in a day's work, for her.

She'd removed the covers from the room's few pieces of furniture—a settee with slender, delicate legs; a small inlaid table; a lamp. The room was much darker than it had been yesterday; she'd drawn the brocade curtains. Well, she'd have to, wouldn't she, Jack told himself reasonably. It would be indecent to leave the windows uncovered; anyone could look in on them from the street. Still, she hadn't drawn them entirely shut; a few harsh golden diagonals of sunlight cut through the space. The upper panes of the windows were cut like prisms; a rainbow splashed and wavered against the floorboards like the sun on ocean waves. The lamp flickered—the rest of the room seemed huge, indeterminate, a pirate's treasure cave of shifting, unpredictable darks and lights. He corrected himself. Not *entirely* unpredictable: as always, the light knew how to find *her*. Her black hair shone almost blue; the short yellow peignoir blazed against the settee's bronze brocade.

The barge she sat in, like a burnished throne . . .

But Cleopatra hadn't arrayed herself on that barge with one black-stockinged leg carelessly curled beneath her. Or had a narrow velvet ribbon tied about her neck.

Nor had there been a cigarette dangling from her fingers when her boatmen had rowed her down the Nile to greet Mark Antony. If the old Egyptian doxy had staged her big entrance this seductively, Jack thought, she wouldn't have needed smiling attendants, purple sails, or "strange invisible perfume" drifting in the wind.

The acrid fragrance of one black Turkish cigarette would have been quite sufficient.

She took a long draw, exhaled, and smiled lazily at him through the smoke, like a girl who'd had an easy day of it so far and might actually welcome a little exercise at the hands of a likely customer.

"Hullo, luv, care to take a turn?"

Impressive. He nodded, flashing his handsome hero smile in return.

To be rewarded with a quick, appraising glance—from head to toe, and especially in between.

"All right, then," she said, "a bit of rantum-scantum, then. They told me about you, you see. Said he likes it more than one way, if you get my meaning, sir. Well, why not, I said, so long's his money's good."

Infinitely more beautiful than any girl he'd ever had, she'd nonetheless managed to present herself as a compendium of all of them. He sat next to her on the settee, pinched her breast where it swelled out from the neckline of her peignoir, and pulled open the knot in her sash.

"Your money *is* good, ain't it, darling?" she whispered. "Because the rest of you don't look too bad."

"My money's good," he murmured. "But let's see the rest of *you*, Cléo."

She giggled and moved to her feet, managing as she did so to wriggle out of the peignoir and leave him grasping the little scrap of yellow satin. Chin high, inky black thatch between her legs, she stood with arms akimbo. Dressed only in a brief corset, a loose shift, and those high black stockings, she held the cigarette between her lips. A slender trail of smoke rose from the tip; she watched him from under heavy, painted eyelids.

The shift's neckline had a drawstring, tied only in a simple bow. Not that it would have mattered; he could have loosened any sort of knot she might have used to close it—he might actually have preferred a bit of a challenge, to uncover, to reveal, to free the fantastic breasts that he now held in his hands. Firm, heavy, ripe: he buried his face in them, slid his hands down to her waist and back around to her arse. He kissed and nibbled, sucked and licked and nuzzled; pulled her closer to him now, clasping her between his thighs, his fingers exploring the parts of her he hadn't yet seen, tracing the curve and the cleft of her behind. And yes, he thought triumphantly, she'd begun to breathe more quickly—she'd gasped—she'd had to take the blasted cigarette out of her mouth.

"Turn around," he told her. "I want . . ."

But she already knew what he wanted to see, the tapering curve, the cleft like one you sometimes find in a perfect white peach, downy, dark, mysterious. In truth, he could have gotten a far better view of her arse if he were willing to let her move a few inches farther away from him. But that would have required him to take his hands from her breasts, his fingers from around her hardening nipples.

Ah well, it was only the first day. There would be time. Everything in due time, but first things first.

"And now turn around again."

He'd moved his hands to her shoulders now, pressing downward. She kissed him lightly, put her cigarette between his lips, and sank down to her knees between his legs.

He leaned back, dragging on the cigarette as she undid the buttons of his trousers. Quickly. *Very* quickly, the buttons undoing themselves, it seemed, the fabric folding itself out of the way as though bewitched by her fingers. Ah, she had him in her hands now. Lovely, her touch. And charming, the way she was smiling down at the flesh she held cradled in her palm.

He didn't usually watch while a woman prepared to take him into her mouth. Sometimes he even closed his eyes; he liked the passive feeling of being serviced. The cigarette she'd given him contributed to the effect—often, at times like this, he liked to fancy himself a pasha in a harem, drawing upon the mouthpiece of a hookah.

But today he found himself gazing down between his legs and into her eyes.

She stroked her face against the length of him, murmured endearments—"oh, but ain't he the pretty fellow?" (Did she really find his cock *pretty*? Did it matter?) He wasn't fully erect yet (had he disappointed her?)—but he could feel the blood gathering, as his flesh rose and stiffened under her touch. She slapped him gently, stroked him underneath, pinched his scrotum—carefully at first, and then a bit more roughly. He moaned and she smiled, eyes alight with the pleasure of discovering him, of learning his tastes and knowing his secrets. She blew him a flirtatious kiss and ducked her head lower between his legs. Oh, very nice indeed—her tongue making long, smooth strokes up and down the underside of his cock. He watched the glint of her eyes behind the spectacle of his own rising erection.

What a mischievous tongue she had: on each downstroke it snaked itself a little farther over his balls. Greedy little beast, going at him quite as though she liked—as though she *loved*—the smell of him. She'd taken his scrotum into her mouth now: he felt his blood coursing to his center, hardening his muscles, engorging his cock; he shuddered, his belly and thighs began to tremble.

She caressed his belly with one hand, stroked his cock between the slender fingers of the other, while her tongue—he cried out to feel it—made its slow, shameless way to the root of his balls, and farther, a bit farther, into the darkness, dangerously close to the cleft of his arse.

A quick retreat from darkness now. A return into the light: he could see her again, licking him slowly and easily on each side of his cock's shaft. More slaps, a little harder this time, now kissing the head that had made its way past the foreskin, and now—oh God, yes, *now*—taking the length of him into her mouth. Calmly, easily, moving her lips and the soft jelly wetness of the insides of her cheeks against him. Caressing him worshipfully, respectfully—*too* respectfully, he thought; "tongue," he growled, "more tongue." Yes, *that* was better; like a tiny flickering torch in the darkness, catching him here and there—egad, especially at *one* particular place—her lips active and mercurial as well, while he moved more deeply into her, probing toward her throat.

The cigarette, long forgotten, had burned down to his fingertips. He snuffed it out and tossed it away. He caught her hair in his hand; she leaned her head back into his grasp; he wanted to lead now, to control the pace and the rhythm of it, to move that gorgeous, astonishing mouth where *he* wanted it to go . . . at least before the pulls and the surges and the deep, deep tremors—the inevitability of his orgasm—took hold of him. Too soon. He could feel it coming. Too soon. But then, forever would have been too soon.

Hovering on the brink of climax, he stared down into her eyes, all his senses dissolved into a blue blaze of triumph as he shot his seed into her throat.

The rays of sunlight coming through the windows had a less defined slant when he regained consciousness—enough consciousness, at any rate, to allow him to find his place in space and time again. An hour had passed, perhaps more, since his arrival. He supposed he could reach for his pocket watch, but he could read the sun's angle well enough.

Her head lay against his thigh, her mouth and cheek close by his spent cock. She might have been sleeping; he didn't want to disturb her. In any case, he liked having her mouth where it was. Perhaps he might recover enough strength to have another go at her. Or perhaps she might simply kiss him there when she woke.

His cock jumped a bit at the thought of the kiss. She laughed, stretched her arms, and raised her head; it seemed she hadn't been asleep after all.

"He's still a lively fellow," she murmured.

"He wants another kiss from you."

A light, girlish kiss, at the tip. And another, more lascivious one, on the shaft, near that spot her tongue was so good at seeking out. It wouldn't be long now; he'd soon be ready for her mouth again.

But . . .

"Are your knees tired?" he heard himself asking her. "Do you want to give them a bit of a rest?"

"Oh no, not at all. Whatever you want, luv."

He could tell that her knees *were* tired. Still, a whore didn't rest while she was entertaining a customer. After all, she'd agreed to do everything he wanted, promised to do her best to please him.

And wasn't that the idea of this bargain they'd struck? After all, he'd laid out a lot of money. Her part of the agreement was to guarantee his pleasure. Better, really, if she had to pain herself a bit to give him what he wanted.

And yet . . .

"Come here." He drew her up to his lap. "*I* want a kiss from you as well."

She shrugged as though it were all the same to her. But he thought he could see a hint of gratitude in her eyes. He reached to kiss her.

"Wait," she told him. "Unless you want me smudging kohl and lip rouge all over your neckcloth."

He laughed as she unknotted the linen and tossed it onto the floor.

"We could have used those quick fingers aboard ship, to help with the rigging," he told her. "And to help in . . ." his voice caught suddenly—he hadn't expected her to begin undoing the buttons of his shirt. "To help in other ways," he said, leaning back to allow her to caress his chest—first with her fingers, and then with her mouth.

"I'm not a very good sailor," she murmured. "The rolling of the waves," she planted a tiny kiss below his collar bone. "The bumping," this time nibbling on his neck. "The sudden jolts and movements . . ."

She stroked his head, tickled his earlobes, nuzzled his cheeks. "All that pitching around, luv, could make me quite giddy," she told him.

"We shall have to see just how much pitching around you can tolerate." He pressed his lips to hers and then forced them apart with his tongue. He could taste himself in her mouth, feel the hard tips of her breasts grazing his exposed triangle of chest. He bit down lightly on her lower lip—it seemed he'd been dreaming of doing nothing else since he'd first laid eyes on her. She breathed deeply, surrendering the moment to him. If he'd *wanted* to draw a drop of blood, he knew she would have allowed it. But he loosened his teeth, relaxed his mouth into a deep, shuddering kiss.

He slipped his hands under her bum, kneading and squeezing her flesh, lifting her, parting her; she was straddling him now. His mouth moved down to her neck. She shifted her center; he moved a bit as well, positioning himself—for he was ready again—to enter her.

She'd opened to him; the lips of her cunt were about the head of his cock. He grasped her waist, intending to pull her body smartly downward. But she resisted him. "Touch me," she whispered, "touch me a little before you fuck me."

He almost slapped her instead. Well, he *was* the one doing the paying, wasn't he? And anyway, he was a man and *he* made those decisions. Well, wasn't he? Didn't he?

It all came from that moment of sympathy he'd felt—for her aching knees. *Stupid, Jack*. Give a woman like her a moment of consideration and there she'd be, ordering him around for her own purposes. He should have bitten her lip until the blood dribbled down her chin.

"Please," she said, "please touch me. Just one finger, for just one minute."

It wasn't much to ask, he supposed. But it was the principle of the thing.

"Please."

He wasn't here for *her* benefit.

Still, she was only asking for a minute of his time and his touch. Just his fingers, after all. Certainly his cock could spare a minute—no reason to be so precipitous, to fear a loss of control. Not when she was touching the head of it as provocatively as she was, kissing it, so to speak, with the lips of her cunt. Certainly he was man enough to . . . just to rub the tip of his finger at the outside of her slit. Lightly. Where the lips came together in front. Where she was swollen, trembling . . .

"Yes, yes, just like that." She moaned, thrashed about—

actually, he found himself rather enjoying the spectacle of her pleasure. Not to speak of knowing just how little it took to arouse her like that. Just a subtle fingertip—had he ever before considered what a mystery the female body was?

"Ah yes, all right. Thanks, darling."

But he didn't like that calm, self-satisfied tone of voice. He liked her better when she was moaning, gasping—not to speak of pleading. He played with her some more—the softer, the more controlled his touch, he discovered, the more profound her response. He ran another finger around the outside of her cunt, lightly pinching the lips, stroking, petting her, like a furry little animal. Her face had become pink, her eyes soft.

By now he had slid his cock within her—or perhaps she'd lowered herself onto him. Did it matter which it was? She was soft, warm, and quite ready, it seemed to him, for some jolting and pitching about. He thrust up into her, quickly, roughly; she cried out, and now so did he, delighted by the bouncing of her bum against his thighs and of her breasts against his chest. "Oh yes, lovely," she called—quite as though he needed *her* opinion of the matter.

He wanted her underneath him now. A quarter turn and he had her lying on her back on the settee; she bent her knees more sharply and he hoisted her legs around his neck. He drove more deeply into her. Excellent—except that the settee was a damn uncomfortable piece of furniture—where was that blasted Elastic Bed she'd talked about? He wanted to raise himself onto his toes, give himself better leverage. His knee ached a bit; there wasn't room to stretch his legs as he wanted.

But even with the knee, he seemed to be managing all right; she bucked under him, twisting and pinching his nipples while he sucked on hers. He could feel her begin to tremble inside. If he could only hold off his own orgasm, he thought. He wanted to see what she looked like at the crest of hers. But he couldn't. He could only fuck her harder and more furiously, too far gone even to notice that one of the settee's delicate legs had cracked, and that the thing was beginning to teeter unsteadily beneath them, even as they continued to rock in their embrace, with him deep inside her, both of them gasping, groaning, even laughing now, in their shared ascent to climax.

The leg had detached itself from the settee's base; the stupid piece of furniture pitched onto its back. Just at the same time she'd screamed her release and he'd discharged into her, collapsing on top of her.

Or to the side of her. Or wherever the ruined settee had deposited them. Jack, for one, was too disoriented to get his bearings for a moment. And both of them were too exhausted even to disentangle their limbs from one another for—well, who knew how long? Except that it seemed that the sun had set; there were no more slants of light coming through the window.

"You *are* all right, aren't you?" he murmured into her neck.

"Umm, I must be," she replied. "Well, I haven't broken or sprained anything, anyway. But the settee will be needing some repair."

He shrugged. "I'll cover the cost."

"That's good of you," she told him. "Thanks."

She was speaking in her shopkeeper's voice once more.

"And we're lucky," she'd rolled out of his arms and onto the floor, "that we didn't upset the lamp and set ourselves afire."

They stared at each other for a moment, both of them considering that they'd come pretty close to doing just that—even without the lamp.

"But it's already evening," she told him. "I must go. And perhaps you have an engagement as well."

He tried to move and groaned.

"Oh dear, your knee," she exclaimed. "I'd forgotten about your knee."

He laughed. "I rather forgot about it, too, for a while.

But it seems all right. No, the problem is that I'm weak. I'm hungry."

For—now that he'd taken the time to think about it—it occurred to him that he hadn't eaten all day.

She'd disappeared into a dark corner of the room. He wasn't surprised; prostitutes often did some secret personal adjustments afterward. Washing themselves, he expected, somewhere inside. Women's stuff; their business.

Her voice rang out from wherever she was. "Didn't eat enough before you came? Poor Jack, how very foolish of you. Well, what would you think about our meeting in the kitchen tomorrow? I'll feed you up a bit—can't have you expiring of hunger on top of me. Do you care for oysters?"

The rules were supposed to be that *he'd* specify the room. But he loved oysters; the feeding-up part sounded quite nice. He grunted. "Yes, yes, oysters, the kitchen." Quite as though he'd had the kitchen in mind all along.

She emerged from her dark corner, carrying her outer clothes and some other items with her. "And then we'll repair to a bedroom, of course."

"Of course." He stared at her, fixing herself up in the lamplight. She'd produced a handkerchief and some sort of stuff in a little bottle, to remove the lingering traces of paint from her face.

And now a loose gown, to slip over her undergarments. She dressed quickly. He expected that she wanted to get home to her Frenchman.

She was looking less whorish—and less approachable—at every moment. Especially after she'd combed the tousles out of her hair. Her face was beginning to fall into the haughty lines he'd seen yesterday. Well, what did he expect? It was only a business transaction, after all.

And as for the cries of pleasure he'd elicited from her—the gasps, the moans, and the way she'd thrown back her head when he'd touched her as she'd asked . . . to look at her now, you wouldn't believe that any of it had happened.

Shoes now, and her velvet cloak again.

"Well, I'll leave you now, Mr. Merion."

He'd liked it when she'd called him *Jack*—though he didn't remember telling her his first name.

But *Mr. Merion* was more appropriate to the terms of their bargain.

"All right, then, Cléo. Tomorrow. The kitchen."

Chapter Three

Tuesday—Later

The Frenchman sighed and shifted a bit in his sleep.

He was going to wake soon, she thought. Time to turn up the lamp. Georges, the valet, had assured her that the gentleman had been resting comfortably for the duration of her absence.

That's how he'd put it: "your absence, Madame." Georges could express polite censure in a very few neutral words. Fiercely protective of her and her companion outside, at home he dispensed with facial expression whenever possible. Of course, given the rough modeling of his face, a little expression went a long way.

Having delivered his message, he'd taken her cloak without even a glance at the unaccustomed dishevelment of her hair and gown, or at the bits of kohl she knew were lingering in the lines at the corners of her eyes.

No question that he knew where she'd been. Georges knew everything, whether he'd been told it or not.

And—ergo—no question that he also knew quite well that she and Philippe had agreed on the necessity of today's errand. They needed to rent the house near Soho Square. It was a pity that *she* had to be part of the bargain, but no more than a pity. They'd each suffered worse indignities over the years: her childhood had been unspeakable, and Philippe had almost died in the Terror. Their time together (a dozen years, as she'd told Jack Merion) had been gay and tranquil for the most part, but not without its financial ups and down, its emotional complexities. No matter. Lovers and companions both, they respected each other. They were adults; when hardships arose, each of them had borne his or her portion of the burden.

They kept no secrets from each other. And it was impossible to keep anything from Georges, who gave his opinion unsolicited and free of charge. Which was only fair, she supposed; these days he was virtually working for free as well. They'd dismissed all the other servants, except for a char who came in for the heavy work. They'd waited too long, hoping that a property settlement in France might go differently than it had. And they'd agreed not to draw upon the money they'd put aside for this brothel business. They couldn't afford anything west of Regent Street; this house was their best hope.

She stroked his cheek—it was pleasantly warm and dry. No clammy sweats today—perhaps he was finally on the mend. His sleeping face looked serene in the light.

Perhaps he'd be able to take some bread and salad when he woke, or even some of the leftover cassoulet. Her own stomach growled at the thought of the cassoulet. Well, it hadn't been any surprise that Jack Merion was an energetic partner. Not only was she hungry, but she quite ached, inside and out, from the vigorous pounding he'd given her. A lovely sort of ache, really.

Demanding was the word he'd used.

Demanding indeed.

Her lips curved into an unconscious smile when she remembered how astonished he'd been by her own modest demands. Astonished, but not intractable—well, *that* was a good thing, anyway. He'd caressed her quite prettily when she'd insisted upon it. And she'd enjoyed those rough, sailor's hands of his.

Of course he'd know more about what a woman liked, if anyone had ever bothered to teach him. He'd been spoiled, no doubt for being so pleasant to look at. Even now. A girl could forgive him a great deal, just for the sight of that smile. Those wide, light, still somehow innocent hazel eyes, too. Not to speak of the fancywork below and his energetic way of using it.

One could take him as he was. Well, *one* could, perhaps. But she wouldn't. She wasn't the naïve, accepting girl she'd once been. She'd bring him round, make a lover of him in the four days remaining to her. She hadn't expected the flashes of kindness and decency under his blustering awkwardness.

No, that wasn't true. He'd turned out to be precisely the man she'd known he'd be.

Four days. Only four days.

But she wouldn't think of it as *only*. These days with him were a gift, and she'd value them accordingly. Do anything she liked with him—even feed him, if it pleased her to do so.

The prince's eyelids fluttered. After supper perhaps she'd read to him for a bit. They wouldn't discuss the events of the afternoon—what mattered was that she was quite safe, that his health was no worse, and that they were a day closer to leasing the property. He liked to see her smiling when he woke. She was surprised to realize that she was already smiling.

Forgive me, Philippe, she thought. But I do have a secret.

A burdensome one. It was hard, bearing it by herself. For a moment she found herself wishing that Georges would use his mysterious powers to divine her thoughts.

Her companion opened his eyes and drifted back to consciousness.

She took his hand. They exchanged smiles. Life was complicated.

Forgive me, old friend.

Wednesday—The Kitchen

Right prompt today, he congratulated himself as he stepped up to the front steps. Well, he could hardly *not* be, lurking around the corner as he had been, anxiously consulting his pocket watch until the hand crept round to three. Pleasant set of streets, actually. The truth was, he found its shabbiness comforting, the buzz of trades and laboring people invigorating. Immigrants had always made their homes in Soho; one heard an interesting mix of dialects and accents around one. It wouldn't be bad to live here, he found himself thinking, before dismissing the thought with an impatient shrug.

He shut the door behind him—it made a nice, solid sound; the house really *was* a fine piece of construction—and started to the back stairs.

Damn, she thought. He was early. The food was ready, but *she* could have used a bit of freshening up.

Damn and double damn.

A splendid aroma wafted up to greet him: mussels stewed with butter, cream, leeks, and some ingredient Jack couldn't identify. He could hear her rattling the pots and pans, singing as she worked, her voice thin but sweet. He waited, just outside the doorway, to hear what she was singing.

A Wife's like a guinea in gold,
Stampt with the name of her spouse;
Now here, now there; is bought or is sold;
And is current in every house.

An insulting ditty, at least to a man who intended to marry. One didn't like to imagine one's future wife being passed around like a gold coin.

No doubt he was especially sensitive to such a possibility, as he'd finally gotten that kiss from Evelina last night. She'd been pleased to see him, concerned about his "touch of malaria," and pleasantly surprised by how well he'd looked. A bit tired, of course, she'd observed, but that was to be expected; he also seemed calmer, more at his ease; bed rest had clearly done him good. Well, *something* had done him good, anyway; he'd blushed invisibly under his sun-browned skin. Perhaps it was his look of confusion that had done the trick. In any case, that's when he had finally gotten the kiss. Hardly a passionate one—in truth, it had hardly been a kiss at all—more like a promissory note, redeemable upon delivery of the marriage contract.

But *now* who was sounding cynical about marriage?

She'd finished the lyric, and was humming softly to herself. He lingered in the stairway, wondering how she'd greet him.

Like the adorable slut who'd wriggled out of her yellow peignoir so obligingly yesterday? Or the distant, self-possessed woman who'd visited him in his sitting room?

He wondered which of the two he wanted.

Each of them. Both of them. The slut in yellow for—well, for obvious reasons. But he also wanted the *grande horizontale* in the dark velvet cloak—for reasons that were quite unfathomable to him.

Today, though, she was neither of those women. She wore a different peignoir today—of some pale, indefinable color, what little he could see of it under her voluminous white apron. Her face was flushed, and a bit moist, from the steam rising from an iron pot on the stove. Her brow was furrowed, all her concentration directed, it seemed, toward the mussel stew. She'd taken a bit of the sauce into a wooden spoon, and was sipping its contents.

Today she was entirely another woman.

Except that she wasn't, he realized. Today he was simply seeing a different side of her. The tormenting half-remembered line from *Antony and Cleopatra* sprang whole into his mind.

Age cannot wither her, nor custom stale
Her infinite variety.

She'd pinned her hair out of the way, but curly tendrils had loosened in front of her ears and at her nape. He moved behind her, buried his mouth in the back of her neck, reached his arms around her and underneath the apron to squeeze her breasts.

She made a low, appreciative sound in her throat, relaxed against him, and then tried to free herself from his grasp. He tightened his arms about her.

"I was afraid you'd be late," she said, "and that the sauce would boil away. And I wasn't sure . . ."

He held her more closely to him, so that he could feel the warmth of her against the front of his trousers.

"Let it boil away," he whispered.

She wrenched herself free and whirled about to face him. "Are you daft?" she asked. "Do you know what mussels cost this week?"

"I'll cover the loss," he said.

"Don't be stupid," she replied. "You can waste your money however you please, but I won't have you wasting food."

She dipped the spoon into the pot. "Taste it," she demanded. "Does it have too much pepper?"

She could have flavored it with brimstone, he thought, for all he cared. He'd lift her up, lay her down on the table, spread her legs, find out—the only way it really mattered—exactly who she was today.

If she would only stop waving that spoon in front of

him. To get the blasted thing out of his face, he tasted the sauce in it.

Blimey. "Did you cook this?"

"Of course I cooked it. I live with a Frenchman, remember? We haven't much money, but we eat well. The pepper?"

"The pepper is fine. The pepper is perfect. The whole thing is perfect. And that other flavor—orange peel, isn't it? Extraordinary."

It was a different smile from any she'd given him thus far.

Well, it was a different sort of pleasure she was offering, he thought. He watched the curve of her arms as she reached to untie the apron from around her neck. He'd thought he'd only be buying sex from her, but it seemed he'd been wrong—odd, how often she made him feel like an ignorant boy again. You think you understand what a man and woman can share, she seemed to be telling him, but you don't know the half of it.

"I enjoy cooking," she said.

She brought the stewpot to the table. The peignoir seemed to change colors as she moved, shading from gray to blue, lavender to the same fleshy pink as the mussels.

"Well, sit down, then, in this big chair over here," she told him. "We'll use the bowls for the stew, after we've finished the oysters."

Two huge bowls, the oysters still in their shells, a loaf of fresh bread, and a pitcher of ale. There were also quarters of lemon and butter melted over a spirit-lamp. He sank down into the seat she'd motioned him to.

"Here's an oyster knife for you," she said. "And you can toss the shells into the bucket."

It takes some concentration to eat an oyster: to grasp it in his palm, swiveling his knife to open it, taking care not to slice through his hand instead. And once he had it open, to be sure not to slop the oyster liquor, pooled in the shell beneath the little creature he was about to swallow.

And so he was saved from the necessity of making conversation. *Coward*, he chided himself, but there it was—he'd bought the right to fuck her every way he could think of, but he was shy about conversing with her across the table while they ate. What could he say, anyway, that she'd find interesting? Nothing, probably. He fell silent, for fear of seeing her eyes glaze and her face fall into delicate, polite lines of boredom.

Well, she wasn't a delicate eater anyway. No more than he was.

And so he simply cut and slurped his oysters, taking time, between twists of his knife, to watch her lips greedily sucking in the gray flesh, the tops of her breasts shimmering above the pale silk of her peignoir, the lines and hollows of her throat moving slightly after she tossed back a shell to get at the liquor and swallowed with gusto.

"It's a very pretty wrapper you're wearing," he told her. She'd torn a large chunk of bread from the loaf, and was mopping up the brine and butter that had gathered at the bottom of her bowl.

She nodded her thanks, chewing all the while.

"But I've seen quite enough of it," he said. "And not enough of *you*."

"I'll get bread crumbs over the front of me," she murmured. "I might even spill some of the butter. I can be a dainty eater when I want to, but it doesn't feel natural. Comes from being hungry as a child, I expect. Philippe was shocked when he took me on. I'd learned to sip champagne elegantly enough, but as for food—he had to teach me table manners, and I still forget them sometimes."

She put down the bread, wiped her fingers on a napkin, and obligingly removed the peignoir. He tried to control his breathing while she loosened the drawstring of her shift.

But he couldn't stop himself from reaching across the table, tugging the muslin cloth down to uncover her breasts.

"Yes," he told her, "much better."

Especially when she leaned over to serve each of them a bowl of mussels.

"I didn't make a lot of it," she told him. "Didn't want us getting full and sodden. The oysters would have been enough, really, but that's not really cooking, is it? And the mussels looked so good when I went to the market this morning—they weren't cheap, but a person gets what she pays for, after all. And I . . . well, I felt like cooking something today. Philippe doesn't have much of an appetite lately."

She looked a bit shy. He hadn't expected her to be shy about anything. "It's an excellent stove," she added softly. "Very easy to control the heat."

They finished in silence. "It was splendid," he said. "And your table manners seem quite adequate to me. Come here, and let me see more closely."

He licked off a few crumbs from her breasts, like a cat grooming its young. She purred under his tongue.

"Were you often hungry as a child?" he murmured. "Or was it just during the hardest times?"

"We had nothing *but* the hardest times," she told him. "But you don't want to hear about *that.*"

He supposed not. In any case, it wasn't what he was paying her for. He supposed they could have talked about it while they'd been eating, though. Odd, he rarely talked of his childhood in Lancashire. It was as though his real life had begun when he'd become a sailor.

"We'd better go upstairs, hadn't we?" She leaned down to kiss him lightly on the head. "It's getting late. Let me just fill a pitcher with hot water from the stove. And—ah, yes—some of those towels that I left to heat there, too."

Silently, he followed her up the dark back stairs to the entryway.

"The Elastic Bed is another flight up," she told him. "I put my gown and cloak in that bedroom as well. I hope the stairs are not a hardship for your knee . . ."

They'd gotten as far as the next landing when he told her to stop.

Chapter Four

Wednesday—Second Story

As she mounted the stairs, she'd been idly trying to calculate how many heavy pitchers of water she must have carried to the upper storys, her first years in the house.

She'd also been wondering (her thoughts these days always threatening to mix up the past and present) if he was looking at her arse as he climbed the stairs behind her. And whether, at her age, her body could really justify such sustained scrutiny. She wished they could get it over with, climb the stairs at a bound—but that was impossible, with his bad knee and his cane.

Too bad she wasn't still wearing her dressing gown. But, as with so many things, she hadn't had the luxury of choosing. She'd tried to put it on again before they'd left the kitchen. But he'd told her to leave it off.

If she'd been cleverer, though, she might have thought to ask him to precede her on the staircase.

Which is what she was wishing she'd done—just as he called out to her.

"Stop, please."

"Is it your . . . ?" She had been going to ask after his

knee, but—a bit belatedly—she'd realized that it wasn't his knee that had caused him to make that request.

"Put down the pitcher and the towels," he told her. "There's plenty of room for them on the floor, at the landing. And now kneel down on the third—no, the second step from the top. That's right, you can rest your head and arms on the carpet. But better push the pitcher farther away, so there's no danger of upsetting it."

The specificity of his demands rather thrilled her, showing, as it did, that he'd been thinking with some precision about what he wanted.

Unfortunately, it also showed that he didn't remember—or worse, had chosen to ignore—the terms of their bargain.

He was kneeling behind her on the step now, his knees on either side of hers. She could feel him fumbling with the buttons of his trousers—ah yes, there he was—not hard yet, well, not as hard as he soon *would* be, anyway, but hard enough for him to nestle into the cleft of her arse. She made tiny arcs with her hips, stroking herself against him, feeling him harden between her buttocks. Lovely, caressing him like that. A pity to have to stop. Lovely the way he'd continue to harden, a bit more with each stroke of her, until he was ready to enter her. Until she was relaxed and open, ready to receive him.

But not so lovely that she'd tolerate such utter disrespect of her wishes in the matter.

Lord, but she wanted him.

Not like *that*, though. Not forced upon her.

"No," she said. "I've already told you. Not without something to make you slippery."

She held herself still and squeezed her legs together. Of course, if he really insisted upon this, she wouldn't be able to stop him. He outweighed her by a considerable amount. At a certain point, she'd have to give way.

But it wouldn't be what she wanted. And—as she'd be

obliged to call off their bargain—ultimately it wouldn't benefit him, either.

He laughed. "It's all right. I do have something slippery with me."

"The bloody hell you do," she told him. "You know, you're not the first imbecile to think his spit will do the job."

"No, really." His voice was warm against her ear. But what was he fumbling with now?

He'd curved his body around hers—she liked his weight and warmth against her, the press of his arms around atop hers on the landing. He brought one of his hands to her mouth, pressed his fingers to her lips. She'd learned over the years that men liked their fingers sucked—odd how each of them seemed to think he was the only one, too. But she'd be damned if she'd open her mouth, or for that matter any part of herself, under the present circumstances.

He forced the tip of his finger between her lips. She bit down upon it.

And was rewarded with the taste of melted butter.

"Will it do?" His voice was a bit anxious. "I brought some with me in a bowl—hid it behind me while you were getting the water."

It would do quite well. "We'll smell of it, though," she giggled. He lifted himself off her, to rub himself liberally with the stuff.

"And rub me, too, dear, yes, that's right, and inside, as well . . ."

A few last rays of sunlight slanted down on her through the skylight at the top of the staircase. She stretched like a cat under its warmth, arched her back under his touch. Lightly, gently, (how quickly he learned!) he massaged her in the cleft of her bottom, touching, tickling, and exploring her, and now (oh dear, yes) creeping inside as the ring of muscle loosened to let him in—a smooth, buttery fingertip, and now the same finger, up to the knuckle. He explored her slowly, carefully—still circumspect, and wonderfully respectful of the private place she'd allowed him to enter.

But it wasn't a finger she was feeling now. She breathed deeply, braced her knees against the thickly carpeted stair riser; it was the head of his cock now and it was inside her. Still moving slowly, he sank into her like spreading darkness, each deliberate quarter-inch of his progress seeming like a new entry, through a new door, into a new secret chamber—each secret, private, scandalous, wicked, and delicious quarter-inch of her.

He stroked her, curved his body around hers, hummed and thrummed with the tremors he felt in her limbs and belly. Given the extremity of their situation, he hadn't thought she'd respond—or even notice—when he kissed her nape, just below where she'd pinned up her hair.

But evidently he'd been quite wrong about that. Grinding with the thrusts of his cock, she writhed and shuddered at the lightest touches of his mouth and tongue—even at the warmth of his breath.

He hadn't really believed her when she'd said she'd enjoy it. But he could feel her muscles opening and relaxing under him, and then squeezing him, hot, tight, dark.

He could drive deeply into her now, as hard as he wanted to, while she gasped and screamed her pleasure, collapsing under him. And now he was gushing into her, collapsing upon her, hugging and squeezing her breasts beneath him, while his cane bumped down the staircase and rolled into the center of the house's entryway.

"I'll fetch the cane," she said softly some time later.

"Sorry," she added, upon regaining the top of the staircase. "I shouldn't have mistrusted you as I did, not when you're so clearly a man of your word."

"No matter," he told her. "It was a bit of a prank on my

part, I suppose. And in any case, you were quite right about one thing: I'm going to stink of this stuff. Well, both of us are. Not to speak of my clothes."

"Come along," she told him. "There's soap in the bedroom. And . . . well, of course, there's also a bed."

He stood docilely, a placid smile on his face as she removed his coat, waistcoat, and shirt.

Becoming a bit less so when she got his boots off.

And flat-out skittish when it came to his trousers.

While *she* (and so expert, too, at untying and unbuttoning—not to speak of peeling a snugly tailored garment down the legs of its wearer) . . . she felt herself growing more graceless, less patient, with every minute.

He looked beautiful silhouetted against the bright blue wall, and beautiful closer up, too, the sculpting of the muscles in his shoulders and belly, the dark brown hair making such a sinuous line down his chest and downward, below his navel, disappearing beneath the waistline of his drawers.

Difficult not simply to rip the linen from his hips and thighs, leave the fine white fabric in tatters.

She reached to untie the string that held them up.

A strong hand immobilized her wrist.

"Leave it alone."

She stared while he made his own adjustments to the drawstring.

"There you are," he told her. "Loose enough so you can wash me and . . . and so forth. But I don't take them off."

His wide eyes were fixed on the room's chandelier. Flickering toward the window now, the molding on the ceiling. Looking everywhere but at her.

"I was burned, one place. And then there are also the stitches the army surgeon put into me, after he decided he couldn't get the metal out of my leg."

"You have scars on your back, too, from a flogging, I should imagine. Old ones. Well healed."

"Yes, just once, a long time ago. But I don't care about those. The ones on my leg are much worse.

"I was lucky it was just my thigh—the deck and not the main mast, if you get my meaning. But it's not pretty to look at. And so I'd rather . . ."

She dipped one of the towels into the pitcher of hot water. "Of course, if you don't wish it."

Clumsy to have to wash him through the openings in the fabric. She did the best she could and dried him carefully, before taking a new towel and scrubbing herself.

"Do you suppose I'd gawk at it or turn away in disgust?" she asked.

He groped for an answer. "No," he told her finally, "a woman as good at your profession as you are would never . . ."

It wasn't the answer she wanted, but it would have to do.

"It's just that . . ." He was frowning now, as though groping for the right word. "Well, I've enjoyed thinking that you like my looks, you see, even if . . ."

Even if it was her job to make every man think she liked his looks. She put a finger on his lips, to stop him from saying it.

"I like a naked man in bed with me," she said. "And after all, Europe has had a terrible war. Scars—especially gotten as you got yours—are a mark of honor."

"Well, tomorrow, perhaps," he replied.

Tomorrow, she thought, *there will only be three more days of him*. She kissed his cheek and pulled down the coverlet, drawing him into bed beside her.

"But we really must go." Sighing, as she pulled herself away from him, an hour later.

"Tomorrow," she told him, "we can use the bigger bedroom upstairs. They named it the Royal Suite when they did it up in that fancy, bright paint. Kept it for special customers. It's another flight up, but it's got a bigger bed. They used to keep it very elegant. It's a very vivid yellow."

He laughed. "Why not? A bigger bed sounds agreeable."

"Tomorrow, then," she said, "in the large yellow bedroom. Third story."

Chapter Five

Thursday—The Yellow Bedroom

It was becoming habitual, he thought, comfortable as expensive boots or a sideboard stocked with good brandy. Today the prospect of seeing her at three hadn't interfered with his normal round of activities at all. In fact, it seemed to make him more efficient, brisker and more confident of his judgment. This morning he'd negotiated for some shares of a wool merchant's business; he could expect a good return on the investment. His courtship of Evelina was progressing apace: Wilson had shown him a few quite likely properties in Marylebone, and today Mr. Oakshutt had clapped him on the shoulder, quite cordially, in the entryway of the big house off Cavendish Square.

He'd eaten a hearty luncheon. Beef and beer were just what he needed, he thought, to keep up his stamina. Though in truth, it wasn't *only* stamina she craved from him. Who would have thought that he'd be able to please her some of those other ways? Astonishing to find himself imagining new ways he might touch her, wring cries and sighs and (then, afterward) sleepy, satisfied smiles from her.

Nice to have such a woman in his life—and remarkably easy to get accustomed to. Well, in a few years he'd be able to do it for real—not her, of course, but someone almost as good. For the next bit, though, he'd have to content himself with getting a wife, making decent, respectful love to her, producing a brood of children to inherit the fortune he was amassing, the solid investments and properties. Not enough surplus, right now, to support a mistress of *her* quality. His blood hummed in anticipation of the afternoon's encounter, his only worry (but mostly he'd kept it at bay) being whether he'd really let her slip off his drawers.

She'd woken early, done her marketing, and taken a load of washing to the laundress. A hen was stewing on top of the range; she'd check on it as soon as she finished totaling the last column of figures she'd drawn up.

Muffled in an eiderdown, Philippe was reading Lord Byron by the fire. Poor darling, she thought, his body didn't retain heat well, and today the air was brisk. The year had passed the equinox; it was unmistakably autumn now, even with the uncertain sunlight making a garish show of itself through the back parlor window, illuminating her calculations. The weather was going to change.

But the numbers, in any case, were reassuringly solid. With luck, the new business would succeed. It would be a difficult undertaking, but possible nonetheless.

Of course, she wouldn't be the sort of generous madam a girl preferred to work for. "Stingy old bawd," she imagined some fresh, young eighteen-year-old muttering under her breath. But after all, hadn't she muttered similar things herself once? Similar and worse.

Well, too bad for them. Make no mistake about it, she told herself, any girl who worked for her would learn to keep her room nice. And not to expect the house to supply bonbons or other luxuries. She paused. No, a desirable girl would demand a treat once in a while. There would have to be nice things, little presents for birthdays and Christmas, anyway. But nothing more; they'd have to depend on their gentlemen for candied violets or Pears Soap.

She changed a few figures, frowned at the higher totals, and shrugged her shoulders. A little worse, but at least the calculations were honest. Better to know now rather than be surprised later.

Still, the general plan was good; all in all, it was a neat piece of budgeting. She'd allowed a reasonable amount for medical care, for example—damned if she'd be one of those madams who were too delicate (or too lazy) to look out for the girls' health. *Her* girls (once she had them) would be able to come to her, consult with her about missed periods, bad discharges, strange itches, and irksome rashes. There would be sponges and all the most advanced potions to douche with. And lots of information about how it all worked.

Sympathy, shared information, and a sharp eye for disease were good investments. Just as long as no one expected her to care about the occasional broken heart.

She sighed. Well, it was the way of the world, wasn't it? You took care of others when you could, but you put yourself first. What was important was her future—and Philippe's, of course. During the hard times, one looked out for oneself. And one was selfish and strong-minded about it. Just look at Jack Merion.

Look at him indeed—without his clothes, if possible.

And in a real bed.

Astonishing, humiliating, and almost wonderful, how much she'd loved having him in a real bed. Staircases and settees were all very well in their way, she supposed, and men seemed to find them proof of a certain impetuosity, but when a woman reached a certain age . . .

A beam of sunlight shone from behind a cloud, slanting across her writing table and blurring her calculations. She pushed the papers away, rather more abruptly than she'd intended. Startled by her sudden gesture, her companion looked up from his reading. She turned to him, pouting so as to create the effect of comic befuddlement. Or so she hoped.

"Well, it's hard work, all these numbers," she murmured. A weak excuse; she'd had very little education, but Philippe knew she could handle a column of figures. Still, she had to blame her emotional volatility on something. Until Philippe's last bout of illness, computing costs had been his responsibility.

He nodded. "You're very good, *mignonne*, to take it on. Perhaps tonight I'll be able to go over it."

If she'd made him feel guilty, he wouldn't burden her with the knowledge.

"Of course. Thank you."

The clock on the mantel struck eleven.

The really hard work, she thought, would be getting through the next four hours.

She was right. After that, it was easy.

For when three o'clock did finally come around, Jack had only to take one look at her, sprawled carelessly upon the big Elastic Bed in a brief, bright dressing gown—red Chinese silk this time—her eyes shining, legs spread open . . .

"Put down the cigarette," he growled. And she had not the slightest difficulty getting him to part with his drawers.

"You distracted me," he told her afterward. "You astonished me, the way you looked in that red thing, with your black, black hair—you know, in the middle of this yellow room."

She hadn't closed the curtains. The room was flooded with rosy, golden late-afternoon light.

Her head rested in the space below his collarbone. She kissed his chest and stroked a finger down toward his belly.

"Thanks, luv," she said. "Glad you liked the red peignoir. It's a bit on the artistic side, I expect.

"But then," her finger was making its slow way downward, "you created quite a distraction yourself, you know, with the whomping big, stiff cock you had on you today. I could hardly spare the time to look at your battle scars."

He laughed, a bit anxiously.

"Well, you're right that they're not very pretty," she added.

She could feel his sharp intake of breath.

"But they're really not as bad as you led me to fear."

His sigh of relief was more intense still.

"Truly," she said.

He relaxed against the pillows.

She touched a smooth and rather nasty bright pink patch of skin on his right thigh, where he'd been burned in the pitch of battle. "It doesn't hurt when I touch it, does it?"

He shook his head. "The nerves are dead."

"So I can't comfort you there, much as I'd like to."

She leaned over to kiss the battered flesh, and then to nuzzle his cock, now spent and docile between his legs. "Still, the nerves are quite alive *here*, aren't they?"

"Quite." He shivered.

"But all in all, you're not as shy about showing yourself to me as you thought you might be, I take it?"

"No, I'm not. Thank you. I thought you might faint or scream, you see. Well, perhaps I've been exaggerating how bad it looks, but . . ."

He stopped, suddenly unsure of what he wanted to say.

"I'm . . . courting a young lady, and . . ."

She smiled. "It'll go fine, Mr. Merion. When you marry the young lady, I mean."

"I expect it will," he said.

"Come here," he told her, pulling her back into his arms. "Of course, I don't know if I can promise you quite so much *whomping* this time, but . . ."

She giggled and mussed up his hair. "You're all right, even when you're not whomping me."

"I want you on top of me this time," he told her. "Yes, that's right. So I can watch you, see you when you come."

Like every halfway competent dolly, she maintained a repertoire of pleased and excited facial expressions, each to be donned in its turn, like a peignoir, for a customer's entertainment and enjoyment. But he'd quickly learned the difference between these and the real ways she had of evidencing her gratification. The way her back would arch, her nipples pucker, her blue eyes turn black and almost opaque, like an opium eater's. Not to speak of how her cunt would open and soften to him, the better to grasp and cradle him when he'd gone deep within her. He'd begun to think that their lovemaking was actually quite a bit nicer after a day's first go-round, when he was no longer so frenzied, so absorbed in his own arousal.

When he was able to make new discoveries. For it seemed there was an infinity to know about her. Places and ways she loved to be touched, sometimes softly, but sometimes not so softly; there were pinches and bites, he'd found, squeezes and tiny slaps that would delight her. Sometimes, making love to her wasn't a soft business at all.

Making love? Could one say one *made love* to a prostitute?

Well, no matter about the words. Sad, though, that there were only two more days of it to go. Less time ahead of them than the time that had gone before.

Rather like their lives.

But she was staring at him curiously—and no wonder, he chided himself, the way his mind had strayed from the business at hand.

Not that he'd ceased his enthusiastic plowing. And not that she hadn't been rolling her hips in perfect time with his.

But there was no doubt that he'd gotten lost in his thoughts—he must have been pretty obvious about it, too.

Smiling apologetically, he put out his arms to draw her closer to him. Slippery, beaded with sweat, her heavy breasts tumbled over his chest while her lips met his in a teasing, biting kiss. He arched his back under her; he caressed her flanks, her bum and thighs. She moaned, paused for a moment, missing a beat or two, almost losing herself in the touch of his fingers.

Almost—but not quite. He marveled at how well they'd learned each other's bodies, how deftly they moved together—the kissing and caressing only enhancing their energetic, rhythmic fucking.

She rose above him now, sitting back onto her haunches, smiling down at him, delighted to have recaptured his attention so totally. Teasingly, she lifted her arms, put her hands behind her neck, as though to give him a better view of her. Well, he *had* said he'd wanted to be able to watch her—especially now, while she was trembling at the brink of orgasm, mightily trying to stave off the inevitable moment of surrender.

If he reached out to touch the tip of one of her breasts, he thought, she'd explode in his hand.

And so he didn't. Thrusting his hips even harder, he simply stared at her with awe and potent wonder, sharing and glorying in her moment of pride and vanity.

Spectacular, that instant when a beautiful woman knew absolutely and exactly how beautiful she was.

But such a brief, narrow, fleeting instant . . . just before . . . for now she couldn't hold back any longer. She tucked back her shoulders, thrust out her breasts. She was all one sinuous line now, curve of neck and spine down to the hot, tight places inside her. Her face, her neck and breasts had flushed bright pink. He heard the low growl in her throat.

Heard her—for he couldn't see her any longer. Now he

could only feel the weight of her body collapsed against his, the soft, shivering, almost sobbing laugh in her throat and against his chest.

And all he could see now was the warm, dark night, the unearthly constellations of his own soaring climax.

"I brought a bottle of claret," he said a bit later. "I could open it if you'd like."

"Ummm." She smiled lazily. "And I brought us some bread and cheese."

They each bustled about, producing their treasures and then arranging themselves against the pillows, treats ready at hand. He'd remembered to bring a corkscrew, but hadn't thought how they'd actually drink the wine. For of course there were no glasses in the room.

"Stupid of me," he said, "not to bring some along."

"I could go downstairs to the kitchen," she offered.

"No matter, we'll drink it from the bottle."

"Passing it back and forth," she smiled here, "like a pair of mudlarks in the gutter."

He took a healthy swig and passed it to her.

As though he'd challenged her to it, she tried to take as large a swallow as he had. The wine dribbled down her chin. "Here," he said, and licked it up. She licked back at him, though there was no wine on his face or neck.

And as difficult as it had been to talk to her in the kitchen yesterday, that's how easy it was today. Perhaps because they weren't staring at each other across a table. He liked sitting next to her, against the pillows; there was something companionable about passing a bottle back and forth.

Whatever it was, he heard himself telling her things he hadn't told anyone, things he hadn't even quite known he needed to tell.

A little about his childhood at first, the village where the men were too stupid not to go down into the colliery. And where lots of them died, too, but he'd be damned if *he* would.

But mostly—perhaps because she'd seen his scars—he discovered that he wanted to explain a thing or two about his supposed heroism. Enlighten her, so to speak, about his so-called marks of honor.

"It was never my intention to go to war. When I was young I was in the merchant force, and did some smuggling, too—well, that's *really* where I made my money . . .

"We were pressed into the damn Royal Navy, see, me and old Eddy, a few years ago, one night when we were out carousing in Wapping. I'd rather be on a ship that actually *ships* something—hauling coal, well, at least it keeps people warm, those who can afford it, anyway.

"No reason to join up to fight Bonaparte, to my way of thinking, not of my own free will. To my mind it was bloody all right, Frenchmen deciding they didn't need a king or lords anymore. I might've been more inclined to risk my neck for England, see, if the lord who'd owned the colliery had risked a few guineas, put 'em to reinforcing the mine shaft."

He shrugged. "Not what 'a grateful nation' wants to hear from one of its heroes, I expect."

"But you did risk your neck. You rescued Viscount Crowden, after all."

"I rescued more men than him. Well, what else could I do, let them die? Nobody cared, though, that I saved some ordinary seamen, and anyway, what did it matter? I couldn't save old Eddy . . ."

But he'd already told her too much. He'd almost told her that he'd thought of Eddy as a sort of dad, his own having died when the mine shaft collapsed. But he managed to salvage a bit of his self-respect by keeping quiet about it. She lit a cigarette for each of them, from the lamp at the side of the bed.

They stared at the white wisps of smoke, drifting about the darkening room.

"I expect you're from London," he said finally.

"The rookery in the parish of St. Giles."

Quite the vilest quarter of the city. He turned to stare at her, with increased respect, for her having survived it.

She laughed. "Good of you not to jump out of bed in horror, or check the sheets for some antiquated lice. I ran away when I was very young. Became a char in this very part of town."

Difficult to imagine her as one of the pale, pinched little girls one saw everywhere, hauling big bundles of washing and pails of water, wielding mops and brooms, scrubbing floors. Or perhaps not so difficult. Something about the lift of her chin, the wariness of her gaze. He leaned forward, to look at her.

She turned her head away. "But in time I found an easier way to support myself, as you see."

"Yes, well, and good for you, too."

"The madam liked to advertise me as a sad case of child molestation—'ruined by a treacherous, villainous stepfather,' that sort of twaddle. As though I'd ever even had a stepfather, or any sort of man staying with my mum longer than a night at a time.

"But the gentlemen loved it. I had to wear pinafores, sing sentimental ditties in the parlor until I was almost twenty, when I finally rebelled against it. I wanted a decent corset, like the rest of the girls. And I hated having to hide my cigarettes."

He'd seen the advertisements the fancy brothels printed up. Crowden had picked up a few that had circulated at his club.

"How did they advertise you after that?"

She hesitated for a moment.

"As the girl whose mouth could accommodate anybody."

"Not very poetical of them."

"True enough, though. Well, *you're* proof, after all."

Uncomfortable, that. Not that he didn't enjoy the implied compliment. But he didn't like thinking of all the men who'd preceded him. Especially the one who actually mattered to her.

But he'd agreed to leave Soulard out of this.

He took a long swig from the wine bottle, passing her the little that was left in it.

"It's an excellent claret," she told him.

"I think so, too," he said. "Well, we've both come pretty far, I expect, even to be able to tell a claret from a Madeira."

She laughed. "Gin's what they drank, where I came from. And gin's what they still drink. Only thing that makes life bearable."

"And these days you've got a prince waiting for you at home. Done quite well for yourself, all in all."

"As you have."

He'd drunk too much wine. Or perhaps it was the unaccustomed cigarette that was making him dizzy. He told himself to calm down, let her cuddle him a bit between the sheets, allow the mild stirring between his legs to gather some energy. After which time she could revive him completely.

She could accommodate anybody. Advertised as such, in all the finest gentlemen's clubs in London.

And she had a prince in her bed at home.

He didn't know which information he found more irksome.

Or perhaps he did know.

"How's Monsieur Soulard's health?"

"Thank you, I believe he's a bit better."

"Good, I'm happy to hear it."

And do you love him?

But he hadn't really asked her that. He'd simply—for the briefest of moments—imagined that he might.

Just as, for the briefest of moments, he'd imagined that he cared.

After all, she hadn't asked him about Evelina. She probably hadn't even been listening when he'd told her he planned to marry.

Why should either of them care? They'd never even meet again, after the two days remaining to them.

It was a business arrangement.

He reached for her, a bit roughly. And as though to prove his point, she did a quick, businesslike job of bringing him off.

Well, what had he expected?

"And tomorrow?" she asked. Her attention appeared to be concentrated on her image in a hand mirror, while she cleared the black stuff from the rims of her eyes.

Tomorrow.

Well, he should take advantage of this opportunity, shouldn't he? Do something different, exotic, a little less personal and mundane than sitting around in bed trading stories of their childhoods.

Tomorrow perhaps he should satisfy his curiosity. After all, he'd probably never have an opportunity like this again.

"Tomorrow, why don't you show me what they'd do in that red room? The one with the . . . the gargoyles, and . . ."

"I know the room you mean. By all means, Mr. Merion. Whatever you want, luv."

Chapter Six

Friday—The Red Punishment Room

"You're sure now?" she asked him.

"Quite sure."

"And have I explained it all quite clearly?"

"Perfectly clearly. Thank you."

"And if, at any time or for any reason, you wish me to stop, what will you say?"

"I shall say 'rhinoceros.' "

"Be sure to remember it, because if you say 'stop,' I shan't pay it the least bit of attention."

It seemed absurd to him, but she'd assured him that it was always done that way. The more ridiculous the special "escape" word, the more likely the customer was to remember it. And the less likely to say it in the ordinary course of events.

Whatever "ordinary" might prove itself to be.

She hadn't worn a peignoir today. Nor even a shift.

Just a very tightly laced corset, piped in black velvet.

Black stockings and tall boots of russet leather. Riding boots, he supposed.

Her breasts were bare, nipples dark and erect. Lips painted a red so dark they seemed black under the skylights.

It's a bit like the theater, she'd explained. Not like real life at all. A girl who's good at it takes you to a place that's safe and dangerous at the same time.

Are you good at it? he'd asked.

What do you think? she'd asked in return.

"Well, then," she said. "Take off those clothes, boy. And be quick about it."

He stared at her, surprised. Somehow he'd expected her to undress him.

"Boy?" Her voice was like ice.

"Oh, yes, sorry." He unknotted his cravat.

"Yes, *Miss Myles*."

"All right, yes, Miss Myles. I'm sorry."

"You're sorry, *Miss Myles*."

"I'm sorry, Miss Myles."

"*How* sorry, boy?"

"I'm *very* sorry, Miss Myles. Please forgive me, Miss Myles."

She nodded, barely countenancing his apology, and far more interested, it seemed, in how expeditiously he'd be able to peel his clothes off.

Which wouldn't be easy with his hands so sweaty. Amazing what a fuss he'd made yesterday, about revealing his scars to her.

"You can sit on the floor," she told him, "to remove your boots."

This time he formulated his thanks so as not to require correction. He was quite sincere, too; if she hadn't allowed him to sit on the floor, his knee wouldn't have allowed him to maintain his balance.

How stately she looked; she seemed to tower over him

while he grubbed about on the floor. It would be easy, he thought, to forget how small she really was.

But one wouldn't want to keep her waiting. Finally disencumbered of the boots, he scrambled to his feet to tear off his trousers, drawers, and stockings. And now to stand quite naked—he felt graceless, and ridiculously, gratuitously tall—endeavoring to maintain an air of calm as he awaited her pleasure.

He could hide the feelings of vulnerability. What he couldn't hide was how arousing he found it all.

Her lip curled. "Well, at least *part* of you knows how to show some respect for what we're about."

"Beg pardon, Miss Myles, but what *are* we about?"

"We're going to auction you off, boy. This is an Arabian bazaar, and you're about to be sold into servitude."

She reached a slender finger to touch him, where the base of his cock met his scrotum. Only a finger, and a bit carelessly, as one might diddle a cat at the bottom of its ear.

He felt himself growing harder.

She laughed softly and pinched him. Not so softly now.

"Wise of you not to inquire what sort of servitude. Or perhaps you've already guessed."

The room had a different look to it than when he'd first encountered it—had it only been three days ago? The light from the glass panes in the roof was livid, almost green; there was a storm imminent outside. She'd made a nice, crackling fire in the grate; he could see flames reflected in the polished surface of her boots. She held a black riding crop in her hand.

Pacing in front of the fire, she weighed the slender black rod in her palm. Frowning now, testing its balance—something didn't satisfy her about it.

She stopped her pacing to open the ebony cabinet. She looked to be considering alternatives to the riding crop. Her concentration was intense; to all appearances it was as though she'd quite lost interest in *him*.

He studied the apparatus on the wall opposite to where he stood. A pair of chains—wrist cuffs attached to the ends—dangled down to . . . well, to approximately the level of his wrists, in point of fact. Three days ago he hadn't fully grasped the mechanics of the contraption, but in fact it was really quite simple. She'd be able to adjust the length of the chains with a pulley, loop it over a hook, and lock it—lock *him*—into place quite smartly.

A certain hinged mechanism had particularly confused him when he'd first looked at it. But the design was clear enough now: the chains could be adjusted to hang at various distances out from the wall. Some customers might be immobilized with their bums or bellies pressed up against the stained red surface; he, however, would not. He wouldn't have that protection; she'd be able to get at him from all sides.

"Ah yes, much better." She closed the cabinet, grinned, and held up a slender branch of rattan; it seemed that she'd exchanged the riding crop for it. She swung it once or twice so that he could hear it whistle. He felt a bit dizzy—the fire was too hot. Or the scent of myrrh—perhaps it lay too heavy on the air.

It's not really a matter of pain, she'd told him. Although for a certain type of gentleman the pain makes it real; sometimes one has to swat at them until one's arm is ruddy exhausted. But a man like you, who's been flogged in the way of naval discipline . . . no, I don't think so.

What you want is a certain quality of attention. Well, you'll understand soon enough.

Still, don't think I won't take a swipe at you now and again.

Feigning more calm than he felt, he stared into her black-rimmed eyes. He wouldn't look frightened or ask for mercy.

She stared back at him. "Turn around.

"Just to make things clear." She whispered it in his ear, as though someone might overhear. She took a step backward then, and gave him a smart taste of the rattan, right across his bottom.

Clear enough.

"Turn around again, to thank me," she said. He complied quite correctly—even rather elegantly, he thought.

"Now keep your eyes down. Head up, though, and back straight. Yes, that's right, that's very pretty.

"We like a modest boy here, one who keeps his eyes lowered. There will be no looking at my face, do you understand?"

"Yes, Miss Myles. I understand, Miss Myles." Obediently, he directed his gaze at her boots, her slender thighs, skin very white above the lace tops of her black stockings.

Hard not to be permitted to look at her face, but in truth he was grateful for the limitations she'd imposed upon his gaze. Better to focus on her commands, concentrate on her low, icy, precisely pitched voice.

It's the voice, she'd told him earlier.

You'd be surprised how much of it depends upon the voice.

He hadn't believed it at the time.

"Over there now." She pointed the switch toward a spot on the floor, near the shadow cast by the dangling chains.

"Open your mouth," she told him after he'd situated himself correctly.

"Here." She placed the rattan between his lips, crosswise—he must look like a dog, he thought, with a bone. "Hold this for me, boy, until I need it again. And mind you don't get it all nasty with drooling. Nor put any tooth marks on it."

Fascinating—astonishing, in fact, how important it seemed to be to follow her instructions. To hold the switch tightly between his lips and keep it perfectly dry. No teeth marks—well, he'd always wondered how a woman . . . All a matter of concentration, he expected.

He concentrated mightily on the task, while she grasped his right wrist and proceeded to shackle him.

His left wrist now. She was amazingly deft with the buckles and obviously familiar with the machinery; his arms were hoisted overhead and his body secured into place before he quite realized it had happened. He was glad to discover that the restraints helped him steady himself; he'd worried about being on his feet for so long without his cane.

She took the switch from beneath his lips and inspected it. No spit or teeth marks on it, none that *he* could see, anyway. He found himself hoping for a word of commendation but none seemed to be forthcoming.

"What's your name, boy? The ladies want to know."

"Jack, Miss Myles, my name's Jack. And the ladies? Beg pardon, Miss Myles, but who are the ladies?"

"Curious, are you, Jack?" She lifted his cock with the tip of the reed.

He wouldn't gasp or moan, he told himself. Not yet, anyway. Not until she forced it out of him.

"Good boy, showing a little control."

More difficult, though, if she were to continue to diddle him in that humiliating way. He'd rather have another swat across the bottom.

He got one.

And decided he might prefer to be diddled.

"The ladies," she said, "well, they're fantasy ladies, Oriental ladies, bored with waiting for the sultan's attention. The sultan doesn't officially ratify this practice, of course. You won't find it in any of the literature. But from time to time he looks the other way and allows them a diversion. And so they need a likely boy, a ready, *demanding* sort of boy . . ."

She chuckled.

"They're insatiable, Jack. The one who gets you will keep you busy from morning till night."

"And they're rich—they don't have any real money, of course—well, why would you need money in a harem? But there are the jewels, you see. They'll pay me a thief's ransom in jewels, for the right boy. A pretty, well-trained boy . . ."

To bring it off correctly, she'd explained, a girl would have to know a bit about the customer. Sometimes they might have a drink or two together, so she can ask him a few questions, find out what's important to him. She looks for ways he's a bit weak, you see, fearful, or vain. Just enough so she'll know what to say. Make it feel personal to him—real, you know—for all that it's just pretend.

It's not that difficult, she'd added. Not so much as you might think, anyway.

"We can see how pretty you are, Jack. It's a scandal, such thick eyelashes on a man—yes, they're quite lovely, especially when you keep your eyes down so sweetly and modestly. And that smile—that shy, honest English yeoman smile of yours. Practiced it hard enough over the years, I reckon—got you out of more than one scrape and lately it's made you rather a pet of the *ton*, hasn't it?

"Smile for the ladies, Jack."

Absurd to be flashing his teeth at an imaginary audience. But it wasn't difficult. It didn't even feel strange to be doing it. It felt to him that he'd been smiling his modest, boyish smile all over London, ever since Lord Crowden had taken him up.

"Now turn, bend. Straighten up now, stand sideways so they can see how nice and tall we've got you at attention."

Still cold and controlled, she raised her voice a bit, as though projecting it outward, to a crowd.

"With a smile and a cock like that, ladies, who could resist him?"

She'd created a perfect illusion. He could almost see the harem ladies' large, liquid, darkly painted eyes peering from beneath sequined veils, the bangles sparkling at their wrists; almost hear their appreciative murmurs, catch a few whispers and giggles.

And perhaps a few hisses as well, from the gargoyles.

She made a slow circle around him, stopping to display him from different angles, prod him into position with maddening little touches of the switch.

"Lovely shoulders, he's a strong one—and," shoving his legs open with the toe of her boot, "may I invite you ladies to turn your attention to the well-developed musculature of the arse and thighs? He can move it, I'll tell you, and then move it some more—it's like a fine piece of engineering, a modern improved steam pump, fully operational and not just for show. Wiggle your arse for the ladies, Jack—grind your hips. Show 'em how you'll pump 'em."

He couldn't. He wouldn't.

"What, suddenly shy? Or simply in need of a bit of instruction?"

At which point she used the switch to prove to him that he could—and *would*—wiggle, grind, and pump as hard and as long as she wanted him to.

And that he would thank her for every stroke of punishment—or *instruction*, as she'd begun to call it. He would thank her loudly, clearly, not forgetting to address her with respect—and, of course, as *Miss Myles*.

He would. And did.

His face and neck were hot. Partly from the pain, though in fact her hand was very controlled; he was sure she hadn't broken the skin. But mostly it was the embarrassment, the total exposure—almost, he thought, like there really was an audience watching. A human audience, and not just the gargoyles, grinning and grimacing at him from their perches on the molding.

And not just her, strutting in front of him so cruelly and deliciously.

It's like a play, he reminded himself. *It's not real.*

Damn if it didn't feel real, though. Real enough to make him sweat. And keep him achingly erect as well.

She gave a low laugh. Her voice was soft. He had to strain to hear it now.

"Well, we can all see how pretty he is, and strong, too, but *pretty* comes cheap, and *strong* isn't hard to find, either. And I won't lie to you, ladies—he's not as young as some boys you could buy for a similar price.

"He's had some experience, life has got to him, for all that he's still a boy some ways, and sometimes"—a light swat of the rattan here—"in need of correction. But a taste of life mellows a person, don't you agree? A little life experience could be a good thing, depending on your taste . . .

"Still, we come to the important thing now, the thing that will make our Jack a prize for some rich, lucky lady. Some very fortunate lady—oh yes, the lady who . . .

"Well, the fact of the matter is that Jack here is the rare sort of man who enjoys providing a lady with some pleasure for herself.

"Of course, he didn't know it himself until quite recently, but he takes instruction well, you see, as I shall demonstrate . . ."

Her voice seemed to falter here.

But perhaps, he thought, it was only a different sort of theatrics. A trap set for him, to make him raise his eyelids after he'd been forbidden it.

He waited.

"I . . . I've trained him myself, and he . . . well, it'll be a pleasure to hand him over to someone who . . ."

Her voice was fading.

He stared at her. She looked very small, her painted face

pale and almost childlike, framed by her tousled black curls.

Frightened.

"Rhinoceros," he said.

She gaped at him as though stunned.

Stupid word. Ridiculous word. *"Rhinoceros!"*

For good measure he yelled, "Stop!"

And then, "Damn it, Cléo, get me out of this rig!

"Come on, that's a good girl, yes, that's right, now unhook the other one . . ."

He had his arms around her. She was shivering.

"What is it?" he said. "Are you ill?"

"P-perhaps," she whispered. "I don't know. My corset's awfully tight, perhaps . . ."

"I'm putting you to bed," he told her.

Easiest simply to pick her up, carry her into the yellow room, and deposit her on the bed. Pull off her boots, loosen her corset. Hell, take it off entirely—luckily, the strings were tied in a bow that was easy to undo. Take off her stockings, too, and tuck her under the covers.

She'd told him, before they started, that there was a flask of water in the red room. He fetched it now, held it to her lips.

Her eyes were dark, defeated. He kissed the ashy skin beneath them, the soft flesh below her chin.

He got into bed with her, pulled the coverlet over them both. Hugging her to him, he tried to restore some warmth and vivacity to her trembling body.

Her voice came in a hoarse whisper. " . . . so sorry. I don't know what happened to me. What must you think?"

"I don't think anything. You laced yourself too tightly, that's all. Tried too hard to give me an adventure. Exhausted yourself, I expect. For a while, though, it was astonishing. *You* were astonishing."

"I lost control. For a moment I thought I was going to

faint. What would have happened to us, Mr. Merion, if I'd fainted while you were chained up like that?"

"I would have had to wait until you revived. Awkward, standing about like that, but hardly life-threatening. And then I would have yelled out the escape word, just as you told me to do, and you would have freed me, just as you did. Don't worry. We're both all right."

She started to say something. He held her tighter.

"And don't call me Mr. Merion. Jack's my name. Call me Jack."

"You're being very good. But I failed. I didn't keep my end of our bargain."

"It wasn't a just bargain I imposed upon you."

She didn't say anything in response.

It was up to him, he expected, to free her from the obligation, propose a rent Soulard could afford, sign the papers, and wish them—what had he said, last Monday night?—ah yes, he'd pompously and sanctimoniously told her he'd *wish them all due prosperity of the property*.

And never see her again.

"It was unjust," he repeated, "unkind, and certainly ungentlemanly, but then, I never pretended to be a gentleman, did I?

"And so I shall hold you to the agreement. You've pleased me very well these past four days. Don't protest—yes, even today, for all its strangeness. Today was . . ."

The sound of falling rain saved him from having to find a word to describe what had gone on today.

"Has the rain just started up?" he asked.

"No, it's been falling for some time."

"I hadn't noticed."

"It began very lightly," she told him. "But I believe it will be quite . . ." She laughed. "Silly of me, to tell a sailor when to expect a storm. As silly as leaving the window open."

Wonderful to hear her laugh.

Wonderful simply to be in the same bed, under the same coverlet, the same good, strong roof.

"I'm glad you left it open," he said. "I like the way the city smells when the weather's stormy."

They lay quietly, listening to salvos of rain beating down across roofs and eaves. Together, they breathed the smells of wet paving stones and of drenched leaves blown from their branches. They held each other beneath the covers.

He could feel the marks in her flesh, impressions the too-tight corset had left on her flanks and lower back. He'd noticed them earlier, when he'd unlaced her. He lifted the coverlet, to look at her. To kiss the angry red ridges. To use his lips and fingers and all his senses to try to understand who she was—in the small ways available to him, by deciphering the marks her life had left upon her.

"I like a naked woman in my bed." His whisper was barely audible above the rain, the winds, and the shuddering of the trees.

They made slow silent love, in the warm yellow room.

The winds had calmed somewhat but the rain was still falling when they finally wrested themselves apart.

She dressed herself quickly.

"Don't go," he pleaded. "Stay the night. You'll catch your death in all that wet."

Lord Crowden had invited him to a late supper. Well, damn Lord Crowden, then.

"I can't stay," she told him. "Philippe would be anxious. And as for getting home, there's a cab waiting downstairs. At least I hope there is. The driver knows to wait for me, should I be a bit detained."

"A cab. Yes, of course. I hadn't been thinking how you get yourself home these dark early evenings. Well, you've run up quite a few additional expenses in the course of this week, haven't you? We can settle them up . . ."

She smiled. "You keep excellent accounts, Jack."

He supposed he did.

It was only after she'd gone that he realized they hadn't decided upon a room in which to meet tomorrow.

Chapter Seven

Saturday

Lord Crowden had found it a fascinating story, excellent entertainment for a late supper on a filthy, rainy night.

"Five days, eh? Well, it only took six to produce heaven and earth. And like the creator, you intend to rest on the Sabbath.

"Sounds like you're getting a good return on your investment, as well. Wonderful, Jack, the head you have for money." He took a pinch of snuff and proffered the chased silver box.

"Thank you, my lord, no snuff."

Permissible to refuse the snuff. But Crowden's patronizing jibes were not to be challenged.

"But perhaps you should have asked for a share in the house. The profits, I mean—or even better, maybe she'd let you . . . hmmm, how would a money man like you put it? Maybe she'd let you take it out in trade."

Damn Crowden, anyway. Though in fact he'd had some similar thoughts himself.

But no, he didn't want her that way. Five days only. An interlude. Real life wasn't like what he'd been experiencing, these last days with her.

* * *

But where was she?

He'd arrived early today, but by now—he checked his watch—yes, it was past three. Only a minute and a half past, but unquestionably past the hour. He owned a very good watch and he kept it precisely set. The fact was that she was late.

He paced the entrance hall.

At ten past, he began to grow angry.

When bells chimed half three, he became alarmed.

Five minutes later, he forced himself to think clearly.

He'd go to the property office, find Wilson if need be, see if they had an address for Soulard. He assured himself that it was very likely—yes, of course there would be an address, or at least some general sense of where they lived.

Find her. Perhaps she was in trouble. Perhaps the Frenchman's health . . .

For the first time, he considered that Soulard might not be well at all. And that she'd spent the past afternoons here in this house, rather than at home with her companion. According to their bargain, she'd had to. She hadn't had any choice in the matter.

Selfish. Even cruel, he thought.

And he'd do it again if he could.

Cane in hand and hat on his head, he was on his way to the door when he heard it rattling from the outside.

He felt vast relief. Followed by fury. How dared she cause him such anxiety?

A rap, now, on the brass knocker—had she lost her key?

He opened the door.

The tall French valet informed him that Monsieur Soulard, Prince d'Illiers, had died in his sleep. Sometime around dawn, they thought.

Madame hadn't sent any other message.

No, none at all.

The property office did have an address. He sent a letter of sympathy. Well, what else could he do?

Anyway, she knew where to find him.

Chapter Eight

Sunday and Through the Following Saturday Morning . . .

He arrived at the house at precisely three the next day. He didn't expect to see her, but his own attendance nonetheless made him feel as though he was keeping faith. They had an agreement. Was he deceiving himself, or did they have something more than an agreement?

He wandered up and down stairs and through the empty rooms. The kitchen was scrubbed, the pots all hanging from their hooks; the only reminder of their feast was a coil of orange rind on the deal table, shedding a faint sweetness as it dried.

I was a char, in this very neighborhood.

In the front parlor, the poor little settee lay supine under its holland cover. He was glad they'd broken it; if he could do it again, he'd break a few more pieces of furniture, create further havoc as a record of what had gone on here.

Touch me. Touch me a little before you fuck me.

He paced the room, breathing the stale fumes of her cigarette.

The next day he arrived at noon.

And earlier still, the following day.

In case she came looking for him. He wanted . . . well, he really didn't know *what* he wanted.

He'd stopped reading the newspapers. Notes, invitations, and inquiries piled up unread in the front hall of his lodgings.

His life had narrowed to this single daily errand. To come here. To wait.

It hadn't been so bad, she thought, while she'd been occupied with the funeral—the arrangements, and then the thing itself; it was gratifying how many of their friends, and even some neighbors, came to pay their respects. They'd had a small, affectionate circle, mostly French. Some, like Philippe, were émigré nobles who'd finally found London more congenial than Paris. Others were from Huguenot families—their great-grandparents had immigrated, establishing homes in Soho more than a hundred years before. Some of the women had started out like her—don't worry, her friend Christine had told her, you won't go unprotected. We'll make up a list of likely men, we'll drink coffee and we'll talk. Next week, *chérie*, when you're up to it.

She wasn't worried.

She was stunned, rather, aghast and even a bit amused by the spectacle of her own foolishness. *All that plotting and planning, the neat columns of figures, the care she'd taken to prepare for every eventuality—except this one, the most likely one, the one that had been staring her in the face all the time.*

She hadn't seen it coming. Her mind had simply refused to countenance the possibility. And then, this past week—well, this past week she hadn't considered anything except her secret, and her guilty and probably futile attempts to hide it.

Had Philippe known he was dying?

Had he guessed the other thing as well?

All too likely, on both counts. He'd been a clever and an

honest man. And he'd been so in love with her that he'd contented himself with her friendship, her admiration, and the pleasure she took in his company, both in and out of bed.

Nothing sharpens the senses like inequity in love. It's a hard thing, she thought, when the person less loved already possesses the finer sensibility. Philippe had undoubtedly known what she'd been feeling these past few days. Probably he'd been able to smell the happiness still clinging to her body, even when she'd bathed herself—scrubbed herself raw—after returning from Soho Square.

How alone he must have felt, in his silent, tactful intimations.

How selfish she'd been, in her stupid, guilty happiness.

And given the chance, she'd do it again.

She'd explain the whole thing to Christine and Bernadette, tomorrow, over very strong coffee. Her woman friends would understand, she thought.

Tomorrow, Jack told himself, he'd give up this hopeless vigil. Tomorrow he'd pay Evelina a visit, see if he could explain away the week's inattention. He supposed another attack of malaria would serve well enough.

Tomorrow he'd also see about subdividing the house and putting it up for rent. Tomorrow he'd get everything shipshape and back on course.

Tomorrow. Or next week for certain.

On Saturday morning she went to the bakery. She'd take the *petits fours* with her on her visit to Christine that afternoon.

Having taken her cloak, Georges reached for the cake box as well.

"You can leave it here, Georges," she told him. "I'll be going out again in an hour."

At least Georges's future was no problem, she thought.

He'd always rather despised her for not loving his master more totally, and he'd easily find employment in some great house west of Regent Street. Philippe had probably already written him a reference, just in case.

"Madame?"

Perhaps he wanted to give notice today.

"Yes, of course, Georges. Let's go into the front parlor."

She motioned for him to sit beside her on a cane-backed sofa. He hesitated for a moment; to her knowledge he'd never sat down in the presence of an employer before. She congratulated herself for having chosen a stiff, straight-backed piece of furniture. He couldn't have managed anything more comfortable.

He allowed himself a small grimace—one corner of his mouth only—before seating himself. The grimace indicated mild appreciation, and not a little surprise at her grasp of the niceties of the situation. He hadn't expected so much, she thought, from a girl who still forgot her table manners once in a while.

"All right, Georges. What did you want to tell me?"

"Two or three things, Madame, that Monsieur had said. He was going to write a note, but he hadn't quite found the words. He wanted me to listen while he worked out his thoughts, but it tired him. He put off writing the note, and then . . . well, he didn't get the opportunity to write it. Still, I've decided you should know what he was thinking about."

She peered warily up at him.

"He was in some physical pain," Georges continued, "though he was quite skilled at hiding it. He was very weak. It worried him, to think of leaving you alone."

She nodded. "He was very good."

His eyes told her not to interrupt. "Which is why Monsieur was grateful that you'd found someone to take care of you."

"*I*? I've found someone?"

"He seemed to think so, Madame."

"What else did he say, Georges?"

The valet hesitated for a moment.

"He said he'd always believed you were searching for someone you lost years ago. And that the man in question must be of the same type. Very English, he said, with that eager, naive English look about him."

"Monsieur le Prince was always a bit too subtle for me, Georges. After all, I'm English, too."

"He understood that, Madame. He accepted that. He wanted to tell you that he took comfort from the fact that he wouldn't be leaving you alone."

"Do you think he really was . . . comforted, Georges?"

"I think he tried very hard to be, Madame."

"Thank you for telling me this, Georges."

"Je vous en prie, Madame."

So Philippe had known. Not everything, of course, but as much as could reasonably be deduced.

Odd that he'd been able to read her so accurately. Before she'd met him, the other girls in the house had considered her a sort of actress—a performer, able to turn herself, chameleon-like, into whatever a particular man might want on a particular day. It was where her exotic nickname came from. Cleopatra, the slutty Egyptian queen who gave her men a lot of variety. They'd called her Cleo, before Philippe had Frenchified it to Cléo.

She'd always enjoyed her little acting turns, particularly in the red room. She'd been glad Jack had asked for a taste of it—she'd imagined herself giving him a splendid time. It had begun well enough—she'd quite thrown herself into her role. And then she'd mouthed that bit about selling him to some lady, and she hadn't been able to continue.

Because in Jack's case there *was* a lady—a rich young lady, no doubt, with a father who'd buy her anything she asked for. Anything or anyone.

She could still feel the moment when her little theater piece had turned real. She'd become choked by bitterness and envy, hating Jack's *young lady* with a cold, paralyzing passion that took her breath away.

Quite spoiled his fun for him, she had. Spoiled *her* fun, too, for she'd been planning to teach him something quite new—force him to learn it, more like. But when the moment had come—well, she'd be damned if she'd teach him to use his tongue to good advantage when the one who'd be benefiting from it would be the *young lady*.

So in the long run, Philippe had been wrong. Yes, she'd once lost someone. But no, she didn't have anybody to take care of her.

Of course she'd manage. Christine and Bernadette would help her. They'd plan it this afternoon over coffee and cake. She'd walk to Christine's house in Soho, pass just a bit out of her way, and return the key she carried in her reticule.

It was the decent thing to do. Leave the key in the entryway, where two weeks ago it had given her such a turn to find him.

Chapter Nine

Saturday—The Housemaid's Room in the Garret

When had he finally figured it all out? There certainly hadn't been a blinding flash of revelation, a stunning moment when everything had changed. The knowledge had crept up on him, during the days' lonely procession, in his aimless wanderings from room to room and up and down the stairs.

And at night, too, in his dreams. He'd had some miserably troubled nightmares at first—pain, catastrophe, and, of course, the gargoyles. But as the week wore on, his dream self learned to ignore the obvious horrors, to search instead for a guide and helper. The little blue-eyed cat padded into view, peeking at him from corners of dream rooms, stroking its flanks against a dream newel post. Sometimes it stood mewing, high up on the dream staircase, as though it wanted him to follow.

"All right," he'd told the cat one night. "All right, I'm coming." The next day he'd climbed to the top of the house.

To this tiny room. Rusty iron bed, straw mattress, one small, high window, walls all mildew and peeling plaster. Tin basin, cracked chamber pot. The memories had been faint—he'd had to keep still and calm, before they lost their timidity and agreed to take recognizable form.

But now he could see them plain as day.

He sat at the foot of the bed, eyes intent on the images: the boy at the door, nut-brown face and hair in a pigtail, the rest of him all grin and swagger and clearly the worse for drink; the girl with long black curls spilling across the pillows, covers pulled up to her neck. Her blue eyes were huge and dark, her skin pale and almost translucent, lit by frightened desire.

Heartbreakingly young, caught motionless in time—did they exist, except in memory?

He didn't hear her footsteps on the stair until she was almost in view.

"I came to return the key," she said. "And then just to . . . to take a last look. I beg your pardon. I didn't know you'd be here."

He was silent for a moment. Then, "You have as much right to be here as I do. Come in if you'd like." He waved his hand at the bed. "Sit down.

"It's a very small bed," he added. "I didn't remember that. Well, of course, I didn't remember any of it, until—I don't know—yesterday, perhaps . . ."

She sat next to him.

"But *you* remembered," he said. "You recognized me."

"The very moment I laid eyes on you downstairs," she told him.

"I'd imagined you a bit different," she continued. "Maybe a bit younger or taller or not quite so broad in the shoulder. But I've imagined you so often over the years. Sometimes, I'd see a man, about your age and height, and with a certain look in his eye, and I'd think, well, it could be Jack, couldn't it? I'd look a bit closer. No, it wouldn't be you, it never was you. But I was always on the lookout, so to speak. I couldn't help it.

"And then, two weeks ago, it *was* you. I knew immediately."

"I thought you were offended," he said, "by how I was staring at you. Bloody indecent, the way I was staring."

"I was glad of *that*—though it would have been better still if you'd recognized me. Still, why should he, I asked myself. And what good would it do, anyway? Probably you forgot me as soon as you left here the next morning."

It hadn't, in fact, been easy to forget that night. But he'd forced himself to do it. Nights in his hammock, he'd think of anything at all—rather than try to reason it out, understand whatever it was he should have known how to give her.

But what good would it have done, anyway? The moment was lost, she *was lost. And so he'd forgotten her. For . . . for twenty-two years he'd kept her out of his mind and even out of his dreams.*

"How bad was I that night?" he asked. "You can tell me—I'm prepared for the worst."

She laughed. "Not the worst. But pretty . . . *rudimentary*, I should say. Boyish, energetic, selfish—and also, sweetly and terribly confused and ashamed of your own lack of . . . um, finesse. But it was my fault, really. Some of the girls warned me that you weren't the best choice for my first time. But you were the one I wanted."

"*You* chose *me*?"

"You were drunk. Too confused to protest."

The small woman took a deep breath.

The man at her side gazed at her with wonder.

No longer trapped in lost time, the images of the two beautiful young people faded from the room.

"The girls in the house would laugh at me," she told him, "the way I'd stare, if I was working anywhere nearby, when you came to the house with your mates. I'd stop my scrubbing or hauling and just, just *stare* at you . . .

"They told me it was clearly time I had a man in my bed, and anyway, wouldn't I like to do some easier work than charring?

"I'd make more money, too, and have some nice things for myself. You're a very pretty girl, Jenny, they told me. You could do well for yourself."

"*Jenny?*"

"Yes," she told him. "My name's Jenny."

"Jenny." He tried it out. "Jenny."

She smiled for a moment before continuing.

" 'All right,' I told Mrs. Allen. 'Yes, all right, I'll do it, but only if it's *him* the first time.'

"*She* laughed at me, too. Well, she wasn't a bad sort, there's lots worse a girl could work for.

" 'I've heard,' she said, 'that he's even prettier with his clothes off, and the girls say he can go on forever. Not gentle or poetical, though. No, he's not the right one, your first time, Jen. The girls've spoiled him—they let him pump into 'em as long and hard as he likes.'

"But I didn't care. And so, instead of sending you to Beatrice's room that night, they sent you to me."

"I remember that part," he told her. "Mrs. Allen told me specially about the bargain I was getting. It wasn't every day that a customer got to have a girl totally fresh like that.

"She gave me more to drink, free of charge, and repeated how sweet and young and beautiful you were. She meant well, I think. But she frightened me out of my wits. I'd never had a virgin, that's for sure. I wanted to refuse, but it was a challenge—a dare, like. Still, I didn't know what to do. I was sure I'd break you."

"You were *supposed to* . . . well, to do something on that order," she said. "And you did. I don't know if you remember that."

"I remember taking off my clothes and getting ready to jump into bed with you. You were watching me, you looked a little scared but mostly calm . . . I never felt so naked in my life . . . until last Friday, anyway, in the red room . . . You looked at me and you smiled and I pulled the cover off you and . . . did I say anything? I remember I wanted to say something . . ."

"You mumbled something. I chose to think that one of the words you used was *pretty.*"

"Well, I was going to be gentle and sweet and kiss you . . ."

"You did kiss me. One time. Almost on the mouth."

"Before I climbed on top of you and forgot to be sweet and gentle. Forgot everything until I woke up the next morning. You were gone."

"I had to work. They hadn't hired a new housemaid to replace me yet. You weren't supposed to stay, but nobody cared, in those garret rooms. I let you sleep, and then you let yourself out without coming to find me. Which made me sad, but not surprised. I remember how tired I was, because I'd spent most of the night just looking at you, sleeping."

"You deserved better."

"Yes, perhaps. But I fell in love with you, anyway."

"And Soulard?"

"We were happy together. But I could never love him as he loved me. Well, that's because I already loved you."

With a houseful of large, beautiful rooms below them—not to speak of a large and well-sprung specimen of Elastic Bed—one might think it foolish that they chose to spend the rest of the day, and the night as well, in that horrid little room, on a thin and moldy straw mattress.

On the other hand, one might think it inevitable.

Odd, how talkative he found himself. Perhaps because he'd spent the week alone, he thought. But he kept thinking of things to ask her. Silly things, he supposed, but . . .

"Did you mean it, when you said I was, you know, of the rare sort of man . . ."

". . . who likes to give a woman pleasure? Of course I meant it. Give me some pleasure, darling."

An extremely long kiss followed. A highly mobile kiss, his mouth beginning next to hers and ending, some time later, entirely elsewhere.

"Ha! Even surprised myself *that time."*

"You didn't surprise me, *Jack."*

And as the afternoon darkened:

"But where are you going? You're not leaving, are you?"

"Not leaving, not yet anyway . . . just going downstairs, luv. There are some cakes we can eat, and I'll get us some water to drink. Oh, and some lubricating ointment, if that's all right with you."

Only she didn't. She brought the butter instead. Giggling as she slipped back into bed, *"I don't mind if we stink of it, do you?"*

And late that night, lying on his back, with her belly curved against his side, staring up at the beams in the ceiling:

"I don't know how long I sat in this room before you came. Well, I could see the two of us so clearly, just as we'd been then. You so innocent, and me with hardly a scar on me . . . oh, no, Jenny, don't cry, I didn't want to make you cry."

"I'm all right . . . s-sorry . . . it's just, well, the years we lost . . . they're all gone . . ."

"They'd be gone anyway, even if we'd had them together. We'd still be preparing to go to sleep this evening, to get a good rest and to wake up together tomorrow."

"You want to sleep?"

"I'm afraid I'm going to have to. Well, I've got my limits, you know. Anyway, how many times was *it today?"*

She laughed. "*I think I'm too excited to sleep. I'll probably stay up all night looking at you.*"

"*You needn't. You'll be seeing quite enough of me. Tomorrow, and the next day and . . . well, as long as we two shall live, I expect. Every night, in this large, solid house. Of course, there is a problem facing us . . .*"

"*Only one problem?*"

"*Only one. To decide which bedroom shall be ours, and which, if there should be a family . . .*"

"*I like that problem. I shall give it some thought. You know, I wouldn't have been a good madam. I'd have worried so about the girls, their heartbreaks, and whether it would come out all right in the end . . .*"

He kissed away a few more tears.

"*Go to sleep, Jenny dear.*"

They stopped in front of the mirror in the entrance hall the next morning to check their reflections. She straightened her bonnet, he his cravat.

"Not bad." He smiled—a private sort of smile this time; the grateful nation could take care of itself.

"Not bad at all," she agreed. "Quite attractive, for a couple entering their later years. Jack . . ."

". . . and Jenny. Common names," he said.

"Wonderfully common."

Their kiss demanded that they straighten bonnet and cravat once more, before stepping out the door and down the steps of their house—say rather, their *home*—into the busy street, in a shabby neighborhood, on a brisk and sunny London autumn morning.

We don't think you will want to miss
Alison Kent's new five-episode series.
Here is a description of all five books.

Meet the men of the Smithson Group—five spies whose best work is done in the field and between the sheets. Smart, built, trained to do everything well—and that's everything—they're the guys you want on your side of the bed. Go deep undercover? No problem. Take out the bad guys? Done. Play by the rules? I don't think so. Indulge a woman's every fantasy? Happy to please, ma'am. Fall in love? Hey, even a secret agent's got his weak spots . . .

Bad boys. Good spies. Unforgettable lovers.

Episode One:
THE BANE AFFAIR
by
Alison Kent

"Smart, funny, exciting, touching, and *hot.*"—Cherry Adair

"Fast, dangerous, sexy."—Shannon McKenna

Get started with Christian Bane, SG–5

Christian Bane is a man of few words, so when he talks, people listen. One of the Smithson Group's elite force, Christian's also the walking wounded, haunted by his past. Something about being betrayed by a woman, then left to die in a Thai prison by the notorious crime syndicate Spectra IT gives a guy demons. But now, Spectra has made a secret deal with a top scientist to crack a governmental encryption technology, and Christian has his orders: Pose as Spectra boss Peter Deacon. Going deep undercover as the slick womanizer will be tough for Christian. Getting cozy with the scientist's beautiful goddaughter, Natasha, to get information won't be. But the closer he gets to Natasha, the harder it gets to deceive her. She's so alluring, so trusting, so completely unexpected he suspects someone's been giving out faulty intel. If Natasha isn't the criminal he was led to believe, they're both being played for fools. Now, with Spectra closing in, Christian's best chance for survival is to confront his demons and trust the only one he can . . . Natasha . . .

Available from Brava in October 2004.

Episode Two:
THE SHAUGHNESSEY ACCORD
by
Alison Kent

Get hot and bothered with Tripp Shaughnessey, SG–5

When someone screams Tripp Shaughnessey's name, it's usually a woman in the throes of passion or one who's just caught him with his hand in the proverbial cookie jar. Sometimes it's both. Tripp is sarcastic, fun-loving, and funny, with a habit of seducing every woman he says hello to. But the one who really gets him hot and bothered is Glory Brighton, the curvaceous owner of his favorite sandwich shop. The nonstop banter between Glory and Tripp has been leading up to a full-body kiss in the back storeroom. And that's just where they are when all hell breaks loose. Glory's past includes some very bad men connected to Spectra, men convinced she may have important intel hidden in her place. Now, with the shop under siege, and gunmen holding customers hostage, Tripp shows Glory his true colors: He's no sweet, rumpled "engineer" from the Smithson Group, but a well-trained, hardcore covert op whose easy-going rep is about to be put to the test . . .

Available from Brava in November 2004.

Episode Three:
THE SAMMS AGENDA
by
Alison Kent

Get down and dirty with Julian Samms, SG–5

From his piercing blue eyes to his commanding presence, everything about Julian Samms says all-business and no bull. He expects a lot from his team—some say too much. But that's how you keep people alive, by running things smoothly, cleanly, and quickly. Under Julian's watch, that's how it plays. Except today. The mission was straightforward: Extract Katrina Flurry, ex-girlfriend of deposed Spectra frontman Peter Deacon, from her Miami condo before a hit man can silence her for good. But things didn't go according to plan, and Julian's suddenly on the run with a woman who gives new meaning to high maintenance. Stuck in a cheap motel with a force of nature who seems determined to get them killed, Julian can't believe his luck. Katrina is infuriating, unpredictable, adorable, and possibly the most exciting, sexy woman he's ever met. A woman who makes Julian want to forget his playbook and go wild, spending hours in bed. And on the off-chance that they don't get out alive, Julian's new live-for-today motto is starting right now . . .

Available from Brava in December 2004.

Episode Four:
THE BEACH ALIBI
by
Alison Kent

Get deep under cover with Kelly John Beach, SG–5

Kelly John Beach is a go-to guy known for covering all the bases and moving in the shadows like a ghost. But now, the ultimate spy is in big trouble: during his last mission, he was caught breaking into a Spectra IT high-rise on one of their video surveillance cameras. The SG–5 team has to make an alternate tape fast, one that proves K.J. was elsewhere at the time of the break-in. The plan is simple: Someone from Smithson will pose as K.J.'s lover, and SG–5's strategically placed cameras will record their every intimate, erotic encounter in elevators, restaurant hallways, and other daring forums. But Kelly John never expects that "alibi" to come in the form of Emma Webster, the sexy coworker who has starred in so many of his not-for-primetime fantasies. Getting his hands—and anything else he can—on Emma under the guise of work is a dream come true. Deceiving the good-hearted, trusting woman isn't. And when Spectra realizes that the way to K.J. is through Emma, the spy is ready to come in from the cold, and show her how far he'll go to protect the woman he loves . . .

Available from Brava in January 2005.

Episode Five:
THE MCKENZIE ARTIFACT
by
Alison Kent

Get what you came for with Eli McKenzie, SG–5

Five months ago, SG–5 operative Eli McKenzie was in deep cover in Mexico, infiltrating a Spectra ring that kidnaps young girls and sells them into a life beyond imagining. Not being able to move on the Spectra scum right away was torture for the tough-but-compassionate superspy. But that wasn't the only problem—someone on the inside was slowly poisoning Eli, clouding his judgment and forcing him to make an abrupt trip back to the Smithson Group's headquarters to heal. Now, Eli's ready to return . . . with a vengeance. It seems his quick departure left a private investigator named Stella Banks in some hot water. Spectra operatives have nabbed the nosy Stella and are awaiting word on how to handle her disposal. Eli knows the only way to save her life and his is to reveal himself to Stella and get her to trust him. Seeing the way Stella takes care of the frightened girls melts Eli's armor, and soon, they find that the best way to survive this brutal assignment is to steal time in each other's arms. It's a bliss Eli's intent on keeping, no matter what he has to do to protect it. Because Eli McKenzie has unfinished business with Spectra—and with the woman who has renewed his heart—this is one man who always finishes what he starts. . . .

Available from Brava in February 2005.